D1388915

THE MIRROR MAKERS

The Mirror Makers

Clare Colvin

HUTCHINSON
LONDON

Published by Hutchinson in 2003

1 3 5 7 9 10 8 6 4 2

Copyright © Clare Colvin 2003

First published in the United Kingdom in 2003 by Hutchinson

Hutchinson
The Random House Group Limited
20 Vauxhall Bridge Road, London SW1V 2SA

Random House Australia (Pty) Limited
20 Alfred Street, Milsons Point, Sydney
New South Wales 2061, Australia

Random House New Zealand Limited
18 Poland Road, Glenfield
Auckland 10, New Zealand

Random House (Pty) Limited
Endulini, 5a Jubilee Road
Parktown 2193, South Africa

The Random House Group Limited Reg. No. 954009

www.randomhouse.co.uk

A CIP catalogue record for this book is available from the British Library

Papers used by Random House are natural, recyclable products made from
wood grown in sustainable forests. The manufacturing processes conform to
the environmental regulations of the country of origin

Typeset by SX Composing DTP, Rayleigh, Essex
Printed and bound in Great Britain by
Biddles Ltd, Guildford and Kings Lynn

ISBN 0 09 179440 4

CONTENTS

Prologue

IN THE shaded room a woman is hunched over a table. She is so still that she seems caught in a moment of time. She is staring into a dark, oval glass shaped like a smooth pebble, which reflects the shadow of her face. She tries to clear the teeming thoughts from her mind, concentrating on the shining surface. The staring hurts her eyes and she clears her mind of the pain as well. Nothing, a black nothingness, is in her mind, is in the glass. And then the shivering begins, like swarms of insects over her skin. As she stares, her eyes see the surface of the glass begin to move like water. She sees a smooth, gleaming lagoon. Water, silky, shimmering, and now there's the sensation of heat on her face. She is looking into a furnace, fierce orange white. There is a dark figure, reaching towards the core of whiteness. The furnace spreads outwards and she is blinded by light. She has to close her eyes, it's like looking at the sun. When she opens them again there is nothing but the dark glass. The insects have subsided and she feels a huge wave of tiredness. She wants only to rest.

She gets unsteadily to her feet, leaning against the table. It is hard to see her in the dimness of the room, for she has drawn the curtains against the light, but from the slenderness of the neck and the tilt of the head she seems young, not yet weighted by the ballast of the years. Recovering from the faintness, her movements are quick and precise. She slides the dark glass into a leather pouch, then opens a drawer in the escritoire, places it inside and turns the key. She hides the key under some papers in the next drawer. She is murmuring something, maybe a prayer or an invocation.

She moves over to the window and draws the curtains back to let in the afternoon light. Now her features and form are clear. She is young, not much more than twenty, and she is wearing a grey dress, full-skirted, the bodice tight at the waist. The collar is of fine lawn, tucked and edged with lace, and a muslin cap perches perilously on her hair, as if she would rather be rid of it altogether. As she turns from the window, the light falls on her face, which has a strange expression, as if half in another world. It is not conventionally pretty, oval with a sharply defined chin, an intransigent pout to the mouth, and she is too pale. The eyes attract people's attention, however. They are green, catlike, with a disturbing gaze. They make people feel a little uneasy, until they remind themselves that she is, after all, only the Marquise's maid.

Claudine seems unhappy with the results of her study. Her brow is furrowed by the train of her thoughts.

The glass hasn't told me anything. Madame will not be impressed by water and fire. One simple question and one only I asked, she will say. One simple answer

I demand. Will the King love me? And then all the subsidiaries will be thrown at me. If not now, when? What should I do? How can I charm him? Just by being beautiful and alluring, I say. But that's not enough. She wants a certain answer, she wants the glass to tell her. The glass tells me what it will. The answer is there but I can't divine what it means.

Claudine crosses herself before leaving the room. It is always as well to protect yourself after invoking the spirits.

PART ONE

The Dark Glass

Paris and Saint-Cloud
1665–6

One

THE MIRROR stands in the middle of the room, facing away from the windows, so that the light falls on the observer and not the glass. The man before the mirror is dressed in ruffled scarlet embroidered with gold thread. His dark hair falls over his shoulders in extravagant curls. He has a high-bridged nose, a well-shaped mouth and eyes with an almost oriental slant. He exudes an aura of regal power, even as he gazes at himself.

Behind him is a man some twenty years older, dressed in black, the only concession to finery being the lace collar of his shirt. His hair is dark, his eyes watchful, his forehead habitually frowning as if calculating figures, his mouth in contrast sensitive, almost feminine. He is the most powerful man in France after the King. He is the King's Controller of Finances. The duty of the most powerful man is to attend on the King, while at the same time running the country. The attending takes up more time than he likes to think about and means interpreting the King's mood as well as his plans. There are days when the King is unusually quick to anger and on these days the all-powerful Colbert is apt to develop a nervous tic to the eyelid.

This is not one of those days, for Louis is pleased with what he sees. He examines his handsome face in the mirror, staring deep into the shining black of his pupils, and stretches out his hand to touch the glass. He can see the newly shaved indentations of his skin, each hair of the delicate moustache that echoes the arch of his brows. He smiles at the reflection of Colbert behind him. 'This is the finest mirror I have seen. From Venice?'

'Inevitably. From the mirror makers of Murano. They are the only people who can make mirrors like this.'

'It is like meeting yourself, face to face.'

He runs a finger around the reflected outline of his mouth. Imagine, he says to his image, imagine a whole wall of these mirrors, no, a hall, a hall of mirrors, reflecting the beauty around them. Imagine five hundred people reflected into thousands, the mirrors facing each other, so your image is visible on all sides. Mirrors reflecting your expression even when you're not looking at them. You will be able to catch them unawares and read their thoughts when they think they are unobserved. Imagine my court surrounded by mirrors. Not one of them will be able to dissemble, their images will betray them. I see that Colbert is frowning. He is thinking of money.

'How much did it cost?' he asks.

'Far too much, Your Majesty will be sorry to know. The mirror makers of Murano are the only ones who know the secret of creating clear mirrors. Their price is exorbitant. It cost a thousand livres.'

Louis looks at his reflection and gasps, 'Venetian robbers! But I am dreaming of my kingdom of mirrors. Exercise your ingenuity, Colbert. Get them here.'

'I have tried. The Venetian Republic knows their value and they are not allowed to leave.'

'You can do it, Colbert. I rely on you.'

The steel grey eyes darken to a fathomless blackness, the anger that lies in the depths of the King like an underground lake. There is nothing to be done, when it begins to rise to the surface, but to agree to the royal will.

The two men turn from the mirror and leave the room. The mirror continues to reflect the space they had filled, images of Baroque carving, of hunting tapestries. Insentient, yet all seeing. There is a click of high-heeled shoes on the marble floor and a new image enters the mirror's unconscious eye. It is that of a woman, dressed in embroidered blue silk, a silver-edged lace fichu at her neck. At a distance, she stops and stares at the mirror, then slowly, as if by magnetic force, she is drawn towards it, until she stands before it, unmoving, locked in her own image. She gazes at herself, taking in the clear skin, the intense blue of the eyes, the chestnut curls of her elaborately dressed hair. She has never seen herself in such detail. 'Why, I really am beautiful,' she murmurs, and then the thought flickers through her mind: how frightening this mirror will be one day. But in the meantime the image is perfect and Athénaïs continues to look at the glass, smiling.

Two

EVERY DAY the boats arrive in the port of Murano, laden to the waterline with wood from the Veneto. The furnaces of the glass factories devour trees with a raging hunger. The men of terra firma spend their days planting and tending them, the men of Murano cut them down. It's a natural cycle of planting, growing, felling, burning.

A black-hulled boat piled high with logs cuts smoothly through the water, as the oarsmen row steadily for Murano. On the prow, his back to the oarsmen and looking across the water towards the island, stands a man, riding the swell of the waves as if he is at one with the sea. In a more populated part of the lagoon people would glance again at the gracefully balanced figure for he is, simply, quite beautiful. His face could have been carved with love by a Michelangelo. The slant of the sun outlines his head with an aureole of gold. He is one of the light Venetians – light-brown hair, grey eyes that reflect the shimmering light on the lagoon. But there is more than his beauty to attract the eye for he radiates youth, health and the confidence that he is immortal. He is around twenty years old.

Andrea had no particular need to make the journey across the lagoon. The boatload of logs would have reached port without his presence on board. But within the body attuned to the sea there is a restless mind. A journey, even a small one like this, eases the restlessness. He was born and brought up in Murano, where his father owns the glass factory in which he works. His days are spent in the infernal glow of the furnaces, his evenings among the enclosed streets and piazzas of the island. No one comes to Murano unless they want to buy glass and no one leaves the island without due cause. Andrea is one of the *specchiai* – the mirror makers – the most treasured and the most guarded of Murano's glass blowers. They have passed through the generations the secret of mirror making. Andrea's father learnt from his father, and expects Andrea one day to teach his son. The art of rendering to man his own image is one that others strive to know, but only the sons of sons, members of the hereditary guild, are permitted to learn the magic alchemy of glass, mercury and tin.

It's a secret that costs some of them dear. Andrea has seen a few of the older *specchiai* in the piazza, lolling about and laughing or mumbling incoherently. They say it's a hazard of the work. You create man in his image through the mirror, as if you yourself are a reflection of God, then one day you become too proud of your creation and you see the devil staring back at you in the glass. Andrea is inclined to think this

11

a myth. The madness is more likely due to years at the furnace, till it cooks your brains to a fricassee.

He's in no hurry to return to the factory on this fine spring morning, and once he has entered the amount of logs and the sum paid in the office ledger, he pauses only for an instant at the entrance to the factory floor, from where the heat reaches him. The furnaces are built of brick, in the shape of a giant beehive, narrowing towards the chimney, and with small doors at the widest part, through which the heat blasts out. He sees in the glow of the fires the shining torsos of men stripped to the waist, each seated on a bench next to an open door. Several of them seem to have only half a face, for they wear a leather shield over the side nearest the furnace.

His father is by the entrance, talking to one of the gaffers, and turns as Andrea is sliding away. 'Where are you going?' he calls.

'Just going to check with the boatman on the next load.'

'You should have done that earlier. Get back here without delay.'

'I won't be long, Signor.'

His father looks at him, in the way he has when he wants to subdue one of his men. Andrea meets his eyes and for a moment there is an almost conscious hostility between the two. The older man resents the impetuousness of youth, the younger chafes at the autocracy of age. But Signor Allegri has other things on his mind than an insubordinate son. He returns to his talk with the mirror maker, dismissing Andrea with his back.

Andrea knows what they are talking about. He is aware of the extra guards from La Serenissima who have arrived in Murano and are patrolling the area near the factories. The rumour is that a Frenchman has been around, offering fortunes to the men to go to France and make mirrors. It is the talk of the *campo*. There have been spies before, but this one is different, for he has the power of the King of France behind him and a seemingly bottomless purse of money. They say he was bargaining with one of the best mirror makers from the Colleone factory, one La Motta, who then started sounding out his colleagues. Old Colleone had told La Motta if he tried to leave, he would turn him over to the authorities as a traitor and let them chain him to the walls of a dungeon, waist deep in water among the rats.

NOT A pleasant fate, thought Andrea, and the subject slid from his mind, as a gang of children surrounded him, demanding pieces of mirror. They haunted the piazza by the factory, begging for fragments so that they could play games catching the sunlight and shining it at each other's eyes.

'Ciao, Signor Andrea!' He felt a pull at his sleeve and looked down at a small dark-haired girl in a grubby red dress, smiling up at him. 'Give me a piece of mirror,' she demanded.

'I have none today,' he said. He knew they regarded him as a soft touch since he had distributed several shards of mirror to the kids on the piazza.

'Tomorrow?' she asked. 'Tomorrow you'll bring some?'

'We'll see,' he said. 'Now leave me be, *raggazi e raggaze*, I'm a busy man.'

'Busy? Ha!' she exclaimed. The children burst out laughing, as they ran away. Andrea walked on, smiling to himself at their cheek. He reached the canal where he could walk along looking at the factories' display windows. Each factory had its own speciality, etched wineglasses in one, coloured chandeliers in another. In the Allegri window was one perfect mirror, its frame of carved glass. Andrea remembered it as the work of Antonio de la Rivetta, one of the master mirror makers. He stood and looked at it for a while, studying its perfection, rather than his image, until he was distracted by another image behind him, that of a small man in black with a high-crowned short-brimmed hat that tipped forward, shading his eyes. Something to do with the hat and the style of his clothes indicated he was not from Venice.

'Beautiful, isn't it?' said the stranger.

'One of ours,' said Andrea, immediately aware, as he turned towards him, of an alert interest in the dark eyes.

'You are from the Allegri factory?' asked the stranger. 'They say of all the factories, the mirror makers of the Allegri are the most skilful.'

'All the mirror makers of Murano are skilful, but we spend time thinking about the design of the mirrors and ways of refining them.'

The man was looking at him, angling his head to one side as if to observe Andrea more attentively. 'Such talented men deserve riches,' he said. 'Instead of being locked away, such men deserve great rewards.'

14

Suddenly Andrea could see that the small man with the dark eyes was the devil in disguise – the French recruiter. 'Excuse me, Signor,' he said, turning to go.

'But, please, one moment,' said the man, moving adroitly into Andrea's path. 'The King of France, who is rich beyond all our dreams, is looking for the best mirror makers to come to Paris. There will be huge rewards for those who have the courage and foresight to accept. There will be travel, celebrations, a life that cannot be imagined in this small island. I can understand older workers being reluctant to begin a new adventure, but you, a young man, with all your life ahead of you? Do you want to spend all those years locked up here, enriching other people, but narrowing your horizons until you are too old to realise any ambition? For I can see that you have dreams and ambitions.'

'Which I can realise here,' said Andrea. He saw the man's disbelieving smile, which was irritating beyond measure. It was also dangerous to be seen talking to a stranger and he looked round nervously for a sign of the guards.

'Excuse me, I must go,' and he stepped round the man, who touched his sleeve lightly.

'Remember where you can find me – Le Sieur de Jouan, staying at Ca' Bellini, on the piazza San Sebastian.'

'*Adio*,' said Andrea firmly.

'Au revoir, Signor Andrea.' The man smiled, as if the two were sharing a joke.

Andrea walked swiftly away. To be seen talking to this person was to run the danger of interrogation. And at the back of his mind an uneasiness nagged him. The stranger knew his name, yet Andrea could not remember having revealed it to him. He returned to the factory, but said nothing of the encounter to his father. He told himself, why bother? I sent the French recruiter on his way. It was strange, though, the way that the man's insidious voice remained in his mind for the rest of the day.

Three

THE BEDROOM of the Marquise resembled a battleground, with billowing silk dresses heaped on the bed like so many fallen bodies. All had been tried and found wanting. Some were hopelessly out of fashion, others needed the attention of the dressmaker to mend a split seam under the arm, or to disguise with a judicious tuck a red wine stain. Most had become a little tight at the waist. Athénaïs knew what perfection was and it hurt to see her wardrobe fall so far short of it. Her dressmaker had found any excuse not to obey her summons. She had obviously heard from Monseiur le Marquis's tailor about the months of unpaid bills.

Athénaïs looked at herself in the mirror, assessing her beauty. The eyes large and of a heart-breaking shade of azure blue, the lips sweetly curved. She thought, despite all, at least my looks haven't suffered. She rubbed at a blemish on the glass. It was so foxed that it sometimes seemed as if there were blemishes on her face, but thank God, she was untroubled by bad

17

skin. She said, looking at herself, but addressing the remarks to the young woman in grey standing behind her next to a small table covered with bottles of lotions, combs and hairpins, 'The other day when I was at court, I saw the most amazing mirror from Venice. I stared and stared, and it was like looking at my double. It was a perfect, unblemished glass. It wasn't like looking at your reflection, but at a living, breathing person. I stretched my hand out and she stretched her hand out to me, and it was a surprise to touch the cool glass. She opened her mouth and I expected her to speak.'

'You were looking at your soul, Madame. Take care they don't steal it away.' Claudine was gazing over her mistress's head into the mirror with abstracted eyes.

Athénaïs waved a hand in front of the maid's face. 'Don't go into one of your trances. Not until I have finished dressing. It will have to be the embroidered blue silk again. Yes, I know I've worn it already this week, but what can I do, my dressmaker is avoiding me. It's still clean, isn't it? Relatively.'

A shadow passed over her face as she remembered the tailor, diffidently and yet at the same time obdurately, presenting his unpaid bill. As if his presence would conjure up the money. She could have told him that the only way to get money out of Monsieur le Marquis was to lie in wait for him at the gaming house, hit him over the head and take his purse before he went through the door. Afterwards, it was always too late.

'I have no objection in principle to profligacy,' she said to her reflection. 'But to be profligate and poor is to make oneself a laughing stock. Now, Claudine' – glancing over her shoulder at her maid – 'help me into the blue silk.'

Laced into her dress and at her toilette table again, she picked through her box of jewellery, holding up a pendant pearl brooch to the mirror. 'If I pin it just here in the centre, that will emphasise my skin. Pearly brooch between pearly bosoms. You may smile, Claudine, but everyone at court notices the least variation. The blue silk again, but with more jewellery. And if we have these diamond and pearl clips, ruching the sleeves just above the elbow, yes? Pearl earrings, where have you put my pearl earrings? Shall I wear the bandeau, or is it too much?'

Claudine stood back, looking at the mirror. 'No, not the bandeau,' she said, 'perhaps ribbons with little combs.'

'Is this friendly advice or are you out to spoil the effect?'

'No, see here, Madame, if we take your hair, like so, and dress it so . . .'

Claudine raised the hair around the comb and threaded the ribbon through.

'Possibly, but I cannot see in this wretched mirror.' Athénaïs rubbed the mirror again with her handkerchief.

'They say the King is going to build a palace of mirrors, so that he can keep an eye on everyone,' said Claudine.

'They? Who are they? If you're going to gossip, I like precise gossip. Names and dates, please.'

There was the sound of the outer door closing, raised voices in the hall, heavy-heeled footsteps on the stone stairs towards the apartment.

'Monsieur le Marquis is back,' said Claudine.

Athénaïs sighed at the glass and said, 'With what new troubles?'

The pearls still gleamed with their subtle lustre, but the sheen was no longer reflected in her skin. They both listened for the sound of footsteps approaching the room and, as the door handle turned, they waited silently for the Marquis de Montespan to reveal his mood.

Four

IT SEEMED they were in the middle of a riot. A carter was shouting furiously at a wagon that was blocking his way. A long whip cracked through the air. The narrow street filled with shouting, gesticulating men. To the Venetians, standing at a loss where their coach had put them down, it appeared that war had been declared at the city gates. Angry men were swirling around them, glaring ferociously, while a torrent of indecipherable French issued from emphatically projecting lips, their shoulders raised to their ears in a mime of disgust.

'What are they saying, Andrea?' asked de la Rivetta. 'What are they so angry about?'

Understanding the French of these street people was far removed from listening to the elegant, modulated voice of the Sieur de Jouan. They couldn't ask the guide who had been with them since Lyon, as he had jumped from the coach and vanished into the crowd without any explanation. Andrea could only shrug helplessly, catching a few words out of the stream of abuse that was being hurled indiscriminately around them. The shock of their arrival in this raucous, aggressive milieu, their nostrils filled with the stench of open drains, the mud that clung to their shoes from the street, and their huge weariness after two weeks of travelling rutted roads in a coach from which the windows were removed for fear of being broken by the constant jarring and replaced with canvas flaps, left each of them longing to be back by the placid canals of Murano, breathing the sea air, instead of gagging on the smell of ordure. The six Venetians stood huddled by their baggage, waiting for rescue while in their minds wondering if they were already being punished by this hostile and confusing city for their desertion of La Serenissima.

But now, just as some ragged men who could have been either porters or thieves were beginning to close in on them, their guide reappeared. With him was a neatly bearded and moustached man in dark-grey gaberdine with a plumed hat who began speaking in Italian, laced with French. He introduced himself as the agent of the glass factory, built, he said, especially for you, and began to organise the loading of the baggage on to the top of a carriage he had brought there for them. He was *désolé* that they had had to wait – the streets had been unusually crowded, but now he could promise them an easy journey in the carriage, pleasant lodgings and a good meal, and then they would meet the head of the new factory, Monsieur du Noyer. They were all delighted, he said, that such talented craftsmen had agreed to make the arduous journey. He snapped at the ragged thieves or porters to be careful with the baggage, and courteously opened the door of the carriage.

The spirits of the men from Murano lifted as they looked out of the open window at the passing scenes of the city. Leaving the narrow streets, the carriage rolled down a grand boulevard lined with trees, past a garden decorated with privet-lined borders and stone statues, the soaring silhouette of a great cathedral on the river, and finally to some more narrow streets, but less crowded, past a great fortress and on to the faubourg Saint-Antoine where the factory was situated.

The doubt that had afflicted Andrea since the beginning of the journey, a doubt that had been so strong among them that four of the original ten had insisted on returning to Venice when they had reached the French border, began to dissolve. In his mind, though, he still heard the voice of his father, ice-cold with anger. That a son of his should contemplate working for a foreign power, giving away the secrets of generations of mirror makers, was insupportable.

'We will make mirrors, not give away our secrets,' said Andrea.

'You won't be able to make mirrors without others learning from you. The French will lean over your shoulder and note everything. Why should they rely on a group of Venetians who will one day decide they've made enough money, get homesick and return to Murano? You're a fool, Andrea, and greedy with it.'

Stung by his father's contempt, Andrea became angry, too. His father never listened to him, he shouted, he rejected his ideas, he could have given much more if he had been prepared to hear him.

'What is there to listen to?' demanded Signor Allegri. 'There's nothing in your mind that I didn't put there and don't you forget it. I taught you everything you know. Why should I listen to some muddle-headed ideas thrown back at me? When you have worked for ten, fifteen years as a mirror maker, when you have learnt most of what there is to know, then I'll listen to you. And then you will say that I was right, it's experience that matters. You could be one of the best, the talent runs in your veins, and now you propose to betray the talent of generations to the French.'

Andrea clenched his fists again as he remembered his father's words. Now he had shaken off the paternal oppression, he was free to become his own man. I didn't come here from greed, he said in his mind to his father. I came here for freedom and for adventure. There is a world outside Murano to explore. As the carriage rolls through the streets, the blood quickens in my veins from the new sights, the strangeness of it all. I'm filled with a vibrant happiness.

He leaned from the carriage window, his nostrils catching the sulphurous stench of the Paris mud, and at that moment a girl selling fruit looked up at the carriage, straight into his eyes, smiled broadly and blew him a kiss.

'Ah, you lucky dog, young Andrea,' said della Rivetta. 'Make the most of it and give us old married men something to envy.'

Oh yes, this wonderful new city, terrifying and entrancing, is waiting for me like a capricious woman, maybe to slap my face, maybe to melt in my arms. Even the ugliness of it is beautiful. What could not happen, as I begin my brave new life?

Five

IN COLBERT'S office two secretaries sit at desks piled with papers near the door. At the window, overlooking a parterre of gravel, is Colbert's desk. The office is on the first floor, level with the tops of the lime trees. At times Colbert turns his back on the room and stares out at the trees and the sky. These are moments when he is making a decision. He doesn't stare for long. He turns back to the room and immediately starts dictating a letter to Secretary One or Secretary Two. There are a dozen clerks in an adjoining room, who send out instructions in quintuplet, sextuplet, to whomsoever they concern.

Colbert has cultivated coldness over the years. His mouth indicates a sensitivity under the surface, but sensitivity wastes time. Be brusque with the supplicants, so that they come to the point. Show yourself immune to flattery and these garrulous aristocrats will eventually shut up and spit out what they want. Then you can simply say yes or no. He is aware of the names they bestow on him. The North, for his icy

demeanour, and also, as he has learnt from an intercepted letter of Madame de Sévigné, Petit. Petit
bourgeois. The son of a Reims shopkeeper running
the great state of France. They, the *noblesse d'épée*, who
are now useless unless needed for war, cannot bear
the thought that a man so far below them in the
hierarchy has become so powerful.

The power is not for himself, but for a grander
design, and one of his schemes has come to fruition.
The mirror makers have arrived in Paris, after several
months of negotiations and cajoling, first from the
French Ambassador in Venice and, when he made no
headway, the roving diplomat, the Sieur de Jouan. He
has received a report from Monsieur du Noyer, who
has installed the men in the factory. With the three
earlier Venetians that makes nine, but they need more
to replace those who turned back. He tells Secretary
One to send a letter exhorting the French Ambassador
to find another six mirror makers and to emphasise
how magnificently they will be rewarded. He has had
a note from the King telling him to have new suits
made in the French style for the Venetians, so that they
will fit in with French life. Secretary Two sends
instructions to the court tailor, omitting no detail of
the King's wishes. An embroidered surcoat, loose
breeches gathered below the knee, the mirror makers'
own choice of colour to be respected, as long as it is
subdued.

That done, Colbert turns to the problem of the tax
farmers. They must be curbed, to stop them lining
their own pockets rather than those of the state. He is
forming a plan, but in the meantime it is a question of

dealing with the most blatantly corrupt. A letter goes to the justice of Bourgogne. And here is a horribly exorbitant bill from the architect Le Vau, and one from the King for a dinner, which he can hardly believe. Colbert feels his heart sink. He looks out of the window for some time at the leaves of the lime trees stirring in the breeze, then composes his most difficult letter of the day in his precise, cramped hand . . . 'I tell Your Majesty that, speaking as an individual, I am given unspeakable pain by a bill of one thousand écus for a single meal . . .'

And so the day continues, as matters that will change the face of France are interspersed with the finest detail of the King's domestic affairs. A servant brings in a bowl of beef consommé, which Colbert eats at his desk. This is the only disagreement between him and Madame Colbert, that he never comes to table for a proper meal. And on the subject of Madame Colbert, where is her report on the royal bastards, with whose care she has been entrusted? The King has to know each day how his little ones are keeping. Finally, a scribbled note arrives from his wife. The elder has a chill and is being wrapped in flannel. *Le petit* is well but fell over while playing and grazed his knee. Colbert's face, as he thinks of his wife, softens from the granite of the north. The good woman, despite the demands of her own children, to be so caring of others, though of course she had no choice.

Every now and then, when he looks at Louise de La Vallière, he can see tears brimming at her eyes. Louise longs to be just a bourgeois wife and mother, with her loving Louis. Colbert has known for some time that the poor girl is not of the stuff of royal mistresses. He knows that the King has begun to realise this too. Still immersing himself in her softness, but increasingly there is a restlessness in the royal eyes. The choosing of a mistress is an affair of state. The King's mistress can help what Colbert is building up, or she can bring it down. For this reason he gets reports every week on whom the King seems to be favouring. It is impossible to tell, for Louis is so good at dissembling and averting the Queen's jealousy. No one will know until it is a fait accompli.

Six

WHEN THE fury of Athénaïs is aroused, the blood rushes to her face and her eyes flash like someone possessed. It's as much as she can do to avoid striking out at whoever has incurred her wrath, but in this case the person she would like to hit is herself. To have had so many advantages in life and to have thrown them away hardly bears thinking of. Her sisters and brother are beginning to think of her as their poor relation, her, the beauty of the family, and all because of a throw of the dice – the dice of fortune and the dice her husband is addicted to. Yes, it's Montespan again and Athénaïs's thoughts rush through her life in a stream of memories, swirling round the latest boulder, the loss of her earrings.

My favourite earrings were taken yesterday – the ones with the three branches, each bearing three large diamonds, with a cluster of little diamonds in the centre. They were a wedding present from my mother and Montespan took them. He had some particularly unpleasant creditors to deal with and now they're sitting in the usual pawnbrokers. Just for a few weeks, he says, but I know I'll never see them again.

I feel angry, I feel foolish. I have no one to blame but myself. After all, I married for love. He wasn't the first choice of my parents, but they didn't stand in my way. He was an ardent suitor, violently in love with me. Standing outside my window all night when I was lodging at the Louvre, refusing to be moved on by the guards. Those innocent days when I was maid of honour to the Queen, the wide-eyed arrival from the meadows of the Charente. The little Mortemart they called me, and then la belle Mortemart. Dancing in the ballets as a shepherdess, while the King played the Sun God.

The days when I was still Françoise, before I was married, before I reshaped myself as a Précieuse, sharpened my wits to duel with words and took the name of Athénaïs. But it's all on the surface, I am skating on glass above a morass of debts, living with my husband, who incidentally drinks too much, in a meagre apartment in the rue Tarenne. My escape is the court. Monsieur the King's brother is a good friend to me. Montespan doesn't come to court, he had relations in the Fronde and the King is still obsessed by that rebellion. So there I am at court, happy, sharp-witted, admired, and then here I am at home, among our depleted furniture, having to say, Louis Henri, what has happened to our carved silver candelabra? Pouf, paf, he says, couldn't stand them any more, took them to the silversmith.

I would never betray my marriage, such as it is, but there are times when I cannot help envying Louise de

La Vallière, for bathing in such an overwhelming love as the King has. But to be subject to all the tittle-tattle that goes with that position, the censure of the Queen, that I couldn't stand.

AT THIS point Athénaïs paused in her reflections. She, a daughter of the Mortemart, intimidated by gossip? She turned to the maid, who was waiting for Madame to decide on her dress for the day.

'Look in your dark glass, Claudine, and tell me, will my husband reform? Will he stop gambling and whatever else it is he spends our money on?'

'*Pauvre Madame,*' said Claudine. 'We know the answer without my looking.'

'*Pauvre* is a word I am tired of hearing. Something will have to be done. I shall learn about business.'

Claudine smiled. Business was just another way the nobility lost money.

'Not even to be able to afford a decent mirror.' Athénaïs sighed. 'This one is as obscure as your dark glass, all blemishes and mottles. One day I shall have a new, marvellous mirror, like the one I saw at court. Now, Claudine, what shall I wear today that won't remind me of the loss of my earrings?'

Seven

IN THE evenings, regrets at the life they had left behind, the abandoned wives, sweethearts and families, passed through the compound of the mirror factory like a sigh. Some of the men shed tears at the loss of their familiar ties.

Even Andrea, who had chafed at his containment in Murano, began to feel a certain nostalgia which surfaced in memories of childhood. There was another mirror maker of his own age, Luca, with whom he talked late into the night when they felt too restless to sleep. 'Do you remember,' he said, 'the games we used to play with mirrors? We'd take fragments to catch the sun and aim the reflected light at another boy's face to see how long before he shut his eyes. We had dark spots dancing before our eyes for days on end. We would signal each other with the mirrors, from one end of the piazza to another, sending messages with flashes of light.'

His father had become in his mind the more benign parent of his childhood, in the days before Andrea's mother had died. He remembered sitting on the bench outside their house on a Sunday, listening to his father's stories. The legend of Archimedes, how he set the Roman warships on fire with a mirror, when they were too distant to be hit by fire arrows. Not the glass mirrors of today, Andrea's father had said, it would have been a shining concave metal mirror of huge proportions, polished so highly it would reflect your face.

Andrea had asked if it would work with the mirrors of today and he said, 'No, you couldn't make a mirror large enough.' It was a question of a powerful ray of light from a very large surface hitting a very small area, no larger than a coin. The ancients knew secrets that were forgotten during the days of the barbarians and now we were only beginning to know them again, as if they were new discoveries.

'That's what I admired most about my father,' said Andrea. 'To most people he was a businessman who knew the worth of each mirror and of each man in the factory. But he was also a seeker after knowledge and he would throw it my way, like scraps, between the day-to-day business. His anger, when he knew I was leaving, was the more painful for this, because he was just as scornful when he realised I, too, was searching for knowledge. Throwing away everything for a chimera, he said. You were taught mirror making so one day you and your brother would manage the factory. Well, too bad, it'll just have to be Federico. And then he invoked the name of my mother, who died when I was twelve. If she had known the son she gave birth to would one day betray Murano . . . Nothing about my journey hit me as hard as that last talk with my father.'

34

'My father was furious, too,' said Luca. 'He had the eldest daughter of the Colleoni lined up for me and she would have brought us a good dowry. Old man Colleoni was so disgusted when he heard that he promised her to the son of Francesco Salviati.'

As if in response to this undercurrent of home-sickness among the workers, news arrived from the Minister's office of generous bonuses for extra quotas of mirrors. It seemed that all Paris wanted to buy mirrors, jostling for orders in the queue behind the King. The hard work and the money lessened the nostalgia to a faint sense of unease in the early hours. It was not long to dwell on, for by six in the morning the first shifts were beginning at the factory, the furnaces having been stoked through the night by the French workers to keep the temperature high. Outside the factory compound in the faubourg Saint-Antoine the early morning sounds could be heard, the rattling of buckets, the sound of iron-clad wheels on the cobbles, voices raised again after the hours of sleep, men coughing and clearing their throats at the start of the new day.

Andrea went to the wash-house. It was in a courtyard surrounded by the living quarters of the mirror makers, behind the main factory. The living quarters were built of red brick with ivy creeping up the walls. There was a small patch of cultivated earth sown with marigolds and artichokes, and a large area of bare earth marked with stones at each end, where the workers would play calcio. The factory in front of the compound was approached from the street by a cobbled impasse. The entrance to the street was barred by iron gates, locked at night and patrolled by a guard during the day. It was designed not only to keep the men in, as Monsieur du Noyer noticed they were apt to wander off for long breaks exploring this new city, but also to keep out the agents of the Venetian authorities.

Only three weeks after they had arrived, one of the mirror makers had been assaulted, as he returned from an evening's walk, and stabbed in the right arm with a sliver of glass. Everyone at the factory was sure the attack bore the mark of Venice. After all, if it had been a common thief, the man would have been robbed of his purse as well. The next day the Venetian Ambassador had sent a message to ask the chief of the mirror makers, Antonio della Rivetta, to meet him. Rivetta had taken with him another mirror master, Civrano, as well as the two youngest men, Andrea and Luca, in case there was an attempt at abduction. They had met the Ambassador in the Place Royale, where he had made crude threats against them and their families unless they agreed to return to Venice. They reported the meeting to du Noyer, who told Colbert, whose immediate response was to increase the workers' pensions. The Venetians had counter-attacked with promised bribes, but it was too late. Colbert had acted first.

That had been in August, and du Noyer had forbidden the men to go out except in twos and threes. There was a lull during the heat of the summer. But now, in mid-autumn, it seemed the Venetian authorities were stirring again. Rivetta, sluicing his large frame in the wash-house, called to Andrea,

'They've sacked that thug of an Ambassador. I heard last night. The new Ambassador is Signor Giustiniani. He wants to have a meeting.'

The new Ambassador appeared to be taking a more conciliatory approach. His invitation was to dinner at his residence, with the solemn oath that no harm would come to them and that the laws of hospitality would be observed.

'It sounds more civilised than being summoned to the Place Royale and threatened with various forms of death,' said Andrea.

'I still don't trust him. We'll meet in a public place or not at all. And not a word to du Noyer,' added Rivetta, 'or we'll be locked in this compound indefinitely.'

Two evenings later, dressed in the new suits ordered for them by the King, they set off by fiacre for the compromise suggested by the Ambassador – a private room in a meeting house near the Seine. A light drizzle settled on their shoulders as they descended from the carriage, spreading a veil over the Ile de la Cité and the cathedral of Notre-Dame. At the door of the building a man in Venetian dress stepped forward to meet them. He introduced himself as the Ambassador's secretary and led them upstairs to the private room.

Ambassador Giustiniani was of a different mould from the previous envoy. He clasped their hands effusively, as if they were his favourite sons returned home, with a cry of 'My dear fellow Venetians!' His small, shrewd eyes twinkled affectionately as he looked from one to the other, naming them in turn, 'Signor Antonio della Rivetta, Signor Mario Civrano, Signor Andrea Allegri. How honoured I am to receive you as my guests tonight. My own cook has prepared a feast for you which, if it doesn't make you wish to return to Venice immediately, will at least fill you with nostalgia. *Risotto con funghi, e allora, luccio al burro, e fegato alla Veneziana, e poi . . . e poi, tutte dolce della Serenissima!*'

The men looked at each other uneasily at the news that the food was being prepared by the ambassadorial cook.

'And of course, I have brought my own taster along,' continued the Ambassador, 'so we can all be sure nothing will disagree with us.'

He smiled again at his visibly relieved guests. 'So unfortunate, your previous experiences, Signori, let us hope that we can make amends.'

The room they were in was in the style of Henri IV – with painted beams supporting the wooden ceiling. Frescos of nymphs and cupids wreathed with roses decorated the walls. The tall windows looked on to the Seine, the glass reflecting back the light of many candles. The Ambassador had chosen the best quality wax candles that burned with a clean flame. A scent of dried rose petals and spices from dishes of pot-pourri pervaded the air.

Andrea warmed to the atmosphere. This was the sort of place he had imagined in his dreams of Paris. Across the table, the faces of his colleagues faded from view. He saw in his mind's eye through the lighted candles an elegantly turned neck, white shoulders rising from a silken robe, frivolously curled hair tied with ribbons. I'll bring her here, this woman who is at the edge of my consciousness. I haven't seen her yet, not among the wenches who hang around the rue Saint-Antoine, or the girls taking the air in the Jardin des Plantes, yet somewhere in this city I know there is a woman I shall love.

The Ambassador was looking at him as if reading his thoughts. 'We would never suggest you leave Paris, where so much awaits you, not until you have had your fill of everything she offers.' He smiled. 'But what we earnestly, wholeheartedly ask of you, plead, beg, supplicate, is never to give away your precious secret of mirror making to the French. Take their money, take as much of it as you like, but keep the secret of the *specchiai* to yourselves. That way you will safeguard yourselves, as well as your colleagues in Murano. For you can be sure that once the French have learnt the secret, they'll toss you aside like used shoes.'

'We agree, Your Excellency,' said Rivetta. 'None of us wishes to harm Venice, as long as Venice doesn't harm us.'

They drank a toast to Venice, to each other, to Paris, to the mirror makers of Murano, to life in general, to absent wives, to love, to the excellent meal and all the sweets of Venice. Then, finally, unsteadily, they took their leave of the Ambassador, who gazed at them with even greater affection, tears glistening in his eyes as he bade them goodnight. In the carriage returning to faubourg Saint-Antoine Rivetta said, 'He is right about the French. Their main aim in bringing us here is to find out the secret and then rid themselves of us.'

'There are already French apprentices in the factory, trying to learn from us,' said Civrano. 'Du Noyer will be furious if we throw them out.'

'The secret of the mirrors is our power,' said Rivetta. 'That's what we must guard at all costs. Du Noyer will have to put up with it.'

Du Noyer cajoled and threatened in turn, then referred the matter to the office of the Minister. A message came back from Colbert, announcing vastly increased pensions for those who agreed to train the French apprentices. The atmosphere of dissension in the factory was tangible. Men who agreed to train the apprentices were cold-shouldered. Du Noyer reported the worsening mood of the men. Colbert sent a message to the French envoy in Venice to try to arrange for the wives to join them, in an effort to diffuse the tension and discourage the men from thoughts of returning to Venice. But in the meantime there was one weapon that might induce loyalty to France rather than Venice, and that was the King himself.

The King was to visit the mirror factory. The word went around the furnaces, around the courtyard, wherever two or three men were talking together. Du Noyer had issued instructions. They were to continue as usual. The King wanted to see the work in progress. They must on no account stare at him, he disliked being stared at, or try to talk to him, he didn't like to be approached. If he decided to speak to an individual, the said individual must bow and keep his eyes directed downwards while replying in a clear voice. For those with no French, the King understood and spoke Italian. In fact, it would probably be best to speak in Italian. The King did not like to hear the French language mispronounced.

Du Noyer's instructions led to a fresh spate of rumours around the factory. The King didn't like to be looked at because he was misshapen. He was horribly fat. He was a hunchback. He had two heads. The speculation expanded into a picture of a monster descending on the factory, a creature so grotesque that the men would have to avert their eyes to avoid being turned to stone.

So on that morning in the spring of 1666, when finally the visit was to take place, the atmosphere in the factory was febrile with expectation. Any sound of a cart or shouts from outside interrupted the process of glass blowing. More glass was ruined on that morning than ever before. Then, like a veritable cavalry, the King's coach and six, and a retinue of riders drew up outside. Du Noyer gave his final instructions. Bow low towards the King as he enters, eyes to the ground, then continue work as normal.

Andrea sat at his workbench, his tools beside him. He adjusted his leather shield over the side of the face against the heat of the furnace. Sweat was beginning to run down the shield as he leaned forward to blow the molten glass attached to the end of the pipe. He shut his eyes against the brilliant orange-white from the mouth of the furnace. When he opened them, the entire band of workers were on their feet, bowing low towards the King.

The first sensation was of looking at another fire. The man before him was dressed entirely in scarlet and gold. He wore a flame-red plumed hat on a head of extravagantly long, curled hair that cascaded over his shoulders, a gorget of gold and a sleeved jerkin covered

41

with gold and silver embroidery. Under the jerkin was another garment of gold brocade, worn over a billowing pale shirt. His knee-length breeches were scarlet, embroidered with gold and fastened with garters of flame-red ribbon. The stockings were scarlet and the shoes soft, pale calf, with scarlet heels, diamond buckles and scarlet ribbons. Andrea stared at the shoes, his eyes downcast as instructed, then his gaze moved upwards, through the flame and gold to the King's face.

The impression was that he was burning with life, that here was a man at the pinnacle of being, no, not a man, a god among mortals. The skin radiated health, confidence and overwhelming power. Andrea stared at the King until the aquiline profile turned towards him. He was aware of dark, narrow eyes fixed on him, the depth in them so fathomless and the force so strong that he could only cast down his own eyes. It was true what they said, you couldn't look at the King for fear of being turned to stone. Andrea turned back to his work, to the furnace that was at least a heat with which he was familiar.

He heard the King's entourage move around the factory and the voice of Monsieur du Noyer explaining various points. He glanced up from his work at the men around the King. There was a stern-faced man dressed in black with a white lace collar, who he guessed must be Monsieur Colbert, the Controller of Finances. There was a diminutive young man, wearing similar clothes to the King but in shades of blue and silver. His hair was long and elaborately curled, his eyes dark and bright. A continual half-smile lit his face as he looked around him, there was a dusting of powder on his cheeks and a beauty spot next to his mouth. Du Noyer was being almost as obsequious to him as to the King and Andrea assumed that he must be a royal relative, a younger brother, perhaps.

The entourage gathered now and then around individual men who were at their benches. The King questioned several of the men about the process of their work and handed out gold coins. Eventually, after some mopping of the brows from the heat of the furnaces, the royal party adjourned to the courtyard, where a table had been laid with joints of carved meat, fruit and flagons of wine. As soon as the visitors had left the factory floor, work forgotten, the men voiced their amazement. Had you ever seen such clothes? How long did it take them to get dressed in the morning? A couple of hours?

Presently, du Noyer's assistant returned to the factory and approached Andrea at his workbench. 'Would you come outside?' he said.

Andrea got up and followed him, in trepidation. Had he committed some form of *lèse-majesté* in staring at the King? Was he about to be dispatched to the Bastille, a reminder, only a mile or so away, of the King's displeasure? He saw, as he entered the court-yard, Antonio della Rivetta explaining something to the King and to Monsieur Colbert. The King's brother was wandering about, peering in at doorways. Two musketeers were standing easy as they chatted together in the spring sunshine. It didn't look as if the scene was set for anything stronger than a reprimand. As he approached the group round the King, he could see they were gathered near the wall against which was the multiple mirror he had forgotten to put away.

'The King wishes to know,' said Monsieur du Noyer, 'what is this curious device?'

Andrea blushed and silently cursed himself for not hiding the instrument. It had been constructed during the summer months from rejected mirror pieces and he had brought it out again, now that the sun was stronger, a relic of his memories of the conversation with his father about Archimedes. Now, to his shame, his childish experiments were being exposed. 'It is just an experiment,' he muttered, looking at the ground, 'to do with heat and light.'

'An experiment?' said the King. 'I am always interested in experiments. Tell me what it entails.'

Andrea looked at him and saw, instead of the blazing icon of his first impression, a man, five years or so older than him, with intelligent eyes, who appeared intent on listening to his explanation.

'Excuse me, Your Majesty, it may seem foolish, but it's an experiment I was working on as a result of the story of Archimedes and the Roman warships. He set fire to a warship, which was at a distance outside an arrow's range, and he did this by means of a burning mirror. One mirror can direct heat if it catches the sun and I was building up a number of mirrors which could be angled, so that the sunlight can be concentrated on to one small spot at some distance. I've managed to set on fire a piece of wood at the distance of ten paces. That's all, it's just an amusement, really.'

'A distance of ten paces?' said the King, ignoring his modest disclaimer. 'So if, instead of having only ten mirrors, you had a wall of a hundred mirrors, you might be able to set wood on fire at a distance of a hundred paces.'

'It may be so, Your Majesty, given the right angle. I can only work through experiment and I wouldn't be popular with Monsieur du Noyer if I used a hundred mirrors.'

Louis laughed. 'Monsieur du Noyer is anxious to make a profit – as are we all. But I like an enquiring mind. What else can you do with mirrors?'

'The angle is everything. You can arrange mirrors in such a way that an image will recur throughout the length of a house and you can watch someone approaching, room by room.'

'That sounds useful. Think of the number of people I could manage to avoid, Colbert.'

The Controller of Finances gave a glimmer of a smile.

'And come to that,' continued the King, laughing as the thought occurred to him, 'how useful it would be to be able to set the courtiers on fire at a hundred metres.'

'You mean the men, as well as the ladies?' said the King's brother.

'An ambitious *duc* vanishes in a puff of smoke. Well, it seems there is a great deal more to mirrors than appearance. What is your name, young man?'

'Andrea, son of Ercole Allegri.'

He was aware that the entire entourage was staring at him as if at an exotic new animal. Colbert's severe expression softened, as of an uncle surveying a promising nephew. The King's brother was looking at him with undisguised interest and murmured to one of the King's officers, 'Italians are either ugly or beautiful and this one is like an angel.'

There was a timeless pause, as Andrea stood there, surrounded by the warmth and interest of the greatest in the land. Then the King said, 'We must move on. Excellent work, Monsieur du Noyer. Good day to you, Signori. A most interesting morning.' And the entourage turned on their heels to follow the King. Andrea felt as if he had been admitted for a moment into an intimate circle and as quickly dismissed.

IN THE days that followed the King's visit the old restlessness assailed him. The circumscribed life of the factory, the daily routine that used to absorb him, seemed part of a small, narrow world. 'I cannot forget the King's magnificence, his grandeur,' Andrea said to Rivetta. 'He seemed to touch everything with gold.'

'A man that rich can afford to and some of it may come in your direction, if you're clever,' said Rivetta. 'I heard him tell Colbert to remember your name.'

A week or so later, du Noyer came over to Andrea's workbench. A consignment of mirrors was to be delivered to the Louvre. Andrea had been deputed to help with the placement.

Eight

THE MIRRORS were packed in cases of wood shavings, to protect them from the jolting of the cart along the uneven streets. A huge road-building project was in progress in the city, the newly paved streets interspersed with rutted and potholed tracks. They passed under the shadow of the Bastille, to the rue Saint-Antoine and then, as it was blocked with roadworks, down by the banks of the Seine, its surface a grey oily sheen under the clouded skies. Presently they could see the leaded roofs of the Louvre.

Labourers, like a besieging army, were gathered around the palace walls and teams of horses were drawing wagons loaded with stone. The mirror factory's cart entered the main courtyard from the east into a building site. The whole façade was under scaffolding. Men swarmed up ladders and on the roof several cranes were hauling up loaded slings of lead sheeting.

In the midst of this frantic work, it was hard to discover where they were expected to go with their consignment. Andrea left the driver and the boy helping with the mirrors, and approached a man in grey serge standing in the courtyard poring over architectural plans, who looked like an official. The man glanced up irritably and shrugged, to indicate that what he was doing was of more importance than the trivial placement of furnishings. A short man in work clothes and broad-brimmed hat standing next to him explained, 'The King's not living here. As you can see, the palace is having a huge overhaul.'

'Try the Tuileries,' said the other man without looking up. 'The King is lodged there at present.'

'The Tuileries? Where's the Tuileries?' asked Andrea.

The official raised his eyebrows and sighed. The man in the big hat said, 'It's just west of the Louvre. Ask someone when you get there. Have you been given a name?'

'They were ordered by Monsieur Colbert.'

'Well, you can hardly expect Monsieur Colbert to be waiting on the doorstep for you,' said the official scornfully. He turned away, muttering, 'Foreign cretins . . .'

At the main courtyard of the Tuileries a palace guard tried to redirect them to the Palais Royal, asserting with the confidence of someone who was talking off the top of his head that the mirrors would undoubtedly be for Monsieur the King's brother. No, said Andrea, who could see their cart making a merry-go-round of these infernal royal palaces for the rest of the day, the mirrors are for the King.

It was beginning to rain and what had seemed like a blessed relief from factory routine now felt like a hopeless mission. 'These mirrors were ordered by Monsieur Colbert for the King,' he said again to the guard, who pretended incomprehension at Andrea's accent. A group of men were walking towards the colonnaded entrance of the palace, among them the black-cloaked figure of the King's Minister.

'Just a minute . . .' said the guard, trying to block his path, but Andrea had already moved swiftly towards the entourage, calling out as he reached them, 'Monsieur Colbert, Your Excellency!'

Colbert turned with the forbidding expression he used to discourage petitioners, then relaxed as he recognised the young man. 'Ah, the mirror maker,' he said. 'Have you brought the consignment?'

'Yes, Monseigneur, but no one seems to know where they should go.'

'No one knows anything,' said Colbert. 'Come with me.'

Andrea joined the Minister's cortège and they passed the great doors into a hall that was over-whelming in its splendour. The wide marble staircase with its gold-leaf statues at the foot of the balustrades, the tapestries of battles on the walls, the confusion of painted gods and goddesses on the ceiling high overhead were an assault on the eyes. Two courtiers in similar, though less richly embroidered, clothes to the King were sauntering downstairs, turning their feet elegantly to display their stockinged calves. They bowed to the Minister, each raising a hand to his hat, without doffing them. Colbert inclined his head curtly, murmuring, '*M'sieur le Comte, M'sieur le Baron,*' then continued up the stairs, followed by his entourage, to the state apartments, where clusters of courtiers chatted together, with the air of passing time while they waited for something more important to happen.

Colbert's group had closed up to form a solid bloc as if to discourage any approaches from the loiterers. They entered a second smaller salon, where Colbert turned abruptly to press a piece of the panelling on the wall. A hidden door opened, which led them across a narrow central passage, to a room of rose and gold, with long windows looking out towards the Seine.

'We're in the Queen's apartment,' explained Colbert. 'The mirrors are for this room. You will place one here, between the windows, and the other two opposite on the walls here. The alignment must be precise. Do you need any help?'

'An extra pair of hands, if possible, then I can watch the alignment.'

'You,' said Colbert, gesturing to a lank-haired page lounging by the door. 'Do whatever Monsieur Allegri tells you.'

The Minister gave a brief nod to Andrea, then turned back through the hidden door, leaving him in the heart of the palace.

The hanging of the mirrors took longer than expected, for under a thin layer of plaster, the walls were solid stone. Andrea stepped back to check the alignment, but somehow he felt the mirrors were not placed to the best effect. He would have liked to angle two of them in each of the far corners, reflecting into the one between the windows, which would widen the range of images, but he knew it would be unwise to countermand the Minister's precise instructions.

He stood on a chair to remove a palm print from the top of the mirror that he had placed between the windows. The mirror was one he had made and he was proud of it. Sometimes there would be a faint ripple in the glass, but this one was smooth as a millpond on a summer's day. He remembered the feeling of elation as he had looked at the glass he had blown when it had first been flattened out. It was not often that you felt the pure joy of perfection, but this had been such a moment.

From the click of the hidden door, he was aware that someone had entered the room, but it was only as the footsteps approached him that his gaze was distracted from the mirror to the image. Reflected in the glass was a woman so beautiful he could not believe she was real. Such perfection must be the dream that haunted the edge of his mind. Transfixed by the lustrous azure eyes that were gazing up at his reflection, almost involuntarily he murmured, '*Bellissima!*'

The vision smiled, permitting a glimpse of white teeth. '*E lei! E anche bellissimo.*'

Her voice broke the spell and Andrea realised with a start that this vision with whom he had been exchanging glances must surely be the Queen. He stepped quickly down from the chair and bowed. '*Scusi, mi scusi* . . . If it please Your Majesty . . .'

She held up her hand to stop him and laughed. 'No, I'm not the Queen, but thank you for the flattering address. So, you are one of the band of mirror makers, *uno degli specchiai? Un uomo da Venezia?*'

For a moment he couldn't speak. The scent of her enticed his nostrils – a sweet, heavy tuberose, mingled with an alluring undertone of female flesh. She stared at him expectantly and finally he managed a reply. '*Sono da Murano, Madama. E lei, è italiana?*'

'No, but all civilised people speak Italian. I like to find any excuse. So, did you make these beautiful mirrors?'

'This one, yes, the one I saw you in. In all modesty, I can say it is a perfect mirror, so it is fitting that it should reflect such perfect beauty.'

She laughed delightedly. 'Ah, you Italians! Not a moment wasted. I love flattery.'

Andrea was aware of the smooth throat which led his eyes irresistibly to the wonderful bosom that filled the bodice of her dress. 'It's not flattery, it's the truth,' he said, averting his eyes from her décolletage to the space to the right of her head, in order not to offend her by his gaze.

'And it's not flattery to say that of these mirrors, yours is the best,' she replied. 'One day you must make one for me, Signor Mirror Maker.'

'Andrea Allegri, Madama. I should be honoured.'

She murmured, 'Signor Andrea . . .' and then to the page, 'Have you seen the Princesse de Conti?'

'She has already left for Saint-Germain, Madame la Marquise,' said the page.

'*Tant pis. Allora, arrivederci,* Signor Andrea of the perfect mirror.' She smiled once more and he saw the white teeth again. Then she walked away towards the gilded double doors into the next room. Andrea watched her retreating back, aware of the rustle of silk against skin.

The page ran to hold the doors open, then returned to Andrea, smirking. 'Well, Monsieur really likes to make a hit with the court ladies,' he said.

'Who is she?' Andrea ignored the jibe.

'The Marquise de Montespan. One of the *dames d'honneur* to Madame, Henriette d'Angleterre. As to what future role she may play in the royal household, well, we're all waiting to see.' The page's smirk widened into a leer.

Without any more words, Andrea and his assistant gathered up their tools and left the Queen's apartment. But as the cart jolted back through the rain towards the faubourg Saint-Antoine, a profound and subtle emotion suffused his whole being. Oblivious to his damp clothes and the rain that dripped from the brim of his hat, he was consumed with the delicious sensation simply of being alive.

Nine

CLAUDINE LOOKS down from the first-floor window of the apartment at the street below. It is evening and she can only distinguish the faces of those passers-by who are carrying flambeaux. There are several shadowy figures picking their way along the edge of the street. Madame has just departed for the Palais Royal and Monsieur le Marquis is at his usual pursuits. She can hear sounds from the street through the glass, but the apartment is quiet, so quiet she can almost hear it breathing. She is surrounded by a listening silence. The past is there, she has only to lift the curtain. She listens to the voice in her head as she remembers Madame in tears.

Yes, last night I saw Madame cry. She has so much spirit that it shocked me when I saw her break down at her dressing table. She had been discussing the placement of a beauty spot, whether near the eye or near the mouth, a *passionée* or a *baiseuse*. I said was she hoping for a glance, or a kiss? And then she said, 'Oh, what's the use?' And then, 'My poor babies!'

It's been like that since the birth of the second, last September. It's induced fits of despondency. Monsieur le Marquis is spending even more time at the gaming tables, which wouldn't matter so much if he won. I said to Madame, 'Poverty, you don't know what poverty is.' And, of course, she doesn't. She hasn't wandered the streets of Paris, starving and sick, offering herself to passers-by to get food for herself and her children until she is too *sale* to interest even the most drunken sot. It happens. It could have happened to my mother but she found another way of making money, through the theatre. So I live in a half-world, knowing there are many more halves than make a whole.

There's another world I live in, too. It's around us all, but few recognise the unseen kingdom that rules us. People pretend they're free, but they are bound by unacknowledged forces. You can only be free by seeking out these forces, by negotiating with them. You strike a bargain and you keep to it. Madame is beginning to reach out in her mind, I know this from the way she seems to think the dark glass can help her. I tell her it may answer your questions or it may not. But it can't do more than that. And then the other day she said, 'Have you heard of a wise woman, by the name of Catherine Voisin? Someone was telling me she could see the whole of your life, present, past and future. I should like to consult her.'

It always comes to that. When they're confused and unhappy with their lives, they think that knowledge will set them on the right path. But knowledge adds to the confusion, for you interpret it according to your own wishes. I know Madame Voisin, as do all the court ladies who find they have women's problems – fears of a pregnancy, a cold-hearted lover, an overbearing husband. Madame Voisin listens, she knows more secrets than anyone else in Paris.

Madame is set on seeing her and maybe it will ease her mind, or maybe she will want more. Madame Voisin doesn't tell all at once. She knows the value of withholding certain information, so the client will return. I promise to arrange an appointment and Madame departs for the ball, a *passionée* by her right eye. She recovers quickly, she knows that at court you must always look buoyant, rich and happy, for otherwise the vultures gather. It is the law of nature, after all.

Ten

As Andrea worked at the factory, his thoughts drifted back to the palace of the Tuileries and to the beautiful Marquise. He recalled the way she looked at him, her voice, the way she had murmured 'Signor Andrea' . . . The sibilance of the 's's and the wonderful drawn-out 'a' echoed in his mind. Each mirror he worked on was made with her as its imaginary recipient, but his lack of concentration spoilt his work. Du Noyer, who noticed his standards had declined, said, 'Concentrate on your work while you're in the factory, Andrea, and forget your outside distractions. You're here to do a job, not chase after skirts.'

Andrea would have liked to have told him that his feelings were altogether on a higher plane. It would be enough just to gaze at the Marquise again, to hear her laughter, to breathe in her presence. It would be happiness simply to see her, to know that such a woman existed.

He mentioned her to Luca, without revealing her name, and Luca sighed in exasperation. They had met two sisters in the botanical gardens who had agreed to see them again, provided they met as a four, but now Andrea was sabotaging this neat arrangement for the sake of an unattainable dream. Luca, ruddy-faced, short and plump, knew he was not to every girl's fancy and he had hoped he might stand a chance with the younger sister. Andrea said, no, of course he would keep to their plan, but the girls knew, despite his attempts to appear interested, that his thoughts were elsewhere.

The beautiful Marquise had expressed interest in a mirror, but he had no idea where she lived and he hesitated to appear to be asking for a commission. He would like the mirror to be a gift, but then again, the only way of doing this was to pay for it out of his own wages. Du Noyer would have a seizure if he tried to make a mirror that was not paid for. It seemed that the Marquise would remain tantalisingly out of reach, occasionally appearing in his mind's eye as he moved about the city. He would see the amused azure eyes sparkle at him as he paused by a flower stall, breathing in the heady scent of tuberoses and lilies. Luca is right, he thought, I'm behaving like a clown.

On a soft, bright morning in May which seemed to hover on the edge of summer, du Noyer called to him as he was taking a break from the heat of the furnaces in the yard. 'You, Andrea, you like getting out of the factory, don't you? You can go to the Palais Royal. Monsieur the King's brother is asking for a large commission of mirrors, but he has no idea how many he needs.'

Andrea felt his heart leap. The King's brother was

married to Henriette d'Angleterre. The page had told him that the Marquise was one of her *dames d'honneur*. It seemed fate was nudging du Noyer into engineering another meeting.

The sun, after the earlier spring rain, lifted the spirits of everyone in the street. The leaves on the trees shimmered with white light and there was an energy in the air that gave impetus to his steps. At the Palais Royal there was a momentary check because of the process of finding the right functionary to take him to Monsieur's apartments. Andrea was happy to wait, studying the mythological paintings in the great hall. He wondered how many other royal palaces the King owned.

Eventually a small, fussy man arrived and took him upstairs to the apartments. Monsieur, he explained, wanted two large mirrors opposite each other in the great salon and he understood that they would have to be made up of several mirrors joined together. That was correct, said Andrea, each mirror measured about one metre in length and half a metre in width, so it was a question of calculating the number they needed. He began to measure the space and make calculations in his notebook. As he made his notes, he would glance up as he heard women's footsteps or the rustling of a skirt. None of them, disappointingly, was the Marquise, but he seemed to be attracting a certain amount of attention, as they would pause and look back at him. More disconcerting was that several young men wearing powder and rouge did exactly the same.

'Monsieur also requires a mirror for his dressing

room, which must be full length,' said the functionary. 'He wants to see himself from all angles.'

They moved through the next two salons to the royal bedroom. A high bed with heavily brocaded blue and gold curtains dominated the room, separated from the rest of it by a marble balustrade. On the walls hung more paintings from mythology, of Arcadian nymphs and shepherds. The next room was Monsieur's boudoir, leading to Monsieur's cabinet de toilette. There was a mirror leaning against the wall and another on the dressing table.

'You see what a problem these small mirrors are for a prince who prides himself on his dress,' said the functionary. 'Monsieur would like the walls mirrored in their entirety.'

'That's unnecessary, I would suggest,' said Andrea. 'Monsieur doesn't need all the walls mirrored if he had mirrors angled in each corner, which would show him every aspect of himself.'

He sketched a plan, made some calculations and said, 'That's less than half the amount he would otherwise pay and it would fulfil its purpose.'

He was about to say that to have a room entirely mirrored would induce a feeling of unreality, then wondered how much reality there was in Monsieur's life anyway.

The functionary placed the sketch in the folder he was carrying. Monsieur would be grateful for the advice, he said.

That seemed to be it. Andrea had spent an hour measuring rooms for a prince's vanity and was about to leave the palace without a glimpse of the Marquise.

There was no way he could ask about her without seeming impertinent, and as the functionary showed him downstairs, he resigned himself to the fact that he would probably never see her again.

In the hall, a flurry of small yapping dogs surrounded a man in a fantastically ruffled costume. Andrea recognised Monsieur at once, it would be impossible, once having met this extravagant dandy, to mistake him. Monsieur was waving his arms and yapping back at the dogs, stamping his high-heeled shoes, until they were almost in a frenzy. He glanced up at the staircase, then froze, as in a game of statues, one arm still extended in the air. 'Mirrors!' he cried, staring at Andrea. 'It's the mirror man from the faubourg Saint-Antoine!'

The functionary, bowing low, said, 'We have measured the salon of Mercury and the boudoir, and I have all the plans and calculations.'

'But what about the temple of Diana, what about my coach? The job is unfinished. I want more mirrors. No one listens to me. I remember telling you I wanted mirrors in the coach. Come with me, young man, your work isn't finished yet.'

Andrea followed him, feeling as if he were yet another dog among the long-haired animals teeming in the wake of Monsieur. They walked across the great courtyard and into a garden of green lawns, gravel paths and avenues of pleached limes. The central path led to a large stone basin. Monsieur paused here and gazed into its still waters. 'This pool could have changed all our lives.' In the midday sun, the powder on his face was like a dusting of flour. He had applied some black ointment to his eyelashes that glued them into little spikes. He was staring at Andrea intensely with his small dark eyes.

'Why?' asked Andrea.

'Aha!' cried Monsieur triumphantly. 'Because my brother fell into it when he was seven and nearly drowned!' His laugh had a hysterical edge. 'Then I would have been King! Imagine! What a farce!'

Realising it was a remark with which it would be dangerous to agree, Andrea said carefully, 'It would certainly have changed your life.'

'Ah yes, so it would,' said Monsieur, his attention caught suddenly by four women playing cards under the shade of a trellis. Monsieur drew in his breath, as if he had seen something unpleasant. 'Madame,' he said, 'gambling.' He bowed in their direction and the lady who was dealing the cards responded with a curt nod, then continued to slide the cards to her companions. She was wearing a necklace of large pearls and elaborate ringlets on her forehead, but her skin was waxen and there were dark circles under her eyes. Andrea guessed that she must be Henriette, wife to Monsieur. It was clear they were not on the best of terms.

Then he saw her, the Marquise, next to Henriette. She had been looking at her hand of cards and now, seeing Monsieur, she smiled and inclined her head towards him. She saw Andrea in the same instant and smiled again, murmuring, '*Buon giorno, Signor Andrea.*'

He bowed and said, '*Buon giorno, Madame. Buon giorno, Mesdames.*'

Henriette looked curiously at him, then at the

Marquise. Andrea heard the Marquise explain, 'He's one of the Italian mirror makers.'

A smattering of Italian words were dispatched at him from the ladies, wishing him good day and asking where he came from in Italy. '*Di dov'è?*'

'Oh, come on,' said Monsieur impatiently. 'You'll be giving them Italian lessons next.'

Andrea bowed again. '*Mi scusi. Arrivederci, Mesdames.*'

He followed Monseiur, who looked at him crossly, annoyed at the attention the ladies had given him. Andrea began measuring the archway behind the statue of Diana, which Monsieur wanted to reflect a vista. As they walked on through the garden towards the coach house Monsieur, recovered now from his fit of petulance, said, 'There's one more commission I should like to place. I should like to order a mirror for the Marquise de Montespan. You'll arrange for the frame as well, which will be carved silver, with a silversmith I use in the Marais. It should be delivered to her house when it is finished. Will you include it on the order?'

'I should be very happy to do so,' said Andrea and it suddenly seemed the whole world was on his side. The sooner the mirror was finished, the sooner he would see her. He felt light-headed. The enticing scent of her, the captivating eyes, the mouth that seemed to draw kisses to it. He no longer wished to deny to himself that he was in love.

Eleven

IT WAS one of Monsieur's friends who told her what
the King had said. Monsieur would not have been
so unkind, but he could not resist gossiping and so the
'friend' passed it on. Athénaïs had been sitting with her
sister Madame de Thianges, watching the King dance.
As one friend of Monsieur asked Madame de Thianges
to join the gavotte, another slid into the vacated place
next to Athénaïs. Without a by your leave. He was
young, but his prominent nose, bulbous pale eyes, slack
mouth and runaway chin promised that he would
mature into a man of outstanding ugliness. While she
was thinking this, he began to pour the poison into her
ears.

What a beautiful couple they were, the King and
Mademoiselle de La Vallière, weren't they? Was it not
inspirational just to watch them? Look at the majesty
of his bearing, the shapeliness of his legs. And La
Vallière, so sweet, so shy. It was a joy to see.

And more in this vein, leading up to what he really
wanted to say. Of course, most of the ladies at court

were in love with the King and it must be very pleasant for him to feel this wave of admiration. Naturally, he was not referring to Madame de Montespan, most certainly not, but even someone as beautiful and spirited as she would never turn the King's desires from La Vallière. The King had been discussing the various ladies at court with Monsieur, as brothers do – which of them was the most beautiful, which the most desirable – and Monsieur, of course, had spoken with great admiration of her, the Marquise de Montespan. Not her, said the King, she is so obviously trying to attract me. She does what she can, but I don't want her.

The young man paused, watching Athénaïs's face. She smiled at him. 'Have you noticed,' she said, 'that those who pass on gossip are those about whom nobody else has anything to say? How odd – I can't even remember your name.'

She left him, staring after her with his bulbous eyes, and joined the group around her brother, the Duc de Vivonne. But despite their distracting *bavarderie*, the reported sentence would not be driven from her head. 'She does what she can, but I don't want her.' Two angry spots burned on her cheeks. To be categorised as one of the ladies chasing after the King was intolerable. How dare the King think she was ogling for his attention! So he assumed every lady at court was after a tumble into bed with him? Well, he would find Athénaïs remarkably unin-terested, less than impressed by the royal physique, the display of his fine calves, the studied elegance of his bearing, the way he held his extravagantly coiffed head. There were others as handsome, though she was hard put to think of any among the powdered dandies at the court of Monsieur.

Back at the rue Tarenne, the anger still coursed through her body as Claudine helped her undress. Claudine, aware that Madame was in a state, suggested a soothing tisane, perhaps Madame's favourite, lime flowers.

'Yes, lime flowers,' said Athénaïs. She raised the cup to her nose and smelt the subtle fragrance. 'It takes me back . . .' she said. Claudine was not listening. Yawning, she had loaded her arms with the warm, crumpled petticoats that Athénaïs had discarded and was taking them to the dressing room.

Athénaïs reclined in the armchair, holding the cup in both hands, watching the petals floating on the surface. Yes, it takes me back, she thought, to days of sunshine and shadows in the Charente. The scent of lime flowers in the avenue leading to the wide open meadows, the sun beating down on my head because I refused to wear a bonnet. Then in the evening when I was too hot and tired to sleep, Nono would brew a lime flower tisane, to shut my eyes, she said. But often I would wait for her to go to sleep, and then I would tiptoe past her bed and up the narrow steps that led on to the turret. I would look out across the trees to the lake shining in the moonlight, and sometimes I would see a dark figure by the water, and I knew it was to do with the stories Nono told us of fairies and goblins and witches. It was strange how her bedtime stories would keep you awake, wanting to explore this mysterious world.

One day I was looking at old Gaston as he was calming one of the carthorses. He had worked with our horses since he was a boy and was known in the Charente for his power over the wildest of them. There was something about the way he stooped, the way his arms hung at his sides, that made me think of the shadowy figure. I said to him, 'I have seen you at night by the lake.' He looked at me with his unreadable eyes and said, 'You have seen nothing, Mademoiselle, you were only dreaming.' I said no more, but there was something thrilling about this unknown world glimpsed in the shadows and I felt the same sense of excitement when Claudine first looked into the dark glass. 'No one must know of this, Madame,' she said and finally she became reluctant to read the glass, saying that it tired her out. So I must go to Madame Voisin, to try to find some reason for the chaos, some pattern to put my life in order. When I go to confession, there's no solution offered, only prayers to achieve unworldliness. If I wanted to be unworldly I would go into a convent like two of my sisters. I am not ashamed to be worldly, I am not ashamed to want everything life can offer.

Athénaïs inhaled the scent of the tisane as she raised the cup to her lips. Claudine returned from the dressing room and said, 'Is there anything more, Madame?'

There was not, 'apart from dealing with my hair which you tangled up so much earlier,' said Athénaïs.

She sat in front of the mirror, while Claudine tugged at her hair with a comb. 'What do you expect, if you want to be at the height of fashion?' said

Claudine. 'You can comfort yourself with the thought that all the other ladies suffer similarly when they try to smooth out their hair at night.'

Athénaïs looked at the mirror. She remembered Nono telling her that on midsummer's night, if you ate an apple while you looked into the mirror and murmured three times, 'Cupid, show me my true love,' you would see the face of your beloved in the glass. Why an apple? Athénaïs had asked. Why not grapes? Nono had said the apple was the fruit of knowledge, as Eve had found out to her cost, so you could see it was dangerous to search for knowledge, rather than accept whatever God brought to you. Athénaïs rebelled against acceptance of God's will. That was the path her mother had followed, deserted by the Duc when he had left her for his mistress. She thought of her mother's grief-ravaged face, of her fair hair turning to grey in a matter of weeks. That she, Athénaïs, should ever be in the position of wronged wife was insupportable.

Into her mind came the image of the gold and rose room in the Queen's apartment, of the mirror on the wall, of the young man looking into the glass, not at himself, as everyone else did, but at the glass itself. She had thought as she saw his reflection that here was a face that had been sculpted by a master trying to capture the profile of a god, of an Apollo. There was a coolness in his perfection, in his absorbed appraisal of the glass, until he had become aware of her and their eyes had met in the mirror. She had felt in that moment a vitality that linked them, as if they were of a similar spirit. She told herself later it was simply that she had been struck by his beauty and by his unawareness of it.

'Italians take it for granted,' Claudine had said when she had described the moment. 'He has no need to confirm from the mirror that he is beautiful.'

Unlike the King, whose every movement was designed to display his splendour. A peacock flaunting his feathers, a cockerel strutting among his hens, a stallion flaring his nostrils. The most handsome man in France, apart from this obscure Venetian glass blower who moved quietly about his business, measuring, drawing diagrams and playing tricks with mirrors.

Athénaïs smiled to herself. She had no intention of encouraging the young man, of course, but it was intriguing, the way he appeared unexpectedly in one palace or another. It was always pleasant to be admired. It made her feel more alive.

Twelve

WORD HAD got about the factory of Andrea's interest in a Marquise. Which comes of confiding in a friend. Every day, one or more of the men would call out, '*Com'e sta, la bella marchesa?*' After his first wave of anger against Luca, the repository of his secret, Andrea would say light-heartedly, '*La bella marchesa* is madly in love with me.' There would be hoots of mirth and warnings of caution – rich women were the worst of all, selfish and unpredictable. They would encourage you, treat you like a plaything and then cast you aside. 'And what about the husband?' said Luca. 'These powerful noblemen have thugs in their pay. You'll end up stabbed in the back and kicked to death in an alleyway by half a dozen bravos.'

Andrea smiled to himself. Even the most jealous husband could hardly take exception to the few words he had exchanged with the Marquise, so it was all amusing speculation. What were half a dozen bravos, he would retort, for the love of *la bella marchesa*? And du Noyer seemed to be acting on his behalf like a benign spirit in sending Andrea on commissions to the royal palaces. He had now given him the weightiest commission of all – the King had asked for the measuring up of a room at Saint-Germain-en-Laye, where the court had migrated for the summer. It was to be a grotto, a bathing place with fountains and mirrored walls. Andrea could ride over there and back in a day.

'I can ride, but not very well,' said Andrea. 'We always travelled by water in Venice.'

'Then get yourself over to the Tuileries and find out when the next coach is going for Saint-Germain. You'll be able to get a seat on the outside, at least.'

It was eight in the morning and the city was crowded with people going about their business. Andrea dodged through the carts and wagons, and skirted round the jams caused by the road building. At the Louvre chains of workmen were still swarming up the scaffolding. At the Tuileries there was the same lack of information and shuffling off of responsibility. A coach had gone a few minutes ago and no one was sure if any other was scheduled. Eventually someone said, 'Try the Minister's office. Monsieur Colbert frequently goes to Saint-Germain. It's the large house with the courtyard on the corner, two hundred paces north of the Palais Royal.'

Andrea walked along the street lined with high-walled buildings, until he came to the house with the courtyard. The iron gates opened on to a paved expanse, with a gravel parterre and several lime trees in the centre. At the steps of the grey stone mansion a coach and four was drawn up. The coach was black, the horses black. Andrea recognised the taste of the Minister, a man for whom colour was anathema. Beside the horses stood a tall, gaunt man whom he took to be the coachman. He explained his commission and was allowed the end of the driving seat, 'provided you don't get in my way'. The coachman didn't like the look of the leather case of measuring tools Andrea had brought with him. The road was rough and you could drop it quite easily, he said. Put it inside the coach, where there's plenty of room for baggage.

At that moment the Minister descended the steps, followed by a secretary. He saw Andrea by the coach door and said, 'You, again. What is it this time?' Andrea explained the commission for the King and the problem with the case. Colbert shrugged. 'Yes, put it inside, it makes no difference,' he said. 'And get up by the coachman straight away.' They hadn't a moment to spare.

It was a heady sensation, travelling on top of the coach, and he soon realised why the coachman had warned him against carrying baggage, for the man drove like a demon. Once outside the city, he laid the whip on to the horses and the coach careered along regardless of other road users. Peasants steered their carts of produce into the hedge to avoid having their wheels torn off by the black coach. A horse shied, throwing its rider half out of the saddle, to be left clinging on to its neck. Dogs and chickens scattered out of range of the iron-clad hooves.

Andrea clung on to his insecure seat above the shining muscular rumps of the horses, from where any moment the jabbing elbow of the coachman threatened to dislodge him. The horses' backs were flecked with foam where the reins rubbed against hide and the pungent odour of equine sweat invaded his nostrils. The road they were tearing along ran through meadows and fields of smallholdings, the aroma of newly mown hay mingling with the riper farmyard smells of cattle and pigs.

He felt a tug at his coat and turned to see Colbert's secretary leaning perilously from the coach window to attract his attention. Shouting over the noise of the wheels on hard earth and the clatter of horses' hooves, he understood the man to be asking him to step inside the coach. Monsieur Colbert wanted a word with him. Andrea turned to the coachman and said, 'Monsieur Colbert has asked me to step inside. Could you stop the coach?'

The coachman laughed abruptly, showing his few discoloured teeth. 'Try stopping these horses yourself, Monsieur. They'll just crash into each other and get tangled up in the traces. I'll lay off the whip for a while and you can slide in at the door.'

For a moment Andrea was spreadeagled, one arm clinging on to the driver's seat, a foot on the mounting step, the other arm hanging on to the frame of the open door, his elbow supported by the secretary who called, with more encouragement than conviction, 'You're all right. I have hold of you.'

Andrea glimpsed beneath him the hard, stony road they were speeding over, let go of the driver's seat, clung on to the door frame and flung himself in, landing in a heap at the Minister's feet.

Colbert looked up from his papers and said, 'Why didn't Jean-Jacques stop the coach?'

'He said he couldn't . . . Your Excellency.'

'Couldn't be bothered, more likely. Well, when you have recovered, young man, I should like to talk to you. You can get up off the floor and sit opposite me.'

While Andrea got his breath back, the Minister continued to read his papers, occasionally making a note in the margin. Andrea watched him surreptitiously, aware that this was an unsought opportunity to study at close hand the most powerful man in France next to the King. Colbert's brows were habitually furrowed, as if his mind were in a state of conflict. Occasionally he would scowl at the figures he was reading and once underlined something so vehemently that the point of his pencil broke. Andrea recognised the scent he was wearing. It was the same his father would use after he had been shaved, bergamot from Italy.

Eventually the Minister sat back in the black leather seat, studied Andrea with deepset eyes and asked him how he was getting on at the factory. Were the men happy? Did they find the conditions and hours of work satisfactory? Any complaints about the living quarters or the food?

No, said Andrea. The men were happy with the conditions and the pay. They had got used to French cooking. They sometimes felt enclosed in the factory and the compound, because there were restrictions on leaving the area during the day.

'What do they expect?' asked Colbert. 'They're there to work and besides, there have been incidents. The present Venetian Ambassador has instructions, as did his predecessor, to disrupt the factory and get the men back to Venice.'

'Some of the men miss Venice and miss their wives.'

'We'll do what we can to bring the wives to Paris. It isn't easy because they are watched by the Venetian authorities. It would be easier for us all, of course, if we were able to train French workers in the art of mirror making. Then those Venetians who miss their homes could get back there, and those who like being in Paris could stay on and profit by the growth of our industry. France is becoming richer by the year and there is no better time to be here, now we have a strong and glorious King.'

Andrea had followed the course of Colbert's thoughts and for a moment the image came to him of the Sieur de Jouan's face in the mirror in Murano. In the black coach, seated before this man in black, whose dark eyes seemed to divine what was going on in his mind, Andrea realised he was once more being subjected to temptation. Colbert was outlining a plan which would ensure Andrea a rich and profitable future. He seemed well informed on the subject of Andrea's family. He knew that Andrea and his brother Federico would have eventually taken over the running of the Allegri factory in Murano, and he knew that he had been disowned by his father, in favour of Federico. Andrea must realise, said the Minister, there was nothing for him to go back to. It seemed only logical that he should profit by the opportunity now before him. If he were to help in training the French workers to make mirrors, not only would he be making himself an immense amount of money, but in due course he would probably have charge of a mirror factory, in which case the profits could be unlimited.

The Minister paused and waited for Andrea to speak. The secretary sat with head bowed, studying the papers in front of him. Andrea was aware in the waiting silence that he had come to a crossroads in his life. He had capitulated, back in Murano, to de Jouan. Logically, there was nothing to stop him taking this next step. A rich factory manager, compared with a factory worker, would open the way to a different style of life. In this swaying, jolting coach, a bargain could be struck that no one else need know.

But curiously enough, despite the compromises he had already made, there was a point he could not pass. This would be a final betrayal of his father, of the men who were left behind in Murano. He remembered the Venetian Ambassador pleading with them, tears in his eyes. 'Do your work, take the money, but don't tell them the secret of your mirrors.' It would not only be a betrayal of those who lived now by mirror making, but of generations of *specchiai* who had guarded their secret, who had refused to let outsiders in on the art of making a living image, whose strength lay in their silence. The men who had come to Paris had already betrayed the factories of Murano, which had lost the greater part of their trade with the French. Yet they had only been thinking in the present. The next step would affect the future and be irrevocable.

'I don't know how I can put this respectfully, Monseigneur, but something prevents me giving away the secret of making mirrors.'

Colbert was frowning in irritation that this man had not understood a perfectly logical argument. It seemed, suggested the Minister, speaking more slowly, that there was not a huge difference between what he was proposing and what Andrea had already agreed to.

'The difference is that I was entrusted with a secret that has been handed down through the generations, over two hundred years. The secret was given to us on the understanding we would keep it among ourselves. I should be betraying not only the *specchiai* of today, but those of previous generations, who lived and died for their work. It's a sacred trust.'

Colbert stared at him coldly. That, he said, was the most illogical argument he had ever heard. To keep the secret, on account of generations of dead mirror makers! Well, there was nothing more to be said, for the time being. But if Andrea came to his senses, he should approach the Minister again. Meanwhile, he was not sure that a man of such divided loyalties was one they wanted to undertake delicate commissions. Perhaps Andrea should not be allowed outside the factory in future.

Colbert noted the anguished expression on Andrea's face, gave him a grim smile and, turning to his secretary, said, 'Will you hand me the folder on the Chambéry case in Bourges?' He settled back to read it, dismissing from further consideration the subject of mirrors. Andrea waited to be told to leave, in which case he would have demanded that the coach stop first, but the Minister seemed untroubled by his presence now that his mind was absorbed in another matter. Andrea bowed and changed places with Dessaix, who began to confer with Colbert on the intricacies of the

Bourges case. There was nothing to do beyond looking out of the window and waiting to see how his fate would be determined.

THE COACH was rolling into Saint-Germain and beginning to slow down. On the left was a stone fortress-chateau, moated, with a causeway across to the great archway that led into an octagonal courtyard. The coach drew up before the main entrance to the chateau and one of the guards opened the door for the Minister. Andrea followed the secretary out of the coach and asked him where he should go now. Dessaix spoke to one of the guards. 'Follow this man, he will lead you through the labyrinth,' he said and sped off to catch up with Colbert.

The way to the King's apartment was via the stone main stairs, through a great ballroom of stone and brick with three storeys of stone carvings. This had been the ballroom of François Premier, the guard informed him, now used for court entertainment of plays by Molière and music by Lully. They ascended some more stairs, walked along a corridor over-looking the central courtyard, past a chapel and finally to the apartments in the north-west wing. These were the King's private apartments, explained the guard. The state apartments were larger, built for an audience. This part of the chateau was for his plaisance, where he could be at ease.

The apartments looked out on to an expanse of gravel patterned with box hedges, lawns and an avenue of lime trees. They were in the antechamber, its walls covered with tapestries of pastoral scenes. There was a pervading scent of jasmine from massed plants in silver jardinières and a fully grown orange tree in one corner. From an adjacent room Andrea could hear the clink of a hammer on metal and looked through the door to see a small, wiry man with a lined, nut brown face tapping a copper pipe that was surrounded by marble floor.

He looked up at Andrea with a grimace. 'I told them not to lay the marble before I had done,' the man said. 'Did they take any notice? How am I supposed to create a fountain with all this stuff in the way? Are you responsible for this cock-up?'

'I am here to measure the walls for mirrors,' Andrea replied.

'*Italiano!*' exclaimed the man and immediately began to talk rapid-fire Italian. He was Francesco Francini, he said, one of the brothers Francini, fountain makers to the King. 'And you? One of the mirror makers of Murano?'

'That's right,' said Andrea. 'At the moment trying to make sense of being in France.'

'Sense? The only sense we need be aware of is that the King is mad for fountains and mad for mirrors, and he doesn't care what it costs. I bless every day I came to France. The Italian princes have grown poor and mean. This King is taking us back to the glory days of the Renaissance. He is Medici, Farnese, Gonzaga, Este, rolled into one.'

'So this is to be the grotto of mirrors?'

'The grotto of Neptune's fountain,' corrected the fountain maker. 'The mirrors are there to reflect the fountain. It's being made by my brother at the moment, in pure silver. Neptune and his tritons spouting water. Very pleasant for the King and his inamorata to refresh themselves on a hot day.'

Andrea smiled. 'Is that what it's for?'

'Young man, wouldn't you like to be King for a day? When you have finished measuring the walls, I'll show you what it means to be King.'

'I'm beginning to understand,' said Andrea. 'His Minister collects the money and the King spends it.'

'But without the King, how would you get people to part with their cash?' asked Francini. 'It's more complicated than you think.'

Andrea measured the walls and made calculations in his notebook. Eventually Francini said, 'Come out into the gardens and see what's going on. That's another of the King's madnesses, gardens. You haven't been to Versailles yet?'

'Versailles? Where's that?'

'Ah, so new, so much to learn. Come, I will show you,' and the fountain maker led Andrea out through the many galleries and stairways downstairs and into the open air.

Across the expanse of gravel, groups of courtiers were walking and chatting together, breaking off from one group and joining another, then drifting on again.

'The King is in conference with his Minister and they are waiting for it to end, to try and have the favour of a word with him,' said Francini. 'Quite often he passes them by just to talk with his gardener. I have heard them discuss for hours the placing of a parterre.'

They walked past the courtiers and Andrea could not help glancing to see if they by any chance included the Marquise. None, he could see, had the beauty and fire of Madame de Montespan, whose image haunted his mind. They reached the lawn at the far end of the garden, which ended in a bluff overlooking the valley of the Seine.

'You see that hill in the distance? That's north of Paris, Montmartre. There's the road you travelled along, there's the bridge across the Seine. Now, look over here,' and Francini pointed towards the south. 'Those are the woods and meadows of Versailles, where the King intends to build the greatest palace in the world – a palace of light and fountains and mirrors. We have started on the fountains and there'll be hundreds more. Yet the most curious thing is there's no water at Versailles. It has to be pumped in from a lake in the next village.'

'That's crazy. Why did he not build where there was already water?'

'Because Versailles was where he first found true love. There was an entertainment, a couple of summers ago, called *Les Plaisirs de l'Ile Enchantée*. We worked for months on the fountains. That's how he sees Versailles, an enchanted island where the elements are in his control. We are fortunate, you and I, in that we don't have the means to realise our dreams, for they devour you.'

They stood on the edge of the bluff, feeling the wind blowing off the valley, bringing with it the smell of freshly cut hay. A hawk hovered overhead, swooping towards the ground as it spotted a movement in the grass.

'To have all this and want more,' said Francini,

shaking his head. 'And you haven't seen Vincennes yet, nor Fontainebleau. But it's good for us, it brings more work, more fountains, more mirrors.'

They heard the sound of music, of the hautbois, flutes and sackbuts of the King's Ecurie that accompanied his walks in the garden. From the open windows of the chateau there was a movement of people and the aimlessly strolling courtiers in the garden all turned their heads. Andrea saw the scarlet plumes of the King's hat and then the King himself as the crowd parted, the figure that he remembered from the mirror factory, walking with slow deliberation. The courtiers gradually started to close in, waiting to be noticed. He stopped and began talking to a few. Andrea could see their heads nodding up and down in unison. 'They are like so many puppets,' he said to Francini.

'And the King is the puppet master,' said Francini. 'But who controls the puppet master? That's the question to which no one has the answer.'

Thirteen

MADAME LA Marquise is safely out of the house and Claudine is going through her wardrobe, holding up dresses in front of her before the mirror. There is the blue embroidered silk, the gold and blue brocade, the blue satin with sapphire clips. Madame likes blue, it shows off her eyes, and besides, it is what the royal ladies often wear. Claudine gathers a gold and cream brocade dress in front of the mirror, and looks at herself assessingly. Yes, the soft tones of the material enhance her face and the agates on the bodice accentuate the green of her eyes. Claudine has discarded her grey dress and is standing in the bedroom in her petticoats and stays. She pulls off her muslin cap and steps into the skirt of the dress. That was the easy bit, but now for the bodice, which she has always struggled with for Madame, when lacing it up at the back.

CLAUDINE CALLED out to Marie, the kitchen maid. 'Lace me up at the back,' she commanded.

Marie giggled. 'I daren't. Madame would be in a fury if she knew.'

'Nonsense, I am Madame now,' said Claudine. 'And you are Claudine. I want you to put up my hair with ribbons and jewels.'

'I don't know how to,' said Marie, picking up the jewelled clips from the dressing table. She ran the teeth of the ivory comb through Claudine's hair.

'Really, Claudine, I don't know how you have become so clumsy,' Claudine scolded Marie. 'And stop tugging at my hair, you will tear it. Why am I cursed with such a clumsy maid?'

'No doubt because you don't pay her enough,' said Marie. 'I'm not playing this game, Claudine. Madame wouldn't dismiss you, she needs you too much, but I would be out of the door without a reference.'

'Go back to your kitchen, then,' said Claudine. 'You'll never be a lady's maid.'

She waited till the door closed behind Marie, then began moving slowly around the room, running her hands over the sumptuous material of the skirt. Such smoothly woven silk brocade, it made you feel like a marquise – no, a princess – to wear it. She paused in front of the mirror. With this costume I could win a prince, thought Claudine. She turned sideways to the mirror. The skilfully cut bodice raised her breasts to a shelf almost under her chin. She looked down at the softly swelling flesh. To think they are usually hidden by grey cotton, what a waste, she thought. I'll cut away the bodice of my dress and show the world that I'm as shapely as the Marquise.

As she sat down at the dressing table, gazing at

herself in the mirror, deciding on her best features, undoubtedly her eyes and her mouth, a shame about the less than refined nose, she heard the downstairs door close and footsteps on the stone stairs. She leapt up in alarm. It couldn't be Madame back already, for she had distinctly said she would be returning in the late afternoon. Now she had to get out of the dress immediately and she had no Marie to help her. She ran into the dressing room and closed the door, her fingers agitatedly tearing at the laces of the bodice. She heard Madame's voice call from the stairs, 'Claudine!'

Mother of God! thought Claudine, damn these laces, and she yanked at them until finally there was enough give to get the bodice over her head. She was aware that the material under the arms was damp with her perspiration. Now the skirt, and she untied the drawstring so that it fell in a heap round her feet. She stepped out of it and laid it back in the open chest. The bodice should be aired but there was no time, so she threw it in on top of the skirt and closed the lid. She heard the door of the bedroom open and Madame's voice close at hand. 'Claudine, where are you?' And then, 'What's this?'

Claudine, standing there in her petticoats, realised only too well what it was. Madame had seen her grey dress lying on the floor. She was trapped in the dressing room in her underwear.

The voice called again, an angry edge to it, 'Claudine!'

Claudine stepped out of the dressing room. 'Madame?'

'What on earth are you doing in your petticoats?

Why is your dress lying on the floor?' Athénaïs was looking at her with growing suspicion.

'It was such a hot day, Madame, that I thought I would work better without so many clothes. It gets very close in here and makes me feel faint.'

'Indeed, and is that why you simply tossed the dress on to the floor? I hope you don't treat my clothes like that. Claudine, you haven't been wearing my clothes, have you?'

'No, Madame, of course not. It was really only the heat. And I felt impatient with the grey dress. It makes me look so dull.'

'That is no bad thing,' said Athénaïs and opened the dressing-room door, looking for signs of recently worn clothes. Claudine waited for her to open the chest, but it seemed that Madame was not going to make a thorough investigation after all. She closed the door and only said, 'And on top of all my troubles, my maid has gone mad.'

Claudine smiled. The storm had been averted but she had had a narrow escape from the famous Mortemart rage.

Fourteen

WHEN NICOLAS du Noyer looked at the men working in the factory, he was reminded of a team of great horses. No one could stay the course as a mirror maker unless he was large and robust. They needed expansive chests for the blowing of the glass, and muscular arms to swing the glass on the end of the pipe and form it into the cylindrical shape. But they had to have the delicacy of a seamstress as well when they took the shears to cut the hot glass, for one slip could ruin hours of work.

Like other men who worked together in difficult conditions, they had become a close-knit guild, jealous of their skill and unwilling to share it with outsiders. For all the financial blandishments Colbert had authorised him to offer, du Noyer had made little headway with persuading them to instruct the French workers in their art. They delegated to the French apprentices the various unskilled jobs of the factory, such as keeping the furnaces stoked. The few Venetians who had agreed to instruct the French had reneged, presumably after pressure from their fellows. He could see that if he himself were a worker, he would not wish to cross Antonio della Rivetta, with his barrel of a chest and head like a bull about to charge. They could not, of course, stop du Noyer looking on at their work and he had, during the course of a few months, come to understand the step-by-step process of mirror making. But the quantities involved and the combination of the materials could not be divined and only an experienced mirror maker could reveal them.

He watched Andrea, back in the factory after his recent expedition and working on the order for Monsieur. He was seated on his bench next to the furnace, his instruments beside him. Like the rest of the workers in this suddenly hot month of June, the young man was bare to the waist, protected by leather gauntlets, arm straps and the leather face shield. His face was red from the exertion and the heat, his chest shining with sweat. What they go through for man's vanity, thought du Noyer. But for the onlooker there was something inspiring about this classical scene of the inferno. Vulcan at his forge; yes, it was a good subject for a picture.

Andrea, oblivious that he was being transmuted through the factory owner's eyes into mythology, drew the molten glass from the furnace, blew until it became a small round globe and whirled the pipe through a semicircular motion, so that the glass began to lengthen to an oblong. He returned it to the furnace to stop the glass cooling, then repeated the process a number of times, turning the pipe swiftly to keep the glass an even thickness, until it had developed into a translucent closed cylinder, the long muff that would be transformed into flat glass. At this point he called out 'Pronto!' to Luca, who was standing by with the shears. Luca pierced the closed end of the muff with the point of the shears and continued to cut as Andrea turned the pipe. They repeated the process with the other end, then Andrea put it back into the mouth of the furnace to soften it again. He drew it out and laid it on the copper-lined table. Luca swiftly cut it lengthways and helped Andrea ease it out into a flat plate. It was always a moment of congratulations, for at this point the glass could easily be ruined.

'Perfect,' said Luca. 'Monsieur will be delighted.'

Remembering Luca's previous indiscretion, Andrea had not told him the mirror was destined for the Marquise. Yes, he thought, it is a perfect glass, of even thickness and without flaws. Now to transform it into a perfect mirror. First, it had to be ground with fine sand, after which came the silvering process. On the silvering table he laid out a leaf of beaten tin and smeared on it a coat of mercury. Then it was a question of waiting till the two metals united.

'Did you see the King when you went to Saint-Germain?' asked Luca, as they watched the foil.

'At a distance. He was surrounded by a swarm of courtiers. Wherever he went they followed him, as if he were the Queen Bee. I had a feeling that without him they would have died.'

'A strange life,' said Luca.

'They would think ours far more strange and not at

all enviable. The metal is ready, now.' Andrea poured more mercury on to the quickened tin foil, then he and Luca carefully slid the glass across the surface, pushing the surplus mercury before them so that there were no air bubbles. They put on weights to press out the extra mercury and winched up the table top so that the glass was on a slope, with a gutter underneath it for the mercury to drain.

Andrea looked at his hands. Pinheads of mercury glistened on his skin. He immersed his hands in a bucket of water and rinsed his face with his hands. Now it was a question of waiting impatiently for the next day and the hardening of the silver. And finding out what progress had been made with the frame, over which Monsieur had been specific.

In the meantime he sent one of the French apprentices to make sure that the household in the rue Tarenne had not yet moved out of town. Word came back that they were still in residence for a few more days. Madame la Marquise would be joining the court in Saint-Germain and might be there for some time. Andrea sent a message to the silversmith to hurry up with the frame. The silversmith replied sharply, did he want the best from him, or did he not? If he wanted the best, then he would have to wait.

The frame arrived two days later, an exquisite piece of work, with curlicues and lilies, that emphasised the beauty of the mirror. They carefully packed the mirror, first in a silk cloth, then in wood shavings in a wooden crate. It was now a matter of getting it to the Marquise, who might or might not be at home to receive it. Andrea had no way of knowing the timetable the

Marquise kept, at what time she might go out, at what time she might receive visitors, or even if he would be allowed to present it to her. He decided the most likely time to find her in would be the mid-morning. A little before nine, he set out with the French apprentice and the cart containing the mirror, intending to be at the rue Tarenne before eleven.

At the door of the building they announced their business to an elderly concierge who confirmed that Madame la Marquise was in residence and they should take the stone stairs to the first floor. The oak front door to the apartment was open, leading through to the hall and a salon. The hall was lit by candles in wall brackets and in the dim light they could see a Turkish rug on the floor planks, a couple of wooden chairs and a chest. It seemed sparsely furnished for a marquise.

A door at the side of the hall opened and a small dark-haired girl in an apron came out. She stared at Andrea, her mouth slightly open. He said, 'We have brought something for Madame la Marquise, courtesy of Monsieur the King's brother. Will you please tell her?'

The girl looked at the crate for a while, as if trying to decide what was in it, and said, 'Madame is not yet dressed.'

'Nevertheless, could you please tell her. She may find this useful in helping her to dress.'

The girl was looking unsure, but retreated to the salon and to the double doors leading off it. Andrea could hear the sound of women's voices and then the girl returned. Madame would be with them shortly, she announced, and leaned against the wall to continue watching Andrea and the crate.

Eventually, the double doors opened again and the Marquise emerged. She was wearing a loose satin gown with lace at the neck and elbows. Andrea saw her surprised expression as she glanced at him and then at the crate. 'I was told that I had been sent something from Monsieur. Are you the bearer of the present?' she asked.

'I am, if it so please you, Madame.'

'Then it must be a mirror.' The Marquise laughed delightedly. 'What else would the mirror maker bring me?'

'I have brought a letter from Monsieur, which he wanted you to receive at the same time,' said Andrea, handing her the sealed letter he had been given.

She sat down to read it and laughed again. 'Monsieur has a great sense of humour,' she said. 'We must set the mirror up immediately. Will you get rid of that wooden contrivance and then bring it through. Have you brought anything to hang it with? There is no one in this house I would trust with such a precious thing.'

'We have brought everything necessary. The mirrors are precious to us too and we have to make sure they are well placed.'

'Such devotion to your craft! Monsieur couldn't have sent a better emissary.' She gave him a teasing look and returned towards the bedroom, leaving behind the lingering fragrance of last night's tuberose. '*Elle est belle, cette Marquise,*' said the French apprentice, raising his eyebrows, '*il faut prendre garde.*'

'What we have to be careful of right now is the

mirror,' said Andrea, mentally cursing Luca for his gossip. They eased the top off the crate and lifted out the mirror in its silk wrappings. Andrea balanced it carefully, then picked it up and carried it through to the reception room.

The double doors opened again, and this time a young woman in a grey cotton dress and muslin cap looked out. She turned back to the interior of the room and said, 'The mirror is here, Madame.'

The Marquise emerged, her hair, which had been loose on her shoulders, now gathered carelessly into a knot, leaving tendrils falling to her neck. Andrea could not help smiling at this little attempt at formality, which only increased her seductiveness. She said, 'Are you going to unveil the mirror for me?'

Andrea lifted it on to the table, to show it to best advantage, and eased off the silk cloth. The Marquise stared at it for a moment, taking in the purity of the glass and the carved silver frame. She stepped forward and touched the silver frame. 'It is beautifully done,' she said. 'And the mirror is perfectly made.' She leaned forward, looking at her face in the glass. 'It could not be better,' she murmured.

'The mirror has the advantage of reflecting beauty,' said Andrea.

She looked Andrea in the eyes. 'The mirror maker is full of flattery,' she said.

'But I am only saying what the mirror says and the mirror tells the truth,' said Andrea.

She looked at the mirror again. 'Is this one you made?' she asked.

'It is, and I made it with the greatest care. It was

made as close to perfection as it was possible to come.'

She ran her hand along the frame again, feeling the indentations of the carved silver. Her hand touched Andrea's and instead of moving away, it lingered almost imperceptibly for a moment, the warmth sending a lightning sensation through him.

He moved his hand, the words of the French apprentice in his mind – *il faut prendre garde*. 'Would Madame la Marquise wish the mirror to be placed on the wall?' he asked.

'Why not? You are the best person to do so, since it was you who made it.'

'It has my initials on the back, in case you should forget.'

She laughed. 'As if I could . . . Claudine, help us. Where should we best place it? Come, Signor Andrea, don't be shy.'

She had moved into the bedroom and he followed, aware of entering some sort of feminine sanctuary. The walls were covered with magenta silk, and the curtains of the four-poster bed were patterned with lilies and roses. A dressing table inlaid with mother-of-pearl, its surface crowded with bottles of ointments and scents, combs, ribbons and a discoloured mirror, was placed in the centre of the room, the light from the window falling on to it. By the bed, a pair of little gold slippers were lying where they had been kicked off.

The mirror should be hung near the natural light, said the Marquise. So it should be on the wall adjacent to the window and the dressing table moved over to be near it.

Andrea measured the siting of the mirror and when he had fixed it into place, the Marquise stood in front of it examining both the glass and herself dispassionately. Yes, she nodded to Andrea's reflection behind her, it was perfectly placed. What did Claudine think?

The maid stood in front of the glass for a long time and said, her voice taut with emotion, 'I've not seen myself like this before.'

It seemed she would never tear her eyes from her image in the glass. Finally, she looked at Andrea's reflection and said, 'It's a very fine mirror.'

'Thank you, Mademoiselle,' he said.

'But you can see more in my dark glass.'

Her eyes had a strange light to them and seemed to be looking through the glass, rather than at Andrea. They had the wildness of the eyes of a stray cat that has grown up without its mother. She began to speak again, as if in a trance. 'I saw this glass being made, there was a furnace, and I saw you reach into it and you drew this out.'

'Claudine!' the Marquise called out sharply.

She continued looking at the glass, unhearing, and said, 'I see poison in the mirror. You must be careful of poison.'

'Claudine!' rapped out the Marquise, the volume of her voice finally penetrating the maid's consciousness.

'Madame?' she said, emerging into reality.

'Claudine, will you pull yourself together! Stop dreaming and find out what has happened to my tisane. And perhaps Signor Andrea would like a tisane as well, or a glass of wine?'

'A glass of wine would be welcome,' said Andrea.

'I'm sorry about my maid,' said the Marquise, as soon as she had left the room. 'She behaves a little strangely during her time of month. You must excuse her.'

'My grandmother had the gift of second sight as well,' said Andrea. 'She would look into still water, but she told us very little of what she saw. She always said it was better not to know the future.'

The Marquise was looking at him curiously. 'You're a surprising man. But no, with Claudine it is simply that she is a little touched, now and again. Full of fancies. As you might be with her surname — Mademoiselle des Oeillets.'

'The demoiselle of the carnations. That's pretty.'

'The mother was an actress, as the daughter should have been, which was the reason for her unusual name. Claudine des Oeillets . . . But she fell into a trance on stage one night and frightened the audience, so she became a maid. I put up with her behaviour – which is by no means the worst I have to put up with. Come into the salon and have your wine.'

It seemed the Marquise was showing another side of herself to him. Underneath the wit and self-assurance, he sensed unhappiness. In one phrase she had told him the state of her marriage. 'By no means the worst I have to put up with . . .' He felt a wave of protectiveness, as of the strong towards the weak, a feeling totally out of line with the reality, he reminded himself. She, the influential Marquise, the recipient of presents from Monsieur the King's brother, he, the immigrant artisan, whose only brush with influence had been to his disadvantage, in the coach of the King's Minister.

But it seemed that she wanted to confide in him. He was, after all, sitting in her salon with a glass of wine, which earlier he would never have dreamt was possible, and she was asking him about the making of mirrors, a subject which surely could be of no interest to her. She asked him to speak in Italian because she would like to practise it, despite the fact he didn't speak the approved Tuscan. All the better, he said, when she met the Venetian Ambassador. She could surprise him with her knowledge of the vernacular.

The Marquise laughed and leant against the back-rest of the chair, which meant that under her loose robe she could not have been wearing the iron cage of stays that most ladies were rigidly encased in from morning to night. Through the satin gown he could see the outline of her unrestrained breasts, which he knew must be as white and as smooth as her arms. He realised that in a moment he was going to do or say something he might regret. She had fallen silent and was looking at him as if at an exotic animal, her eyes travelling upwards from his legs to his face, in open curiosity. They were now dwelling on his mouth, which seemed to burn under her gaze. It was more than flesh and blood could bear.

He was saved by the maid, who came in at that moment to say Madame's dressmaker had arrived. The heightened atmosphere, when the only sound had been their breathing as they looked at each other, dissolved into the air.

'At last,' said the Marquise, 'I've been waiting months for her. What excuse did she give?'

'I must take my leave,' said Andrea, getting to his feet. 'You have been very kind, Madame. I leave my mirror in the best home it could have.'

'My thanks to you, *multi grazie,* Signor Andrea, *arrivederci,*' she said, extending her hand graciously. 'Will you see the Signor out, Claudine?'

He bowed over her hand and followed a subdued Claudine out into the hall. 'Your workmate got tired of waiting,' she said. 'He took himself and the cart back to the factory.'

Andrea could foresee more hilarity in the mirror works when he returned. He said goodbye to the maid's downcast eyes and descended the stone stairs. Halfway down, on the landing, a man in expensive but dishevelled clothes was leaning against the balustrade. He was holding in his hand what seemed at first sight a long-eared brown spaniel, but was the wig that he had torn from his head in frustration at the heat. His own hair was lying damp with sweat close to his skull. His face was red from the heat and from his choleric mood. He glared at Andrea. 'Where are you going in such a hurry, garçon?' he demanded.

Incensed at his lack of courtesy, Andrea said, 'What's that to you?' but the man was now standing in his way and he was forced to halt. He could see a sword at his side and he experienced a sudden sense of danger. These noblemen, for that was what he must be despite his uncouthness, were a law unto themselves.

'What's that to me? It's my house, that's what it is to me. My house, my wife. What was your business there?'

'Only to deliver a mirror, Monsieur, as you will see when you return,' he said quietly, though he was seething with anger.

'What mirror? I ordered no mirror. What new extravagance is this?'

'I cannot tell you, Monseigneur, I only delivered the mirror. I know nothing more about it.'

The man looked at him suspiciously but stepped aside, to allow him to continue on his way.

'*Merci, et au revoir*, Monsieur le Marquis,' said Andrea and descended the rest of the stairs, resisting the temptation to look back and fix in his mind the face of the Marquise's husband. He heard the Marquis shout some insult after him, recognising the word 'Italian' but not the rest of it. He paused for a few moments outside the building to subdue his agitated breathing. It was not only his encounter with the Marquis that had disturbed him but the whole tenor of his meeting with the Marquise. She had encouraged him, she had flirted with him, and then she had left him in unresolved expectation. He had been simply a diversion to amuse her until the dressmaker had arrived.

His anger turned from the husband to the Marquise. She was just a woman playing tricks out of vanity. A vain flirt with a mad husband and a mad maid. He was glad he was not likely to see her again. And then, as he continued walking back to the factory, he remembered the moment when she had seemed to want to confide in him, looking into his eyes as if for help. It was not her fault, he thought, that she was so dangerously attractive. He should, instead, be angry with himself. He who stood every day at a furnace should know better than to play with fire.

Fifteen

THE MIRROR has found an audience. Three women stand in front of it watching their every move. Athénaïs is to the left and Claudine to the right. In the centre, staring into her reflection, is Madame de Thianges. She steps forward and raises the palm of her hand to the mirror, as if to test out the reality of the image.

'No,' said Athénaïs. 'Don't touch it.'

'Why not?'

'Because I shall then have to fetch a cloth and clean it, Madame,' said Claudine.

'This is a very delicate mirror,' said Gabrielle de Thianges. 'Perhaps it's better for me not even to look at it, in case it breaks.'

'It is a perfect mirror and Monsieur is a perfect friend. He couldn't have known of anything I would have wanted more.'

'Monsieur is judging you in his image. He can't get enough mirrors. He has been lining the Palais Royal with them and now he's going to start on Saint-Cloud. Anything his brother has, he wants too.'

'Of course, Montespan was extremely put out,' said Athénaïs. 'He came back from one of his unsuccessful nights out, had a set-to with the mirror maker and then began accusing me of being unfaithful.'

'Unfaithful with the mirror maker?' exclaimed her sister, looking incredulous.

'No, with Monsieur.'

'Even more unbelievable. Doesn't he *know* about Monsieur?'

'If you saw the mirror maker, you wouldn't find the idea of seeing more of him so distasteful, Madame,' said Claudine.

'Mademoiselle des Oeillets is very chatty today,' said Madame de Thianges. 'Who is this mirror maker she is recommending to me?'

Athénaïs smiled at the mirror. 'A charming young Venetian with a face like an angel. A flatterer par excellence, for he utters all his remarks with such sincerity, as if he truly believes them.'

'He does believe them, Madame,' said Claudine. 'I can tell he is in love with you.'

'No, really!' said Madame de Thianges. 'That's too much. What a scoundrel!'

'Take no notice, Claudine is full of romantic notions. He's simply a charming young man who makes beautiful mirrors, which he can hardly bear to part with, because he then comes round to hang them.'

'So it is the mirror he loves?'

'But I must admit, he's as beautiful to look at as his mirrors. He has the most wonderful white teeth when he smiles, and brilliant eyes, and a profile like a statue of Hermes.'

'I can hardly believe I'm hearing this,' cried Madame de Thianges. 'Some stray Italian glass blower?'

'And Madame, he has a perfect figure,' said Claudine. 'Broad shoulders and a slim waist. He was wearing loose breeches, so I couldn't tell more, but his calves were as fine and as well shaped as the King's.'

'And it's not only my maid who is struck by him,' said Athénaïs. 'Henriette d'Angleterre remarked that she would be very happy to have some Italian lessons with the mirror maker.'

'Madame l'Anglaise probably has similar déclassé tastes to her brother,' sniffed Madame de Thianges. 'What is it about these Italians? Look at Lully. One moment a valet de chambre, the next composer to the King. Well, Athénaïs, I had come round to invite you to dinner with two *ducs* and a *vicomte*, but it seems you would prefer to go slumming.'

Athénaïs laughed. 'No, I've no objection to meeting your *ducs* and even a *vicomte* or two. But I can tell you, Gabrielle, that if the young Italian were called il Principe Andrea di Castelgrande di Monted'oro and arrived at Saint-Germain in a coach and six, the entire court would be at his feet.'

'My fanciful Athénaïs, you always had a wild imagination, one moment thoughts of the King, the next . . .' and Madame de Thianges shrugged expressively.

'I think nothing of the King,' said Athénaïs, an angry redness diffusing her skin. 'He is vain, conceited and unfaithful to the Queen.'

Gabrielle raised her eyebrows, but forbore to comment. Marie the kitchen maid looked round the door of the bedroom, to say the tailor for Monsieur le Marquis had arrived with his bill. He seemed to be in a state of distress.

'The poor man, but what can I do?' asked Athénaïs. 'It is the Marquis de Montespan's bill and he's not here.'

Marie nodded, and returned to the hall. Athénaïs sighed. 'Enough of fancies. The reality is that Louis Henri is at this moment with our brother, trying to borrow more money.'

'What an appalling man!' said Madame de Thianges.

'Before you criticise my husband, when did I last hear you say a good word about yours? At least Montespan has some fire to him.'

'It's time I left, before I am tempted to cancel your invitation for tonight,' said Gabrielle. 'Au revoir, beautiful mirror. I hope, for the tailor's sake, that your husband is successful with his begging bowl. If I had a husband like yours I would be considering a visit to Madame Voisin.'

Athénaïs made a face at her sister's departing back.

Marie returned with the tailor's bill. 'He says he's being pressed for taxes and pleads for part payment at least. He has a wife and children to support, Madame la Marquise.'

'What can I do? There's no money in the house. He's come at the wrong time. Why did he allow this bill to mount up to such a huge sum?'

'Because Monsieur le Marquis ordered more clothes before he had paid the previous bill.'

Athénaïs unlocked the drawer of her dressing table and drew out a small leather bag. She counted out ten livres and gave them to Marie. 'Will you apologise to him and say the full amount will be with him next week. Tell him I am *désolée* that I can do no more at the moment.'

Marie departed with the money. Athénaïs said to Claudine, 'I can't bear to see the tailor's sad face. This time I must make sure to get hold of the money before Montespan spends it. I don't understand what my sister meant when she said I should visit Madame Voisin because of my husband. How can she help?'

Claudine busied herself with tidying the dressing table. 'It may be because Madame Voisin is a wise woman,' she said, not looking at Athénaïs.

'I should like some wise advice. Then I must see Madame Voisin. I can feel it now, it will be some sort of turning point. When your confessor fails you, then take another path.' Athénaïs looked at her reflection in the glass. 'I must do it while the mirror shows me what I want to see.'

Sixteen

THE KING'S *grand lever* was taking place in the state bedroom. Near the door, discreetly behind the courtiers, stood Francini and Andrea. It wasn't difficult to get admission, just a little sweet-talking to a guard whom Francini knew. The King, wearing a gold and blue brocade dressing gown, was seated at a table having breakfast.

'He's already been washed and given his under-garments before everyone was admitted,' Francini whispered to Andrea. 'He knows what's fitting to be seen.'

One of the courtiers in front of them muttered, 'What are you doing here? This is not a public show.'

'*Scusi, Signor*, we belong to the household.' And then, whispering to Andrea again, 'Not a public show with nearly a hundred people watching?'

A boiled egg was placed before the King. He sliced off the top with one stroke of the knife, to appreciative murmurs and a smattering of applause from the courtiers. He consumed a brioche and a glass of wine and water before embarking on the next part of the *lever*. Under the dressing gown he was wearing stockings and knee breeches. Now one of the valets de chambre was helping him off with the dressing gown, to reveal the King in his nightdress. The other valet stepped forward and the two of them held up the dressing gown as a shield against the eyes of the courtiers while the King divested himself of the nightdress. They lowered the dressing gown again to reveal the King clad in a fine white lawn shirt. A third valet stepped forward with the King's waistcoat.

The King sat down, as the decorative flourishes were added of jabot, ribbons and a final hairdressing to the long dark curls of his abundant hair. During this time, several of his courtiers entertained him with anecdotes and sallies of wit. He listened and laughed occasionally, his eyes scanning the watching faces. He looked over towards the door and Andrea felt the sharpness of his glance. Whether the King remembered him he could not know, but the eyes registered the stranger near the door and Francini standing next to him before moving on.

'He knows everyone at the *lever*, and checks to see who's there each morning,' whispered Francini. 'Anyone who is supposed to attend and does not, loses his standing with him.'

The King had had enough. He rose from the chair while the hairdresser was still adjusting the curls under the feathered hat. Acknowledging the assembly, who bowed to him, he walked towards the door that led to his study. A few of the courtiers followed him, the rest moved towards the door to the guardroom. Francini touched Andrea's sleeve and said, 'It's time to go. But now you've seen the morning ceremony of the Sun King.'

'It's the strangest thing I have seen,' said Andrea. 'If I were king I should abolish it. Every day to stand in front of a hundred people in your nightdress . . .'

'He's been doing it since he was a child, though the crowd of spectators grows by the year. Come now, I must get back to the grotto and the fountain of Neptune. What brings you here today?'

'I'm measuring for a mirror over the fireplace in the state bedroom and then a mirror in the King's study. It seems he has to see himself wherever he is going.'

'Never decry the King's vanity. The love of his image will keep you in work and out of trouble,' said the fountain maker, shouldering his bag of tools. 'If *you* reigned in glory, you'd also like to witness it.'

Andrea asked for a ladder and set to measuring the wall above the fireplace. As he did his calculations, his mind returned to the Marquise. Maybe she had arrived at the court of Saint-Germain. Of course, he was aware that all it was possible for him to do was to smile and make pretty remarks if she looked in his direction, yet he knew – and he suspected she might too – that their bodies had already acknowledged their attraction. He remembered the folds of the satin robe, the vitality that seemed to course through her, giving a shimmering aura to her skin. He remembered the timeless moment when they seemed to speak to each other in the silence. And yet, and yet, wasn't she just exerting her power over a man, and in perfect safety too, for she must have known that he wouldn't dare respond? He was reined in by the great divide between them.

The debate for and against continued as he worked. Was the Marquise a lost soul looking for the love she could not find with her boorish husband? Or was she a knowing flirt? Was admiration just food for her vanity? One moment he saw himself, like the knights of chivalry, loving her in silence. The next moment a scene flashed into his mind of the Marquise escaping from her husband and flying to his arms on a moonlit night, all discretion cast aside.

'Three metres by two metres, to take mirrors of one metre by half a metre.' Andrea scribbled his calculations. Damn the Marquise, she has ruined my arithmetic. Back up the ladder again, he remeasured, trying to concentrate on the work in hand. He heard a door open and the sound of voices. Looking down from the ladder, he saw beneath him the King and Monsieur Colbert.

His immediate reaction was that no one should be higher than the King and he scrambled down the ladder, to make a deferential bow. Louis raised a hand in acknowledgement, saying, 'It's not necessary to interrupt your work. If everything came to a halt whenever I entered a room, we would never be done.' The eyes narrowed as he looked at Andrea. 'You're the mirror maker who experiments, aren't you? Isn't this the one, Colbert?'

An expression of weariness drifted over Colbert's face at the sight of the young Venetian. 'Yes, this is the one, Sire.'

'You can set fire to wood at ten paces. You say you

could do so at a hundred paces, given an increased number of mirrors. With more mirrors, could you set fire to a greater length, or does the strength of the beam diminish with the distance?'

'Your Majesty, that is difficult to answer, for I don't know if there's a point at which the strength of the light becomes weaker. Archimedes set fire to a ship at a hundred paces, but at a greater distance . . . it may be possible, it may need more mirrors. It could be done with a practical experiment, given the necessary space and mirrors.'

'Isn't this an experiment our new Academy of Science should be working on?' Louis said to Colbert. 'It would be more interesting than seeing how long a bird can live without air.'

'It would be both difficult and expensive to arrange, Sire,' replied Colbert.

'I can't see why,' said the King. 'Imagine if you could use this burning mirror at a distance greater than cannon fire. What if you were faced with the Spanish fleet on a hot day in the Mediterranean and were able to burn them with the mirror before they could reach you with their cannons?'

'That remains an academic question, Your Majesty,' said Colbert uneasily, 'in a hypothetical case.'

'An academic question? That's what the Academy of Science is for,' said the King. 'A practical experiment to resolve an academic question. How would we best conduct this experiment?'

'Over a level uninterrupted surface, Sire, preferably over water,' said Andrea. 'Its success would depend on the strength of the sun and the angle of the mirrors.'

'And you know about the angles.' The King, not waiting for an answer, turned to Colbert. 'Something to consider at the next meeting of the Academy. Ask our distinguished scientists to apply their minds, then we'll decide on a practical experiment.'

Andrea bowed. 'I am at your service, Your Majesty.'

The eyes of the King seemed to burn through to Andrea's soul, as if he were divining the form of his character and thoughts. Finally, Louis said, '*Bene, allora, una sperimentazione con tanti specchi*, Signor Specchiaio.' Louis smiled at his little Italian phrase and turned away, followed by Colbert.

Andrea stared after them. The domain in his mind that had remained with him during all his months in France, of the lagoon of Venice, had been burned by the brilliance of the sun. He knew that from now on he was not his own man any more, that part of him belonged to the King.

Seventeen

THE TICKING of a clock was the only distinct sound in the room. The clock was made of ebony with carved figures supporting the timepiece, on one side a nymph, on the other a skeleton in a shroud. On the clock face itself was an engraving of a monster devouring a human form.

Madame Voisin was looking at Athénaïs, reading her face, and then she shut her eyes, clasping the necklace Athénaïs had given her in both hands. For some time the sound of her breathing could be heard in the quietness, in rhythm with the clock. The curtains were drawn against the daylight and the room was lit by candles in brackets on the walls. Athénaïs waited, trying to curb her impatience. These things took as long as they took. She examined Madame Voisin's face while the woman's eyes were closed. She had plump, smooth skin, a roundness of the chin and her iron-grey hair was covered by a muslin cap. It was only when she opened her eyes again that the peaceful, motherly look disappeared.

'There are several men in your life.' Madame Voisin's eyes were pale and slightly prominent, with a curious glazed quality.

Athénaïs felt a twitch of irritation. Any fairground fortune teller would have said as much. She had thought this woman would have been more perceptive.

'But you know that already,' continued Madame Voisin. 'Beautiful women never have only one man in their lives. There was a man you might have married and you still think he might have made you happy. But he's no longer in your life. And then there's your husband. I can see a lot of pain there. He is full of anger. You're bound by ties of pain. There's something you wish to do about your husband, is there not? Would you like to see him go away? Is his presence preventing you from realising happiness with another?'

'It would be enough for me if he were to stop being such a spendthrift and improve his temper,' Athénaïs replied.

Madame Voisin looked at her steadily. 'You don't wish to see the last of him, then? That is curious, for you know your life with him will get no better. I'm afraid, Madame, he will never reform. But I see a dazzling aura around you, as brilliant as diamonds. You are destined for a great future, but only if you reach out for it. You must be bold, you must strike out and care not what people think. I can see a man who loves you, but he denies it. He is afraid of the consequences of declaring his love. Do you know who I am talking about?'

'Perhaps I do.' Athénaïs smiled. 'My maid says he is in love with me, but he would never dare tell me. It's no more than a fancy. We are too far apart in society.'

'You're closer than you think and he has a key to your future happiness. There's something about this man – I can see an aura like flames around his head . . .'

'Like a furnace?' interrupted Athénaïs.

'Flames . . .' emphasised Madame Voisin, but her vision had been dissipated by the interruption. 'He has gone . . .' She closed her eyes again, breathing deeply as if to revive the link to her other world. There was silence again for a while and then she suddenly said, 'The blonde woman, there is a blonde woman who will call for you. When she does, fly to her side at once. Don't hesitate.'

'The Queen?' queried Athénaïs.

Madame Voisin opened her eyes as the window on the other world was closed from her vision. She said, 'The link is broken now. I can't see any more. You'll have to visit me again, another day.'

'I'm sorry, I shouldn't have interrupted,' said Athénaïs. 'You might have told me more if only I had stayed silent.' She rose from her seat and moved over to the clock, which had been fascinating her.

'It is unusual, isn't it?' said Madame Voisin. 'A present from one of my clients. The theme is appropriate – time devours us all. That's why people come to me. They know life is not infinite, they want their wishes fulfilled now. What I'm trying to divine is what you want now. I feel that you're not admitting your true desire. Some of my clients think they know and then find it's something completely different.'

The door opened and a man stood on the threshold, looking enquiringly at them, as if waiting to be invited in. He was dressed in black clerical robes,

114

and a sleeveless overgown embroidered with red and gold dragons. He had a face like pale, crumpled paper and red hennaed hair.

'May I introduce Father Mariette,' said Madame Voisin. 'He officiates at some of my ceremonies, to great effect.'

Father Mariette smiled and bowed to the Marquise. 'I am at your service, Madame, whenever you have need of such a ceremony.'

Athénaïs felt a shiver run through her, a mixture of repulsion and excitement. Looking at his robes, she realised that he must be one of those who invoked unseen powers through blasphemous masses. The image came into her mind of dark figures at a lakeside at night, their shapes defined in the light of a fire.

'The time is not right for Madame la Marquise,' said Madame Voisin. 'But one day she will call for you. Madame, remember Father Mariette. He can invoke a greater power than the power of prayer. One day he will help you to your destiny.'

In the open air, outside the hermetic atmosphere of Madame Voisin's consulting room, Athénaïs was aware of her normal perceptions returning to her. She had felt mesmerised, almost as if she were drugged, while she had been there. It would be better not to call upon these people again, said her rational mind. But at the same time she was filled with an immense curiosity. Madame Voisin had seemed about to reveal something of great importance, but at the end there were just a few cryptic sentences, which could only be interpreted in the light of future events . . .

Eighteen

A S THE early morning sun slants over the city, the church bells ring out, from one spire to another. The heavy, clanging bell of Notre-Dame is joined by a chorus of peals in varying tones and intensity, proclaiming their message of joy in the Divine. It is the feast of Saint Anne, the mother of the Virgin. Though it is only seven o'clock, there's a haze over Paris that promises another oppressively hot day.

In his house near the Palais Royal, Colbert is already at his desk. He is studying the letters from Murano, which were intercepted on their way to the factory. The wives of Civrano and della Rivetta are pleading with their husbands to return. The writing is so fine that they must have been written by a professional scribe, the language so flowery that he can almost hear the voice of the Venetian Ambassador composing them. It's another ploy to create dissension in the factory and all the more reason for the French Ambassador to renew his efforts to bring the wives to Paris. The deep-toned bell of the Louvre joins the clamour of the early

morning but hardly impinges on Colbert's consciousness as he moves from his desk to his ebony writing
table, and reaches for a quill and inkwell.

The sound of the bells increases in volume as the
bell-ringers fall into the rhythm of the movement.
They ring across the Seine to Saint-Cloud, mingling
with the birdsong in the garden, infiltrating through
the window of Monsieur's bedroom. It is not the
sound that wakes him, though, but the fact that
Madame has inadvertently touched him in her sleep
with her foot. Monsieur sits up in bed and furiously
berates her. Henriette wakes from a pleasant dream to
the reality of her hysterical little husband, still wearing
the remains of last night's make-up, to whom she is
shackled in bed until such time as they produce an
heir. She shouts back, in a crescendo of rage and
frustration ending in a long, agonised scream from the
depths of her being. Thus begins another day in the
married life of Monsieur and Madame.

Over at Saint-Germain Louis wakes in the bed of
the Queen, where he usually spends the remainder of
the night after visiting his mistress. Louise de La
Vallière is indisposed and Louis has last night given
proof of his ardour to the Queen. Marie-Thérèse hears
her husband begin to stir from his sleep and reaches
out a little hand in search of more love. Louis opens his
eyes to look into hers, which are milky with adoration.
She smiles at him, open and trusting as a baby, and he
sees her teeth, blackened from eating chocolate. The
bells commemorating the mother of the Virgin Mary,
which call him to early mass, save him from having to
prove his love again.

In her large, solitary bed at Versailles, where she has fled from court, Louise lies gently weeping. The haven of their early love, the enchanted island of their pleasure, now induces a profound melancholy for it's a reminder of what she is losing. She listens to the bells and thinks of those mornings, when the chateau was just a pleasant country house, before the elaborate building works began to envelop its pretty brick façade with monumental stone. When all that occupied their minds was the prospect of a day's hunting and the accompanying games of love as they lost themselves in the forest. Louis has changed, he wants more than she can give him, but she won't accept that it might be over. She will find some way of clinging on to his affection, of making him acknowledge that, however dazzling the other court ladies might be, she is his one true love. She raises herself from bed and goes to the window overlooking the parterre. She can see the shirt-sleeved figure of Monsieur Le Nôtre, the King's gardener, surveying his domain. It would be her dream of bliss to live here with the King, to have only conversations with Monsieur Le Nôtre and the other keepers of Versailles, not to be subjected to the spiteful maelstrom of the court. But the enlargement of the chateau means only one thing — that in a few years' time the court will have moved here and she will have lost her enchanted island. She looks with envy at Monsieur Le Nôtre standing solidly on the gravel below, contentedly taking the morning air.

Contentment, too, is the dominant emotion for Athénaïs as she stands at the window of the old manoir bordering the grounds of Saint-Cloud. The bells are only faintly heard through the summer foliage of the trees, the air alive with a chorus of raucous frogs from the nearby pond. Their croaking has such a unison about it that she imagines a chief frog, like an amphibious Monsieur Lully, conducting his band with a staff made from a bulrush. Monsieur has been kindness itself, to have understood that she needs a little peace and space after the difficulties of the past year. Later she will walk through the gardens to the chateau, to sharpen her wits, laugh at the gossip, discuss with him his most serious topics of clothes, jewellery and etiquette, play cards with Henriette. But in the meantime it's enough to savour the wonderful freedom of being without her husband, who has gone to his estates in Gascony, gathering troops for a border skirmish with Spain. And her babies have been taken by their nurse to stay with her aunt near Vincennes, so she is truly free of any responsibility. She stretches her arms above her head with a feeling of release and, as she turns from the window, her nostrils scent the chocolate which she has left to cool. She can resist it no longer and raises the cup to her lips, inhaling first the smell and then tasting the rich sweet darkness of it. Happiness spreads through her in a warm, enveloping wave.

In Paris, the air is already fetid with the smell of ordure. Despite the edicts over the last two hundred years against people throwing the contents of their chamber pots into the street, there are still enough disregarding the law to make it hazardous for walkers. Andrea has learnt to use the broader streets where possible, but the streets and alleys near the faubourg

Saint-Antoine are like an obstacle course. You have to look down to make sure you are not about to step on to a turd or a dead dog, and at the same time watch out for what may be coming your way from above. There seems no way of solving the problem of a mass of people living at close quarters and all subject to the laws of nature. It is the time of year when anyone who has the means to do so gets away from the city.

Andrea has the means to escape, for he has been told to go to Saint-Cloud where Monsieur is crying out for mirrors. The factory is closed for a fortnight, to clean and overhaul the furnaces, and the mirror makers have been left idle. Andrea has it in mind, after he has measured up at Saint-Cloud, to go over to Saint-Germain and look up Francesco Francini, in the hope of getting a few days of country air. As he walks along carrying his bag over his shoulder, he smiles at memories of the previous evening. The younger of the two sisters from the botanical gardens was very sweet to him. They had gone out together as a four, the sisters, Luca and himself, but then she had drawn him into a courtyard, away from the others, and kissed him. When he had put his hand inside her bodice, she had held it there. He is sure she would have let him go further, but as luck would have it they were interrupted by the owner of the house, who had heard their sighs and whispers from his bedroom window. She had turned shy again after that, but Andrea feels she is close to being his. When he returns, revitalised by a few days away from Paris, and she has become the fonder for his absence, he will see her again and they will continue where they left off.

He smiles at the passers-by, for he feels blessed at being strong, young, warm-blooded and in love. The physical certainty of last night's encounter has driven from his mind all thoughts of the Marquise. It is, as Luca keeps telling him, the bird in the hand that matters, not the impossible dream of an enchantress. He is in the best of moods by the time he reaches the Palais Royal where he will find a cart or coach, whatever departs next for Saint-Cloud. The bells ring all around him, the clear wild pealing punctuated by the deep measured tones from the Louvre. Their pervading clamour resonates through his head, obliterating all further thought.

Nineteen

ATHÉNAÏS HAD had her fill of reclining on the daybed that had been brought into the garden. It was all very delightful, looking up at the green light filtering through the leaves of the lime tree shading her, but she was in need of company. She felt a sense of regret for times past when she was a child and it was enough to be in the country with the sun shining overhead, but those were days of unsophisticated pleasures, of splashing in the lake, or running through the hay. When you grew up you put away such simple diversions. Your enjoyment was planned, you corseted yourself into a habit for hunting, you walked around the gardens and parterres, which were designed to allow staging posts for conversations, viewing of the panorama and the display of fountains. You took part in bucolic meals in cultivated groves, noting from the seating arrangements how you ranked in the favour of your hosts. And you made conversation to a background not of birdsong but of stringed instruments playing music by Jean Baptiste Lully. Athénaïs did not decry sophisticated pleasures, far from it, but you became dependent on them for your entertainment. An idle day under the lime tree, a jug of lemonade at her side, however glowingly perfect to start with, would leave her fretful by the evening. So it was back into the stays, on with the stockings, the petticoats, the muslin and lace, to achieve the required pastoral effect for the court in the country. She wavered between the pearl necklace or the amethyst, then decided the pearls would appeal more to Monsieur, who would be quick to remark on any error in taste.

Monsieur had sent one of his young friends to escort Athénaïs to the chateau. A sprightly, bright-eyed little fellow, he filled her ears as they walked through the gardens with chatter about Monsieur's new fountains, about the King's plans for Versailles, Monsieur's plans for a *galerie* of paintings for Saint-Cloud and so on. There was a rivalry between the two royal brothers over who would build the most lavish palace, leading to arguments over architects, painters and garden designers. Le Nôtre had remarked that he wished he had two bodies, for he felt as if he were being torn in two between the demands of Saint-Cloud and Versailles. And so on, the young man's voice running like a brook over pebbles, Athénaïs listening with half an ear while her eyes took in the well-groomed beauty of the garden.

It seemed that she had missed some thread in the conversation, because suddenly she heard him say, 'But, of course, that won't be a consideration when we are at war next year.'

'At war?' queried Athénaïs. 'Why are we going to war?'

The young man's eyes lit up. He enjoyed possessing knowledge ahead of others. It was to do with the King of Spain, the Queen's brother, he said. The greater part of her dowry remained unpaid. If it was not paid by next year, Louis would take payment in kind, from the Spanish colonies of the Netherlands.

'So the King intends to go to war against the Queen's brother? What does the Queen think about that?' asked Athénaïs.

The young courtier found the question puzzling. Why, the Queen would agree with whatever the King decided, he said, and then, as if the subject had been dismissed, 'Would Madame la Marquise like to see the orangery,' which was half in flower, half in fruit, so you could smell the scent of the flowers and of the oranges at the same time. It was the inspiration of Monsieur and a work of genius by the gardeners.

The day at Saint-Cloud passed in an atmosphere of prickly gaiety. As soon as Monsieur saw Athénaïs, he said disparagingly, '*Pearls*, with all that white. You should have chosen a contrast. Something darker, purple perhaps, or emeralds.'

'Perhaps you can find some emeralds for Athénaïs,' said Henriette, 'lying around in one of your jewellery boxes.'

'*Madame*,' said Monsieur, emphasising the word as if it were disagreeable to his ears. 'In *excellent* humour, as ever.'

The heat affected him, for he would not sacrifice one item of his elaborate clothing. Another disagreement that exercised Monsieur and Madame was his liking for a shaded room and hers for being en plein air. For the greater part of the day he remained indoors with some of his friends, occasionally coming out on to the terrace to complain that Madame was not only unsociable but also was keeping Athénaïs from him. He seemed determined to continue the day as it had started, in an atmosphere of recrimination.

'I cannot concentrate on the cards, if you're always distracting me,' said Henriette, as if to a fractious child.

'Good,' said Monsieur. 'Perhaps you will stop playing cards, then.'

He spun round on his heel and returned indoors. Henriette raised her eyebrows and continued to deal. It was late in the afternoon and the shadows were lengthening. Athénaïs was beginning to tire of the game, as earlier she had tired of Monsieur's dissertation on etiquette, one of his pet topics. The whole day had been out of kilter. People who usually amused her seemed, seen through the distorting glass of disaffection, shallow and artificial. In this mood she gazed towards the end of the terrace where she could see a young man talking to one of the new demoiselles at court. They, at least, seemed to be enjoying each other's company.

She looked again – for a moment she had not recognised him. He was, in the most casual way, leaning against one of the stone pillars by the steps into the garden. He was talking to the girl, she said something in reply and he laughed, with a splendid flash of white teeth. Athénaïs stared in disbelief. There, at the end of the terrace of the chateau, as confident and assured as if it were his domain, exchanging words and glances with one of the young girls at court, was the Venetian mirror maker. Athénaïs felt a conflict of emotions, surprise at seeing him there, a twitch of chagrin at his seeming familiarity with the girl, who could be no more than seventeen, and an acknowledgement that there was something changed about him. No doubt, she thought, he has had some sort of success with a girl. Perhaps even that one.

She experienced a stab of proprietorial jealousy, which surprised her even more. She could not help but stare at him, for in a realm of popinjays in ruffles and ribbons, this handsome, muscular man was like an exotic animal. An image came to her mind of their last meeting, of the moment when she had almost provoked him into indiscretion. And now she was aware again of unseen filaments of desire, a longing to be closer to him.

It seemed that one of those filaments had touched his consciousness, for he suddenly looked from the girl straight at Athénaïs, his eyes meeting hers in recognition. His face was suffused with lightness and he smiled, and bowed, murmuring, 'Madame la Marquise.' But then, instead of approaching her, he turned back to the girl and continued to talk to her, his face now slightly turned away so his expression was obscured. Athénaïs thought, you clever young man. This time you don't come running.

'Your turn, Athénaïs,' said Henriette. 'Hearts are trumps. And I see that the pretty Venetian is back. Monsieur keeps finding him new mirrors to measure to keep him here. But I have a feeling he is not one for

Monsieur's camp. He is more likely to create havoc among the ladies, don't you think?'

'Very likely,' said Athénaïs. 'I think you should send him packing.'

The two women smiled at each other in understanding and continued their game of cards.

Twenty

THE PATH to the manoir was overgrown with thorn hedges. Low-hanging branches obscured the daylight and created a tunnel of foliage. You could imagine you were going into a dark wood, until you saw the stone posts ahead of you, each with a griffin, and the iron gates. As you approached the gates, you could see through the trees a brick façade and mullioned windows framed by stone. The house had been there years before the chateau at Saint-Cloud and Monsieur had allowed it to remain, neglected but not forgotten. It had been useful for discreet assignations, in the days when he had hidden from his wife the extent of his preference for men.

Andrea walked along the track to the iron gates, and paused to take in the whole view of the house and gardens. In front of the house was an expanse of gravel and a box-hedged parterre, filled with herbs. From the end of the gravel there was a lawn, neatly mown for about twenty metres and then left to run wild in a field of long seeded grass and marguerites. To one side was a small lake, edged with rushes, and nearby a spreading lime tree, under the lime a wooden bench, a table and a day bed. On the daybed reclined the Marquise.

He was not sure how she would receive him. She had been courteous to him when he had talked to her the previous day on the terrace of Saint-Cloud. It had been a conversation of slight acquaintances, fittingly formal, and he had not assumed anything more, until she had mentioned the hidden manoir in which she was staying and the difficulty of finding the path to it from Saint-Cloud. It was like the setting of a fairy tale, she said, the one where the handsome woodcutter's son hacked his way through the thorns to find the enchanted maiden and rescued her from the ogre. At this point Henriette smiled and said, 'My dear Marquise, I can see you are longing to be in a fairy tale. I think Signor Andrea should play the part of the woodcutter's son and find his way through the woods.'

Both women had laughed, looking at each other and then at Andrea with an indulgent expression. The Marquise said, 'It would certainly be a change from the little chevalier who usually comes tripping up the path in his high heels to escort me here.'

'There you are, Signor Andrea,' said Henriette. 'The enchanted maiden is just waiting to be rescued.'

'I would go through a thousand forests of thorns,' said Andrea extravagantly and they laughed again. But he had noticed when he said goodbye that the Marquise, who had always been so self-assured, cast her eyes down, as if she had revealed more than she had intended.

So now, he felt that not to make his way to the

manoir would be to lose the only chance he had to discover the Marquise's feelings for him. Just as his encounter with the girl from the botanical gardens had momentarily eclipsed his passion for the Marquise, now the sight of her, and her implicit encouragement, filled his mind to the exclusion of the girl.

She had seen him at the gate and, still reclining on the bed, she turned her head to him as he walked towards her. On the wooden bench nearby the maid was also watching him. The Marquise's expression of mild interest at the new arrival did not seem to indicate an overwhelming passion beating inside her breast and the maid's cold, catlike stare was positively discouraging, but Andrea was filled with a young man's optimism that could not envisage rejection. He reached the lime tree and bowed before the Marquise, who extended a languid hand towards him. 'I am here at your command,' he said. 'I fought my way through the thorn trees, past the wild animals and circumvented the ogre. But you don't look as if you need to be rescued.'

She looked at him silently with wide azure eyes, her face expressionless. For a long moment he waited and then he saw her mouth twitch, as she struggled to hide her amusement. Finally, she smiled and said, 'Bravo, Signor Andrea. I applaud your courage, for you had not only the wild animals to overcome. Claudine, the gentleman will be thirsty after his long journey. Bring some citron pressé from the kitchen.'

She waved to Andrea to sit on the bench the maid had vacated. He sat down and, leaning towards her, said, 'It is well worth the journey, to find you at the end of it. Every time I see you I am overwhelmed by your beauty.'

The Marquise sat up abruptly. 'I don't care for such extravagant talk,' she said. 'And besides, I know you said exactly the same thing to the young girl you were speaking to yesterday. I saw the way she gazed after you.'

'I said nothing of the sort,' protested Andrea. 'You're the only one who has been in my thoughts, since I first saw you, in the mirror, at the Tuileries. Do you remember?'

The Marquise smiled. 'Andrea, you advance too fast. You should take a lesson from the art of war. Reconnoitre first. You know nothing about what I think of you and yet you assume you can carelessly talk about love. I have to forgive you your Italian impetuosity. If you were French, you would have been out of here and on the road back to Paris a few seconds ago.'

'Madame, please forgive me for expressing so readily what is in my heart,' said Andrea apologetically and bowed his head, but at the same time he felt renewed confidence in her interest. For what could her remark about the young girl gazing after him mean, except that she had suffered a pang of jealousy? Her rebuff was not about his declaring his love, but about who should control the course of events.

The maid had returned with the citron pressé. She placed it in front of him on the table and then, since Andrea had taken her place on the bench, fetched a kitchen chair and placed it to the right of the daybed, so that she could hear the conversation while she occupied herself with some sewing. Every now and then she would stare at his face with her cat's eyes, as if assessing him. Andrea stared back at her, at which she lowered her eyes, her cheeks pink, and concentrated on her sewing.

The Marquise suddenly rose to her feet. She declared herself stricken with ennui, which could only be cured if something exciting happened in the next few minutes. But as this was unlikely, it would be enough to take a walk around the estate, so that she didn't become as rooted as the lime tree. She held out her arm to Andrea. 'You must speak to me in Italian. Nowadays, I don't hear it enough and I must practise it or I shall forget it all. We'll have an Italian lesson, as we walk.'

This was beneficial for Andrea as well, for the closeness of the Marquise and the way her hand rested on his sleeve, the warmth of it penetrating the linen of his shirt to his skin, made it difficult for him to concentrate on speaking French correctly. Having permission to use his own language allowed him an emotional range that wouldn't otherwise have been possible. Now, instead of censoring him, she smiled at the extravagance of his conversation. A sublime happiness filled his soul. Everything he said seemed to please her.

They had reached the far end of the lake and paused to look along its length towards the house. Its waters shone dark in the sunlight, the smooth surface only disturbed by a rising fish.

'It's smooth as the mirror I made for you,' said Andrea. 'I often think of you looking into it and wonder if you're reminded of me.'

'Ah, I think I hear someone in search of compliments,' replied the Marquise. 'Your mirror is very dear to me. It has a perfect reflection, I look into it as if at my twin. I only fear that one day I'll return home to find that it has disappeared.'

'Why should it do that?' asked Andrea.

But the Marquise was suddenly annoyed, as if she had revealed too much. 'Indeed, why should it?' she said, reverting to French, and began to move away.

Andrea said to her back, 'Madame, I would do anything in my power to make you happy. It's my only wish in the world to serve you. You may ask of me whatever you will.'

She turned to him again and he could see tears in her eyes. She said, 'That's a dangerous promise, which you would be wary of making if you were any older. We're entangled by fate from the day we are born and we struggle all our lives to escape it, to set ourselves on another course. My sister, the Abbess, would tell me to accept the will of God. But I've always questioned the will of God. It invites despondency.'

Andrea could find no answer to her change of mood. He raised her hand to his lips and kissed it. She made no move away from him. He slid one arm round her waist, almost breathless with tension. Surely now the Marquise would assert herself, slap his face, remind him of his lowly place in the universe? But she only looked into his eyes and he could feel that her breathing had quickened. He thought, she is going to let me kiss her.

She had glanced suddenly towards the house. He followed her gaze and saw a small man in the ruffled

133

clothes of the court watching them across the lake. The Marquise sighed. 'There is no escape from the little chevalier. This means Monsieur has been asking for me.'

'Stay a little longer,' pleaded Andrea.

But she shook her head. 'That wouldn't be wise. You may return tomorrow, now that you've found your way here.'

'Tonight?'

'Oh, Andrea.' She smiled. 'You're too impatient. Tomorrow, for heaven's sake. Come, walk with me to the house. My chevalier of fire, you will have to learn forbearance.'

He felt light-headed. She had agreed to see him tomorrow and he would wait, if impatiently, a subject to his lady. They reached the house, under the bright-eyed gaze of the little courtier. He looked quizzically at Andrea and raised his eyebrows. Then he turned to the Marquise and said, 'Madame, much as I hate to tear you away from pastoral pleasures, Monsieur is in urgent need of your company. All I have heard this morning is "Why is Athénaïs not here to amuse me?" So eventually, to save him from going into a decline, I undertook to fetch you.'

Athénaïs . . . At last Andrea had learnt her name . . .

He watched her as she walked towards Saint-Cloud, the courtier leaning towards her with a parasol against the sun. Athénaïs, a strange and beautiful name, pagan in its origins. Athénaïs . . .

He murmured the name to himself that night, repeating it like a charm, under the lime tree, watching the darkened house until all the candles had been extinguished. The night was alive with the croaking of frogs in the lake, the screech of an owl in search of prey and then, in a moment of stillness, the piercing sweetness of a nightingale's song. He felt a sense of contentment, just to be near the house where Athénaïs lay sleeping. He stayed there until he, too, was almost asleep before walking back to his lodgings in the village.

Twenty-One

UNDERNEATH THE pergola of jasmine, a plot was being hatched. Henriette poured a dark liquid from a silver pot into a porcelain cup and handed it to the Chevalier de Saint-Cyr. She and Athénaïs watched him as he drank it. He grimaced and said, 'It's bitter. Even with syrup in it, there's a taste of wormwood. Where does this vile drink come from?'

'From Venice, but originally from Turkey. The pashas claim it heightens their perceptions and makes it possible to solve all manner of equations.'

Saint-Cyr took another sip and said, 'It's truly disgusting and it's making my head go round like a spinning top. What is it called?'

'Coffee. Courtesy of the Venetian Ambassador. He's hoping we will put in an order and encourage everyone to drink it, as the new fashion.'

'It will never catch on,' said Saint-Cyr. 'My mouth feels like the inside of a parrot's cage. I must have a glass of wine instantly to wash away the taste. I should be careful of the Venetian Ambassador, he is trying to poison you.'

'We thought we would have some amusement with him. That's what we wanted to talk to you about,' said Henriette. She and Athénaïs exchanged a conspiratorial glance.

'Ah, so you ladies are having an intrigue. You'd better tell me all.' The Chevalier sat back in his chair, stretching his legs in front of him, and waited.

Monsieur was to give a ball to celebrate the *grandes eaux* of the Cascade and the Great Jet, Henriette explained. The gardens would be lit with flambeaux down to the Seine, which would illuminate the waters as they were switched on. Everyone had been invited, including Signor Giustiniani. As it happened, though, there was a young Venetian . . . He was known to the Ambassador, they would like to invite him, but he had no formal clothes with him and there was not enough time to get them made.

'Then the unfortunate young man will have to remain in the background and watch the fountains,' said Saint-Cyr. 'Why are you telling me about this fellow?'

'Every time we meet, you have a wonderful new set of clothes. We thought that somewhere, in one of your storerooms, you might have a set that you were tired of wearing, but that would suit him perfectly well.'

'Who is this young man? I don't lend clothes to just anyone.'

Athénaïs took up the explanation from Henriette. The young man was from a respectable Venetian family. He was a specialist in making mirrors and was staying at present in the village of Saint-Cloud.

'You wish me to lend my clothes to an artisan? To have them returned awash with his sweat and God knows what else. You must be mad, both of you, Mesdames.'

'He is as clean as any Chevalier and a great deal cleaner than the Duc de Vendôme,' said Athénaïs, her voice rising a pitch in anger.

'I wouldn't lend my clothes to the Duc, either,' said Saint-Cyr. 'He lets his dogs mess in his bed, farts like a cannon and pisses in the fireplace. Excuse my language, Mesdames. It would be difficult not to be cleaner than the Duc. How do you know the young man is clean, anyway?' He looked at the two women, who had now fallen into a confusion of laughter and embarrassment. 'Ah,' said Saint-Cyr, understanding finally. 'Is the young man attractive?'

'Very,' said Athénaïs.

'Like an angel,' said Henriette.

'Ah, you ladies, whatever will you think of next?' Saint-Cyr was smiling indulgently. 'As it happens, I have a suit I no longer wear. I had more bad luck at cards when I wore it than at any other time, so the young man can have it, with my compliments. As long as he doesn't play cards, he will find it perfectly acceptable.'

'You are an angel, Chevalier,' said Henriette. 'We are everlastingly grateful.'

'I shall look forward to the ball, especially as I'm not sure which of you has the young man in her sights,' said Saint-Cyr. 'Now, please may I have some wine, before my tongue rots completely from this poisonous coffee?'

Twenty-Two

THE HEAT of the day extended into the evening, the haze over the landscape resembling a gauze, as in a theatre spectacle. As the guests began to arrive for the grand ball at Saint-Cloud, the dust raised by their carriages added swirling particles to the air. The grooms attempted to direct the different parties towards an orderly disembarkation in the stable yard but were thwarted by the guests' reluctance to walk any distance to the chateau. It was a matter of pride for those arriving in a coach and six to disembark as near the entrance as possible, regardless of the unwieldiness of their transport. The grooms desperately shouted instructions, which the cream of society, for the most part, ignored.

Andrea edged around the mêlée to the main entrance of the chateau. He ascended the double-sided stone stairs and stepped into a new and exotic world. To be in one of the royal palaces at the time of a fête was to be immersed in a jungle of luxury. The flames from the candelabra lit the hall in a glorious blaze. The crystal of the chandeliers sent sparks of light in a dancing pattern over the painted ceiling. Massed tubs of lilies and jasmine filled the air with their heady scent. The lights, the chatter of excited guests, the whirlpools in which they moved, circling each other in the hall and on the stairs, until they were drawn towards the state apartments and an orchestra conducted by Monsieur Lully, induced a wave of giddiness. He was reminded of his arrival in Paris, of the moment when he descended from the coach into a maelstrom of street people. Those who were now jostling around him engendered the same feeling of danger. They were alien and he had stepped, in a most foolhardy way, into their world. He could only hope not to be drowned in the whirlpool.

It had seemed a harmless enterprise when he had first agreed to it. The Marquise had decided he should attend the ball and had even arranged for a suit of clothes so that he could feel at ease among the other guests. Claudine had taken him into the manoir to a bedroom where the clothes had been laid out on the bed. She had remained there, disconcertingly, while he had dressed, then adjusted the long waistcoat so that it was even on both sides. She tugged at the sleeves of the shirt so they billowed out from under the short sleeves of the surcoat, and tied his jabot for him. Then she stood back and surveyed him, with a secretive little catlike smile, and said, 'You look every inch a marquis.'

The Marquise then entered the room and gave her verdict. He looked like an Italian prince, she said, and he must have a fitting Italian title.

'If he wore a wig, he would look even more imposing,' suggested Claudine.

'He has excellent hair, but a wig would add a certain authority,' agreed Athénaïs. 'I'll see what I can do. It must not be too light, nor too dark. A chestnut shade perhaps, like a magnificent horse.'

'That's just what I feel like at the moment, like a horse being judged at a market,' muttered Andrea.

'At the ball, we're all horses at the market,' said Athénaïs. 'Each one judging the other. That's why it is so important to appear in the best light from the first. Who wants to be ignored?'

He had thought he had escaped the wig, but on the evening of the ball, just before he set out, there was a knock at the door of his lodgings. He opened it to see Claudine holding a rectangular box. Madame la Marquise had found this wonderful creation, she said, property of a prince and hardly worn. She was so looking forward to seeing him in it.

Claudine lifted out of the box a mass of glossy, curled, dark-chestnut hair. 'Isn't it beautiful?' she said, stroking it. 'Feel its softness. Many wigs are made from horsehair, but this is the real thing, this is human hair.'

Andrea's hand recoiled from the wig as images came to mind of its origins. A poor woman of Paris, with nothing left to sell, leaving her tresses on the wig maker's floor for a few sous, emerging from the shop as shaven-headed as a convict. Or the corpse of a young girl, whose family could only afford the burial fees by selling her hair. 'I can't wear this,' he said.

'Please, Signor Andrea, Madame la Marquise went

to such trouble for you and she would be so disappointed. It will make her evening.'

Andrea conceded. He sat on a chair while Claudine combed his hair, fastening it in a tail at the back, and then placed the wig on his head. Her fingers flicked out the tresses and she combed the top of the wig into shape, one hand resting on his forehead, breathing deeply with concentration. It struck him that the most beguiling part of being an aristocrat was to have your grooming done for you. It reminded him of childhood when his mother had washed his face and combed his hair. But there was an extra attraction to this service from Claudine, who had now moved in front of him to adjust the wig, her bodice a few inches from his nose, which brought to mind the thought of pashas being ministered to by slave girls. He had never thought of her as comely, with her wan complexion and green eyes, but it had to be said that any youthful female flesh in such close proximity exerted a certain magnetism.

She stepped back, looked approvingly at the wig, then caught his eyes and looked away quickly. 'The wig looks fine, let's hope you can live up to it,' she had said abruptly.

Now, in the grand salon, he felt overwhelmed by what was expected of him. As he moved through the groups of people he was aware of eyes flickering in his direction. They all must have realised he was an outsider who had strayed into their enclosed circle. His scarlet-heeled shoes felt too tight, the suit of clothes sat on him as on a stranger, the wig was horribly uncomfortable on a hot night like this and he could feel the dampness of his own hair underneath. Yes, everyone must be assessing him as an interloper and, before long, he would be shown their backs, or even the door.

One of the liveried servants offered him a glass of wine from a silver tray. He took it and the servant smiled as if to tell him he knew who he was. Andrea moved on through the salon towards the orchestra, where he could watch the musicians. Monsieur Lully was beating time with a staff, his back to the room, and the musicians were bowed over their instruments. Twenty or so of the guests were dancing a gavotte. Andrea drank the wine and watched them. They were like performing animals at a circus, he decided. A man in an oversized wig twirled round, pointing his toes and flourishing one arm in the air, accompanying each flourish with a toss of the head as if trying to dislodge the hairpiece. His partner, who was heavily powdered and coiffed with ringlets, was bestowing glutinous smiles to the room. There is no one here who is not playing a part, thought Andrea. They are all counterfeit, living in an artificial world.

He continued his circulation of the room, examining the courtiers with censuring eyes. As he reached the end, he was suddenly confronted by a man who looked intently at him. Startled, Andrea stared back. The face, which was oddly familiar, was framed by a magnificent wig and the man was wearing a fine suit of steel blue embroidered with silver and black thread over a billowing silk shirt. As Andrea looked at this princely vision, he realised it was his own reflection in a mirror. His interior doubts, his feelings of clumsiness, his cramped feet, none of this was evident in the image before him. For the first time he saw himself as a stranger would, as a man confident of his attraction. This was the person of whom the other guests had taken note, about whom eddies of speculation drifted like wisps in the air. The image was all.

As he took this in, one of the guests detached himself from a group and approached him. Andrea could see by his lined, weather-tanned face and determined stride that this was not an indoor courtier, but a man of arms. He looked at Andrea's image in the mirror and said humorously, 'It's worth staring at. That's a splendid suit you're wearing. You must let me know who your tailor is.'

Andrea smiled and shrugged. He would certainly tell him if he could only remember, he said.

'So young and problems with the memory already? I shall introduce myself and hope you will remember my name. Chevalier Edouard de Saint-Cyr. And you?'

'Andrea Allegri, Monsieur, at your service.'

'Allegri . . . Italian . . . Strange, I could have sworn you were the Count of Montebelluna. A relation, perhaps? But you're on your own and so I must introduce you to some friends. Come with me.' He put his arm lightly round Andrea's shoulders and guided him towards a group by the open window. 'I must introduce you to the most fascinating and beautiful lady at court, the Marquise de Montespan, when she arrives.' Saint-Cyr glanced with amusement at Andrea's face. 'What, you know her already? But do you know the Venetian Ambassador, who is here? You should do, as a fellow Italian. Come.' And Saint-Cyr's grip tightened on Andrea's arm, as he steered him into the heart of the group. Andrea found himself face to face with Giustiniani, who looked at him with shrewd eyes that seemed to hold a glimmer of recognition.

'Your Excellency, may I introduce a compatriot, whom you should know,' said Saint-Cyr. 'He has recently arrived in Paris and I'm taking him under my wing. Le Comte de Montebelluna.'

'No,' protested Andrea and then stopped himself from correcting Saint-Cyr, for he realised if he revealed his identity it would end in his ignominy, that he would be seen as the butt of the Chevalier's joke.

Giustiniani was smiling at him. 'Ah, Signor Conte, I am delighted to meet you. Montebelluna, it's in the Veneto, isn't it?'

Andrea had no idea, but improvising again, he said, 'It is not far from Vicenza.'

'Nearer Treviso, I think,' corrected the Ambassador. 'So do you come to Venice sometimes? Your accent is Venetian.'

'Everyone in the Veneto comes to Venice. It's a city I love.' Andrea saw Saint-Cyr's expression of benign interest, as the two Venetians talked in Italian. What perversity had caused the Chevalier to give Andrea a false identity he could not fathom, but now he was irretrievably il conte di Montebelluna, and Giustiniani was questioning him about families he knew in Venice and where he stayed when he was there. Not in the fashionable part of the city, said Andrea, intending to keep away from any territory known to the Ambassador. He preferred being in Dorsoduro, for the freshness of the sea air. 'Ah, Dorsoduro,' cried the Ambassador, 'it's one of my favourite areas. Do you know . . .' And he was off again on a litany of names and places. Andrea, in order to head him off, introduced the subject of the Carnival, declaring it his favourite time in Venice. It was at least, he reckoned, something he knew about, having taken part in the Carnival since he was a child.

'Ah, the Carnival!' exclaimed the Ambassador. 'It is carnival most of the year in Venice. We never stop enjoying ourselves. Masked balls, assignations with flighty ladies in gondolas, it makes me nostalgic for Venice, but I'm getting old. Carnival is a young man's sport, isn't it, eh, Signor Conte?'

Andrea realised he was now labelled in the Ambassador's eyes as a libertine. Saint-Cyr had a lot to answer for. The Ambassador was inviting him to call upon him at the embassy when they were both back in Paris. Andrea bowed and said, 'I should be delighted to do so, Your Excellency.'

'The pleasure is mine, Signor Conte,' said Giustiniani, bowing in return. 'I shall look forward to seeing you.'

As the Ambassador moved away, Andrea whispered to Saint-Cyr, 'Why did you make up that nonsense about a title? You know it's not true.'

'A momentary lapse . . . You reminded me of Montebelluna,' said Saint-Cyr, unabashed.

'I don't believe there is such a person. And I don't want you to use that name again. I have no wish to be an imposter.'

'I promise,' said Saint-Cyr. 'And besides, I have no need to, for the Marquise has won the bet.'

'What bet?' Andrea stared at him.

"That the Ambassador wouldn't recognise you. Madame Henriette said he was very sharp and would spot you instantly. The Marquise said it was clothes that defined the person and that, combined with your natural grace, you would be able to fool him. So, it is a compliment, there is no need to be put out.'

'It could have been a disaster,' said Andrea.

'Instead, it was a success. Come now, have a glass of wine to settle yourself, and let us go in search of the Marquise.'

THERE WAS an excited edge to the chatter of several hundred voices. The news, like the early flames of a forest fire, leapt from the hall up the stairs and into the salon. The King had arrived. He was in the hall. He was being greeted by his brother. A score or so of the guests hung over the staircase and sent the despatches back to the salon where the crowd had congregated near the door, leaving the far end of the room empty. Monsieur Lully glanced over his shoulder, understood immediately what had happened and snapped quick instructions to the musicians. The tune switched from a light gavotte to a triumphal march.

He was coming up the stairs. He had stopped, he was talking to Olympe de Soissons. No, he was moving on. He had reached the salon and everyone who had crowded near the door gave way to allow him space to enter. Now he was in their midst, his eyes adeptly noting who was there. Those who were there similarly noted the favoured courtiers whom he had chosen to accompany him to Saint-Cloud, significantly, it was whispered, the dark-haired woman, glittering with diamonds, the Princess of Monaco. So much for poor Louise.

Monsieur bustled along behind the King, indicating to some to step forward and be introduced. He flourished his arm from courtier to King and back again, talking animatedly. Louis looked affectionately at his excited brother and murmured an aside to Henriette, who smiled but with a sadness in her eyes. Those who had overheard passed on the bons mots. The King had compared his brother's conversation to the Cascade they were about to see.

'It's piquant to watch the three of them together,' said Saint-Cyr. 'When she was first married to Monsieur, it was Louis she fell in love with. There was nearly a scandal, until he was distracted by La Vallière. If you're going to be a courtier, Signor Allegri, you have to know these things, otherwise you'll never understand what is going on.'

Monsieur had looked in their direction and was now staring hard at Andrea, as if trying to place him. Andrea was aware as their eyes met that he had been recognised. The smile on Monsieur's face puckered into the beginnings of a kiss, his eyes gleamed darkly, he mouthed something at Andrea and raised his eyebrows. The royal entourage moved on.

'Later?' said Saint-Cyr, who had lip-read. 'Is that a promise or a threat? I suppose it depends whether you are of Monsieur's persuasion. If not, perhaps you should leave now and save yourself embarrassment.'

But the Marquise had arrived and there was no question of leaving. She had never looked more beautiful in Andrea's eyes. Her skin had the luminous sheen of the pearls she wore at her neck. A fine gauze under her bodice, far from hiding her breasts, drew attention to them, for as she breathed the gauze quivered transparently. Andrea's nostrils, assailed during the evening by so many perfumes and odours in the crowded salon, breathed in the tantalising scent of tuberose, heightened to a sensuous richness by the Marquise's body. He bowed over her hand and said, 'Now you are here, I cannot tear myself away.'

'And why should you?' said Athénaïs. Her eyes were very bright as she saw him for the first time in his court dress and wig, and she seemed young and vulnerable, as if uncertain of her control over events, which made her all the more enticing. But her hesitation was only for a moment and then she recovered, wondering aloud and dangerously close to earshot from whom the Princess of Monaco had borrowed her jewellery.

The royal entourage was moving by again towards the door and down the stairs. The entire salon of guests surged after them, leaving the orchestra playing to an empty room. The word was that the *grandes eaux* were about to be switched on and the Great Jet was to be seen in action for the first time. Slowing down, in order not to tread on the heels of the King, the courtiers jostled each other, those at the head of the procession unwilling to give way, as those behind pushed against them. The King reached the main entrance and stood in the doorway talking to his brother. The pushing on the stairs had become unbearable and a few began to stumble, clutching for the banisters, as they could no longer move forward.

Finally, the King moved out on to the terrace and there was an audible sigh at the easing of the bottle-neck, as the throng dispersed into the wider space.

The terrace, on the high ground of the chateau, overlooked the stepped gardens leading down to the Seine. In the evening sun the river gleamed tranquilly and, on the other side, fields and woodlands, bathed in golden light, stretched towards the distant spires of Paris. From the terrace the garden sloped steeply towards the lower ground, intersected by the stone steps of the Cascade. At the end of the Cascade was a large square pool, of which the central fountain was the Great Jet. The entire party was now assembled looking expectantly at the stone steps and the still pool.

Monsieur, in a show of deference, asked the King to give the order to switch on the *grandes eaux*. Louis demurred, for after all, he said, Monsieur was the host and they were his *grandes eaux*. The rules of politesse having been acknowledged, Monsieur stepped forward, stood high on his heels, raised his right arm with a flourish and called out, 'Let the *grandes eaux* commence.'

There was a moment's pause while everyone waited in anticipation, almost fearing that the *grandes eaux* would fail, then a rush of water burst forth below the terrace, down the steps of the Cascade, increasing in volume until it became a white torrent. The guests applauded and Monsieur Lully, who had nipped down a back stair to reach the assembled garden orchestra, struck the ground with his staff. The musicians began to play a composition he had devised for the occasion, 'Le Marche des Grandes Eaux'.

Monsieur raised his arm again and called for the commencement of the Great Jet. The entire court directed their attention to the pool at the end of the Cascade. There was a trickle from the fountain, a spurt, and then a gurgling noise, as of air in the pipes. Monsieur stared ferociously at the fountain, willing it into life.

'The Great Jet seems in need of a little help,' said Louis with a smile.

'It will come,' snapped Monsieur, the anxiety on his face foreshadowing impending humiliation. 'Give it time.'

The fountain spurted again, a little higher, then with a crack like a pistol shot, a jet of water exploded into the air. The volume and the force of the water were so great that in the space of a minute it had reached an extraordinary height, spraying out a mist all around it. Monsieur's guests applauded and cheered. Monsieur turned to his elder brother and said, with an expression of tremulous pride, 'The water can reach forty-five metres. There has never been such a high jet before.'

'Well done, brother!' Louis exclaimed. 'A proud boast.'

Behind the assembled crowd, the servants had been lighting candelabra on tables set out for dinner on the terrace. Monsieur led the King towards the most elaborately decorated table near the Cascade and the guests dispersed to find their places. Saint-Cyr organised a table near the King's for his party, which included the Marquise and Andrea. It was a good vantage point, he said. They could watch the *grandes eaux*, they could watch the King and they were near one of the flambeaux so that they could see what they were eating when it grew dark.

At each place setting was a present of a silver and enamel box containing sugared almonds. 'Monsieur is the most painstaking of hosts,' said the Marquise. 'This is a perfect evening and worth dressing up for, isn't that so, Andrea?'

Andrea agreed that it was more than perfect. Earlier she had apologised for her little bet. She would never have undertaken it, she said, had she thought there was any danger that Andrea would be exposed to ridicule. And then, as the Great Jet erupted in its explosive, glorious spurt, she had moved close to his side and had gazed up at him with such a sweet look. They stood side by side in closeness, as if they were lovers.

'Monsieur is indeed a great host,' said Saint-Cyr, while the servants poured wine into their glasses, 'and this is a perfect setting, though unfortunate for those with weak bladders. Fountains and cascades in front of us, fountains on the parterre behind us, I can see a number of people having to answer the call of nature.'

Men were heading for the *bosquet* on the other side of the parterre, while the ladies took the longer journey to the *chaises percées* behind the stable block. A strong bladder was one of the essentials of court life, declared Athénaïs. Particularly if you were required at any time to travel in the King's coach. His endurance was superhuman, she had heard. He could travel for eight hours without needing to relieve himself.

At the royal table Monsieur was serving the King with food brought by the servants, carefully selecting for him the best cuts of meat. How curious that an accident of birth should cause such a discrepancy in their estate, mused Saint-Cyr, and, if Monsieur had not been schooled as he had been, he might have been a rival to the King, in more ways than one.

Athénaïs declared the story was just malicious gossip. On the contrary, said Saint-Cyr, he had it on the best authority. No mother would have allowed that to be done to her son, said Athénaïs furiously. Andrea, bemused by their argument, asked for an explanation. Saint-Cyr, lowering his voice, said, 'It is to do with your compatriot, Cardinal Mazarin, who was the power behind the Queen Regent when Louis was a boy. They encouraged the younger brother to be effeminate, gave him jewels and dresses, introduced him to sodomy. It was done so that he would not be a rival in power to Louis.'

'Don't listen to him, Andrea. It's all lies and tittle-tattle,' said Athénaïs, so loudly that the other guests at the table began demanding to hear the tittle-tattle.

A large woman in bright yellow with feathers in her hair, whom nobody knew, called across to Saint-Cyr, 'Is it about Monsieur?'

'Keep your voice down, for God's sake!' said Saint-Cyr. The royal table had fallen silent and were looking in their direction. Everyone averted their eyes and stared at their plates as if the food had become the most interesting thing in their lives.

'I was just saying that Monsieur is an excellent host and his chefs have excelled themselves,' said Athénaïs, projecting her voice distinctly.

'We were praising Monsieur's taste and generosity,' added Saint-Cyr.

Behind them, they could hear conversation being resumed at the royal table. Saint-Cyr muttered to Athénaïs, 'That cow in yellow could have done for us. Keep your voice down, in future.'

'Oh, so it's my fault? Who started the gossip? And what is the woman dressed like a *fauteuil* doing at our table, anyway? She has obviously had too much to drink.'

It would have been difficult not to drink, for the servants brought one glass after another of different wines, from pale muscat to rich dark burgundy. In the balmy night air the spirit of the grape spread its warm glow through the veins of the guests. Now Monsieur Lully struck up the royal triumphal march as the King departed with his entourage, escorted to their coaches by Monsieur. There was a perceptible release of tension and the guests, as their presence was no longer required to witness the King's glory, began to drift off towards the darkening garden for various natural pursuits. Others followed Monsieur Lully towards the great salon, where the band struck up a sarabande. Saint-Cyr escorted the Marquise on to the floor, leading the procession. Andrea watched, absorbed at the way her delicate feet in their satin slippers turned out at the beat of the music. The large woman in yellow was bearing down on him with a determined look in her eyes and, to avoid the danger of her asking him to dance, he moved away towards the door, almost colliding with the diminutive courtier whom he had seen earlier at the manoir.

'Just the man I was looking for,' said the courtier. 'May I introduce myself. Chevalier Jean-Baptiste de Saint-Eustace. We thought you might have left.'

'No, I'm still greatly enjoying Monsieur's hospitality,' said Andrea. 'I have never been to such a magnificent party.'

'He does them well, doesn't he?' said Saint-Eustace. 'But come with me, you can tell him yourself.'

He placed a small, well-manicured hand on Andrea's sleeve and drew him towards the next salon, where a number of guests were talking and playing cards. At the end of the room there was a hidden door in the wall. Saint-Eustace pressed a catch, and hop-la! there they were on the other side of the chateau, he said, as they crossed the interior passage and entered another room, smaller than the great salon, but intensely decorated, with Japanese lacquer and paintings of mythical scenes. On the tables were displays of semi-precious stones, rock crystals and agates on small stands. Jewelled pagodas from Siam stood on pedestals between the windows, from which could be seen the orangery.

'Such pretty apartments,' said Saint-Eustace. 'Do you like jewellery? Monsieur has a wonderful collection.'

Andrea could think of no reply to the Chevalier's odd remark and followed him, dazed by the surroundings, as he opened the gilded double doors to the next room.

They were in an opulently furnished bedroom and his first image was of the bed, a four-poster of immense height, with rich, dark, crushed-velvet curtains and a heavily gilded frame. In the glow of the candles, for the curtains had been drawn against the dusk, he could see gold and silver glinting threads in the tapestries of bucolic scenes that decorated the walls. Then his eyes were drawn to the candelabra on the dressing table and the mirror in the centre. Seated in front of the mirror he could see the figure of, it seemed, Henriette. She had her back to him, and was absorbed in her image of the glass. She was wearing a rose silk dress and a little lace cap perched on the back of her head.

Andrea stepped backwards towards the door, fearing he was committing an indiscretion in observing Madame at her toilette. Then he heard, coming from her direction, the voice of Monsieur, 'Don't run away. You're not disturbing me.'

The figure at the dressing table turned and now he saw the unmistakable face of Monsieur framed by curled hair dressed with ribbons, the lace cap perched on top. He was wearing diamond earrings, a diamond and ruby necklace at his throat, his face was powdered, but there was no mistaking his sex, for above his rouged lips was the dark line of his moustache, waxed and curled at the ends. Andrea stared at him, horror mingled with rising hysteria that threatened to burst out into laughter. Then he saw in Monsieur's face, under the powder, an expression of such vulnerability that the laughter died within him.

'Well,' said Monsieur, standing in front of him and looking into his face with eyes that demanded approval, 'do you like what you see?'

Behind him, Andrea heard the door close, as Saint-Eustace left the room.

'Well?' said Monsieur, inclining his head coquettishly to one side.

'You look much changed,' said Andrea eventually, his throat dry with tension. He was aware of the silence in the room, all sounds muffled by the heavy curtains and the tapestry, which induced a feeling of enclosure, of imprisonment, like being inside a velvet-lined box. He could hear his own breath, uneven for the increase in his heartbeat.

Monsieur heard, too, and smiled. 'I like what I see, as well,' he said. 'How sweet of you to go to so much trouble for me. Such fine clothes on such a fine figure. All you need is a little jewellery to set it off. Earrings, perhaps.' His hand touched Andrea's face, stroking his cheek, then reached under the wig to his ear lobe.

Andrea stepped back and said sharply, 'There's been a mistake. I didn't come here for — it wasn't for you. I must go, please excuse me.'

Monsieur smiled again. 'Of course, of course, I'm always too fast and it frightens you. I mean no harm, it's just that I love beauty. You mustn't mind if I get a little overenthusiastic. You can always tell me to stop, I know the meaning of the word no.'

'Even so, I should like to leave,' said Andrea. 'If you please, Monsieur.'

An expression of annoyance at having his will thwarted fleetingly appeared on Monsieur's face, followed by one of conciliation, as he said, 'Just stay a few moments more, my handsome signor. I need to ask your advice, not about love, I promise you. It's a matter of furnishing this room. You're the man who knows about mirrors, aren't you? I have been wondering whether to get rid of all these tapestries and have the walls completely mirrored. What do you think?'

Andrea looked at the tapestries, noticing that most of the bucolic scenes showed a tangle of semi-clad nymphs and shepherds in the throes of Bacchic joy. He couldn't help smiling at the thought of Monsieur attempting to emulate them with Madame. One of the nymphs bore a passing resemblance to the Marquise, as she would be if she unlaced her bodice and exposed her breasts. He had a sudden desire to get out of the room and to find her. 'The last thing you should do is get rid of these tapestries, they're so well suited to a bedroom,' he said. 'You need no mirrors, beyond one over the fireplace. The room is perfect as it is.'

'You may say it can't be done, but I must show you where I should really like to have mirrors,' and Monsieur put a hand on his sleeve, as Andrea was looking towards the door, drawing him towards the bed. 'No, don't worry. I'm only asking for advice.' Monsieur clambered on to the bed, hitching up his silk dress, and pointed at the tented canopy overhead. 'Tell me if I'm being absurd, but what I really, really want is to have mirrors over the bed. Imagine seeing yourself and your lover like twins above you. No, I'm not asking your opinion of whether you would like that, just whether it is possible. Could you make a frame of mirrors that would stay in place above the bed?'

Andrea began to laugh, as he imagined Monsieur's energetic cavorting bringing the mirrors crashing down upon him. He leaned backwards against the edge of the mattress and looked up at the canopy. 'Excuse me,' he said, 'but I can't help laughing because, well, the whole idea is absurd.'

Monsieur laughed, too, in surprisingly deep and resonant tones. Then, so suddenly that it was impossible to recall how it had happened, Andrea was flat on the bed, his legs kicked from under him, and Monsieur was astride him, his hands grasping Andrea's arms, as he looked down into his face. He murmured, 'Oh, you pretty little macaroni,' and bending his face towards his, 'I've wanted to do this ever since I first saw you.' Andrea saw above him the powdered face, the moustache, smelt the scent of sweet cloves on the breath, then the two eyes merged into one as Monsieur's mouth descended on his. He struggled to get out from under him, but the man's delicate appearance masked an unexpected strength.

The hands gripped Andrea's arms all the tighter, his thighs encircled Andrea's torso with the muscularity of an expert horseman. 'Don't worry, my angel, I won't do anything you don't want,' he whispered in his ear, then one of his hands loosened its grip on Andrea's right arm, slid downwards to his crotch and felt for his member through the cloth of his breeches. 'Oh, *you like it*, you lovely, lovely . . .' breathed Monsieur, just before Andrea's right fist hit him in the face. He cried out in pain, recoiling from the blow. He grasped at Andrea's arm, but Andrea's knee came up forcefully, jabbing into his belly. Monsieur lost his grip and fell off the bed, landing on the floor.

'You devil!' shouted Monsieur. 'You attacked me, you thug, you hooligan!' Blood was trickling from a cut to his mouth. Monsieur put a handkerchief to his face and looked at the blood staining the white linen. 'There,' he said, thrusting the handkerchief in Andrea's face, 'you will hang for this, shedding the blood of a royal prince.'

Andrea had already grasped the implications of

what he had done and felt a chill through his body. He said, 'There is also a law against sodomy, Monsieur. I shall leave now. Have me arrested, if you will.'

He turned towards the door, and heard Monsieur cry out, 'No, don't go. Don't leave me.'

He looked back to see Monsieur had sunk to the floor again, tears trickling down his blood-streaked face. He was tearing at his bodice like a girl trying to retain a reluctant lover. Andrea reached the door and as he shut it behind him he heard Monsieur's furious imprecations hurled after him. 'Bitch! Piece of shit! *Salaud!*'

'Sodomite!' retorted Andrea and repeated it as he walked swiftly through the apartments looking for the door through the wall. He railed at himself. 'Stupid, stupid, idiot, idiot.' He had walked straight into an ugly, unnecessary, dangerous and compromising scene. Saint-Cyr had warned him to leave, but he couldn't tear himself away from the Marquise. Now he began to feel angry with her as well. He found the door and passed into the dimly lit interior corridor, feeling his way for the other door into the state apartments.

It opened into the room where the card players had been. There were fewer of them now and those who remained had the set, feverish appearance of addicts. A red-faced man in a sumptuous brocade coat was peeing in the fireplace. On a sofa near the window a woman reclined, half-conscious, while a man massaged her feet.

'Why in such a hurry?' he heard one of the card players call out as he passed by, and then laughter from the others, as if they guessed what had happened. He had now reached the great salon and as he entered, he saw Monsieur Lully, in front of his orchestra, playing on the fiddle. Lully's dark, saturnine face was absorbed in the music as the bow teased the strings into the sweetest, most heart-piercing notes. Then he glanced towards Andrea and gave him a complicit smile, his fingers trembling on the strings.

So he knew as well. Andrea, in a fever of agitation, was intent only on getting out of the chateau and into the anonymous night air. As he walked down the stairs, he tore off his wig and threw it, half-skewed, on to a marble bust of Plato. May they all rot in hell, he thought, as he reached the hall, then, to avoid the milling crowd and carriages in the main courtyard, he turned into the garden salon and left by one of the french windows on to the terrace overlooking the orangery.

Once outside he paused, for the night was beautiful and calmed his soul. In the moonlight, the white of the flowers had a ghostly luminosity. He could hear the fountains splashing, the sound of laughter from the *bosquet* and the hoot of an owl in the direction of the woods. He murmured to himself, 'Athénaïs,' and was suffused with sadness at the opportunity lost.

As he looked on to the orangery, catching the scent of the flowers, he heard footsteps on the gravel behind him, and knew in the quickness and lightness of their tread that he had been saved. He turned and saw her walking towards him, her skin as luminous as the flowers in the moonlight. In her hand she was holding the wig.

'Why did you leave in such a hurry, Andrea? It's not courteous to do so. And what offence has the wig caused you, to be cast aside like that?'

He could hardly speak for a moment, for the confusion of feelings inside him. She had been looking at him in her mock imperious way, which gave way to an expression of concern. 'Why are you so agitated? Why, you're trembling! What has happened?'

'Monsieur is a sodomite,' said Andrea at last.

'Well, that's not news to anyone,' said Athénaïs, laying the wig along the edge of the balustrade. 'So he attempted to persuade you to his views? Well, that's not a surprise, either. So you told him to go to hell. So what? These things happen all the time.'

'It was so shaming,' said Andrea.

Athénaïs raised her hand to his cheek and murmured, 'There's nothing to be ashamed of. If you're young and beautiful, people want to possess you. Would you rather be old and ugly and undesirable? Can you imagine what that will be like?'

She was smiling up at him, her eyes dark and shining in the moonlight. Andrea moved closer, bending his head towards hers. Her hand encircled the back of his neck. He sank his mouth on to hers and her lips opened to his tongue like a sea anemone in search of food. Her grip on his head tightened, her body moved against his, he could feel her heartbeat and her breasts in a warm shelf of flesh against his chest. His hand moved to caress them and now he was trembling with another emotion altogether, a fire coursing through his blood demanding love.

'I love you, Athénaïs, I love you so much,' he said, as

his hand found its way through the thin veiling to her breast and his other hand slid down the curve of her back.

She drew back and whispered, 'Come to the manoir tomorrow. I shall be waiting for you.'

'But why not now? Why wait? Let's go there now.'

'We can't. We would be seen. I have my reputation to think of and it would be dangerous for you as well.'

'Who cares for reputation or danger?' said Andrea wildly.

But she raised her hand to his mouth to hush him. 'It's a serious business. Come to the manoir tomorrow, I shall be waiting for you, I promise.'

He looked at her doubtfully, but said resignedly, 'Tomorrow, then?'

'Tomorrow.'

'At the manoir?'

'At the manoir. Come towards evening.'

'You'll be waiting?'

'I promise.' She traced his lips with her finger and added, 'Leave now, through the garden. You don't want to run into Monsieur, do you?'

He kissed the palm of her hand and said, 'I'm not the least concerned about him now.'

'How could Monsieur have made such a mistake?' She smiled and then, 'Don't forget your wig.'

He watched her walking back across the terrace to the chateau, feeling the sensation of her body in the gentle sway of her dress. Tomorrow, Athénaïs, tomorrow evening at the manoir, I shall see beyond your image, I shall know you to your depths. He saw her reach the windows of the chateau, framed for one moment in the candlelight, and then move inside, lost to view. He noticed a shadow move near the windows. Someone else had been watching the Marquise. Best to leave now, he said to himself, through the garden, quickly.

Twenty-Three

'WHAT HAVE I said? What have I done?' The refrain in Athénaïs's mind as she drank her morning chocolate, seated beside the parterre. The scent of thyme warmed by the sun mingled with the aroma of the chocolate. Her face was shaded by a wide-brimmed straw hat but the sun's warmth enveloped her body. She thought of Andrea.

Madness, she said to herself. In the daylight, and with the haze of alcohol diffused from her mind (what did Monsieur put in the wine that made it so potent?), she could see she had made a rash promise. And yet, was it not at moments like that you knew the truth of your feelings? She had given way to a desire to show him that, whatever Monsieur had assumed, he belonged to the world of women. And then his mouth had touched hers and her flirtation had been consumed in tongues of flame coursing through her body. Arrows, Cupid's arrows. At times like this, the old gods laid claim to you. Venus, Aphrodite, Cupid, Eros, as potent as ever.

'I think this evening I might give the servants time off. They had to wait up late for me last night,' she said to Claudine, who was mending a tear in her shawl.

'So Andrea is coming here this evening?' said Claudine, looking up from her sewing to catch her mistress's expression.

Athénaïs felt the tell-tale blood rise to her face. 'As it happens, yes.'

Claudine smiled. 'So the signor will get satisfaction?'

'What is it to you, Impertinence?' said Athénaïs.

'It is so long since Madame was happy,' said Claudine. 'Monsieur le Marquis deserves to be cuckolded.'

'Don't talk about my husband,' said Athénaïs. 'He has nothing to do with this.'

'Nevertheless, it will pay him out, even though, of course, he will know nothing about it.'

'Exactly,' said Athénaïs. 'I rely on your total discretion. If a word gets out to anyone, you'll be out of the door.'

'I am the keeper of secrets,' said Claudine. 'By the way, I see your little Chevalier is arriving. He's early today.'

The Chevalier de Saint-Eustace raised his plumed hat, flourished it over his chest and bowed to the Marquise. 'Madame, I trust you slept well last night?' he said, his alert, bright eyes seeming to ask quite another question.

'I slept well for what was left of the night. It was a magnificent party and Monsieur is a superb host.'

'Monsieur is concerned for nothing but the welfare of his guests, and none more so than his favoured guest and great friend, Madame la Marquise,' said Saint-

Eustace. 'That is why Monsieur has sent me to request your presence at the chateau.'

'But of course,' said Athénaïs. 'Once I'm groomed and dressed.'

'No, to stay at the chateau. Monsieur feels that the manoir is too remote and primitive for favoured guests. He has also heard that it is infested with rats and he would not wish you to stay another night in such conditions.'

'There are no rats. A few field mice, perhaps, but that doesn't worry me. I was raised in the meadows of the Charente, after all.'

'Monsieur didn't wish me to frighten you,' said Saint-Eustace, his bright eyes hardening, 'but it isn't only the rats that worry him. The manoir is not secure for ladies. There have been some ruffians in the area, who have been breaking into houses. Monsieur would be devastated if you came to harm. He would rest much easier in his bed if you were under his roof.'

I see what all this is about, said Athénaïs in her mind, and to Saint-Eustace, 'I appreciate greatly Monsieur's concern, but will you please tell Monsieur I am perfectly capable of looking after myself. We're not entirely alone in the house and the reasons Monsieur so kindly let me stay here still apply. I haven't been well, and I need to have peace and seclusion.'

'Monsieur will not be happy,' said Saint-Eustace, bowing again, before he departed.

'Too bad,' said Athénaïs, as soon as he was out of earshot. 'Monsieur is like La Fontaine's dog in the manger. I'm not going to give way to his little jealousies.'

An hour later Saint-Eustace returned with two large servants. He was *désolé*, he said, but Monsieur had insisted that Madame la Marquise move to the chateau. He had sent two men to help move the trunks. Athénaïs knew when it was unwise to hold out against Monsieur's will. An hour after that, several trunks of clothes were on their way to the chateau.

THE APARTMENT in which they were installed looked over the main courtyard. It was approached through a series of public salons, which gave on to the main staircase. At the entrance to the first of the salons were two footmen permanently on duty. Athénaïs looked down from the window at the carriages in the courtyard below. She could see everyone who was coming or going from the chateau. It was not the sort of place where you could arrange a tryst unnoticed, particularly with one who was now *persona non grata* at Saint-Cloud.

Claudine had taken a note from the Marquise to Andrea's lodgings. He had been out and reluctantly she had left it with his landlady, trusting the seal would deter her from reading it. She then walked around the outside of the chateau, noting each entrance and its proximity to the wing in which they were installed. She observed the kennels and the dogs within, mastiffs with jaws like traps. She chatted to the kennel boy, expressing admiration at his ability to control such man-eaters. He told her quite a lot about the keeping of dogs. On her final tour of the chateau, she watched as a man let himself in at the low wooden door of a narrow round tower. A few minutes later he emerged, adjusting the belt of his breeches, and she guessed that the tower was being habitually used as a latrine. It was sited near the far end of their wing. She returned to their apartments, and began to search for the interior door that enabled the servants to take away chamber pots and ewers without having to go through the public salons. She found the break in the wall and pulled at the small brass ring. It led into a narrow dark corridor, lit intermittently by tallow candles. There was a door in the wall opposite, leading into the section overlooking the garden, possibly, she thought, Monsieur's apartments. She tiptoed along the corridor away from the main apartments, until she could see daylight from a slit in the end wall. The corridor's exit was through the round tower, she was sure of it, and this was confirmed by her nose as she reached the stone spiral stairs. So there was an unguarded way into the chateau. Now it only remained to see whether the door was locked at night.

She returned to the apartment where Athénaïs was trying to distract herself from the ruination of her plans by reading a book of fables. She said, 'I am finding curious analogies in the story of the poison dwarf who kidnaps the princess and locks her up in a tower guarded by goblins with two heads. Did you see any two-headed goblins on your travels? We know, of course, the identity of the poison dwarf.'

'Don't be despondent, Madame,' said Claudine. 'All fortresses have a weak point and I may have found the way through. If it works, it will be one in the eye for Monsieur.'

Athénaïs smiled. The idea of entertaining the forbidden lover a short distance from Monsieur's apartments was irresistible. It overrode all other considerations, including what would happen if they were caught.

THE NEXT morning Claudine visited Andrea's lodgings again. The landlady told her he had borrowed her husband's rods and gone fishing. Claudine walked down to the banks of the Seine, where she found several men occupied in the business of gazing into the middle distance while waiting for a bite on the line. Andrea was on his own, leaning back against a willow tree, some yards from his fishing rod, to which he was paying little attention. He watched Claudine approach him, without greeting her. As she drew near, instead of getting to his feet, he simply looked up and said, in a tone of unsmiling coolness, 'So what's the news?'

Some bridges to mend here, thought Claudine, and conveyed the Marquise's deepest apologies for not having been able to keep their appointment. It was all the fault of Monsieur, who had insisted she moved to the chateau, and of course it was far more difficult to meet in these new circumstances.

'So it's off, then?' Andrea interrupted.

Claudine, taken aback by his abruptness, protested, 'No, of course not. Madame is as much in love with you as ever. She can't sleep, she can hardly eat . . .'

'I am sure Madame la Marquise is still able to drink her morning chocolate and eat her brioche, and then take a little light sustenance of a roast guinea fowl for lunch, and some peaches, and a few strawberries . . .'

'Oh Andrea, please don't be angry.' Claudine put her hand on his sleeve in supplication. 'I'm trying to arrange things. It just takes a little more, well, arranging. If you listen, I'll tell you.'

'Yesterday evening I went to the manoir,' said Andrea. ' "I'll be waiting," she told me. "Come towards evening." I arrived to find it shuttered and empty. Eventually a churlish old guardian came out and told me the Marquise had left, he thought, for Paris. I didn't know what to think, except that she had meant not a word. And then I returned and found the note from her, which the landlady had forgotten to give me. It wasn't at all loving, just cryptic and full of initials. M this and C that.'

'She has to be careful. A note is always dangerous. Someone else might have read it. She couldn't have written what she really felt.'

She felt the tension in his body subside and he looked directly at her. 'As she couldn't put it in a letter, then you will have to tell me. What does she want me to do?'

'She wants to see you. She loves you. And I can tell you how you can find her.' Claudine began to outline her plan for getting into the chateau. It had to be after dark and he would have to take the long way round through the *bosquet*, avoiding the kennels with the mastiffs.

'So I'm going to be chewed over by Monsieur's watchdogs?' said Andrea.

'The guards don't let them out at night any more, not since they tore one of Monsieur's spaniels to pieces. They only take them out if they suspect there is an intruder. In any case, they're more interested in playing dice than keeping watch.'

'I hope you're right,' said Andrea. 'And what happens then, once I have found my way through the *bosquet*?'

With the aid of a scribbled map, Claudine showed him the route through the tower, to the inner corridor with the doors leading off. He would know the door to the Marquise's apartments, because she would leave a vase of flowers outside.

Andrea began to laugh. 'This is crazy. Why don't we just meet somewhere in the gardens, by the lake at the manoir, for instance? Why should I risk my life trying to get into the chateau? Have you thought what Monsieur would assume if I were caught? That I was trying to steal his jewellery, no doubt.'

'There are always people in the gardens, and in the woods and fields. You can't expect her to fall into a hedge with you like a milkmaid. There'd be a scandal. I promise you, Andrea, it's not that complicated. And think of how the Marquise is longing for you. I have seen her standing at the window, her breast quivering with emotion as she gazes out, her face suffused with blushes as she thinks of you.' Claudine leant towards Andrea, touching his sleeve again, and whispered into his ear, 'She is very passionate and she loves you. How can you be so faint-hearted?'

She was aware that his desire had overcome his caution. Andrea's eyes had darkened. 'She said she would be waiting for me. Do you promise that she will be?'

'I promise.'

'Then tell her I'll be with her tonight.' A smile suffused his whole face with light. Claudine left him and returned to the chateau to give the news to the Marquise.

ATHÉNAÏS WAS in demand. Monsieur wanted her to be with him while he discussed architecture with Monsieur Le Vau, who was working at present on plans for Versailles. Henriette wanted her to play cards. There were any number of people who had discovered she was now at the chateau and were trying to interest her in various diversions. As the day lengthened, her tension increased. Suppose, she said to Claudine, suppose Andrea were caught, what then? He won't be, said Claudine, that man is born lucky. Athénaïs crossed herself, touched wood, spun round three times. 'Never talk about luck, you'll be heard by malign spirits. You, more than anyone, should know that.'

In the afternoon a letter arrived for the Marquise. She was winning at cards and put it to one side until she returned to her apartments. There, while Claudine was fetching her clothes for the evening from the closet, she broke open the seal and read it.

Claudine returned to find her looking out of the window. 'Is all well?' she asked. 'It's not bad news, is it?'

'No, it's of no significance.' Athénaïs looked at the clothes on the bed. 'I thought I was going to wear the cream and gold tonight. What's wrong with it?'

'It has some stains which need to be treated. But the blue and silver will suit you well tonight. It brings out the colour of your eyes.'

173

'Why should the other dress be stained? I hardly ever wear it.' Athénaïs picked up the blue and silver bodice and held it against her face as she looked in the mirror, staring into her eyes as if assessing their colour. Then she said, apropos of nothing, 'It's dangerous to look into the future, for it only reveals itself when it arrives. And then it seems blindingly obvious and we wonder how we could not have known all along.'

Claudine waited to hear more, but Athénaïs had returned to the present and simply said, 'Well, the blue and silver it will have to be, then. Where is the hot water for my bath?'

Twenty-Four

THE NIGHT was overcast and the countryside was submerged in darkness, shapes only revealed dimly by the moon through clouds. Most of humanity was indoors for the night, the candles in the windows extinguished. An owl hooted and from the nearby wood there was a sudden screech of a nightbird or small animal. As Andrea drew near the walls of the chateau's park, he heard a chorus of croaking from the frogs. He was startled by the rush of wings passing overhead and looked up to see against the sky the owl cruising towards the lake. Flickering shadows darted close to his head. The trees were infested with bats.

The thought passed through his head that he had agreed too easily to this hazardous enterprise. But to have insisted on other terms would have been to lose Athénaïs. It was part of her game. She had chosen him to play the role of the hero in the fairy tale she had created. It was not so difficult, after all, to get into the grounds from the back. He knew at what point the wall became lower, designed so that the eye could travel easily from gardens to the countryside beyond. When he reached it, he clambered over and dropped down the other side. As his feet hit the ground his knee cracked, sounding to him like a pistol shot. He waited, trying to control his breathing, for sounds of voices or dogs barking. There was only the frogs' chorus and a nightingale singing. The night air was warm and a breeze from nowhere caressed his cheek like a passing spirit. It seemed that the air was alive with a presence, as if the darkness had become a tangible form. There was rustling in the undergrowth nearby, which he supposed to be mice or rats, though he touched the cross at his neck for reassurance.

An expanse of grass stretched before him towards the formal paths of the *bosquet*, which he remembered as having a grit surface. Then came the parterre. This was where any sound would most likely be detected, just before he reached the tower. He touched the cross again and moved slowly towards the chateau, uncertain of the ground beneath his feet. The chateau was in darkness, the windows blanked out by shutters. He heard the crunch of his feet on the grit of the path. No matter how softly he trod, he couldn't be completely silent and he was thankful for the volume of the frogs' chorus. Edging closer to the chateau he reached the parterre, near the door to the tower. There were just a few paces to go and he walked more swiftly, feeling exposed in the open space. From the kennels, a dog barked. He reached the door and raised the latch. It was unlocked, thank God, and opening it he stepped inside.

His nose was assailed by the acrid smell of urine. He trod cautiously, fearing something slippery and soft underfoot. To arrive at the Marquise's bedchamber with shit on his shoes didn't bear thinking of. He began walking up the spiral stone steps, his palm against the rough-hewn walls for balance. In the darkness, the circular ascent seemed to continue indefinitely. Finally he reached a half-landing, with an open door leading into a narrow corridor.

Here there was a little light. Two or three candles in wall brackets were guttering to their end, smelling of hot tallow. He stood for a moment, getting his bearings. There was something familiar about this corridor, which brought back to him the memory of Monsieur's bedroom. If he were to open the wrong door, what then? Where was the vase of flowers she said she would leave? He tiptoed a little further, his nerves on edge as each step sounded in the silence. Now he could detect the scent of flowers, and see dimly a vase of pale tuberoses, lilies and carnations. This was the door, then.

He opened it a few inches, but could see nothing in the darkness. He edged in and closed the door after him. The scent of tuberoses was overwhelming. The scent of Athénaïs. He called out her name.

'Ssh, no sound,' from the far side of the room. The voice of Athénaïs, light and high.

'Where are you? Please light a candle.' He had stumbled against a piece of furniture. 'Athénaïs, I can't see a cursed thing.'

'Over here,' came her voice again. 'Be quiet, we mustn't be heard.'

'Who'll hear us?' he asked, dropping his voice to a whisper.

'They're on the lookout. Be quiet and come to me.'

He heard the sound of bedclothes being drawn back and of bare feet on the floor. He was aware of a movement in the darkness and then she had reached him. Her hand touched his chest and she murmured, 'How your heart is beating!'

'All for you,' he whispered. Then, as he drew her to him, he realised she was entirely naked. His hands found her unrestrained breasts, her smooth belly, her soft damp mount of Venus. Overwhelmed by the goddess made flesh, he sank to his knees in front of her, his arms encircling the roundness of her, and worshipped her with kisses.

She made a low, moaning sound, but when he called out her name, she whispered, 'Ssh, we mustn't be heard.' And then, curtly, 'Take your clothes off. You must be naked, too.' Small hands pulled at his shirt and slid inside his breeches. She murmured, 'Ah, you feel so wonderful,' and, as he pressed against her, 'No, all your clothes off. Your shoes and stockings, too, for heaven's sake. Don't be in such a hurry.'

'How can I not be, when I have you in my arms, *bellissima* Athénaïs.' He kicked off his shoes, pulled off the stockings, the breeches, the undergarments, lifted his shirt over his head. 'There,' he said. 'Now I'm naked, but you can't see me. Light a candle, Athénaïs.'

'I can see with my hands,' she said.

So that was how they made love, as if they were blind, knowing each other through the sensation of skin against skin. The sweetness of tongues touching, the hotness of their bodies coming together, the scent of tuberose and sweat. The intensity of touch in the darkness. Then she began to moan as he pushed into her, she wrapped her legs round him and moved with him, until that moment when all his love became a liquid fire that spread from somewhere in his lower back through his loins and in a flood-tide deep into her body. She cried out as if to wake the whole chateau and this time it was he who whispered 'Ssh,' as he caressed her face, which was damp with tears and sweat. He murmured, 'Athénaïs, *bellissima*, you have all my love now. All the love that was in me is in you.' She laughed and then began to cry a little. He asked, 'There's nothing wrong, is there? You're happy, aren't you?' And then, as he was trying to say something else, a wave of fatigue overwhelmed him and he fell asleep, his head resting on her breasts. Through a semi-conscious haze, he was dimly aware of her shifting from under the weight of him and getting out of bed. There was a click of a door in the wall, as she went to the close room. A few minutes later she was back in bed again, nestling against his back. She whispered, 'I love you, too,' and kissed him between the shoulder blades.

He awoke later, unsure what time of night it was, for the heavy curtains blocked out all light, but he thought it must be dawn because he could hear the birds. She had changed her position again and was now curled up near the edge of the bed, her back to him, the sheet half covering her head. He bent to kiss the back of her neck and said, 'Athénaïs, I must be leaving, or I'll be discovered.' There was no response from the sleeping form, so he felt his way from the bed towards the closet she had used. An impression came to mind, and as fleetingly faded, of there being something odd about her inertness, and then he opened the closet door and stepped inside.

He could see by the dim light of a candle in a wall bracket a *chaise percée*, and a table with a flask of water and a glass. He poured himself some water and was about to return to the bedroom when he noticed a mirrored door in the wall opposite the door he had used. His attention was first taken by his image in the mirror. He had never seen his naked reflection before and he gazed at it appraisingly. Then he examined the door more closely and finally, unable to resist, he turned the handle and pushed it slightly ajar. It led into another bedroom, but as the curtains were drawn, he could see only the shape of the four-poster bed. He listened for the sounds of someone breathing, then, realising his rashness as an intruder, withdrew and pulled the door to. The chateau would soon be awake. He needed to get his clothes on quickly and go, yet his body was telling him otherwise. To make love in the morning, to immerse himself in the depths of her being, it was impossible to leave without loving her one more time.

Back in the bedroom, he saw a thread of grey light at the edge of the curtains and moved over to the window to draw them open. The sky was pale at the horizon and the light was becoming clearer by the minute. He looked down at the courtyard, where there were already signs of life. A stable lad was carrying a bale of hay over his shoulder. A man wearing the King's livery was standing in the middle of the courtyard. His head was inclined towards a woman who was talking to him intently. Andrea wondered what subject could so concentrate their minds at such an early hour. He watched the woman, whose back was turned to him. She was wearing a cloak with one of those voluminous hoods that ladies of fashion favoured to accommodate their hair. He watched until she turned away from the officer, and at that point she glanced up towards the chateau and the hood slipped back from her head. He was looking into the face of Athénaïs.

For a moment he thought he had conjured her out of his mind, and that it was an apparition born of his passion; that every woman he looked at now would take on the appearance of Athénaïs. As quickly, he told himself, no, it was her double, perhaps the sister whom she had mentioned. And yet there was no mistaking her, for there could be no one quite like her. Now she was looking directly up at the window and it was as if her eyes were seeing through him into his soul, though she gave no sign of recognition. Thoughts came to his mind of witchcraft, of stories he had heard of sorceresses who were able to appear simultaneously in different places. Athénaïs was looking up at him from the courtyard. Athénaïs was asleep in the bed where they had been making love. She had not left it, for he could hear her stir and her voice murmur, 'Andrea . . .'

Athénaïs here, Athénaïs there . . . if not Athénaïs, who? He walked swiftly over to the bed, treading on the clothes he had cast on the floor a few hours earlier, and pulled back the sheet. She grabbed at it to stop him exposing her nakedness and looked up at him with supplication, waiting for his reaction. She whispered, 'Andrea,' and gave him a little uncertain smile. Then the green light in her eyes darkened as she saw the anger in his face. She said, 'I love you, Andrea. That's all that matters. Don't be angry with me.'

And Claudine bent her head, as she waited for the storm to break.

Twenty-Five

THE COACH to Paris left at eight in the morning and Andrea was on it. He shared the journey with two clerks dressed in grey who discussed interminably a complicated set of tariffs, in which they seemed to think lay the future welfare of France. There was also an elderly widow and her maid, and a sharp-faced man with a portfolio that intruded on everyone's space. He had refused to have it strapped to the top of the coach. Andrea began to wish that he had walked, a feeling reinforced every time one of the clerks looked out of the window at the slowly passing countryside and remarked to his companion, 'It would have been quicker to have walked.'

And it would have been more of a distraction, to have used his energy in walking rather than sitting in this jolting carriage reflecting on the events in the bedroom at Saint-Cloud. The question nagged his mind, why? Why had she deceived him? What did she know of Claudine? Had she realised what had been going on in the night? Claudine had told him she had not, but he could not trust her any more than he could trust Athénaïs to tell him the truth. He turned his face towards the window to hide his expression from his travelling companions as the pictures of last night came into his mind.

Claudine pulling the sheet up to her neck as she looked pleadingly at him. 'I love you, Andrea, that's all that matters.'

The effrontery of it. As if his love were to be had indiscriminately, as if it were perfectly reasonable for him to service any woman who took a fancy to his body. 'You may love me; I loved Athénaïs.' He noticed, even in his fury, that he had used the past tense, as if the love had gone. Yet from the pain he felt in his heart he knew this wasn't so. Athénaïs, Athénaïs, why did you deceive me?

Claudine was crying now and looked up at him with red-rimmed eyes. No, Madame hadn't deceived him, she said. It was all down to her, Claudine. Madame hadn't deceived him, she had changed her mind.

'Oh, very nice,' Andrea had said. 'She swears love to me, gets me to risk my life climbing into the sodomite's chateau and then coolly says she's changed her mind. Oh, and as you're all primed up and I wouldn't want you to be disappointed, Andrea, here's a substitute.' He yanked the sheet away from Claudine. 'Why, she's even got tits the same size as mine, what more do you want, you Italian stud?'

Claudine snatched the sheet back and now she was angry. Andrea was not a gentleman to treat her like that, she said. If he couldn't accept a gift of love from her, then she was sorry to have wasted it. He would never get Madame now and he might as well forget her.

'Why are you so sure?' asked Andrea. He sat down on the bed, aware that he would get no more information if he continued to rage. He said more gently, 'Claudine, you must tell me, out of fairness, what I have done wrong, to turn her away from me. I shan't leave here until I know.'

Claudine looked doubtfully at him, weighing up his temper, then said, 'I don't know myself, I only know it is so. She was in a strange mood yesterday. There were so many people wanting her attention. After Monsieur's lunch party, she seemed very thoughtful, almost cast down. Then, later in the afternoon, a letter came for her, and she became distracted and restless. I helped her dress for the evening and suddenly she said, "Claudine, you must tell Andrea not to come tonight." So I tried to dissuade her, but she wouldn't hear of it. "No, he mustn't come, tell him I've changed my mind." '

'Who was the letter from?' asked Andrea.

'I don't know. She didn't say. I couldn't ask. I left the chateau to come to your place, and then I . . . I decided not to. She thought I had gone to tell you, but I hadn't.'

'She must have known,' said Andrea. 'You're trying to excuse her, to make her look less deceitful. Unless she spent the night somewhere other than this apartment she couldn't have failed to have known what was going on.'

'The walls are very thick,' said Claudine.

'Led astray by a vase of flowers.' Andrea laughed

briefly. 'The flowers placed outside the wrong door. How simple, how clever. What a clever little whore you are. Keeping me literally in the dark. He won't notice, you said. When men are in that mood, they'll fuck whatever is there.'

'You had better go, Andrea.'

'Don't worry, I'm going, as soon as I've got my clothes on, I'm getting out of this stinking chateau of deceit.'

Andrea picked up his clothes and pulled them on roughly. He held the shoes in his hand, to move more quietly in the corridor. 'Well, let's hope I don't get caught after this wasted night,' he said.

'One day, Andrea, you will realise it wasn't wasted. One day you'll come back to me.'

'Dream on,' said Andrea. Reaching the door, he turned just before he opened it, for a parting shot. 'My regards to Madame la Marquise and I trust she slept well, in whichever bed she was at the time.'

Claudine gazed at him with eyes like a baleful cat.

Andrea shut the door behind him and stepped into the corridor. The candles had long gone out and there was only a glimmer of daylight in the distance from the stairs. He stepped on something warm and furry that let out a succession of agonised yelps. One of Monsieur's dogs had got into the corridor.

'Fucking hound,' muttered Andrea. He felt sharp teeth in his ankle and kicked out, which made the animal yelp the more. He swore to himself again, reached the stairs and walked down to the last flight, making sure to put on his shoes before reaching the latrine. There was a besom by the door and it seemed a good idea to take it so that he looked like a worker at Saint-Cloud, rather than an intruder. The air was already warm outside. He walked, at a measured pace, across the lawn, shouldering the broom. On the other side of the wall was real life, ordinariness. He could hardly wait to reach it.

Now, as he sat on the hard seat of the jolting coach, his face flushed as he remembered what he had said to Claudine. It was wrong of him, he thought, cruel, yet what did she expect, after she had made a fool of him? But if she had made a fool of him out of love, was that so bad? Her legs wrapped round his back, her body moving with his, her hot flesh engulfing him. The disturbing images rose in his mind, stirring desire, obliterating the droning of the clerks and the plaintive voice of the widow. But how could he have been so deceived, how could his body have told him it was Athénaïs? The scent of Athénaïs, the voice of Athénaïs. The maid had picked it all up by living with her. She knew what it was to be Athénaïs. She had practised until she had become her mirror image. Well, there you were, a man in love was a fool and it was a lesson well learnt. The coach had jolted to a halt, as a herd of cattle blocked the road. Andrea said to the clerks, 'You're right. It would be quicker to walk.' He shouldered his bag, stepped out into the road and set off with long strides towards the city.

Twenty-Six

THE FURNACES were stoked to their highest temperature. In the heat of the city in late August, the mirror factory was like an inferno and Andrea's workmates were tormenting demons. 'How is the Marquise, Andrea?'

'Don't ask.'

Luca found the embroidered suit crumpled up in the holdall. 'A present from the Marquise, eh?' He insisted on hanging it up to get out the creases. 'You may want it again,' he said, 'when she invites you to a ball.'

Andrea immersed himself in the everyday life of the factory. The orders he had taken, the measurements he had made, were translated into hard manual work. Blowing the glass while sweat ran into your eyes and your face scorched from the heat, cutting and levelling the glass, spreading the mercury, tilting the glass to the right level. Then the mysterious element that gave some mirrors more clarity and lustre than others. Something to do with timing and the position of the planets, they said. The planets affected both the glass and the men.

Andrea felt his planet was in the descendant. He had been allowed capriciously into an enchanted territory, a *paradiso* on earth, and had found himself arbitrarily ejected. Pinpricks of memory reminded him of what he had lost. In the botanical gardens, birdsong would transport him to the manoir, under the lime tree, listening to the high, light voice of Athénaïs, soaring into realms of fantasy, her azure eyes looking not at him, but into him, as if prospecting for his soul. She was, he decided, a witch stealing men's souls and his was just one more that she was nailing to the wall, like a gamekeeper notching up vermin. At other times his body would remember the night of passion, when his entire being became part of hers – because he had believed he was loving her. He experienced a disorientation of his feelings, which was impossible to confide to anyone, for he knew what their reaction would be: 'Well, if the maid's such a good lay, go back to her. A bird in the hand . . .' To return and become an object of laughter between the maid and her mistress was more than a man's pride could bear.

He took to wandering the streets of Paris by himself. There was a rule against workers going out alone, because of fears of Venetian assassins. But nothing had happened recently and besides, he was not in a mood where he cared. He avoided the area of the Louvre and the Tuileries, and wandered down by the river, finding a measure of tranquillity in watching the passing boats and imagining the lagoon at Venice. Then he would turn eastwards from Notre-Dame, cutting back from the river to the faubourg Saint-Antoine. There was often an element of danger. He would note the assessing gaze of a chancer, weighing up a potential victim for his likely worth. He would glance back sharply, as if to say, I know what you're about, and see the other man turn his face away, like a cat pretending lack of interest in its prey.

One day he became lost as he tried to make his way back to the factory. He had wandered further east than he had intended and had reached the area of the tanneries. The stench from the drying skins was nauseating and he tried to cut through a narrow alley of shops, avoiding the open drain in the middle, to get back to the territory he knew. Turning into another street, he was caught up in a flow of people moving relentlessly in one direction, away from the area he was trying to get to. There was no alternative but to move with them and hope that he could cut away when they reached the next crossroad.

There was something strange in their mood, a subdued excitement, not the usual buzz of conversation that accompanied such gatherings. They were pushing ahead as if not to be late for an event, tension in their faces rather than expectation. He asked one man where they were going and received a glance as hard as pebbles. The street narrowed and now Andrea was jostled shoulder to shoulder with the crowd as the pace quickened. There were more people at the end of the street and he realised he was in danger of being crushed by the numbers behind him. His ribs were already constrained by the people who were hemming him in. There was nothing to be done but to keep moving and avoid tripping, for those immediately behind wouldn't be able to stop, propelled as they were by the human flow. At the end of the street, the space widened and he was in a large square. Ahead of him the crowd spread out, then converged again towards the centre, where there was a platform, on which were several soldiers, a man in a black mask and three sets of gallows.

He understood, now, the strange excitement of the crowd. They were there to witness the death of their fellow humans. He looked around him, but could see no way through the crowd and instead made his way towards a gap kept free of people by the soldiers. There was no way out here, either. He asked one of the guards whether he could cross, but the man snapped, 'Don't be stupid,' and pushed him with his musket butt.

He heard a voice near his ear mutter, 'You'll have to wait till it's over.' He turned to see next to him a slight, sharp-faced man in black, whose features seemed vaguely familiar. His eyes assessed Andrea's expression and he said, 'You don't have to look.'

'Who's been condemned?' asked Andrea.

'The usual thieves and sinners, but there's someone from my guild as well. A tailor. Condemned for killing his children. Here come the carts. You'll see him in a moment.'

Two men in chains were driven into the square. One of them stared ferociously at the crowds and cursed them. 'The brothers Deshayes,' said Andrea's neighbour. 'Bastards.' They had ambushed the wagons of merchants and had made a good living for years. No one need mourn their passing. The second cart was now moving by, within a few metres of where Andrea was. A thin, frail young man, hands clenched on to the front rail, stared towards them, but the blankness in his eyes seemed to say that he was already in another world.

The man next to Andrea crossed himself and recited a prayer. 'It will be good for him when it's all over,' he muttered. 'No one could have been a better father. He worked day and night at his tailoring, but he couldn't get these bloody aristos to settle their bills. I told him not to take on more work from bad debtors, but he believed their promises. Just one more suit, they would say, and then I will pay for the others at the same time. Poor fool. There was a marquis, who everyone knows is a gambler. The money he owed Jean went on the tables. Jean couldn't pay his taxes. The bailiffs moved in and took the lot – work table, chairs, bed. Everything. He couldn't work, didn't have a sou to buy bread. He fell into despair, into madness. Crying out that he would save them all from destitution, he slit the throats of two of his children. The wife snatched up the baby and ran out of the house, screaming her head off. So they arrested him and that was that. We're looking after the wife, but she's half mad as well.'

'How terrible,' said Andrea. 'The marquis deserves to be punished.'

'So he does, but he will go on as before – though I doubt if he will find a new tailor very easily.' He looked hard at Andrea. 'I've seen you before, haven't I? You were on the coach from Saint-Cloud with me.'

'Briefly. Then I decided to walk. I work at the mirror factory.'

'You'll be all right, then. The King pays his bills. All he has to do is tell his Minister to squeeze the country for more taxes. Never the rich, mark you, only the poor people. Like my friend who's about to swing. His baby will grow up hating the King. In two generations there will be enough people who hate the King to make an army. You mark my words, the rich won't have it their way for ever. But it's all right for you. All you foreign workers just rake in the money and go back home. Never enquire where your wages came from, or you may start seeing blood on your hands.'

The steady drumbeat reverberated round the square, like a wildly beating heart. There was a shout and the drums stopped. Then came a sound like a wave breaking and retreating on a shore, a sigh from a thousand throats. One of the Deshayes brothers writhed at the end of the rope, but the tailor hung like a broken rag doll. Andrea turned away, feeling sick to the stomach. He looked for the man he had been talking to, but he had slipped away into the crowd. The drums began again, at the oddly upbeat tempo of a march. Andrea eased his way through the crowd, as if following a thread out of a labyrinth. The drumbeats sounded in his ears, an insistent reminder that he could still hear and see and feel – that his heart was beating, his lungs were breathing. He was filled with a strange elation at being alive.

BACK AT the factory, he didn't talk about what he had witnessed. It was partly not to draw attention to the fact that he had been outside on his own, against the command of du Noyer, but also because he did not want to describe the hanging and his own reactions. Luca said to him, 'What or who were you chasing after this time?'

'Nothing, nobody. I was just taking the air.'

'Odd, considering how the air stinks. Do you remember the sisters from the botanical gardens? I was seeing them while you were away chasing your Marquise. The younger one is very sweet, I'm in love with her.'

'The younger one? Suzanne?' Andrea remembered their moment in the courtyard, her little pointed tongue in his mouth. 'I thought Suzanne was the one who liked me.'

'She knows you're otherwise engaged.' Luca smiled broadly at him.

'Luca, my friend, you don't know the first thing about women,' said Andrea. 'But I'll keep out of your way. Pursue the sisters, whichever you fancy, on your own.'

But in the end, on that Sunday, against his better judgement, Andrea came along. The sisters had told Luca that they wanted to hear about Saint-Cloud, about the gardens, the fountains, and was it true that the chateau was crammed with precious jewellery? They had heard that the King's brother had a more wonderful collection of paintings than the King himself. And what about the ladies? They wanted a full description of their dresses.

Afterwards, vignettes from that day would flicker into Andrea's mind and be as quickly suppressed. The moment when Luca, fresh from the barber with shaven face and pomaded hair, asked Andrea, 'How do I look?' He was wearing a clean linen shirt and a jerkin edged with green braid over his bulky frame. The barber's razor had smoothed his cheeks but added to the heightened colour of his furnace-reddened face. His eyes shone with confidence and expectation. Andrea had thought, Luca has a loving soul, let's hope the girl is kind to him. 'The barber seems to have been generous with the eau de toilette,' he said.

'Lemon and rosemary. He splashed a lot on so that it would last through the day. Do you like it?'

'Very piquant. I expect the sisters will be all over you.'

'It's Suzanne I'm interested in, don't forget,' said Luca.

The moment when they met the sisters by the gates to the botanical gardens. The elder one, who reminded Andrea of a mouse, glancing shyly at them and then smiling, with a sudden warmth, adding colour to her face. The younger one looking at Andrea and smiling too, her lips parted to show a glimpse of her tongue as a reminder of their last meeting. Luca noticed nothing, as he stood next to her, his arm slipping round her waist in a proprietorial gesture. Andrea thought, he's an idiot, and I'm an idiot, too, for imagining she might have forgotten.

At the fair on the left bank, where the students were celebrating the feast day of Saint Jerome and their return to university, stalls had been set up selling sweets, gateaux, ribbons, lace and other little presents with which men could make a gesture to their ladies, without spending much money in the process. Andrea bought some chocolate for them all and Luca asked the sisters to choose ribbons that he then presented to each sister. The elder gave a discreet, mouselike smile and tied the ribbon round her neck. The younger said, oh, it was so difficult to tie ribbons on oneself, would Andrea help please? 'I should like the bow in front.' Andrea stood in front of her tying the ribbon, his fingers hovering above the breasts that seemed to rise towards him as she breathed, inviting his touch. He tried not to catch her eyes but when she murmured, 'Thank you, Andrea,' he couldn't help but glance and see the enticement in them.

This time Luca noticed. He said to Andrea as the girls' attention was drawn to another stall, 'What the hell are you playing at?'

'It's not my fault,' said Andrea.

'You're spoiling everything, I thought you were my friend.'

'Perhaps it would be better if I left,' said Andrea, but the sisters were now suggesting it was time to eat and they found a table on the square. The two men sat side by side on the bench, the girls on the bench opposite them. Suzanne was in front of Andrea, so it was impossible for him not to look at her. He noticed she had loosened the drawstring of her chemise under her bodice, which exposed more of her breasts. The waiter brought them a jug of wine and several dishes at the same time: artichokes, roast pork, tomatoes. She pulled at the flesh of each artichoke leaf, leaving behind the ridge marks of her teeth. Underneath the table the instep of her stockinged foot caressed

Andrea's calf. He shifted his leg and saw Luca look suspiciously at him.

It was a perfect early autumn day, the air still warm and a golden light over the river. A band of musicians was playing dance tunes and some of the students were dancing in ragged unison, their arms linked, while others clapped to the beat. It was, they all agreed, a wonderful day, but underneath their conversation ran an undercurrent of jealousy, rage and chagrin, which only erupted after they had seen the sisters to their aunt's house. The liberal-minded aunt was used as an alibi in order to escape the watchfulness of their parents. 'If they knew we were seeing Italian men, we would be locked up or sent to a convent,' said the elder. 'What a waste that would be,' said the younger. She clasped her hands behind her head, revealing damp patches on the chemise under her arms, and smiled at Andrea.

'We'll escort you to your aunt,' said Luca abruptly.

Afterwards, as they walked back, Luca fumed. How could Andrea pretend to be a friend and then try to steal the girl Luca loved? Andrea replied that he couldn't steal her, because she didn't belong to Luca in any case. You couldn't decide for women whom they would love – they made their own choices.

'She was loving to me while you were away,' said Luca.

'She's a kind-hearted girl,' said Andrea, at which point the pent-up emotion in Luca's breast erupted in a torrent. He would never have believed that Andrea could have betrayed him in this way, he shouted on the Pont-Neuf, oblivious of passers-by. Andrea could have any woman he fancied, he had the devil's own luck, yet he must go after the one Luca had set his heart on. Why, he had been planning to talk to the girl's parents, he had been thinking of marrying her.

'The more fool you,' said Andrea, 'she would have led you a dance. Come on, Luca, you've had a lucky escape.'

Luca's eyes were brimming with tears. If Andrea only knew, he said, what it was like to have a heart full of love, only to see the beloved turn away. He had never felt such pain. He hoped Andrea would know what it was like one day. But no, Andrea just had to smile and they came running. He could really hate him for what he had done, he could kill him. He moved forward as if to hit him.

Andrea stepped back and raised his hands in supplication. 'Luca, none of this was intended. I told you that it was a bad idea for me to come with you. You can't control the feelings of women. And as it happens' – he hesitated a moment, remembering Luca's gossiping tongue, before continuing – 'as it happens, I do know what it's like to have love rejected. I know the pain and confusion, and I know that it doesn't last. You'll get over it, I promise you.'

'So what happened with the Marquise?' asked Luca instantly, his eyes brightening.

'Never you mind. But whatever happened, it's over. And we have both been left in confusion by the games these Frenchwomen play. We neither of us understands the rules.'

Luca's anger subsided as he shifted the blame from his friend to the women. Yes, now he saw how they amused themselves by driving men mad. 'Tarts,' said Luca.

'Deceivers.'

'But even so it hurts. Let's have another jug of wine.'

'At the next tavern.'

At the next tavern . . . the waiter dusted down the table under the tree with a wine-stained cloth. Inside, in a dark recess, a group of men were playing cards. One looked up, the whites of his eyes glinting in the candlelight. Instinctively Andrea and Luca retreated to the open air. The waiter brought over a jug of wine, two glasses and a dish of bread and olives. '*Santé*,' he said, and stood over them until they paid.

'Not the friendliest place in town,' muttered Andrea in the Venetian dialect.

'But the wine's drinkable,' said Luca.

The waiter, checking the change, said, 'You're from Venice, are you?'

'Is it so noticeable?' said Andrea. 'We're from Murano.'

'*Bien*.' The waiter slipped the coins into the pouch at his waist and retreated back into the tavern.

'*Santé*,' said Andrea, raising his glass. The sunlight passing through the wine cast a rosy reflection on the marble-topped table.

'*Salute*,' said Luca. He took a long gulp of the wine. 'To the ladies of Venice.'

'The ladies of Venice.'

'I'll earn as much money as I can and next spring I'm going back to Venice. I've had it with Paris.'

'Next spring you'll find reasons to stay,' said Andrea.

'I don't think so. I miss my home. I miss my parents and my sisters. We're isolated in the factory, there's no home life. Everyone has started quarrelling. Maybe you haven't noticed because you've been able to get out. There was a fight the other day when La Motta discovered we were all being paid more than him, though he was the first to come to Paris. The men want to go back, but we're trapped. No one will be allowed to leave until the French have wheedled out our secret. Meanwhile, we're paid more than we have ever earned in our lives. More than we're ever likely to earn again. So we're trapped by the money as well.'

'Be glad that it's such a comfortable trap. Have some more wine.'

One of the men who had been playing cards emerged from the tavern and glanced at them as he went by.

'Strange eyes that man has got,' said Andrea. 'You notice the whites first, like a horse that's about to kick.'

Luca shrugged. The sun glimmered through the leaves of the tree, so that the patchwork of light and shadows on the jug of wine, the glasses and the dish of olives took on the quality of a picture. 'If I could paint,' he said, 'I would paint this jug. And look how the light changes the colour of the wine. We don't create images with our mirrors, it's the onlooker who does that.'

'But we provide the glass in which they can see the truth, what their portrait painter daren't show.'

'If that was what they saw, they wouldn't keep ordering. No, they create their own image when they look in the mirror. They see only what they want to see. They ignore the fat and the wrinkles. They think, what splendid clothes I'm wearing and this is the best wig at court. They obscure the truth of our mirrors with their powder and paint and jewellery. They can't see their souls.'

'My dear Luca, you're in danger of becoming a philosopher.'

Luca laughed. 'Wine loosens the tongue.'

'And our mirrors feed their delusions. A man looks into a mirror and sees a beautiful woman gazing back at him, even though he is wearing a moustache.'

'Maybe *you* should lay off the wine, too,' said Luca.

'Did you realise that the King is nowhere near as tall as he appears?'

'You're wrong. You forget, I saw him at the mirror factory. He towered above everyone.'

'Everyone was bowing and feeling small. It's all down to the plumes on his hat and the high heels. He has created the illusion of height and no one would ever contradict the most powerful man in France.'

Luca gazed reflectively at his glass. 'I wouldn't mind being seen as a dwarf if I could be the most powerful man in France. And I could have my pick of the court beauties. We've finished the wine. Shall we move on?'

'To the next tavern.'

Towards evening, they arrived at the market place which led into the faubourg Saint-Antoine. Now only a few rotten vegetables were scattered on the ground below the empty market stalls.

'I'm gasping for a drink,' said Luca. 'What I wouldn't give for a glass of fruit juice.'

'There's the answer to your prayer,' said Andrea, pointing out a man lounging on a bench with a basket of fruit beside him.

As the two men approached he glanced towards

them, and called out, 'Messieurs, I see you have come to relieve me of this fruit. Come and try the oranges.'

'Oranges,' murmured Luca, 'what I was praying for. Where are they from?'

The man shrugged. 'Who knows? Somewhere in the south. Try them and see if you like the taste. You can have the whole basket, I don't want to take them home.'

Luca examined the fruit in the basket. 'And you have some grapes as well.'

'The grapes are not so sweet,' said the man. 'You're better off with the oranges, take some for your friend as well. For all your friends. Half price at this time of day.'

'Why half price? Is there something wrong with them?' said Andrea.

The man glanced up at him, one eye very bright and dark, the other covered with a white film. He had skin like a wizened apple and when he smiled, he revealed gaps to his discoloured teeth. 'Feel the fruit. Judge for yourself.' He held up an orange. 'Firm and ripe. The very best. There's no market tomorrow and I want to get rid of this batch before another lot comes in. Would you like a taste?'

Luca took one of the oranges and held it to his nose. Then he bit into the peel and sucked at the fruit. The juice ran down his cheeks and dripped on to his shirt. 'We'll have the lot,' he said. 'I'll take them back for the factory. We're starved of fruit.'

'For another sou you can have the basket,' said the man. 'You're a generous man, Monsieur, to give your friends a treat.'

Luca handed over the money and took the basket.

'Good day to you, Monsieur, enjoy the fruit.' The one eye shone darkly, the other opaquely with the pale blankness of a stone statue.

Andrea said, as they walked away, 'There's something wrong with everyone's eyes today. He reminded me of that man at the tavern.'

'What man?' said Luca. He was peeling the skin back until he could divide the orange into segments, which he stuffed into his mouth. 'Have an orange, Andrea.' Luca's face was smeared with juice.

'I have too much respect for my shirt. I'll wait till we're back.'

'We're late. We spent too long at the second tavern. We must hurry, we'll miss dinner.'

They were nearing the factory gates when Luca stopped suddenly and leaned against the wall of a house. 'I feel strange,' he said, shutting his eyes.

'You drank too much,' said Andrea. 'Just hold on, we're almost back.'

Luca stumbled, put a steadying hand against the wall. 'I was all right till just now,' he said. 'Maybe it's a fever.'

Holding the basket in one hand, Andrea grabbed Luca's arm. They had just reached the gate when Luca bent almost double, clutching his side. Beads of sweat were standing out on his face and his eyes stared like a frightened animal. 'What's happening to me? Oh God, Jesus, Maria.' He began to retch. 'I've such a pain, Andrea . . . the oranges.'

One of the guards at the gate, seeing them in trouble, came out to help Andrea support Luca into the compound. Andrea put down the basket of fruit by the guards' hut. They took Luca up to their rooms and helped him on to the bed. He lay staring up at the ceiling, groaning as a spasm shook his frame, and he leaned over the side of the bed, vomiting on to the floor.

'I'll find a doctor,' said the guard, retreating quickly from the room.

'There was something in the orange. It tasted bitter,' said Luca.

Andrea remembered du Noyer's various warnings when they had first arrived. Don't go out alone, don't eat any food you are offered. Over the months, they had shrugged off such stories as simply the manager's way of trying to control the men, of discouraging them from leaving the compound. Now, as he looked at Luca's grey-tinged face, he realised that finally, after months of tricks and false letters, the Venetians had become serious. He thought of Giustiniani's face, of those shrewdly twinkling eyes, and somewhere at the back of them a calculating hardness.

Andrea ran down to the guards' hut and saw one of the apprentices crouched by the basket. 'Don't touch them,' he shouted, 'they're poisoned.'

Immediately, the word went round the compound. Others gathered, staring at the fruit. The doctor arrived and gave Luca a purge, which caused him to vomit all the more, then bled him, filling two bowls with blood, and went off to have dinner. Later he returned to apply the knife once more.

Andrea stopped him. 'You've done enough,' he said. 'He's already fainting from loss of blood.'

'And what qualifies you to give an opinion?' snapped the doctor. 'The poison comes out with the bleeding.'

'That's no use if you bleed him to death.'

'I'm sick of lay people thinking they know better,' said the doctor. Luca raised his head from the pillow, staring at the doctor with eyes that seemed to have sunk right back in their sockets, and whispered hoarsely, 'Don't bleed me.'

The doctor shrugged. Very well, the patient must then commit himself to divine intervention, he said. He could help no further. Andrea, fearing the worst, sent one of the apprentices to fetch the priest. While they waited, he sat by Luca's bed, wiping his face with a cloth dipped in lavender water.

Luca suddenly went into a violent spasm and began to writhe in pain. 'I'm going to die, aren't I, Andrea?' His voice was barely audible.

Andrea said through his tears, 'God will spare you.'

For a few moments Luca lay there peacefully, as if the struggle were already over. Then he stared at his friend with burning eyes. 'Promise me, Andrea, promise me that you will avenge me. Make them pay for this. Make Venice pay.'

Andrea was afflicted with a sense of helplessness. One man against the Venetian Republic – it couldn't be done. But Luca was no longer interested in what was possible. He whispered again, 'Make them pay. Avenge me.'

'I will,' said Andrea. His tears fell freely on to Luca's hand, which clutched at his shirt.

Soon after, the priest arrived to administer extreme

unction. He prayed by Luca's bed, holding out the crucifix for him to kiss, and anointed him with oil. Luca gazed up at him like a trusting child, lulled by the sonorous Latin of the Indulgentium. At the same time it was as if his body, now that he had been absolved of his worldly sins, wanted only to shake off its physical self. The convulsions became more violent, then he began to vomit blood. He turned his eyes towards Andrea again, but seemed not to recognise him. He looked beyond him, as if the room and those in it were no longer part of his world. Then he was shaken by another convulsion and fell back on his pillow. The priest and Andrea listened to the silence that followed the rush of air from his lungs. He was no longer breathing. Andrea leant forward and closed his eyes.

AFTER THE funeral, Monsieur du Noyer was quick to point out the dangers of leaving the compound and to remind people of the necessity to be watchful at all times. He was preaching to a group of sullen and angry men. The mirror makers held a council among themselves. They had had enough of Paris, they were frightened, no amount of money was worth the terrible death Luca had suffered. Della Rivetta and Civrano wrote to the Venetian Ambassador to negotiate a return. Giustiniani wrote back, offering large pensions all round and no reprisals. No one had expected such generous terms for what the Republic had hitherto considered a betrayal.

Giustiniani proposed a meeting but Andrea told Rivetta that he would not be able to trust himself to attend. This was the man who had given the orders that led to Luca's death. The sequence of events ran through his mind. He knew now that they had been recognised at the tavern and the fruit seller near the factory had been waiting, as if for an appointment. If Luca hadn't greedily demolished two oranges before they reached the factory and suffered the consequences, how many others would have been poisoned?

'We could stop them from leaving, but there's no point as they refuse to work any more,' du Noyer said to Andrea. 'Too bad for the factory, and for the French workers. I suppose you will be going, too?'

'Luca was a good friend,' said Andrea. 'He didn't deserve to die like a rat.'

The next day du Noyer called him over as he was wandering aimlessly around the compound and said that Monsieur Colbert had asked Andrea to attend him. 'Get over there as quickly as possible, don't keep the great man waiting,' he added.

COLBERT HATED anything in his office to be out of order. The ebony and mother-of-pearl inkwell had to be placed just so on his escritoire. The papers he had to deal with were neatly stacked in files. That morning the clocks were trying his patience. There were two, as an insurance against mechanical failure. And they were out of sync. As one went tick, the other went tock. Dessaix was charged with synchronising the ticks. Colbert was trying to suppress his irritation at the time Dessaix was taking to chase the elusive half-second, as he dictated a letter to the other secretary.

Now there was a further interruption. A Monsieur Allegri was downstairs, said the footman. An *Italian*, he added with disdainful emphasis.

'Fine, send him up,' said Colbert. 'Dessaix, if you can't get the ticks right, stop one of the clocks altogether.'

'Which one, Monseigneur?'

Colbert raised his eyes to the ceiling and muttered, 'Dear God, I am surrounded by imbeciles.'

He looked towards the door, as the mirror maker entered. Yes, he remembered the face well, it was more handsome than it had the right to be. He was standing there in a perfectly respectful way, and yet there was a certain independence about him that was at the same time admirable and irritating. Colbert was reminded of his eldest son, who seemed to think that the universe was fashioned for him. As with his son, he felt an almost irresistible urge to slap down this young man, to remind him that the world was a complex place and he was but a small cog in an infinite series of the wheels of time, a tiny tick that could be stopped at will.

It seemed, though, glancing at the young man again, that Monsieur Allegri might already have learnt something of this. The face he remembered in the coach to Saint-Germain had been like a beautiful blank canvas, unmarked by trouble or time. The man standing before him now looked different. His mouth was set in a harder line, his eyes were more watchful. He was no longer an overgrown boy.

He gestured to Dessaix to fetch a chair and watched as the young man hesitated a moment before sitting down. Pride and wariness, thought Colbert. He had been the same in his early days, well aware of the rebuffs that might suddenly be visited on the son of a draper, as they had called him then. And now those same people were pleading with him for favours.

But to business. Colbert extended his condolences to the mirror maker over the tragic death of his friend. It seemed all the more bizarre to him that the mirror makers had decided, despite the criminal poisoning of one of their number, to return to the city that had instigated it. He appreciated the fact that they were frightened of staying, in case there was a similar incident, but to give way so quickly to the murderers . . . The King would have been more than willing to give as much protection as they needed.

'They're homesick as well,' said Andrea.

Colbert noted Andrea's detachment in the use of the third person. The young man himself was not homesick. 'Unlike you, your friends have not seen for themselves the magnificence of our palaces. They have not wandered through the apartments of the Louvre, of the Tuileries, of the Palais Royal. When a man possesses knowledge that is needed by those who have both power and riches, he can have much to gain.'

He saw comprehension in Andrea's face. This time, he thought, there will not be pious talk of guarding the secret of his departed ancestors. The young man was hardly breathing, he was looking at Colbert with eyes in which the pupils had dilated. Colbert smiled, a glimpse of sun in the face of the icy North. 'Of course,' he went on, 'we already know something of the secret of mirror making simply from watching you at work. But it would take much valuable time to discover the whole process. If you were to return to Venice, we wouldn't be lost, but if you were to stay, if you were to instruct our men in the making of mirrors, you would benefit from the King's gratitude.'

Colbert noticed Andrea's eyes flicker around the office. The furniture and the pictures in his office could have graced the Louvre.

'You, Monsieur Allegri, are on the edge of the greatest opportunity of your life. Remember, the King has a special interest in mirrors. He realises, as you do, their amazing properties. You would be able to experiment with their uses.'

Colbert sat back in his chair and waited for the young man's response, which was frustratingly slow. What more did he want to hear? 'Of course, the Venetian Republic would not be delighted to lose their monopoly. It would cost them dear.'

Andrea leant forward, his face shining with excitement, fists clenched. 'We'll make them pay,' he said in a low voice. Then he straightened his back, looked Colbert in the eye and said, 'Let us discuss the terms.'

AFTERWARDS, ANDREA lingered for a while in the main courtyard. He felt disorientated and numb. The prospect of never seeing Venice and his family again had not occurred to him before, but this was what it amounted to, the action he had taken. He was to become a stranger to his own country, his fortune depending on a foreign land. A shiver, light and thrilling, ran through his body at the enormity of his decision. 'So, Luca, you are happy now?' he said to himself. 'They'll pay and pay again. You will be well avenged.'

He looked up at the piano nobile. The long windows of Colbert's office were open to the air and

Andrea could see Colbert at his writing desk. He watched the black-clad shoulders move slightly as he came to the end of a line and went on to the next one. He saw Dessaix take a paper from him, but the writing continued with hardly a pause. This was the man to whom he was now beholden, who in turn was beholden to a King whose mind could be read by no one.

Andrea realised that the guard was looking at him suspiciously. He left the courtyard and turned right into the street. Confused images flickered through his mind as he walked along. The King's plumed hat like a fiery beacon as he moved through the sea of courtiers. The Minister's dark austerity amid his gilded sur-roundings, the scent of bergamot emanating from him, a reminder of Italy. The burning heat of the glass furnaces, the smell of sweat and stale wine. This was to be his world from now on, in this unpredictable, capricious city. He walked on, in the direction of the Tuileries, when a picture came unbidden to his mind of the rose-pink salon, him with his back to the room hanging the mirror, the reflected azure eyes looking into his, the scent of tuberose that tantalised his nostrils. His first glimpse of her – and how long ago it seemed. He had become a different man.

PART TWO

The Island of Happiness

Saint-Germain and Versailles
1666–74

Twenty-Seven

O NCE UPON a time there was a king who was young and handsome, and who wanted everything. The fairy Mazarine watched over him as he grew up and taught him the secret of how to have anything you desire. 'There is only one drawback,' said the fairy. 'You will have to lose your heart.'

'Not a problem,' said the king, who enjoyed losing his heart to any number of ladies.

The fairy Mazarine said, 'That's not what I meant.' But the king was already off on the chase, so the fairy shook her head sadly, before gathering her crimson robes around her and flying off to the heavens, though not before she had bequeathed to the king an industrious black dwarf who would go down the dirtiest and most dangerous mines to dig for gold, which he brought up in great hoards.

'Always keeping a portion for himself,' interrupted Madame de Thianges. 'Though discreetly, not like the unfortunate Fouquet. I heard the other day the poor man's health is completely wrecked. His hair has turned white, his teeth have fallen out, he coughs blood. Madame Fouquet was devastated when she saw him last. He lives in permanent darkness, damp and cold. Such is the fall of the richest man in France.'

'Once upon a time there was a cruel and powerful king,' began the Chevalier de Saint-Cyr, 'who delighted in selecting favourites, in making them believe that they were the most favoured and trusted of his subjects, and then, one day, when they least expected it, he would send his guards to drop them from a great height into a dungeon where they spent the rest of their lives up to their waists in effluent . . .'

'Excuse me,' said Athénaïs. 'I was in the middle of my story. You must wait your turn.'

'My apologies, Marquise. *Désolé.*'

'One day the king said to the black dwarf, "You must bring me all the gold from under the earth so that I can build the most beautiful palace that has ever been seen. It will be made of marble and the salons will be gilded with gold, encrusted with rubies and diamonds. The gardens will be filled with the most rare and beautiful lilies from the Orient, with fountains and cascades, caves and grottoes . . ." '

'Decorated with pearls from the deepest oceans,' added Saint-Cyr.

'But of course. And the palace will be built on an island where all is happiness and joy, where the sun always shines. And no one will be allowed in who is ugly and old . . .'

'I can already see a problem here,' said Saint-Cyr, 'which time will exacerbate.'

'The palace is decorated with great golden sunbursts

and in the middle of the sun, a man's face. You look closer and you see it is the face of the king,' said Athénaïs, her eyes seeming to fill with the vision.

'Ah, Versailles!' exclaimed Saint-Cyr. 'So you have been there recently?'

'No, I was hearing about it, from the King's architect. When it's completed there will be no palace in the world as grand and as beautiful, so he said.'

'Well, he would, wouldn't he? There is no greater proponent of his own work than Monsieur Le Vau.'

Athénaïs smiled, as she remembered the *déjeuner* at Saint-Cloud that day last summer, Monsieur Le Vau's jowls quivering as he had described the delights that he was creating, Monsieur's sidelong conspiratorial glances at Athénaïs as he encouraged Le Vau to ever greater flights of eloquence.

'I don't quite understand,' Monsieur had said, furrowing his brows in a caricature of puzzlement worthy of one of Molière's troupe. 'What is this sunburst motif you refer to?'

Monsieur Le Vau seemed to swell visibly, like a marsh frog, and sat back in his chair, his eloquent hands painting the picture before him. 'Imagine,' he said, 'just imagine. There are the great doors to the state apartments before you and on the doors the relief of a man's head surrounded by the rays of a sun, a great sunburst of gold flames round the beautiful golden head – you are standing in front of the palace of the Sun King.'

'He always did enjoy playing Apollo in the court masques,' murmured Monsieur, raising his eyebrows at Athénaïs.

'The great doors open before you, and you are in the magnificent salon, the walls decorated with the exploits of the gods and above them the King overlooking the scene, his sceptre outstretched. You walk through the salon and you come to the next set of doors and there, again, the golden head surrounded by the sun. As you pause, gazing at the stern but beautiful face of the godlike man, the doors open and you are in the next salon, likewise magnificently decorated. You pass through this salon, admiring the decor, and you are before the next set of doors and there, bam! the gilded head is before you once more. And so you process through one salon after another and there is the gilded head, again and again. Bam! Bam! Bam! One after another, at each set of doors.'

'So there's no danger of forgetting whose palace you are in,' said Monsieur.

'The palace bears the stamp of one man, of His Majesty. I am like his instrument, playing the rhapsody in his mind. He says, "Build it this way." I say, "Sire, it can't be done." He says, "But this is how it should be. This is what I want." And so you find a way. I told him time and again that we should demolish the old hunting lodge and start anew, but no, he wouldn't hear of it. He had to have it enveloped by the palace, not a brick was to be disturbed.'

Le Vau continued in this vein, with Monsieur adding an occasional aside. Athénaïs, meanwhile, was experiencing a series of confused speculations. The head in the centre of the sun's rays – this was the vision Madame Voisin had described to her in the curtained room. The man surrounded by flames. It had never occurred to her before. Everything was unchanged, to outward appearances, as she heard the voice of Le Vau and acknowledged with her eyes Monsieur's little asides. She was the Marquise de Montespan still and yet her sense of herself had shifted. Somewhere in her mind her image of herself was undergoing a change. It was as if she had been lost in the dark woods and had become aware of a path ahead which, if she took it, would lead her to her destiny.

That afternoon she had received a letter from Louise de La Vallière. It was difficult to understand what Mademoiselle de La Vallière was on about, the letter was so confused, but she kept referring to Athénaïs as her 'dear friend' and declared how much she would like to see more of her and hear her amusing repartee. Athénaïs guessed that the mistress, whose conversation was said to make the King yawn, was anxious to sharpen her intellectual skills. But how very strange, thought Athénaïs, as she held the letter in her hand, gazing out of the window at the courtyard of Saint-Cloud. Didn't Madame Voisin predict that a blonde woman would call for my help?

A hand waved in front of her face and she became aware of Saint-Cyr's voice. 'The Marquise seems to have lost her way,' he said. 'She went into a reverie while describing the golden heads in the palace of pearls and diamonds, leaving us all on tenterhooks.'

'I'm not lost, you are simply impatient. A good fairy tale cannot be hurried. So, the palace was built, the envy of all the world, but the king was not content, for he was looking for a matchless princess who would be worthy of it . . .' She paused, appearing to lose the thread, then said, 'I'm sorry, Chevalier, you are right, my inspiration is not up to much today.'

'The problem is that Louis is building the palace, he is creating a fairy tale of which he is the centre. He has made reality out of imagination and so our tales become shadows of the substance.'

'Very nicely put, Chevalier,' said Madame de Thianges. 'So if we are now considering the substance, who will be chosen as the matchless princess?'

'I'm not going to endanger myself by such speculation,' Saint-Cyr laughed. 'Who do you think, you ladies who are more expert on men's hearts than I?'

But suddenly the women had become strangely reticent. Madame de Thianges remembered a dressmaker's appointment and the Marquise a visit she had promised the ailing Madame de C. November was a cruel month, she said, not all the parties in Paris could keep ill health at bay.

NOVEMBER WAS a cruel month. Montespan, back from his skirmishing on the Spanish border, was kicking his heels in Paris. Their marriage was at a point where Athénaïs found it difficult to remain in the same room with him.

Claudine had been moody, ever since that night at Saint-Cloud. She reproached her mistress, her eyes filled with tears. 'I'll never forget the look on his face when he saw me. To have been so deceived . . . Do you not feel guilty?'

'For heaven's sake, you were happy enough about it at the time, playing the counterfeit marquise. It was months ago and I'm sure he's nicely fixed up with a girl by now.'

Claudine, incomprehensibly, cried all the more. Athénaïs sighed. A droopy maid was the last thing she needed at a time like this. It was strange how that adventure, on a warm summer's night, had been so unsettling. It had been only one night, after all. But he had been an unusual and handsome young man. She remembered the moment of seeing him on the terrace at Saint-Cloud, the curly head of hair, the smile that lit up his face. He looked, she had thought, *bien-aimé*. Once upon a time there was a woodcutter's son who fell in love with a princess. . . . Well, it was just a fairy tale, after all.

In the meantime there was the reality of the ogre husband. If only Montespan did not care for her there could be a way of inhabiting the same house. His love had turned to anger and to reproaches. 'Once you loved me, too,' he had said, 'or had you only been pretending?'

'You abused my trust,' she replied, 'you took my jewellery, you took my money for your gaming and now we're only one step ahead of the bailiffs. How can I feel love for you when you've brought us to penury?'

'It was only a temporary hitch,' protested Montespan, and then, when she turned her face aside as he tried to kiss her, he raged, 'You're a cold, heartless woman. You've got a lover, haven't you? Who is he? It's Monsieur, isn't it?'

Now it was her turn to rage at his impugning her honour, and with such a ridiculous accusation. *Monsieur*, of all people . . . The scene ended with his slamming out of the house, his need for gambling justified in his mind by his cold, unfaithful bitch of a wife. And that's

221

how our life is at home, she thought. A grain of happiness to a cartload of pain.

But at the same time there was, within her, a sensation of coming change. It kept her from despair, that narrow ray of light which had illuminated the dark woods in her mind. I am walking towards the light, she thought. So when Montespan declared that the household would decamp to spend the winter on his estates in Gascony, she knew this was a deviation to be avoided. Her dear friend Monsieur intervened, to tell the difficult husband that the Princess Henriette could not spare her most valuable lady-in-waiting for the winter season of parties and balls. The price for Athénaïs was high – her pearl necklace – but then Montespan departed swiftly for the south, just ahead of his most pressing creditors. And Athénaïs was free.

Twenty-Eight

WHEN DID the King first turn his thoughts to Athénaïs? Afterwards, the whisperers suggested it was around November, for wasn't it then that he had appointed Athénaïs lady-in-waiting to the Queen? Hitherto he had seemed indifferent to her charms. He had danced with her at court masques, she had played a nymph to his Apollo and the Sun King had remained aloof. But now, if you had eyes in your head it was clear that something was afoot. At the balls and masquerades at Saint-Germain where the court was spending the winter, it was piquant to watch the pastoral ballet des muses, where the King played the Shepherd, with Mademoiselle de La Vallière and Madame de Montespan as the two shepherdesses. You would only notice if you saw in a certain way that his hand held hers a moment longer than was necessary, that when his eyes met hers they didn't look away. Saint-Cyr, whose livelihood as a gambler depended on anticipation of other people's thoughts, noticed. Gabrielle de Thianges, Athénaïs's knowing sister, noticed. Others didn't. Louise de La

Vallière had no idea, when she appeared in the court masque as Diana the huntress with a quiver of arrows at her back, that Venus, in the form of Athénaïs, was in the ascendant. After all, the Marquise was her new best friend. Louise was growing fonder of her by the day. Athénaïs's wit and charm caused the King to spend more time in their company. The King's mistress and the new lady-in-waiting were almost inseparable.

When did Athénaïs realise his mood had changed from indifference to a speculative interest? There had been the moment during the lunch with Le Vau when her superstitious mind had remembered the cryptic words of Madame Voisin and had understood them anew, with brilliant clarity. But there was, she realised later, another moment, earlier, at Monsieur's party at Saint-Cloud. It came back to her now, like a picture.

THEY ARE in the middle of supper on the terrace, on that summer's night. The air is warm and heavy with the scent of jasmine. She feels imbued with a sense of *bien-être*, she is bathed in admiration, she sees herself mirrored in the young Venetian's eyes as a goddess of beauty. She feels loved. The despond of the last few months falls away from her like a dusty veil. She is the butterfly emerging from the cocoon. Then the woman in yellow shrieks across the table for gossip about Monsieur. The royal table has already fallen silent, their attention drawn to the noise and laughter that has been emanating from Saint-Cyr's party. The woman's voice, cutting across everyone, stops the conversation on their table as well. They are struck dumb by the enormity of her faux pas. They are all looking at their plates. Saint-Cyr's foot nudges Athénaïs under the table. She knows he is asking for help. 'Ah yes,' she says, projecting her voice clearly, 'we were just remarking on what an excellent host Monsieur is and how his chefs have excelled themselves.'

The conversation resumes and after a few minutes she cannot resist glancing at the royal table. The King is watching her. As their eyes meet, he continues to look at her. It is an expression without emotion, as if he is observing an interesting species at his menagerie. He turns away to talk to the Princess of Monaco and the moment has passed, but the image remains in the back of Athénaïs's mind. Much later, she sees that expression again. It is one of assessment, the moment the King marked her out.

SHE WAS now in dangerous territory. Dancing and flirting, but discreetly. The Queen's jealousy of Louise was expressed in ferocious unpleasantness whenever she was given an opportunity. Louise's eyes often filled with tears, though her distress was forgotten when she danced with her Louis. The shepherd and the two shepherdesses pirouetted in the ballet of the two muses. Athénaïs heard the words of Eurydice's lament – '*Mais que c'est un mal dangereux / D'aimer et de ne le pouvoir dire!*' And too dangerous to look at the King, who had also heard the words and murmured, '*Que c'est vrai.*'

So the *jours gras* came and went, the carnivals and balls before Lent, and the relationship continued like tightrope walkers who knew that one false step would result in catastrophe. At least, Athénaïs had that sensation, conscious of her proximity to unlimited power and of feeling that power bend towards her will. She saw the abyss into which it was possible to fall. She heard in her mind the mockery of the court – 'There goes the lady-in-waiting who tried to supplant the King's mistress. Well, she's still waiting . . .' And the future, debt and more debt, a move to a smaller apartment and eventually out of the orbit of the court, into obscurity. It didn't bear thinking about.

'WHAT DOES your sister think she's doing?' Saint-Cyr said to Madame de Thianges when they reached an impasse at chess.

'She's returned to being a Précieuse,' said Gabrielle. 'She seeks to rule the King with her wit. I gather he's under her spell.'

'It's a dangerous game to play with a man who has the appetites of the King. Twice a day, on average, with La Vallière. Twice a week with the Queen.'

'Less often with La Vallière now, I hear.'

'I'm told she's pregnant again. Athénaïs should be careful that she doesn't become a mistress of convenience while Louise is *enceinte*.'

'Athénaïs is not stupid. In any case, the King's thoughts are about the coming war with the Netherlands,' said Madame de Thianges. 'There'll be no time for love once he is embarked on the campaign. Which I hope he conducts better than yours, Chevalier. You've left your queen uncovered to my knight.'

THE KING, though, was not intending to go to war without his court. What was the point of winning glory in battle if there was no audience to applaud?

The Queen and her ladies-in-waiting were to make the journey to the Netherlands as well. But before their departure a significant event occurred.

Athénaïs arrived at court in a pale and agitated state. Montespan had returned from Gascony and had already borrowed twenty thousand livres. Later that day the King had departed for Versailles, taking with him one person in the carriage – Athénaïs. Five days later Louise was created a duchess and her daughter was legitimised. When she was congratulated on her ennoblement she began to weep. She felt, she said, like a servant who was being paid off. Even Louise, the most innocent of souls, was aware of the turning tide in the King's affections. And then – another sign that the King was conducting a very different campaign from war – Montespan was given a commission to serve in the Pyrenees, on the borders with Spain, a very long way from the court. All these points were duly noted by Saint-Cyr who had a bet on the likely date of the succession by the Marquise de Montespan to the post of mistress to the King.

CLAUDINE WATCHES the moods of Madame change from day to day. There is a heightened gaiety about her and, when she comes back from some event at which the King was present, she has a positively luminescent glow. She does not confide in her maid. Claudine only knows from the flashes of Mortemart temper when there has been a setback. Perhaps the King has shown some favour to Louise that indicates the fading mistress still has a hold on him. If things go as Madame hopes, however, Claudine will profit as well.

This is no great comfort. To see another woman on

the edge of a grand amour while being desolated in love herself is bitter indeed. At times Claudine has the sensation of carrying around with her a huge aching hollowness somewhere in the region of her stomach and her heart. Sometimes it is a sharp pain, as a particular image comes to mind, sometimes it's just a terrifying emptiness. There are a succession of images from the days at Saint-Cloud, leading to that one magical night of closeness, of her watching Andrea's face at rest after passion, of willing those invisible filaments between their bodies to link and intertwine so that they would always be part of each other. Of murmuring her prayer to the spirits and hearing in her mind their voices. Yes, this man belongs to you. And then, Andrea ripping away the threads that bound them, his anger murdering her hopes, reducing her to nothing more than − what was it − a clever little whore. And after that to have to keep her lost love secret, not to be able to tell a soul, for to do so would have been to betray Madame and bring her wrath down upon her head. Madame had not been in the least sympathetic, either. Silly and deluded were the words she had used. Madame, said Claudine to herself, once you are the King's mistress you will recompense me for the hurt you have caused.

SAINT-CYR noted the moves of the secret game of chess that was going on during the campaign. On 16 May: King, Queen, knights and pawns to Amiens, in a travelling display of royal power and riches, of gilded carriages, parade horses with plumes and gold-embroidered harness, and similarly plumed and gilded courtiers. Monsieur, of course, in his mirrored coach, and the King's cousin, La Grande Mademoiselle de Montpensier, with her retinue. On 25 May: King to knights, to inspect the troops, while Queen moves in straight line to Compiègne. King takes two pawns into his carriage – Madame de Montausier and Madame de Montespan. A break for the business of war before the chess game resumes – the first siege was to Armentières which surrendered almost immediately, as did Charleroi. Eckelsbeke and Furnes resisted for a few days, which brought glory for the French when they fell and comparatively little bloodshed. On 7 June: Queen rejoins King. Pawn, which should have been out of the game, arrives at almost the same moment – Louise de La Vallière in her coach and six, regardless of her pregnancy and orders to stay at home, desperate to block the other pawn before it takes the King. A nice spectacle for gossip – Louis's sharp discussion with her, ending with words that were overheard and passed on around the court – 'Madame, I do not like to have my hand forced.' Queen's next move is to force pawn off the board, with orders that she is not to be served dinner. Queen leaves in carriage with Madame de Montespan and other pawns. 'I should die of shame rather than behave like that,' declares Athénaïs. La Grande Mademoiselle smiles at these pious words, until she sees tears rolling down the cheeks of the Queen. Yes, there's a difference between this and a real game of chess. People are getting hurt.

So when did it happen, that first time? When did the pawn take the King, or the King take the pawn? There were only two people, apart from the lovers, who knew for sure. One was Madame de Montausier, with whom Athénaïs was lodged at Avesnes, in a room on the same floor and next but one to the King. The other was the Marquise's maid.

Claudine could tell you when it was. She always helped Madame to undress at nights and, to do so, had to walk past the guards outside the King's room. On that evening they weren't there and her relief at not having to run the gauntlet of their coarse remarks was mixed with puzzlement as to why the King's room had been left unprotected. Madame had chosen an embroidered white silk nightgown for the night, and wore over it a satin white and gold robe. Madame de Montausier was already undressed, sitting in a chair and wearing a woollen shawl over her shoulders. Her hair, which had overcome the effects of age through henna, was still knotted and curled. She was looking indulgently at *la belle* Athénaïs. The thought came into Claudine's mind: she is like a mother surveying her daughter on her wedding night.

'Would Madame la Duchesse like me to comb out her hair now that I have done Madame's?' asked Claudine, for the Montausier maid had gone sick.

Madame de Montausier said no, there was no need, she would do it herself later. As Claudine turned down the sheets on both sides of the bed, she was struck by the lack of conversation. At this time of night the two of them were usually avidly gossiping about the day's events. Madame de Montespan slid into bed and said, 'That will be all, Claudine.' Madame de Montausier remained seated in her chair. As

Claudine left the room, carrying a bundle of their linen for the laundry, she thought, there's something odd about these ladies tonight. They couldn't wait to be rid of me.

Claudine retired to the attic room she shared with three other maids. It was a warm, stuffy night, but one of the maids insisted on the window remaining closed. At one in the morning she woke up in a sweat, her nostrils filled with the smell of foul air. She wrapped her shawl round her and climbed down the narrow stairs to the first floor. There was a window overlooking the main stairs and beside the window an armchair, in which she had planned to spend the rest of the night, but she saw it was already occupied. Seated in it, asleep, was Madame de Montausier, a book she had been reading by the light of the now extinguished candle lying open on her lap. Claudine tiptoed past her and then paused outside the door of the room that the two ladies occupied. At first there was silence, then she heard the sound of murmuring, a man's voice, subdued but with that unmistakable deep resonance, then a woman's voice, lighter, replying, then the man's again, and so on, a conversation that was going on and on, through the early hours of the morning. Well, whatever is happening or not, the two of them are in there together and whatever they are doing excludes Madame de Montausier, thought Claudine. She heard a movement from the armchair and froze for a moment, but then there was a gentle snore. Claudine edged back past Madame de Montausier, whose head was now lolling back against the headrest, her mouth gaping open, and crept up the stairs again to the noxious attic room.

EVERYONE REMARKED how light-hearted and gay the King had become. It was the joy of the campaign, they said, he was a man who loved the life of the soldier. Nothing gave him more pleasure than being with the troops, of feeling a manly camaraderie. And they treated him not only as King and their supreme commander but as a brother in arms to be protected. He came back from the thick of the fighting one evening with mud all over his coat, having been pushed into a ditch by one of his soldiers, who had objected to the risks he was taking, exposed in the midst of the enemy, his scarlet plumes a signal to any musket man. At night there were, so he said, reports to be made and papers to be read. What was he doing, the Queen asked in the carriage one day, that kept him till four o'clock in the morning? Reading dispatches, he said, and turned his head away, so that no one but his cousin La Grande Mademoiselle saw him smile.

CLAUDINE NOTICED how the mood and appearance of her mistress changed from day to day. She spent most of one day asleep, exhausted, she said, from the travelling. Then she went to confession and afterwards seemed more carefree. A convenient confessor, thought Claudine, who believes in absolution rather than penance. One morning she asked Claudine to massage an extra quantity of cream of comfrey into her face, as her skin was roughened from the weather. Obviously the King could do with a shave, Claudine thought, as she smoothed the cream on to the Marquise's reddened cheeks. I wonder when the Queen will guess what's going on. In the event, the Queen learnt, not from the behaviour of the King or Madame de Montespan, but from an anonymous letter.

Madame de Montausier rose to the occasion splendidly. What a nonsensical accusation, she said. The Marquise has been at my side in bed every night, I'd be the first to know if she were other than innocent. Athénaïs, her eyes brimming with hurt feelings, asked how could the Queen think for one moment that she would betray Her Majesty? There were too many jealous little people at court who liked causing trouble. Claudine thought, let's see what happens when they return to Paris from this campaign, which has been more like a holiday than a war. The great test is whether a love survives on familiar ground.

Twenty-Nine

How fast is the path from triumph to defeat. Athénaïs was aware of the fragility of their secret love, in the way that the King went to such lengths to keep it from being generally known. To her mind, this was not what being the King's mistress was about. The King's mistress should be proclaimed to the sound of trumpets, should descend the great staircase with diamonds blazing. The reason given for the secrecy was to do with her unpredictable husband, who might commit some hideously embarrassing act, like challenging the King to a duel. But there was more to it than that, for Louis was at heart a religious man, his sins graded according to their seriousness. Adultery was one thing, especially as he didn't deprive the Queen of her marital rights. Double adultery was another, the sin extended to wronging another man. Morally, it was indefensible.

But there was something else again, which had to do with fear. Love with Louise had been comfortable and sweet, love with Athénaïs was making hitherto unknown demands. To possess was part of his life, to be possessed was to be in danger. She knew from his sharp reaction to one of her light-hearted remarks – God knows, she hadn't meant to be rude about the Queen but occasionally your tongue runs away with you – the familiar sensation of treading on thin ice. The next day he disappeared off to Fontainebleau with Louise, for some hunting. Everyone knew what that meant – the pair of them diving into the undergrowth whenever the fancy took them. Athénaïs couldn't compete with Louise the huntswoman, whose trick was to ride a horse bareback. She was excluded from the King's passion for the sport, for she was a creature of the salons, of conversation, music and dance.

She didn't watch them leave for Fontainebleau, but she could imagine Louise's expression, that sweet, smug look that tied Louis to her side. Now everyone was saying nice things about the Duchess, having for the last few months shrugged their shoulders at the mention of her name. Athénaïs had the sensation of her destiny slipping away. Her whole being was concentrated on the necessity of binding the King to her. It was at this point that she heard Claudine mention Madame Voisin. The name had been running through her own head and it was as if Claudine had picked up her thoughts as she stood behind her, watching her reflection while she arranged the curls on her forehead.

'Madame Voisin? The fortune-telling woman?' said Athénaïs, as if the name could not have been further from her mind.

'I'm told she makes very effective love powders,' said Claudine. 'Powders for every occasion. If you want someone to love you . . . if you want someone to stop loving you . . .'

'How can I feed powders to the King?' But into Athénaïs's mind came another image, that of the red-haired priest standing on the threshold of the door and the words of Madame Voisin, about a greater power than prayer. She had felt repulsed at the time, yet now she experienced again that undercurrent of excitement.

'Of course,' said Claudine into the mirror, 'there is another way.'

Athénaïs looked at the maid's reflected eyes, which had a curious glazed quality as she spoke, like the eyes of Madame Voisin. 'Another way?'

Claudine smiled. 'You remember Father Mariette, Madame? He said he would help you to your destiny.'

'How do you know? You weren't there at the time.'

'They say his ceremonies are very effective.'

Enough of this hesitation, Athénaïs thought. Either it would work or it wouldn't work. She said, 'I'm not sure if I could bear the journey to Madame Voisin's horrid little house in the suburbs.'

'There's no need, Madame. Father Mariette knows his way to Saint-Germain.'

IT WAS near midnight in the apartment of Athénaïs's sister, Gabrielle de Thianges. Father Mariette had said it would be the most effective time for his ceremony. He arrived with another man, small and emaciated, whom he introduced as Monsieur Lesage. Lesage was carrying a bag in which were Father Mariette's special aids for the mass – the dragon-embroidered robe, incense, a chalice, a flask of wine. He set the wine reverentially on the table that had been prepared as an altar. It came from the church of Saint-Séverin, where he served during the day.

Father Mariette looked at Athénaïs with eyes the colour of burned caramel. His face was as blanched as a plant grown in darkness, his hair a fiery red. She had half a mind to ask him if he used henna, but he was now telling her that this was a serious undertaking, solemn and dangerous. He looked at Athénaïs, at Gabrielle and at Claudine, one by one, as if gauging their commitment, then to Athénaïs, 'Marquise de Montespan, have you done your part?'

She had. Claudine stepped forward with a dish in which lay two small, bloody pigeons' hearts that she had managed to pluck from the offal in the kitchen. Father Mariette took them from her and placed them on the table, next to the wine and the chalice. Lesage helped him on with his dragon robe, over his habit, and began to swing the censer from side to side. The room filled with the heavy and cloying smell of incense. Father Mariette stood very still in front of the table, his eyes closed.

Presently he began to intone a prayer in a language that none of them recognised. But the mysterious words seemed imbued with a power that ran through the veins like a dark current. The levity that Athénaïs had felt a few minutes before, as Father Mariette had arranged his hair after putting on the dragon robe, gave way to rising tension. She could feel a change in the atmosphere of the room, as if some unseen presence were materialising in their midst.

Father Mariette opened his eyes. He looked at Athénaïs and said softly, 'She is with us now, the goddess Astaroth. She is listening. Tell her what you will. Come to the altar.'

Athénaïs knelt. She felt intoxicated from the incense that Lesage was now gently swaying towards her. 'I want the love of the King,' she said, looking towards the chalice on the table. 'That he should love only me and no other.'

Father Mariette whispered, 'That is not all that is in your mind; there is much more. Say all that is there, you are safe in the presence of Astaroth.'

Yes, there was much more. Louise de La Vallière should go away, the King should think no more of her, the Queen . . .

'Yes,' prompted the priest, 'the Queen . . .'

'The Queen should have no more children, I should marry the King, my children should inherit and I should reign with the King . . .'

She was shocked by the force with which she said the words, as if it came from somewhere else, this over-whelming hate, this all-consuming desire for power that could never be taken away. She felt the listening presence around her, saw Gabrielle cross herself, heard Claudine murmuring a spell or a prayer. She looked at Father Mariette again and saw infinite understanding in his eyes.

'My child, you said what you had to say. Astaroth was listening.'

Father Mariette stood in front of the altar and held up his hands as if in blessing. He poured the wine into the chalice and held it out to Athénaïs to drink. Then he picked up the dish with the pigeons' hearts and held it above his head. 'O Astaroth, hear our prayer, may the two hearts be as one. Beating with one accord, never to be separated. Hear and grant our prayer.'

Athénaïs heard a loud sob and saw Claudine overcome by emotion, her face in her hands and shoulders shaking. Father Mariette moved over to her and softly touched her head, that the goddess should heal her troubled heart. The clock struck one.

'Heavens, is that the time?' exclaimed Father Mariette, 'I really must be going.'

Lesage helped him off with his robes, and put away the chalice and wine. He wrapped the dish with the pigeons' hearts in a cloth, for Father Mariette had promised to bless them during a mass at Saint-Séverin.

The priest turned to Athénaïs and bowed. 'Madame la Marquise de Montespan, I trust that you are content.' He bowed again as he accepted the purse of money, gave another blessing to the three women and left, they knew not where, whether to someone he was lodging with at Saint-Germain, or back along the moonlit road to Paris.

Gabrielle, her face still pale, said, 'Well, Athénaïs, I trust you are content and that we shall all share in your good fortune.'

Athénaïs turned and hugged her sister to her. Her tension began to subside and she laughed. 'Well, we shall see whether he's an honest rascal or not. What is it they say, never trust a red-haired man?'

'An expensive adventure,' said Gabrielle. 'Not to be repeated too often, I imagine.'

'Never again,' said Athénaïs, but deep in her heart

she knew that her desires had been heard, that there *had* been a presence in the room, that she *would* triumph over her rivals and attain her rightful destiny, and that her life had changed for ever.

Thirty

THE MIRROR never lies, yet the mirror plays tricks on the mind. Andrea experimented with mirror boxes and angled mirrors in the time he had left after training the French apprentices. Monsieur du Noyer took no notice of his occasional absences into the small studio he had set up. Andrea had, after all, rescued the factory from an uncertain future, and it was also a relief to have got rid of his compatriots. Now that the Venetians had gone, du Noyer had to admit what a pain they had been, what a set of prima donnas, encouraged by the largesse emanating from the Minister of Finance. He had suggested to Monsieur Colbert the folly of allowing the men to overvalue themselves. They had become spoilt, their work had slackened. It only needed one of them to go sick and the whole lot would down tools, claiming danger of an epidemic. Then there was the problem of *les femmes galantes*, as Monsieur Colbert called them. Sneaking in past the guards and further impeding their work. At night the place had been like a bawdy house, squeals and laughter disturbing the neighbourhood.

The young French glass blowers whom Andrea was training had a different attitude altogether. They were not there simply to line their pockets, they believed themselves to be part of a new age of industry, which would enrich the entire nation. They worked with undivided attention, free from the residue of guilt that had afflicted the Venetians.

Andrea had heard nothing from his fellow mirror makers after their return. It was from du Noyer that he had learnt that his father and brother had been placed under house arrest, but when the guild of *specchiai* had protested to the Venetian authorities and threatened to make no more mirrors, they had been released, though not before his father had publicly denounced his son as a traitor to the Republic. At nights Andrea would wake up in an agony of regret. The idea that they would remain unreconciled until death was something he had not envisaged.

Winter gave way to spring and the King, he heard, was doing battle again in the Netherlands. He had already captured the Spanish-held territory in lieu of the Queen's unpaid dowry, but he wanted more. There was patriotic fervour in the voices of the French workers as they discussed the latest bulletins, and some dissension as to whether the King should have ceded the newly conquered Franche-Comté under the terms of the peace treaty. But there was no doubt, they agreed, that France had a great and glorious King and brilliant generals in *le grand* Condé and Turenne. They would show the Spanish, and the Dutch too, who was the master of Europe.

Andrea left the men to their triumphalism and retreated to his studio. In the time since he had fallen into the quicksands of love, he had tried to save himself by grasping on to the area of his life that he knew so well, that followed set patterns and yet was still capable of surprising him. The world reflected in a mirror. He had devised a long tube, with parallel mirrors set at each end, which he demonstrated at a meeting of the Scientific Academy. The gentlemen took it in turns to look through the end of the tube, and expressed varying degrees of sceptical interest.

One of the doubters said he couldn't see the use of such an instrument, unless it was to spy through a bedroom window to check if your wife had a lover. Andrea suggested the seeing tube could be most useful in war, you could survey the land from the battlements without the risk of getting your head blown off. The members smiled. One of them suggested patronisingly that Monsieur Allegré had some interesting ideas and he might profit by delivering a paper at the same time on his practical demonstration. Andrea took the point, without offence. He returned to his studio and began to write a new treatise, under the heading 'The Strange Case of the Burning Mirror – the Truth of Archimedes's Secret Weapon'.

VERSAILLES WAS en fête. Ostensibly, the Grand Divertissement Royal was to celebrate the Peace Treaty of Aix-la-Chapelle. In reality, those in the know were aware it was a homage to the King's new mistress. The evening vibrated with coded messages. The words of *The Triumph of Bacchus and Amour* were nothing to do with peace treaties – '*Chantons tous de l'amour le pouvoir adorable.*' Those in the know exchanged significant looks. They glanced towards the King and the Queen, and then at the Marquise de Montespan, who seemed, they said, to exude a luminescent glow. Truly, the King was bewitched.

Andrea watched the royal cortège as it arrived at the entrance of the theatre in the gardens. The dwarfish, heavily pregnant woman with fair hair and a mass of jewellery was, he realised, the Queen. Her mouth was downturned glumly. The King's plumed hat was visible in the midst of a cluster of courtiers, who were buzzing around him like so many bees around a honey pot. And there, on the left of the King, was the face engraved in his memory: Athénaïs, in a dress of gold tissu, diamonds scattered over it like raindrops sparkling in the sun. She was alight with love triumphant. For a second she glanced in Andrea's direction and her azure eyes looked straight into his, but he could not tell whether she recognised him. They were as unseeing as if she were truly blind with love.

'Magnificent, what a heartbreaker,' said a voice by his ear, that of Francesco Francini, the fountain maker.

Andrea bit his lip but continued to observe her. Yes, there was that familiar quick turn of the head he remembered, but heightened by the splendour of her new role. If ever there was a woman born to be the King's mistress . . .

'Do you want to see the play?' asked Francini.

'I don't see how we can. They're even turning away

the ambassadors,' said Andrea. By the archway to the open-air theatre, one of the Swedish entourage was being manhandled by a guard, who had been transported back to the field of battle. The Swedish Ambassador protested in French, swore in Swedish, then turned on his heel and left with his entourage. The guard's expression was of self-righteous belligerence at having repulsed a foreign enemy.

'It's easy if you don't mind the view,' said Francini. 'We can find a way through the wings.'

Past the wall of foliage hung with tapestries that separated the auditorium of the theatre from the garden there was an open space on a slope next to the wings. Here they could see the front of the stage and the first few rows of the audience. Two of the actors, wearing enormous wigs and face paint, were already there, watching the audience jostling for their seats.

'This is as good a place as any, isn't it?' said Francesco.

'Provided you don't get in our way,' said the one with the ebony staff.

'We'll be as quiet as mice, Monsieur Molière. My friend here is newly arrived from Italy.'

'Then he'll enjoy the harlequinade.'

Which was true. The long, convoluted speeches of the play were interspersed with ballet and songs, which to Andrea's mind were the only entertaining moments. Looking at the front row of the audience, he could see they thought so, too. The King was wearing an attentive, but slightly bored expression while George Dandin declaimed; Monsieur, two seats along, was fidgeting and glancing around at the rest of the audience; the Queen was glummer than ever, which emphasised her Hapsburg jowls. Only Athénaïs de Montespan, sitting with other court ladies to the right of the royal party, looked amused – as if a thousand delightful thoughts were passing through her mind. She turned to smile at the King, who for a long moment gazed into her eyes with such loving absorption that they seemed to be in a world of their own. Andrea remembered looking at her in the same way that summer's night in the garden of Saint-Cloud. What an idiot he had been, how ridiculous.

'You'll enjoy the next bit more,' said Francini, who had interpreted Andrea's impatient movement as boredom. 'It's the contest between Bacchus and Amour.'

'*Chantons tous de l'amour le pouvoir adorable . . .*' the Harlequins sang to the nymphs. The followers of Bacchus, draped in vines, leapt on to the stage to extol the '*attraits glorieux*' of their god who had subdued all the world to his power.

'No, love is the greatest pleasure. Anyone who lives without love leads a dreary life,' sang the supporters of Amour.

'Life without drinking is more like death,' responded the supporters of Bacchus.

The Harlequins somersaulted before the nymphs, the Bacchi turned cartwheels, the singers tried to drown the voices of the opposing team. Then a shepherd stepped forward to reconcile the quarrel because, after all, he said, Bacchus and Amour went well together – let us not separate them. This sentiment delighted the audience. Glasses were raised in a toast to the two gods. The King turned towards Athénaïs, laughing. The Queen stared straight in front of her.

Francini said, 'She must be regretting the days of Mademoiselle de La Vallière, though they say it's still not over with Louise. How would you like to be King and have three women to choose from? One's less trouble, that's what I tell Signora Francini when she starts getting jealous.'

The night darkened outside the circle of chandeliers in the theatre. The air had cooled and there was dew on the grass. Andrea, leaning back, his hands splayed out on the ground behind him, was aware of the damp hem of a skirt brushing his fingers as a woman walked by. She paused, as if looking for the best place to view the play, then sat down on the grass to the left of them. He could only see her silhouette in the darkness. Her dress spread voluminously over her hips, tightly in at her waist, and as she shrugged off the fichu round her shoulders he could see the fullness of her breasts.

Philène was singing, 'It is your supreme grace that holds my eyes captive.'

Yes, there was a grace about the way the woman held her head that reminded him of the Marquise. The fichu was now lying on the ground and she had turned slightly, as if to watch the audience but at the same time making a better display of her figure. He was aware of her awareness of him and waited to see what she would do next.

'If you decide to make the first move,' sang Climène, 'it's just possible I might follow.'

Andrea smiled – she was about to make the first

move. The cloud that had been obscuring the moon drifted past and now he could see her clearly as she turned her head towards him, and he realised why, under his sense of intrigue, there had been a frisson of uneasiness. Of course, he had recognised her first in his unconscious mind. She was looking at him with those unnerving eyes, like a cat. She had changed from that time in Saint-Cloud. There was an assurance about her, a sense of display. Claudine had done very well through the Marquise's change of fortune. They stared at each other for a moment without time. Neither of them spoke as the memory of their last meeting in the dark rose between them. Then Andrea got to his feet and walked away. He heard Climène singing out, 'Expect a sweet end to the pains that torment you' and Tircis retort, 'I expect no cure.'

No cure – the rational man, the researcher into matters scientific, the dissector of mysteries, had deluded himself in imagining he could shun Amour. She caught you when you least expected it.

Thirty-One

SHE CAUGHT you when you least expected it. Claudine knew that the night at Saint-Cloud must be turned to her advantage rather than remain a barrier of anger between them. She was aware of the change in Madame since she had nailed the man of her dreams. There was no doubt that nature had designed certain men for certain women and if you didn't grab the opportunity, if you let the man slip away and turn to someone else, you would spend a lifetime regretting it.

Claudine had noted the radiant complacency of Athénaïs after the King had succumbed to her charms. The doubts about his love were no more. Louise de La Vallière remained in her apartment. The courtiers would see the King visit there twice a day. But her rooms opened into the apartment where Athénaïs was now lodged. The King would be charming and conciliatory to his former mistress, then move on. Louise was left with his hunting coat, or a stray dog that had followed him. 'Poor Louise,' Claudine had said, after she had watched her help Athénaïs to dress one evening. 'To be reduced to being your maid.'

'Poor Louise nothing,' the Marquise had retorted. 'I am charming to her, the King is charming to her, she lacks for nothing, she is a duchess. And what is wrong with being my maid anyway? Have you any complaints?'

'Of course not, Madame,' replied Claudine. And then, 'It's strange how everything has changed since we saw Father Mariette.'

'Father Mariette nothing,' snapped Athénaïs, but Claudine could see an uneasiness in her eyes. There you are, Madame, she thought, just a reminder I know things about you that you would rather others didn't know. It's as well we establish that.

The next day she had called the dressmaker while the Marquise was out, and carefully went through the swatches of fabric and drawings, choosing a number of pretty and low-cut dresses to show off her figure. When the dressmaker had gone, she cut down the neck of her grey dress. We'll start now, she said to herself. There's no point in living at court and dressing like a nun.

And now, she thought, after the night of the Divertissement, there's no point in dressing like a court beauty and not having the man you want. She was tired of fending off pages and footmen, even the occasional courtier, who were drawn to her décolletage. But how to attract someone who had turned on his heel the moment he recognised her? It was time to try the other way.

AT SAINT-SÉVERIN the day followed an ordered course. After early mass Father Mariette retired to read the Scriptures and to contemplate the nature of eternity. At around ten, he was present again in the church and his red-haired, black-clad figure could be seen gliding through the ambulatory under the fluted Gothic columns. Shafts of light through the jewel-dark stained-glass windows reflected fleeting patches of crimson and lapis lazuli on his pale skin. At eleven, Father Mariette went to the confessional and sat behind the curtained window to await the procession of penitents. This part of the day now held few surprises for him, so accustomed was he to hearing of man's perversity. More usually, he had to endure tedious moans over petty jealousies, embarrassed mumblings about lusting after someone's wife or envying a neighbour's good fortune, though some- times the dullness was enlivened by a repentant murderer or rapist, for whom he could devise long and onerous penances.

It was particularly trying, on this sultry day in mid- August, to be closeted in the stuffy darkness of the confessional, as a succession of penitents brought their mouths close to the grill, exhaling with their sins the smell of garlic, bad teeth, poverty and dirt. So much misery in this city, he thought, as a thief confessed to stealing bread for his children. The poor and the rich living cheek by jowl, giving envy so much to feed on. Father Mariette mused on the transforming quality of money while he gave out penances and absolution in equal measure.

'*Mea culpa*, Father, I have sinned . . .' He heard a woman's voice at the grill and guessed before she said another word that he was about to be treated to a story of fornication. She continued, 'Father, I love a man who doesn't love me but has only had eyes for another woman, and I shall die if he refuses to return my love . . .'

Envy and Lust, to name but two of the deadly sins, thought Father Mariette. And Anger as well. Pride in assuming that the man should return her love and Gluttony for what she can't have. That leaves just Avarice and Sloth. It was enough to be going on with.

'Father Mariette, I want you to help me.' He sat up from his semi-recumbent position. This was most irregular. The confession should be treated anonymously to protect both sides, but as he was about to remonstrate, she continued, 'You helped the Marquise de Montespan attain her desire. I was there that night. I want you to help me with your special mass.'

He put his head close to the grill, seeing beyond it the face of the young woman. 'What are you talking about?' he muttered. 'Who are you? What are you doing here?'

He could see her smile at him through the grill. 'I am Madame de Montespan's maid and I want you to perform the same mass for me.'

'This is no place to talk about such matters. In any case, you wouldn't be able to afford it.'

'Perhaps there's someone else who would perform the mass for me. Perhaps I should ask the Bishop?'

He felt a chill to the back of his neck. This young woman was dangerous and even though his word would be believed rather than hers, he couldn't allow any doubts to be thrown over his conduct. He said, 'If you insist on this mass, then meet me tonight at the charnel house.'

With any luck, he thought, she will be too scared to come. But when he arrived at the hour, just to check, she was there already, waiting for him.

Thirty-Two

COLBERT'S WORST fears have been realised. The maison de plaisance, sited in flat, undistinguished land, is to become the jewel in Louis's crown. They are to drain the swamps and the royal coffers to build the dream. Colbert has pleaded with the King instead to complete the work on the Louvre. Such a palace, dominating the capital, is the only place for the King of France, he argues. A monarch should be seen by his people. If he desires fresh air and hunting, he can always go to Fontainebleau, Chambord, Vincennes, Saint-Germain. They need only general maintenance. But to create this new chateau around the old hunting lodge requires the sort of money that makes Colbert blanch. It is agonising, after having set up so much new industry in France, to see its profits swallowed up. And, as the King has appointed him Surintendant des Bâtiments, he has not only to agree to the expense, but also to make a full report of building progress on this unnecessary chateau. While the King was campaigning in the Netherlands, Colbert had written to ask if, in the midst of his other concerns, he would prefer to receive shorter reports on the work at Versailles. The answer came back, scribbled in the margin of his letter: 'Long – the detail of everything.'

Colbert's discontent is shared by the courtiers. Life is comfortable in the court and town of Saint-Germain. A summons to Versailles means camping out in makeshift rooms, long queues for the few *chaises percées* available, tripping over workmen and all their paraphernalia, being woken up in the morning by the sound of hammering, breathing in builder's dust. It's no comfort that the King has to suffer this as well and there is huge relief when he desists from staying there during the height of the construction. He inspects the works twice a week with Monsieur Le Vau and the gardens with Monsieur Le Nôtre. In his campaign to create the most beautiful palace in Europe, they are his generals.

Le Vau and Le Nôtre understand the King's search for perfection. It allows them full rein to display their genius. Athénaïs de Montespan understands the dream. Louis is not just creating a fairy tale, but a myth. It is to be a temple to the Sun God. She has seen the plans for the gardens, for the fountain of Latona, mother to the god, and the fountain of Apollo. Athénaïs will take her place, blazing alongside him, unlike Louise who is rooted like Daphne transformed into a tree, dripping misery from her leaves.

Athénaïs triumphant is also vulnerable. She is so in love with Louis that just to see him makes her weak with desire. It's his custom to visit her in her apartment in the afternoon, throwing his plumed hat on the table, his hair long and extravagantly curled – he only wears a wig for state occasions. They laugh and talk for a while, often to the detriment of various courtiers who have been petitioning him. Then there's a pause. They look at each other and, smiling, he says, '*Venez à moi, Madame.*' They move over to the bed and into each other's arms, sometimes prolonging the moment by undressing each other, sometimes in their haste making love fully clothed. She cries out as if she's dying of love and sees his eyes brimming with tears. They lie together, as if nothing will ever part them, but soon he resumes his role as King. There is a meeting of ministers to attend and by the time he leaves the apartment, his hair combed, his clothing rearranged, the man who not very many minutes ago was over-whelmed by his passion has assumed another persona.

What also gives Athénaïs joy is helping his dream become reality. When she first visited the building site that Versailles had become, she experienced a frisson of power. A thousand workmen were swarming over the place, shifting blocks of stone, pushing carts of timber, hammering, sawing, shouting, in the process of creating the chateau of Louis's dreams, and now hers as well. She does not impinge on Le Vau's work, but there are follies and frivolities that her imagination can play with. And a delightful little Italian who is master of the fountains, and who listens to her ideas with bright, receptive eyes.

'Monsieur Françine, I have in my mind the vision of a tree, with bronze branches and silver leaves which will emit little jets of water, like an endless stream of tears.'

'That sounds very pretty, Madame la Marquise,' said Francini. 'Silver, though, will tarnish. Tin would be more suitable and would glitter like silver in the sun.'

So her first creation at Versailles is to take place and meanwhile she is aware of another creation within. Her body has responded to the fullness of the King's love and she is with child. A son for Louis, and one day her wish would be fulfilled and her children would rule France. Already, and it is hardly two weeks since she was sure of the pregnancy, she feels the little one there inside her. He will have eyes like the King, a mouth like the King. She is creating another King.

'YOUR MADAME de Montespan is quite something,' said Francini to Andrea, who had arrived to discuss mirrors with Charles Le Brun, the King's decorator.

'What do you mean, my Madame de Montespan?'

'Just a figure of speech. The King's Madame de Montespan. She has style.'

Andrea felt a surge of relief. Of course no one knew or would ever know. And anyway, what was there to know? Perhaps it had been fortunate that he had not achieved his desire. How difficult it would have been not to confide in someone. How tempting to have boasted of his success. But no one knew what had happened, apart from Athénaïs herself and her maid. Neither of them would reveal the secret. He was safe.

'She certainly displayed style at the Divertissement.' Andrea sat next to Francini on the *bassin* of Latona, looking towards the canal, the meadows and the distant trees. The afternoon sun cast a gauze of shimmering gold over the land.

Francini appeared worried. 'The Swan is to become the *bassin* of Apollo, and even now they're working on the statue of the Sun God, his chariot and four horses. Think of the number of jets it will need. And here, there'll be Latona and a host of peasants being turned into frogs, each spewing forth water. Then there are about thirty or forty other fountains, I have lost count. There are to be cascades of water in the garden ballroom, the mirror pond will extend over two acres and from Apollo's fountain, as far as you can see, we will lengthen the grand canal. Where is all this water going to come from? We have horse pumps working day and night to bring it here from the *étang* at Clagny. It's not enough, I keep telling them. What will it be like once all my fountains are in full spate?'

He stared gloomily over the landscape. 'Not your problem, of course, just mine and Monsieur Le Notre's. You only have to make sure your furnaces keep burning and the glass keeps turning.'

That was the sum of it, agreed Andrea, not feeling concerned enough to compete over who was dealing with the most capricious element – fire or water. Anyone who worked with furnaces knew their unpredictability. You stoked them up to searing white heat, then you would add more fuel and suddenly the furnace would sputter from undetected damp in the wood. They called it sulking and for a while the furnace would be useless for glass blowing.

Back at the factory, he found Monsieur du Noyer in the courtyard, talking to a man in black, wearing a black high hat, the uniform of a doctor, though it was not the brusque fellow who had attended Luca. One of the workers, Guillaume, had been taken ill, du Noyer said, and they were puzzled by his symptoms. They indicated poisoning, yet the young man had eaten the same food as the others and appeared to have no enemies. He had been stricken with vomiting and diarrhoea, and for some time before that he had complained of giddiness, blurred vision and a tremor in his hands, which had affected his work. He had become confused in his speech.

Andrea remembered a curious, rather disjointed conversation he had had with the young man only a few weeks ago. It had reminded him of a few of the older workers at Murano, who were pensioned off and would be seen around the piazza, in a state of dazed confusion. It was said they had fried their brains at the furnace, or, more fancifully, that they had seen the devil in the glass. But these symptoms were unusual in a young worker, though Guillaume was a narrow-chested type who had not enough lung-power for glass blowing. Because of this, he had been deputed to work on the amalgam of mercury on to tin, at which he had been proficient enough, until the last few weeks. When Andrea had reprimanded him for slap-dash work, he had become angry and offered a string of jumbled excuses – something, Andrea remembered, about the moon and mercury. What was it? The moon and mercury were the same thing, Guillaume had said. They were round and silver, and they drove men mad.

Andrea had called him an idiot, a spouter of drivel. Now the words came back into his mind. Guillaume had spent his working day smoothing mercury over the tin surface, his hands glistening with myriad pinheads of silver. Sometimes he had played idly with the mercury in the bowl, pressing the round shining surface till it broke into smaller globes, and then watching them rejoin.

'Doctor,' said Andrea, 'if Guillaume had swallowed some mercury by mistake, could it have poisoned him?'

The doctor shook his head. If he had eaten large quantities, then of course it would have done him no good, but that would have meant he was mad anyway. No, in small doses, mercury was medicinal. Look at the mercury treatment they gave syphilitics. Would they do that if they thought it would kill them?

Du Noyer's face was impassive. Andrea thought, he's wondering, too, but he's not going to say anything. Du Noyer shook the doctor's hand and said, 'Do what you can for Guillaume. The health of our workers is important to us.'

He walked away, ignoring Andrea's call, 'Monsieur du Noyer, please . . .'

Andrea retired to his small studio in the back courtyard. He stared at the charts and measurements on the wall, which indicated refractions of light on a mirrored surface. Here was a plan he had devised for Monsieur Colbert, in which by the aid of angled mirrors he would be able to see his petitioners from the moment they entered the building and be able to follow their progress up the stairs. Monsieur Colbert had rejected the idea as a waste of time. He knew already, he said, that they all hated him. And that they only pasted on an ingratiating expression as they reached the top of the stairs.

Lying on the table were squares of mirror, shining silver, like the mercury. He picked one up and looked into it. Clear and truthful, clean glass, cool mercury, forged in purifying flames. Was this perfect mirror really the source of some kind of poison? Were they paying with their lives for man's vanity? Best not even to consider it, yet the thought came into his head: that doctor talked of how syphilitics are treated with mercury, yet how many of them are cured, how many go mad and die?

Thirty-Three

THE ROAD to Versailles is blocked with trees. On long carts drawn by teams of horses lie chained a succession of great poplars. The leaves trail in the dust of the road and the roots are encased in sacking. At Vaux-le-Vicomte there are dark pits of freshly dug earth, like so many raw wounds, from where the trees have been wrenched. If news of the desecration of his chateau's gardens were to reach Fouquet in his cell, it would make little difference to him, locked up as he is with no view and little daylight, but the gardeners at Vaux-le-Vicomte were in tears as they watched the uprooting.

Versailles needs trees. Grand, fully grown trees. The King is not going to wait twenty years for saplings to grow. He wants them now. He is in the full summer of his youth and nature must bend to his will. He is building his dream in a land with no trees, so they must come from elsewhere. The procession moves with infinite slowness, the cartwheels creaking with the load. It raises a cloud of dust as debris and insects are dislodged from the branches, and brings to a halt any other traffic on the road, apart from those on horse-back who can make a detour over the fields.

THE MARQUIS de Montespan had made several detours, first to Fontainebleau, where someone had told him the King was staying with the Marquise. Then, when he realised he had been misinformed, to Versailles, where he came across the line of moving trees. He learnt from the overseer that the King was not at Versailles. It was nothing but a building site at present. He suggested Monseigneur would find him at Saint-Germain. Montespan spurred his horse on, the letter he was itching to deliver burning a hole in his pocket.

David and Bathsheba – the aptness of the biblical story struck him with full force. There he was, serving his King in a far-flung outpost, endangering his life, sent there deliberately so that the King could satisfy his lust with his wife. He couldn't wait to see Louis's face when he read the letter. It would be worth several years in the Bastille. Montespan rode on, his face reddened with anger, with righteous anger, he told himself. Never has a husband been so wronged.

In the courtyard of Saint-Germain the sentries had to leap out of the way as the horseman came hurtling through the archway. Montespan pulled up the horse by the great door, unhitched his wig from a hook on the saddle, slapped it on to his head and threw the reins to the sentry who was about to ask him his business. His eyes blazed with such insane fury that when he shouted, 'Marquis de Montespan – my wife's my business,' no one felt like questioning him further.

The progress of the Marquis through the state apartments was sensational entertainment for anyone who was not the object of his wrath. Roaring for the new David to show himself, Montespan glared to left and right at the fascinated courtiers. 'He has dressed himself like Alceste the misanthrope, even his nails are black with grime,' said Saint-Cyr, before hurrying away to warn the Marquise.

Upstairs in Madame de Montausier's apartment they heard him before they saw him. There was a shout of 'Where's the King's procuress?' and the Marquis burst into the room, gesticulating at the Duchesse. There she is, the brothel keeper, the old trollop, and thrusting his face close to hers, he poured out a torrent of abuse.

On the terrace, Athénaïs was already being warned by La Grande Mademoiselle of her husband's intemperate behaviour. She made a joke of it, but the colour had drained from her face despite the light tone of her voice and she felt tension coil in her stomach. Supported by one of her ladies, Madame de Montausier came across the lawn towards them. Her eyes stared in disbelief from a blanched face and she could hardly speak for shortness of breath. 'Athénaïs,' she gasped, 'I've been abused and insulted by your appalling husband. If there had been a man in the room to hear what he said to me, he would have thrown the Marquis out of the window.'

She subsided on to a nearby bench in a storm of tears. 'This is too much,' exclaimed La Grande

Mademoiselle. 'Where is the King?' Gathering up her skirts, she ran off towards the chateau.

Athénaïs put her arm round Madame de Montausier, who was shivering as if with cold. 'I saw murder in his eyes,' the latter said. 'If you had been in the room with me, he would have killed you.'

'No, he would just have shouted all the louder,' said Athénaïs. 'He's a loud-mouthed hooligan, nothing more.'

'He's insane with jealousy, which makes him capable of murder. You must be careful, Athénaïs, he would stab you without thinking twice. I can't forget his face, like a demon in a nightmare.'

'Calm yourself, forget about him. Here comes the Chevalier, looking as if he is bursting with news.'

Saint-Cyr bowed to the ladies. 'The Marquis has given the performance of his life,' he said. 'Molière wants him to join his troupe.'

'How can you laugh?' exclaimed Madame de Montausier. 'The man is insane and violent.'

'But like a summer whirlwind, he has blown away, so you can breathe again. The King sent for the guards but he had already stormed off, towards Paris, I gather.'

'So,' said Athénaïs, 'all the world will know now. He did this just to shame me.'

'My dear Marquise, most of the world who matters knows anyway. It's time to be *maîtresse déclarée* and to have a separation from your ridiculous husband. In your condition – I know that you suppose it to be a secret but there are some horribly observant people here – in your condition any other course would be to your disadvantage. It is wonderful living in an enchanted land of festivals and fireworks, but there are hard facts, like rocks in the sea of fantasy, which could wreck your dream, and a jealous husband who could claim your child as his is one such rock.'

'Chevalier, eloquent as always.'

'You know I'm right, Marquise.'

FOR THE sake of the dream, it was necessary to negotiate the hazardous rocks of reality. Athénaïs remembered the evening of the Grande Divertissement, that extra-ordinary moment when, in the early hours of the morning, after the theatre, the feasting and the dancing, she and the King had drifted from the darkened alleys of the gardens towards the chateau. The air was filled with the chatter of the guests and the croaking of frogs from the Grand Canal. They emerged from the *bosquets* to see the chateau and the statues glowing with an unearthly phosphorescent light. As they stared, enraptured, fireworks exploded in a blaze of gold, lighting up the entire land. The water in the fountains seemed to catch fire and then, as the flames died down, a thousand rockets roared into the sky, with explosions like cannon fire, breaking into great sunbursts of light, to trace across the sky the letters of the Royal Cipher. Frogs and courtiers were silenced by the magnificent pyrotechnics of it all. Athénaïs's eyes filled with tears, partly from the sheer splendour, partly from the acrid smell of gunpowder and smoke.

The King turned towards her and said softly, 'For you, Madame. This is our enchanted island.'

From the east, daylight began to suffuse the sky, dispersing the artificial sun of the night.

Thirty-Four

THAT WASN'T the last of the Marquis, who aspired to an even greater scandal. His plan was to attack the King's person through his wife. Montespan haunted the brothels of Paris for several weeks until he noticed a nicely suppurating sore on his member, then descended on Saint-Germain, to arrive at Madame de Montausier's apartment where Athénaïs was taking a morning cup of chocolate.

No one had taken any notice of the Marquis this time, for he had walked silently and swiftly through the chateau. Andrea had passed him on the stairs, after he'd finished measuring for mirrors in the Queen's apartment, and remembered their previous meeting. There was no mistaking the choleric face, the glaring eyes, the dishevelled wig. Montespan stared right through him, as he strode up the stairs. Andrea continued to descend, but stopped when he met Francesco Francini, who launched into a tirade about being torn away from his fifty fountains in Versailles to do some little job that any *plombier* could have done.

The drains of Neptune's grotto in the King's apartment were blocked.

Francini departed for the grotto and Andrea had nearly reached the foot of the stairs when he heard a woman scream. Two courtiers who had begun to ascend the stairs, ribbons and frills swaying around stockinged legs, continued their leisurely progress, without taking the slightest notice, beyond a raised eyebrow and a shrug. The sound of a woman in distress seemed to cause them no alarm. The woman screamed again, louder this time. Andrea ran up the stairs, two at a time, to the first-floor landing.

The doors to the apartment on the left of the stairs were flung open and a woman dashed out, shouting, 'Guards! Help us!' He ran into the salon, straight into a scene so grotesque that his eyes almost denied what he was seeing. Montespan, his breeches unbuttoned, wig cast on the ground, was tearing at the layers of petticoats and skirts of the Marquise, whom he had trapped half-seated, half-lying in a chair. Claudine was clinging to his back like a monkey, pulling at his hair and beating him around the head. An older woman, hands clasped to her bosom, was screeching like a peacock. Montespan shook off Claudine and hit her in the face. She fell to the ground, clutching her eye, and Montespan turned back to the Marquise, pulling her skirts up to her thighs, exposing the garters on her stockings. Andrea reached the tangled bodies and yanked Montespan back by his collar, as if restraining a fighting dog. 'Take your hands off me!' Montespan shouted and swung out at Andrea. The punch caught him on the mouth and as Andrea reeled from the blow, still clinging on to Montespan's collar, two of the King's guards, alerted by the commotion, arrived, saw the struggling men and leapt on them both, pulling them apart from each other.

'This hooligan attacked me!' roared Montespan.

The Marquise, pale and shaking, raised herself unsteadily from the chair and smoothed down her disarrayed skirts. She said, 'My husband is mad and tried to rape me.' Madame de Montausier subsided sobbing into a chair, while the guards forced the struggling Marquis to the ground, pinioning his arms.

'Get your hands off me, you vermin!' shouted Montespan. 'I've done nothing wrong. I'm entitled to my conjugal rights, even if my wife's a jade.'

'Shut up!' said one of the guards and the other, more formally, as befitted the status of the arrested man, 'If Monseigneur le Marquis will please come quietly with us.'

Montespan, eyes still blazing, clambered to his feet and they marched him off to the guardroom. A silence descended on the salon, as all three women looked at Andrea. The sleeve of his shirt had been torn by Montespan and blood was trickling from a cut to his lip. Then the Marquise led the tributes to the timeliness of his appearance and his bravery. The azure eyes welled up with tears and her voice trembled as she spoke. 'Signor Andrea, I can never thank you enough for saving me. If you had not been there ... God knows what would have happened. You have my profound gratitude, from the depths of my heart.'

'Andrea is a hero,' Claudine said, her cheeks reddening. 'Come, you must let me clean the blood from your face.'

'It's nothing,' said Andrea, wiping his face with the back of his hand.

'No, that's not good enough,' said Claudine and, taking a handkerchief from her bodice, dabbed it at the cut. He shifted his gaze to one side to avoid meeting her eyes and found himself gazing directly at the Marquise, who despite, or because of, her ordeal had a lively sparkle in her eyes. What is it with these infuriating women, he thought, they're a pair of witches.

Madame de Montausier's apartment was now filling with courtiers who wanted to know what the commotion was about. 'You can see for yourselves,' said the Marquise. 'This brave gentleman has been hurt. So has my maid and the poor Duchesse is deeply shocked.'

At this point Madame de Montausier, who was being attended by her ladies, fainted. Andrea, taking advantage of the diversion, began to move away.

'Stay a while longer,' said the Marquise.

'Now you are safe, Madame la Marquise, there's nothing to detain me.' He bowed and turned towards the door, where the two flamboyantly attired courtiers who had earlier ignored the screams were watching the scene with interest. 'You would have seen more if you'd arrived earlier,' he said as he walked by and heard one of them mutter, 'Impertinence!' He reached the stairs he had earlier been walking down, his mind a turmoil of sensations. That he should have been here, just at this point, when the drama erupted

. . . Whether it was chance or fate that was weaving a web around him, he had the uneasy feeling of a force outside his experience, drawing him into unknown territory.

MONTESPAN WAS swiftly dispatched to the prison of For-L'Eveque, charged with a crime that did not implicate the King's relationship with the Marquise, though what had happened was common knowledge at court.

The drama suited Athénaïs. Once she had recovered from the assault she transformed the experience into the tale of the priapic ogre for the scandalised entertainment of her sister and Saint-Cyr. Claudine, too, bore the light of combat in her eyes for days afterwards. She had beaten the Marquis around the head and kicked his arse, which she had been longing to do for years, and even had battle scars in the scratchmarks from his dirty fingernails as well as a purple bruise round one eye to prove it. Madame de Montausier, however, suffered a nervous crisis. Years as a Précieuse, playing exquisite word games and delighting in romantic poetry, had been obliterated by this hideous scene. Once she had been the inspiration of poets. 'Guirlande à Julie' had been written in her praise. Now she couldn't excise from her mind the insults he had rained on her – procuress, trollop, lubricious old cow. He had torn away the delicate veil she had wrapped around her life and left her with an overwhelming sense of ugliness. When she looked in the mirror, it was as if he were holding it up to her. For years she had seen only the bright eyes and smile of her youth. Now the glass showed her a mouth like a prune, an age-freckled skin, a lizard's neck. 'Old trollop,' she murmured. 'Dreadful old bat.'

Thirty-Five

SPRINGTIME, AND the gardeners at Versailles are planting out pot after pot from the hothouse. The weather is still cold, but the King has decided that it should be spring and the air must be filled with the scent of flowers. Colbert writes to the Intendant de Galères in Marseilles, desperate for jonquils. A wagonload of three thousand plus two thousand hyacinths arrives from the south. They are planted out in the gardens of the new pavilion Le Vau is building in the furthest area from the chateau. The pavilion is in the Chinese style, faced with blue and white porcelain tiles – the Trianon de Porcelaine, a place of seclusion for the King and his new love. There they will breathe in the heavy scent of the flowers, mingled with the Marquise's tuberose perfume.

Athénaïs has been delivered of a son, who has been despatched to foster-parents. The Queen would never tolerate his presence under her roof. She has had her own misfortunes in childbirth. There was the one heir to the throne, the Dauphin, followed by a miscarriage and a stillbirth. Since La Montespan has filched the love of her husband, her body has suffered ill luck.

Colbert has received another letter from the King, with an order for seven hundred mirrors. If it had come from one of his subjects, or a foreign prince, it would have been a coup for the mirror factory. But mirrors for the King are paid for by money that should go elsewhere, on strengthening the Navy, for instance. Colbert could almost curse himself for his skill at raising money. It has given Louis the impression that he has access to a never-ending fountain of gold.

The order comes through to the factory. Andrea is despatched once more to Versailles to discuss it with the King's decorator who has clearly miscalculated the measurements. He is, in any case, intrigued to see the progress at the chateau and to take a tour of Francini's fountains. It's spring and a restlessness fills the air after the long, dark winter.

OF NECESSITY, Andrea had learnt to ride. From Monsieur du Noyer's stable at the factory he borrowed the grey, Mouette. The first part of the journey through the older streets was always the most hazardous, as his head was almost on a level with the first-floor windows, from which someone too lazy to carry a basin downstairs might sling the contents into his face. He did as others did when seeing a window open, shouting '*Faites attention!*' before the intentions of the householder became clear. Seconds afterwards it could be too late.

Past the Tuileries, he reached almost open country-side, with a few grand houses and gardens, and an avenue that was being built to one side of the formal gardens. The road led onwards, one section branching towards the chateau of Saint-Cloud, rising in splendour on a hill overlooking the Seine, the other towards Saint-Germain-en-Laye. He crossed the bridge at Saint-Cloud and took the road to Versailles. It was a road less travelled than the one to Saint-Germain and at this early hour it was deserted. The air was fresh and the dew on the meadows sparkled with points of light in the sun. The birds were singing as if they would burst their hearts and he felt a surge of joy to match theirs. He began to sing one of the songs he had known from the time that seemed so long ago, in Venice, 'Dolcissimo usignolo'. It occurred to him that the song now seemed foreign. He had become so absorbed in the French way of life that he had begun to think in French. Even when startled, he would reach for a French word – *Ça suffit!* rather than *Basta!* But the small cloud of regret at the loss of his past was dispersed in his general feeling of well-being at the present. He had the privilege of being involved in the building of what would be the greatest palace in the whole of Europe; indeed, in the whole world. He was confident of his position, as one favoured by the Minister. Du Noyer had even broached the subject of marriage with one of his nieces for whom, he suggested, Monsieur Colbert would supply a generous dowry. Andrea could not help smiling to himself at the time, for the implication was that du Noyer's brother would thus save himself a great deal of money. Mouette flicked pointed grey ears forward and back, as the metal of her bridle jingled and her hooves thudded on the earth. After the upheavals of the past couple of years, life was working out for the best. The still, small feeling of discontent, which came from he knew not where, had been obliterated.

At Versailles, he found the King's decorator Charles Le Brun perched high up on the scaffolding, a paint-stained cotton smock over his clothes, applying his brush to one of the King's legs. An assistant was standing lower down on the scaffolding working on the background to the epic painting. Le Brun was frowning with concentration as he outlined the curve of the calf. He glanced down at Andrea and called out, 'What brings you here, Monsieur de la Glace?'

'More measurements for ever more mirrors,' he called back.

'Just wanting a day out from Paris, no doubt,' said Le Brun. 'And to see the latest work I'm doing. Come up here and get a better view.'

Andrea climbed up the ladder to the platform where Le Brun was working and looked at the image of the King. He could see the allusions to Apollo in the wreath of laurel, the golden aura, the musical symbol of a lyre at his feet. He noticed that the lesser figures of gods and goddesses were substantially smaller than Louis. 'It is a great work, undoubtedly,' he said, 'but is it not strange how much taller the King seems in his paintings?'

'Of course he's tall,' said Le Brun impatiently. 'He is greater in stature than anyone else in France. Therefore he is tall. You would not expect him to be shorter than any others in the painting, would you? The King's true height is irrelevant. You'd know that if you were an artist.'

The King's face was in half-profile and there was a classical cast to his features. 'It's not quite right yet,' said Le Brun. 'I've still got some more work to do there. Stay and talk to me, André de la Glace, I've been up here for three days and I need someone to talk to me or I'll go mad. My assistant never says a word.'

Andrea watched Le Brun as he returned to the King's calf. 'You have to be an anatomist to be an artist,' said Le Brun. 'I know exactly the structure of the muscles, I can feel them with my brush. That's years of looking at flayed corpses for you. I used to have spare arms and legs pickled in brine lying around my studio. The landlord thought I was a cannibal. He couldn't see why I needed stinking dead flesh to paint beauty. D'you know anything about art?'

'I studied with an artist in Venice when I was a boy,' said Andrea, 'but my father wanted me to be a mirror maker, like him and his father before him. Artists were two a penny in Italy, he used to say, whereas the guild of mirror makers was confined to those who had inherited the knowledge. So I never learnt anatomy. I went to work in the factory instead.'

'And did very well at it, which means your father knew best even if you didn't think so at the time.' Le Brun smiled. 'And your mirrors reflect the world around you, so you create a picture of a sort. They have one fault, though. They're not large enough. Imagine if you could see an entire image without the joins.'

'It would be impossible to blow the glass to a larger size,' said Andrea. 'It would become too thin to use.'

'Nothing is impossible with material that can be shaped or moulded. Think about it, dear boy.' Le Brun turned his florid face to him and closed one eye meaningly. 'If you work out how to do it, imagine the riches and acclaim. There's a seed blowing in the wind, for anyone whose mind can fertilise it.'

LATER IN the morning, after he and Le Brun's assistant had pored over plans and measurements, Andrea walked out into the gardens, through the parterre and down the great flight of steps to the *bassin* of Latona, from where he could see two dozen men digging out the Grand Canal. He took a path to the left through a *bosquet*, under the fresh green light of newly unfurled leaves, past the fountains that would play when the King arrived but now, without an audience, were dark pools reflecting the sky. The path led him into a wood and he wandered along an avenue that formed a canopy of branches overhead, like the vaulting of a cathedral. This part of the garden was wild, as if a reminder of the natural forces outside the order imposed by the will of the gardener. The path led on to another avenue, which opened out to a space that dazzled him with light from a calm body of water, smooth and metallic, reflecting the trees on the edge and the vastness of the heavens in its shining surface. Andrea gazed into this huge natural mirror, gradually drawing to its edge and crouching over it to study his reflection. The image was darker than in a mercury mirror, but it had an unnerving clarity, as his face stared up at him. He ruffled the surface with his hand and watched his face undulate into ripples before settling again to stare back at him. Behind him he heard footsteps, but he only turned when they were close, so absorbed was he in this strange, still lake. Standing there, watching him as he looked at his image, was the Marquise's maid.

'Mademoiselle des Oeillets,' said Andrea, getting to his feet. His first thought was of leaving and he gave her a perfunctory bow. But it was not so simple to turn his back and walk away. She was looking at him silently and the silence made a claim on him. He hesitated, for she seemed about to speak, and in that moment he lost the impetus of the turn of the heel that was to have followed the curt bow. Eventually, to break the stillness, he said, 'I trust you're fully recovered, Mademoiselle.'

She smiled, 'As you can see, there are no bruises and no scratches.'

Her eyes glanced down, as his did, to her bosom, encased and emphasised by a grey and white silk bodice edged with lace. A fleeting image came to his mind of the heat and softness of flesh in the dark, and he could see as his eyes met hers that she was aware of the memory. A flush had risen to her cheeks and she murmured, 'Whatever happened in the past, I never intended to offend you. I don't want you to go on being angry with me, Andrea.'

'It's all over − all forgotten. Thank you for the apology, Mademoiselle,' said Andrea and he turned to go. But after only a few paces, he heard a voice clearly in his mind, 'Why walk away, idiot?' He glanced back at her and she was looking at him with such intensity that he realised he was incapable of moving out of her field. She was drawing him towards her, like a fisherman reeling in a salmon, like a horseman reining in a colt, like a cat willing a bird towards its claws. He

279

felt a dryness in his mouth, an increased beating of the heart, then an uncurling of desire, as the voice in his head said, 'This woman wants you.'

He was now standing directly in front of her and for a moment it seemed that the world around them was waiting in silence, the universe centred on this one spot beside the mirror pond. 'Will you walk with me?' he said and held out his arm. The two of them walked arm in arm beside the water until they came to the woods.

Thirty-Six

THE MAID hums to herself as she tastes the hot chocolate before taking it in to the Marquise. Sweet and strong, she thinks, like her lover. The taste as sweet as his tongue in her mouth. Well, Madame, now I have the man for whom you once felt *un petit amour*. Let me tell you, Madame, how he fills you up more satisfyingly than a gallon of hot chocolate, his sweet juices flooding through your body. And thank God it was just before my time of month, or I might have been in trouble.

CLAUDINE RAN her tongue over her lips to remove traces of chocolate, placed the porcelain cup on an enamelled tray and took it into the Marquise's bed-chamber. There she was, her hair tousled on the pillows, her eyes, lustrous from her night with the King, sleepily watching the progress of the hot chocolate to her bedside.

'I'm so exhausted,' said Athénaïs, 'I'm not sure if I have the strength to drink my chocolate. Just put it to one side, there, where I can smell it.'

Claudine placed the tray on the table by the bed. She noticed a pillow lying on the floor and picked it up. Clearly, the bed had been well pummelled last night, but no matter how prolonged and passionate their sessions, the King was never there in the morning when she arrived. He would have had to make two bed hops since then, first to the Queen's bedchamber and from there, when the time came for the *grand lever*, to his own state bedroom. At this moment, while his mistress lay languidly in her rumpled bed, he was being attended by a hundred courtiers as he put on a freshly laundered shirt and selected his jabot for the morning. He would have listened already to a number of jokes and been solicited by several courtiers eager for favours.

That's how it is, Madame, thought Claudine. We're the ones who are left in the aftermath of passion. Whereas men, no matter how eager beforehand, how driven by their lusts into helpless supplication for their mistress's favours, afterwards they're like any dog. Once satisfied, off they go, busily on the scent, barking at passers-by, just to show they are their own animal.

Not that she felt like that about her lover, for he had stayed with her, lying on the ground under the trees until the earth began to chill them and it was she who had said she must go or she would be missed. He had let her leave with the sweetest reluctance, extracting the promise of meeting again. She could see, though, the obstacles in their way. She knew Saint-Germain and Paris were not so many miles apart, but a maid took a lover at her peril. A pregnant maid was useless as far as a mistress was concerned. She would have to be careful, to keep an eye on her chart of the lunar cycle, perhaps seek advice from Madame Voisin on prophylactic herbs. In the meantime she would do everything in her power to make sure that every time she saw Andrea he fell more and more under her spell, until he could not bear the thought of life without her.

'Where did you get to at Versailles yesterday, Claudine?' said the Marquise, now sitting up in bed and revived by the chocolate to her customary alertness. 'I wanted your advice on the arrangements at the Trianon de Porcelaine, but you simply disappeared.'

'I went for a walk, Madame, and then I felt very tired, and I sat down under some trees and slept for a while.'

'With whom did you sit under the trees?'

'Oh, Madame, that's unfair. I was on my own.'

'Hmm,' said the Marquise disbelievingly, but was too absorbed by her own emotions to pursue the enquiry any further. There were more pressing matters to deal with, like what to wear for the morning, what to change into for lunch and what to amaze the court with for the evening. This was no frivolous occupation, for the well-being of the King's mistress was judged by her appearance.

ATHÉNAÏS HAD gone for her game of cards with Henriette, Saint-Cyr and two or three other enthusiasts. The cards took up hours of their time, for it was not only a game, but a sparring of the intellect and of the irrational emotions underlying their actions. The sparring was at its height during the post-mortems over the mistakes. Why did the Chevalier play a jack, when he could have trumped them all with an ace? Madame Henriette's fault, said Saint-Cyr. She kept kicking me under the table and distracted me. No true card player should ever allow himself to be distracted, declared Athénaïs. Look at Dangeau, oblivious to everyone's chatter. He sits there, totally immersed in the game, and wins every time.

WHILE HER mistress played cards that afternoon, Claudine was immersed in her own game. She had half drawn the curtains in the Marquise's bedchamber and had taken the dark glass out of its velvet pouch for the first time in several months. Her mind was troubled. What was her future with Andrea? Did he love her? Would they find happiness together? She stared deep into the glass, waiting for the familiar sensations. It lay before her, gleaming but opaque. Then she started to feel the insects swarming over her skin, like moving particles of matter. The surface of the glass began to undulate like waves. In the centre, a pinpoint of light spread in flickering strands, red and gold. She must think nothing, her mind must empty, she was reaching another plane, the room was falling away. She was in a universe of nothingness.

She didn't hear the door open and close, nor the footsteps. She was unaware of anyone else in the room until a shadow fell into her line of vision. She jolted from her trance and cried out in alarm. She looked up into the eyes of the King. They were as black and shining as the mirror.

'What are you doing, Claudine?' he asked, but she knew he had guessed.

It was forbidden, of course, to attempt to look into the future, to solicit the help of spirits. It was against the teachings of the Church. It was a form of sorcery, something she knew the King abhorred. She pushed the glass back into its pouch in confusion. 'It is nothing, Your Majesty. Just a pretty piece of glass. I was trying to see my reflection.'

The thought came into her mind that it was odd to hear him address her by name. He continued to look at her, his eyes shining with an attention she now understood. She glanced into the blackness of his eyes, and knew that one moment more and she would be in territory too dangerous to contemplate. 'Please excuse me, Your Majesty, I'm late for Madame la Marquise.' She gave a curtsy and moved cautiously wide of him, towards the door. She was half expecting him to obstruct her, but he didn't move, as if he could afford to wait.

Once outside, she walked swiftly away, then paused for a moment by a window, assailed by a feeling of breathlessness. She felt light-headed, from the inter-rupted trance and the strange episode with the King. And what ironical timing, the day after she had gone with her lover. As she gathered her wits again, the thought came into her mind: When one comes running, they all come running.

Thirty-Seven

THE ENCHANTER waved his wand and instantly there rose up a palace of porcelain encircled by a parterre of jasmine that scented the air so strongly that all who entered the gardens fell into a swoon. They forgot the world outside as they listened to a thousand nightingales singing exquisitely and time stood still, enveloping them in a state of eternal perfection.

'I think a thousand nightingales is excessive,' said the Chevalier de Saint-Cyr. 'Their exquisite voices would become a cacophony, and you would have to cover your ears.'

'I won't have less than a hundred,' said Athénaïs. 'It spoils the story if you say half a dozen nightingales.'

'Why not one perfect nightingale, created by the Enchanter from rubies and diamonds, with a voice so sublime that all who hear it forget their homes, their wives and husbands, in order to listen to it for ever?' suggested Madame de Thianges.

'Then one day, as with all these musical contraptions, it develops a mechanical failure, and those who have fallen under its spell become sick with sorrow and chagrin, fading away among the jasmine bowers,' said Saint-Cyr.

Henriette cried out suddenly and they turned to look at her. She had the pallor of a Renaissance *peinture en gris*. The shadows under her eyes emphasised her sockets. Her eyes were filled with pain. 'I have a terrible stitch in my side, please excuse me,' she said. 'Continue with the story.'

But now everyone was distracted with advice as to how to alleviate the pain, from lying on the floor, to having warming pans applied to the area, or an emetic administered by the doctor. Henriette said, 'No, please take no notice,' and retired to a couch where she lay with eyes closed.

Athénaïs looked at Saint-Cyr who looked at Madame de Thianges and without speaking they conveyed their thoughts to each other. Henriette had been having an appalling time with Monsieur, who had accused her of being instrumental in the banishment of his favourite, the Chevalier de Lorraine. His jealousy had been heightened by Henriette dabbling in matters of state between her brother, the King of England, and her brother-in-law, the King of France. He, the King's brother, was excluded from any decision making, had even been kept ignorant of Henriette's negotiations. Every day at Saint-Cloud, Henriette woke from a dream to a nightmare, as she saw the hatred in the face of her husband. No wonder her stomach-aches, which had troubled her for several years, had become more acute for, with unhappiness, the first part of the body to suffer was the stomach.

Thus they voiced their concerns, after Henriette had left, but there seemed no answer to the problem. Monsieur and Madame were married indissolubly until death, after all.

THE INNER circle of the court was beginning to visit Versailles more often. The chateau was still a ferment of building works, but the gardens had taken shape in a delightful way. A succession of open-air salons linked by avenues of fresh young trees meant that during the summer you could conduct your life with consummate elegance under the open sky. There was so much to admire. The grotto of Thetis, with its fountains that ambushed the unwary, the labyrinth with its painted animal statues inspired by La Fontaine's fables, the menagerie that housed an elephant, lions, deer and ostriches, and the perfumed garden of the little palace of porcelain.

It was on one of those days when the Marquise and the King had retired to the Cabinet de Parfum of the Trianon de Porcelaine, to breathe in the scent of tuberose and jasmine, that Claudine wandered through the garden, towards the mirror pond, which had become a meeting place for her and Andrea on the infrequent occasions when they were both at Versailles. Inside her bodice she secreted the most recent letter he had sent, full of sweet phrases, which made her long to reach the solitude of the mirror pond so that she could read it again.

As she neared the fountain of Apollo, she saw the unmistakable figure of Monsieur, small, flamboyantly dressed and moving among a flurry of overexcited spaniels, which weaved around his high-heeled shoes as if trying to trip him. Beside him was his little confidant, the Chevalier de Saint-Eustace, and another young man she had not seen before, wearing a large plumed hat. She curtsied as Monsieur came nearer and expected him to pass by, but he stopped and waved a hand of greeting. 'If it isn't Mademoiselle des Oeillets. That means the Marquise must be here today.'

'She is indeed, Monseigneur, ensconced in the perfumed garden with the King.'

'How touching,' said Monsieur. 'What joy there is to be found in a garden.' He looked around at the avenues, the *bosquets*, the fountains and the newly installed statues of gods and goddesses. 'And what a garden,' he said, 'though of course it sadly misses a view. When I think of Saint-Cloud and the panorama from the terrace, over the Seine, the spires of Paris and the land around. But there you are, he doesn't need a view. He is the view. *La vue, c'est Moi.* How is my dear friend, the Marquise?'

'She is extremely well, Monseigneur. She flourishes at Versailles.'

Monsieur stepped towards Claudine and said, 'There's something I wish to speak to you about, a little delicate, perhaps.'

He took her arm lightly to indicate they should move away from his companions. A shock ran through her at his touch. Not Monsieur as well? One comes running, they all come running. And the irony of having Andrea's letter stuffed down her bodice, for she had heard from him about Monsieur's attempted seduction. But no, Monsieur was obviously up to something else, for as they moved away he said, 'The Marquise is in such good form and the King has eyes for no one else.'

'That is indeed the case, Monseigneur.'

'Of course it is love, but love is sometimes aided by a little magic.' He stood in front of Claudine and looked directly at her. His eyes were as hard and brilliant as jet, his tongue flicked his lips like a serpent.

She thought, someone has betrayed us about the mass with Father Mariette, but kept her face composed as she said, 'Love is magical. One needs nothing more.'

He smiled. 'You're a clever little baggage, Mademoiselle. But you know what I'm talking about. Like a few other ladies at court, the Marquise has obtained some magical powders from a certain wise woman. I have long been curious to try these powders, but you can imagine the embarrassment if I or one of my courtiers were to be seen going to that establishment. I only tell you because I know you are discreet.'

'I never break confidences, Monseigneur,' said Claudine, feeling a wave of relief flood through her. So it wasn't to do with Father Mariette after all, only Madame Voisin's love potions. Monsieur either wanted someone to fall in love with him or to increase his potency. Madame Voisin had a powder for every aspect of love. 'I have occasionally been sent on errands to a certain lady, but I shouldn't say for what powders.'

'I'm not asking you to betray any secrets, just to make a little errand for me next time the Marquise sends you there. The Chevalier will bring you a note. You don't even need to know what I am asking for.'

Claudine smiled and glanced coquettishly from under her eyelashes at him. 'I couldn't begin to guess, for I'm certain Monseigneur has no fears for his potency.'

Monsieur gave a resonant laugh and slapped playfully at Claudine's rear. 'That's the least of my problems, Mademoiselle Méchante. Now don't forget, not a word to anyone, particularly the Marquise. I'm afraid she lacks your discretion.'

Monsieur gave an exaggerated bow and wave of the hand, then rejoined his companions and they strolled off towards the Grand Canal, their lapdogs gambolling around them. Claudine touched her bodice, where Andrea's letter lay secure, and thought, 'How he will laugh when I tell him.' For telling your lover a secret was not breaking a confidence and that was why Monsieur had been so anxious that she did not mention the conversation to the Marquise — it would have gone straight to the King.

As she walked towards the mirror pond, she wondered at the extraordinary lack of confidence the Marquise had in the King's affections. With such beauty and wit, why did she need to have recourse to Madame Voisin's medicine? She must know she had his love and yet, despite her outward assurance, there was an uncertainty deep inside her. She wanted to have him exclusively, whereas he seemed not to understand the meaning of monogamy. For her to have become pregnant at the same time as the Queen and as Louise — particularly Louise whom he had sworn he had rejected — was a peculiar humiliation.

Claudine reached the mirror pond and sat down on the grass, her back against the trunk of a tree. She drew the letter out from her bodice and began to read it again. *Mia gattina birichina* – my naughty kitten – she loved the way he mixed Italian with French, it heightened the romance of the words. She gazed at the reflected clouds that drifted across the water and thought about him.

Thirty-Eight

ANDREA'S MIND was not on his work. Sometimes he was devising an excuse to visit either Saint-Germain or Versailles, depending on where the court was at the time, sometimes he was writing love letters in his head. In his spare moments he would sit among the fragments of mirror in his studio, pen and paper before him, images in his mind of her eyes which had first reminded him of a baleful cat and now seemed like a kitten in need of affection. He couldn't work out his feelings towards her. He felt waves of tenderness while he wrote his letters and an urgent desire for her when they were together. So it must be love, then. And yet it was a feeling that ebbed and flowed, almost as if, like a woman, he were controlled by the moon. Sometimes he felt he would go mad if he couldn't be with her, sometimes, immersed in his work, her image in his mind seemed more like a distracting gnat, to be swatted. The sacred possession of his being, the holy joy he had felt in his love for Athénaïs, was no longer there. Perhaps love altered with age and experience, and with different women. Love with Claudine was different again from his dalliance during the previous winter with the wife of a clockmaker in the Marais, whom he had met when he had been drawn into the shop to take a closer look at the curiously embellished clock he had seen in the window. It's after the Greek legend, she had said. Time devours us all – which is why we must make the most of it while we're young. There had been no mistaking the invitation in her eyes and it had been a pleasant affair, until she had started to develop a conscience about her husband.

Monsieur du Noyer, he could tell, was disappointed with his non-committal response to the proposal of marriage with the niece. He could imagine him discussing it with his brother. Italians, they would conclude, were unreliable. They might dress as Frenchmen, speak as Frenchmen, but underneath they were still foreigners. The niece had had a lucky escape, but it was a pity about the dowry, for Monsieur Colbert favoured Andrea and would have been generous.

'I cannot wait to kiss your pretty lips again and much else besides,' wrote Andrea and drew a series of kisses beside his signature. The letter would reach her in the royal post the next day and a few days after that they would be together again. He imagined them at Versailles, like the first time, walking by the mirror pond and then into the woods, their pace quickening as they looked for a peaceful place where they would not be disturbed. Sinking on to the ground while in mid-kiss, his hands negotiating the flounces of her petticoats, her removal of his hands with a little slap, then, soon after, abandonment of the token resistance as she clung to him, crying out with desire. She was ingenious at finding different places, for, she said, that way they would remember, that was the time in the long grass behind Monsieur de La Quintinie's potting sheds, or that was the time when we were in the *bosquet* near the menagerie and heard the lion roar as we came. There was one alarming occasion when she had taken him into the labyrinth, along the winding paths until they came to a glade in the centre with a stone bench. She was sitting astride him when they heard the noise of yapping dogs and men's laughter. 'Monsieur!' she had gasped. 'Let's get out of here.'

Strangely, their encounters, which varied in their intensity according to her time of month, never evoked that first time of all, in the chateau of Saint-Cloud. But then it had been dark, she had been unseen and naked. Now they made love in the daylight, their bodies impeded by their clothes, and he could see her face as she cried out. 'No,' she said, when he had asked to see her naked, 'if someone came along I could never get my clothes back on in time.' And once they couldn't make love at all, because wherever they went there seemed to be gardeners or workmen around. He counted the times on the fingers of one hand. Twice in the woods by the mirror pond, once behind the potting sheds, once near the menagerie, once, interruptus, in the labyrinth.

Thirty-Nine

HENRIETTE HAS died. The court is seething with rumours. Had she not said when she was dying that she believed she had been poisoned? People talk about the Chevalier de Lorraine as the likely suspect, for he was vicious enough and ruled both Monsieur and the whole household at Saint-Cloud. In order to quell the murmuring at court, an autopsy takes place on an August evening. As the knife slices into her stomach a stench of corruption fills the room. The doctors pronounce the liver and lungs so rotten that it was a wonder she lived so long. But the doubts remain. Was not the pain she had suffered that evening so agonising it could only have been poison? The doctors may talk about natural causes, but the English Ambassador is convinced she was murdered. The Chevalier de Lorraine is seen at court, looking supremely self-satisfied.

CLAUDINE REMEMBERED her conversation with Monsieur and wondered what was in the order for Madame Voisin that Saint-Eustace had brought to her.

She could still see Madame Voisin's face as she read the letter, the absent-minded look in her eyes when she gazed at Claudine and said, 'This will take us a little longer. You'll have to return for it and I need payment in advance.'

It had been a large sum, almost all the money she had been given by Saint-Eustace. But who had written the order, Monsieur or someone else? And who would have administered the poison to Henriette, surrounded as she was by her ladies, all of whom were loyal to her? It was better to believe the doctors' verdict, that Madame had died of the corruption of her innards. If it were otherwise, Claudine thought, I should be guilty of complicity in murder. The wisest action was to keep very quiet.

A shadow remained over the court at Saint-Germain after Henriette's death, and there were murmurs about the buying and selling of lives. In Paris, the enemy of shadows was talking to Colbert. Nicolas de La Reynie, Lieutenant of the Police, had been lighting the darkness with tallow lanterns hung at regular intervals through the newly paved streets. His watch arrested the criminals who profited from the night. He had accumulated a mass of files, listing trials, verdicts, length of sentences, time served and date of release. Until now, criminals often remained forgotten, languishing in prison for years after their sentence had expired. La Reynie was casting light in the darkest corners. No one was more aware of the Paris underworld.

One trial in particular had attracted his attention – or half a trial, as there appeared to be no sentence on the two accused, despite the fact that the crime was a capital offence. The dossier, from the year 1668, came from the chambre criminelle de la Tournelle. One of the accused was l'Abbé Mariette, the priest at Saint-Séverin. The other was a certain Adam Lesage. They had been accused of conducting blasphemous masses, on several occasions for a number of aristocrats. They had been arrested by the watch in the spring of 1668 for being abroad in the early hours, with no good reason. In their bag they carried the chattels for mass, together with some noxious-smelling powders. Father Mariette claimed to have been at the bedside of a dying man, but later confessed, under interrogation, to blasphemy. La Reynie found it odd that the full confession was not attached to the papers.

The president of the chambre criminelle was Monsieur de Mesmes. The name seemed familiar. Yes, said Colbert, when La Reynie asked him, he is sometimes at court. He is the father of Madame de Vivonne who is sister-in-law to Madame de Montespan.

La Reynie experienced such a marked sensation of being on the scent of something that he felt a twitching of his nose. So the president of the trial that found insufficient evidence against the priest and his accomplice had the highest connections at court, and the priest's confession had gone missing. The two *coquins* had slipped through the prison gates. La Reynie had a strong desire to haul the priest in for further questioning, although aware that such a move might rebound on him. And besides, these people had a wide network. The only way to learn about their accomplices was to leave them at large. He could not anticipate what would come of keeping an eye on the priest, but it was always best to accumulate more knowledge than you might need.

THE MARQUISE was pregnant again. It was becoming almost an annual event. Claudine was despatched to Madame Voisin for her special powders against morning sickness. These trips to the wise woman took her to Paris and to Andrea. Arranging their meetings had become difficult, for Madame de Montespan was particularly exacting when she was with child. When Claudine had once suggested that she too might like to marry and have children, the result had been explosive. How could she desert her, the Marquise demanded, when she was at her most vulnerable, *enceinte*. With all these female vultures perched around the palace . . .

'No one will get their claws into the King,' said Claudine, 'because he's in love with you. And I know someone who's in love with me and I'd like to marry him.'

'You would do so without my blessing,' said the Marquise. 'This is no time to talk of leaving me. In a year or two it will be different. Then I'll give you a splendid wedding. Who is the man you're after?'

'After is not the right word, Madame. The gentleman also loves me and if we aren't very careful, we'll have to marry in a hurry.'

'So I have a maid with no morals. Well, you'll just have to ask Madame Voisin's advice. I need your help and I should be very, very disappointed if you let me down now. There's no one else I can rely on.'

Claudine thought, you wouldn't find anyone else who would put up with your little tantrums, but at the same time she felt a certain pleasure in being found indispensable. She said, 'I could always marry and continue to be your maid.'

'Not with squalling babies, you couldn't,' said the Marquise.

You can't even bear the sound of your own babies crying, thought Claudine, you are quite happy for them to be farmed out with the Widow Scarron, so you can just visit them once a week with the King and coo over them. No mess, no loss of beauty sleep, only the pleasure of looking at your pretty little creations for an hour or so and then back to the palace for another game of cards.

THEY BORROWED Monsieur du Noyer's grey mare, Mouette, for the journey to Madame Voisin's house. Claudine perched sideways behind Andrea, until she complained the edge of the saddle was digging into her vital parts. So she rode while Andrea walked beside her, leading the horse. She watched him as she clutched at Mouette's mane, absorbed by the shape of his back under his shirt, the long curling hair, better than any wig, the easy way he walked and the wonderful smile he gave her from time to time. She reflected on her situation with the Marquise. If she married Andrea without her permission, no dowry. If she waited for a year or so, there would be a generous dowry and a gorgeous wedding. She had to juggle these two factors in her mind with the need to ensure that there was a marriage and that in delaying she didn't lose him – there were so many harpies around. She could see even now a passing trollop giving him the eye.

Andrea waited for her in the hall while she consulted Madame Voisin in her enclosed room, its curtains drawn against the sun. The old witch smiled at Claudine, but her eyes had an absent expression, as if her mind were turned inwards. Eventually she said, 'I see you are one of us. I can tell from your eyes. You can see the other world.'

'That may be so, but I don't need a glass to know what will happen if I fall pregnant before it's convenient for Madame la Marquise. She has sent me for some medicine for her morning sickness and I want some medicine to prevent me from getting morning sickness in the first place.'

'A sponge soaked in vinegar during and a douche after the act are the cheapest preventatives,' said Madame Voisin. 'My herbal pills are costly, as they come from the Americas and you have to take them at the right time to be effective. But there, if it's important to you . . .'

She gazed at Claudine for a while in silence, then asked, 'Are you weaving a web for this young man? I see him in some sort of danger. I can hear the crackling of flames . . .'

'I'm here about the morning sickness,' Claudine said impatiently. 'I don't want my fortune told.'

'It wasn't yours. I was concerned about the young man's. I could say more, but there, you probably think you know enough. One day you'll come running and say, "Madame Voisin, why didn't you tell me?" '

She left the room to measure out the ingredients, and returned presently with some small packets wrapped in paper and sealed with wax. Claudine counted out the Marquise's money for both purchases. Madame Voisin said, 'Will you give my regards to the dear Marquise and I trust her health improves. Perhaps she would like to pay me a visit one day for a consultation.'

'I'll pass the message on,' Claudine said, though she remembered the Marquise's clearly expressed distaste at the prospect of the journey. She opened the door into the hall and almost collided with Father Mariette who was standing just outside.

He started, then, recovering himself, said, 'Ah, Mademoiselle des Oeillets, I trust all is well.'

Claudine blushed, at the memory of their last meeting near the charnel house and the fact that she could see Andrea looking at them with a curious expression. 'All's well, Father,' she said.

He nodded his head in the direction of Andrea, raised his eyebrows at Claudine and murmured, 'The one in question?'

'Discretion, Father Mariette,' she said. 'Best for both of us.'

He smiled and inclined his head, then passed into Madame Voisin's consulting room.

'Who was that priest?' Andrea said as she joined him.

'Only Father Mariette. I have seen him before at Madame Voisin's.'

'He may wear the cloth, but I don't like the look of him. And I may say,' he continued, as they returned to where Mouette was tethered, 'I don't like the whole area. There's some fellow over there lurking on the corner, watching this house. I don't like the thought of your coming here, it's not safe.'

'But with you, I'm safe,' said Claudine. 'You can come with me in future.'

'And the place stinks of cats,' said Andrea. 'Let's hope the morning sickness powders work, so we don't have to come back.'

Claudine smiled down at Andrea, as he helped her back into the saddle. The dear, sweet man, she thought. Like them all, completely unaware of what lies underneath the surface.

Forty

THERE WAS once a king who suffered from a confusion over words. When someone said the word Fire, he heard the word Water, and wondered why his horse leapt back in agony when he took it to quench its thirst in the flames. When the word War was pronounced, he heard the word Glory. He would ride into the field of battle in gold brocade and red plumes, and the more they were stained with blood and mud, the greater the glory. He only needed an enemy to fight. In a small country next to his lived a people too industrious for their own good. They were solemn, clad in black, their minds like calculuses. Their sea captains, who cared nothing for comfort, would go on long voyages and return with spices and gold. Their country was flat and could be ridden over in a few hours, the men were more exercised in counting their money than in fighting. It seemed to Bel-Amour, the great King, that they were simply waiting to be the instruments of his Glory.

The court went with him to witness the Glorious

War against the Dutch. And to the people who watched the procession of the royal coaches pass through their lands on the way to the border, it seemed like a veritable *conte de fées*. The King on his fiery horse riding beside a golden coach in which sat, not one Queen, but three. In the coach itself, the atmosphere was tense. Louise de La Vallière drooped with depression in one corner; the Queen, face screwed up with jealousy, glared at both her and Madame de Montespan, heavily *enceinte* and wincing at each jolt of the coach.

At Versailles, another battle was being fought, the war against Nature. The master of fountains, Francisco Francini, had predicted correctly that there was not enough water to supply the *grandes eaux*, despite an elaborate recycling process. Moreover, the *étang* at Clagny from which the water was drawn received the effluent from the nearby village, together with various dead animals. Now that the gilded fountains of Latona and Apollo had been installed, and the Théâtre d'Eau, with its ballet of fountains, was in operation, the problem of water was acute. An overseer was appointed whose sole job was to anticipate which part of the gardens the King would visit next and to get there ahead to make sure the fountains were turned on. The King was not impressed by this haphazard arrangement, and found time in the midst of his war against the Dutch to write to Colbert of his exasperation at the frequent breakdowns of the *grandes eaux*.

The small, flat country next to France was proving as intractable to deal with as the Versailles water system. The great King left the war in the charge of his generals and returned with his court to more comfortable quarters. Madame de Montespan deposited her new infant at the house of the Widow Scarron, who she noted with some irritation was beginning to behave as if she were the natural mother. Claudine remarked that she couldn't understand why the Marquise carried on with this subterfuge, considering that the Queen had already seen her bursting with fecundity. And wasn't it about time, now that the Marquise was so firmly established in the King's affections, for her maid's marital prospects to be considered?

She said as much to Andrea as they watched the lion cubs playing in the menagerie. Last summer they had heard the lions roar while they lay in the grass nearby, and now three lion cubs were blinking their golden eyes in the sun. She looked up at Andrea and said, 'What if I were to have a little cub in here?' and drew his hand to her belly.

She waited for him to look alarmed, but he smiled and said, 'Do you have a little cub in there?'

She said, 'It could always happen,' and he smiled again and began kissing her neck, his hand on her breast, until they moved with one accord towards the shelter of the *bosquet*.

'I want to see you naked,' he said.

'When we have our own bed,' she replied. 'Until then you'll just have to see bits of me.' And she raised her skirt, as slowly as a theatre curtain, while her audience of one knelt in front of her. Now, she thought, it's just a matter of catching Madame in the right mood.

★

'WHERE HAVE you been and what have you been doing?' asked Monsieur Le Brun, as Andrea arrived in the Mars drawing room. Le Brun was leaning over a desk, examining some architectural plans. On the scaffolding overhead one of his artists was working on the painting of a child, sword unsheathed, playing at war games. 'I can have a pretty good guess,' continued Monsieur Le Brun, 'judging from your dishevelled clothes and the expression on your face. Well, if you can just get your mind in order for one moment and look at the plans on this table. This concerns you ultimately. There, what do you see?'

Andrea examined the meticulous drawing. He said, 'It's a long gallery with many tall, arched windows, or are they doors?'

'You tell me, Monsieur de la Glace. They are neither, they are mirrors. Seventeen of them, each made up of eighteen mirror panes, set in gilded frames. In the ceiling before each one, a chandelier. Opposite each one, a window of the exact same size. And where will you find such a great gallery in this fine chateau? Come with me and I'll show you.'

They walked together through the apartments towards the west, Le Brun holding a handkerchief to his face against the dust of the stone masons, and swearing under his breath at the obstacle course of builder's materials, wheelbarrows, heaps of rubble, gaps in floorboards. An assistant scurried after them, carrying the plans.

'I'm reaching the conclusion,' said Le Brun, 'that this chateau will never be finished. No sooner do we appear to have the final plan than another larger variation comes over the horizon. This is not going to be a palace at all. Eventually, it will be a city.'

They arrived at the door leading out on to the terrace, which ran the length of the west side, between the two end salons of the apartments on the north and south sides of the envelope. From the balustrade there was a panorama of the gardens in their entirety, looking over the parterres, to the fountain of Latona, down the steps, along the *grande allée* to the gilded fountain of Apollo, on to the Grand Canal and in the distance, on one side, the Trianon de Porcelaine, its tiles glinting in the sun. On the other side lay Monsieur de La Quintinie's vegetable gardens and beyond that the menagerie. In the centre of the marble-floored terrace on which they stood a fountain was playing. A pair of white doves preened their feathers in its spray.

'It's one of the prettiest places from which to view the gardens,' said Le Brun. 'But it will have to be sacrificed to the magnificence of Majesty. The *galerie* will be a fitting tribute to the most powerful king in the world. After the Netherlands, the King's eye will be ranging towards Franche-Comté, the Palatinate. And I will be here for ever, painting his great victories on one ceiling after another. So you see, we shall need the *grande galerie.'*

THE DOOR from the War drawing room opened and the King emerged on to the terrace, accompanied by a young man with a smooth, complacent expression.

'Jules Hardouin Mansart, nephew of the great Mansart,' muttered Le Brun. 'Young architect in a hurry to step into the shoes of the deceased Le Vau.'

The King touched his hat, with elaborate courtesy, as he approached them. Andrea had not seen him at close quarters since the day at Saint-Germain when he had been measuring for mirrors and dreaming of the Marquise. That dream had dissolved in a mist of regret and foolishness, but he remembered how he had at that moment felt the King make claim to him. It was the way he had looked into his eyes, as if demanding his loyalty, the moment when Venice began to slip inexorably away from him.

He doubted that the King remembered, too, but Le Brun had already introduced him as Monsieur de la Glace from the faubourg Saint-Antoine, and Louis smiled directly at him. 'But of course. Our valuable mirror maker. As you can see, we're asking more and more of you. How many mirrors have we ordered so far, Monsieur Le Brun?'

'Five thousand, Sire.'

'And how many do we need for the *galerie*?'

'Roughly five hundred, Sire.'

'No more? But it will be the effect, after all, rather than the quantity.'

The assistant held out the plans and the King studied them, hand on chin. Eventually he said, 'Mirrors or windows opposite? If we have mirrors opposite, we will see reflections ad infinitum. Monsieur my brother multiplied a hundred times. That would be extraordinary. All those images lit only by chandeliers. What do you think, Monsieur de la Glace?'

Andrea looked out over the gardens, touched with gold in the afternoon sun. He would have liked to have said that it was a pity to close off the terrace at all and didn't the King already have enough splendid rooms? But despite the informality of the meeting and the friendliness in the King's face, no one would be unwise enough to tempt fate. He said, 'Look at the way the sun is lighting up the terrace, Your Majesty. Imagine its rays slanting through the open windows and striking gold on the mirrors. The silver of the mirrors becomes gold, the *galerie* is filled with the glory of the sun.'

Behind the King he saw Le Brun pursing his lips to suppress his mirth, but the King was laughing, too. 'Bravo, you have the Italian eye for the wonders of nature. But of course, it's the only answer, nature illuminating the beauty of our architecture. You wouldn't have thought anything else, would you, Messieurs?'

'Of course not, Sire,' chorused Le Brun and Hardouin Mansart.

Louis laughed again and said to Andrea, 'When are we going to see your mirror to the sun, the one that burns? Will you have it ready for our next fête?'

'Yes, Your Majesty,' said Andrea, unsure of the King's meaning.

'Good, it will be on the day of the feast of Saint Louis, provided the sun is shining, but I see no reason why it should not do so. Arrange everything with Monsieur du Noyer.' He looked at him with the direct gaze that demanded unquestioning fealty. 'So, Chevalier of the Burning Mirror,' he said, 'that's settled.' Then he laid a hand on Andrea's shoulder for a moment, leaving a sensation of heat and energy that lingered after he withdrew. Andrea looked after him, almost in a trance, as the King, followed by Hardouin Mansart and Le Brun, walked the length of the terrace until the doors of the War drawing room were opened for him and he stepped inside.

So that was how the demonstration of the burning mirror was arranged at Versailles. At the mirror factory Andrea and an assistant cut and ground one hundred mirrors to precise measurements. They constructed a circular framework, over two metres in diameter, and attached the mirrors to a network of adjustable wires. When the instrument was finished, they wheeled it out on a trolley into the yard and positioned it opposite a stone wall. Dancing reflections of light scattered over the wall as they adjusted each mirror, until the reflected light was confined to one small circle. Then Andrea leant a plank against the wall in the path of the mirror ray and they waited. After a few minutes a wisp of smoke rose from the spot where the light was focused, increasing in density until a flame flickered in the midst of the smoke. The mirror workers, who had gathered to watch the demonstration, cheered and one of them shouted, 'Now set Versailles on fire!'

On the feast day of Saint Louis, at one in the afternoon, the court gathered by the Grand Canal to hear the Secretary of the Academy of Science expound the theory of the mirror, beginning with the legend of Archimedes burning the Roman ships. In the heat of the sun, the courtiers' faces glistened with sweat, their aching feet swelled in their leather shoes, their clothes began to steam from their perspiring bodies. But no one felt able to leave this scene of a scientific experiment, devised by the Italian mirror maker, Monsieur André de la Glace. The whisper went around that the King had made him a Chevalier.

'Chevalier? Are you sure?'

'Yes, he's known as the Knight of the Burning Mirror.'

'You're joking!'

'It's true – I heard it from Le Brun.'

Andrea, unaware of the undercurrents running through the assembled courtiers, concentrated on the success of the experiment. He raised the black cloth which had covered the instrument, to expose all the mirrors to the sun. A hundred paces away, becalmed in the middle of the Grand Canal, was the sacrificial boat, fresh tar applied to its sides and mast. Andrea adjusted some of the mirrors which had been displaced, until they were focused on to the prow. Now it was a matter of waiting. There was an expectant silence for a moment, then the courtiers began chattering again. They had assumed the boat would explode into flames instantly. Someone yawned loudly, but stifled it on realising the King was staring intently at the vessel without the slightest sign of impatience.

A wisp of smoke rose from the wood on which the reflected sun was directed. Andrea, watching it curl like a grey wraith through the air, felt an intense relief. To have been exposed to the ridicule of the court and the crushing displeasure of the King had seemed a distinct possibility. The sweat that ran down his brow in runnels had been caused by fear as much as by the sun.

The smoke thickened and a small flame flickered, then another. There was a crackle from the tarred wood, and a larger flame shot out and disappeared. The boat was alight.

Now he could hear the applause. He turned to see a blur of faces, all of them well disposed towards him as a result of the afternoon's entertainment. The Secretary of the Academy of Science announced, 'The experiment is concluded. Is it your wish, Sire, that the boat continues to burn?'

Clapping and cries of 'Burn it!' from some of the courtiers.

The voice of the King cut across, 'That's enough. Extinguish the flames.'

Andrea and his assistant covered the mirror with the black cloth, then turned to acknowledge the applause and bowed low to the King. It seemed that he had become, for a moment, the centre of attraction, as Louis extended a gracious arm towards him and announced to the court at large, '*Voilà* – the power of mirrors.'

Afterwards he went over the scene in his mind, the instant of triumph. Among the applauding courtiers the Marquise, whose diamonds rivalled the light of the mirrors. She had caught his eye for a moment, in an instant of amused recognition, a smile that had more significance for him than the watching courtiers would have imagined.

There were a few other faces he had recognised – and many that he didn't. One imprinted itself on his mind, a face that was brutal in its cold-eyed force. It belonged to a man in his mid-twenties, whose thick neck and broad shoulders under the brocade coat reminded him of a bull. He was standing in the King's circle and, unlike the other courtiers, his face didn't soften into an ingratiating smile as he spoke with him, but remained unyielding, the mouth set in a line of pride and discontent. Andrea pointed him out to Francini who said, 'Oh yes, that's our Minister of War. The Marquis de Louvois. They don't come any tougher than him and he's always on the lookout for enemies. Monsieur Colbert detests him.'

As if he had realised they were talking about him, Louvois's head turned in their direction. Andrea felt overwhelmed by a black wall of hatred emanating from the man. He muttered to Francini, 'I don't think he likes me.'

'He doesn't like anyone,' said Francini. 'But it's as well to stay out of his way. Anyone whom Monsieur Colbert favours is looked on with disfavour by him. In this court, Andrea, you must learn that the art of survival is knowing whom to avoid.'

Forty-One

As to Athénaïs – the Diamond Marquise, la Reine Sultane, she knows the names they call her, not usually to her face. La Belle Armide, the beautiful enchantress, and for some reason, Quanto. That's Madame de Sévigné's little joke. Quanto – how much? An important question, whether it applies to diamonds or to love. With the King, the one is the expression of the other.

Athénaïs's apartment enjoys the best vantage point on to the marble courtyard in front of the palace. It is almost like being at the theatre, especially when the King is with her. Then it's a comedy. They sit beside the open windows, laughing at the clothes, at the postures and pretences of the passing courtiers.

'There's the Duc de Vendôme, still not recovered from drinking himself under the table. He can hardly find one foot to put in front of the other. You must send a page after him with a chamber pot to stop him pissing in corners.'

'Oh, what have we here? The Marquis d'Effiat. Did

you ever see such a ridiculously large hat? It's as if he has an ostrich sitting on his head.'

And so on, their laughter audible on a fine day, when the windows are open. Athénaïs knows how to amuse and she knows the King has to be amused, to keep the demons deep inside him at bay. She knows, too, of his need to live in a heightened atmosphere of beauty, of scents and sensations. In her apartment she has collected massed tubs of jasmine and tuberoses, and the tuberose follows them in her scent as they take the gondola, given to the King by the Venetian Ambassador, the length of the Grand Canal to the Trianon de Porcelaine. The scent of flowers pervades the garden. Monsieur Bouteux, the gardener, spends his days repotting plants, so there is always a new display. He's rumoured to have a store of nearly two million flowerpots.

Athénaïs can still arouse the King's passion as strongly as in their early days. Monsieur Colbert has to abandon his ledgers of taxes to chase after diamond merchants when the King takes it into his head to festoon her with more jewellery. Court gossip often centres on the burning love the Beautiful One continues to inspire in the King. It seems it will blaze for ever. In her beauty she is the mirror to his sun.

There are moments of disquiet, though, especially during her pregnancies. He is not a man who likes to be deprived and she suspects the Queen encourages her ladies to flirt with him, just to make her feel insecure when she is at her most vulnerable. Louise de La Vallière has finally taken herself to a convent, where she has become known as Sister Louise de la Miséricorde. But there are others, all of them younger, who would like to tip the favourite off her pedestal. And there's an older woman, as well. Athénaïs is beginning to feel seriously irritated with the pious governess, Madame Scarron, who is forever conferring with Louis about the health of his children. There are times when her temper gets the better of her and people are astonished at the things she can say to the King. Anyone else would have been banished from court but instead, Quanto appears glittering with more jewellery.

As to Claudine – she is indispensable, so her wish to be married is hugely inconvenient. And to the mirror maker, as Athénaïs has now discovered. Had it been one of the court servants, or even one of the actors with whom she used to resort, Claudine could still have helped out on occasion. She could have undertaken those little commissions that the Marquise would entrust only to her. Once married to the Italian, she would live in Paris, have half a dozen babies and that would be that. Athénaïs is also aware that there might be other reasons why the marriage to Andrea displeases her more than a match with some other court servant.

WHAT DOES Claudine feel about the continued impediment to her marriage plans? That morning, on a particularly sultry day, Claudine was feeling rebellious. She was being less than careful with the cleaning of the Marquise's satin gown. She was dabbing spirits at a grease mark in such a way as to make the stain larger. '*Merde*,' muttered Claudine to herself, and '*Putain*.' *Putain* gown, *putain* Madame. Does she expect me to live as if in a convent? No, she knows what I am doing and she doesn't care that I'm in a state of sin. But then, so is she. She wants me to be as *putain* as she is.

Claudine had taken off her own gown, which would be next to receive some dabbed spirits, and was dressed only in her stays and shift, but with a *déshabillé* of Madame's over, in case of interruption. She heard, before she saw, the nails of the King's lapdog on the polished floor in the salon next door. It trotted up to her, wagging its tail. 'Ah, Malice,' she said, 'what have you done with your master?' Malice, she thought, well named for a court dog.

She heard the King calling for the animal and quickly gathered the *déshabillé* around her as he entered the bedchamber. There's the little dog sniffing around, followed by the big dog, she thought. 'I'm afraid Madame la Marquise is not at home, Sire,' she said. 'She has gone for a drive with Madame de Thianges and the Duc de Vivonne.'

'I know,' said the King and he sat down in the armchair. He leant back, splaying his legs, his eyes fixed on Claudine.

'Your Majesty will excuse me for continuing to work. I have a lot to do,' she said.

'That's a very pretty robe you're wearing. Haven't I seen it somewhere before?'

'No doubt you have. It belongs to the Marquise.'

'It suits you well, Claudine.'

Claudine said nothing, as she concentrated on the

318

grease mark. There was silence for a while, then the King said, 'Why are you not being friendly?'

'Your Majesty, I have an understanding with someone.'

'Don't we also have an understanding, Claudine?'

An understanding that Madame la Marquise is indisposed again with her monthlies, thought Claudine.

The King rose to his feet, called to Malice as if to leave, then pushed the dog out of the room with his foot and closed the door. 'Malice will keep watch for us,' he said. 'Come to me, *ma mignonne*.'

'No.'

He began to move towards her. She was aware of the decreasing distance between them and the increasing magnetism of his being. She noticed, as if in a picture, the shape of his face, rounded at the cheeks, high-coloured from the hours spent in the hunting field, the sensuous mouth, the strands of curling dark hair that fell over his shoulders. She saw him pause, take off his coat and drape it over the back of a chair. She saw him smile at her, she saw the brightness of his eyes as he stood before her and untied the bow of her *déshabillé*, of Madame's *déshabillé*, and drew it open. Still she did not move, not as he put his hand on her breast, not as he leant forward to kiss her on the mouth, not as his arm drew her towards him, so that she was aware of his erection against her stomach. She didn't move because she was filled with desire, a melting submissiveness to his majesty. She allowed him to ease her on to the bed and to lie beside her, and to run his hand from her calf to her thigh. Then he eased himself on top of her as she opened her legs to him and he murmured, '*À l'horizontal, tout le monde est égal.*'

Forty-Two

Francini was giving a demonstration of the Théâtre d'Eau in its full glory for his audience of two. Andrea and Claudine sat on the grassy steps of the auditorium to watch the fountains as they were turned on to the *grandes eaux*. In front of the stage of finely raked sand, nine small fountains played. At the back of the stage, double avenues of fountains sprayed high into the air. On each side, high jets of water spurted from gilded fountains of dolphins and Cupids. The mist blown by the breeze from the fountains cooled the air. Francini laughed as the jets rose to their full height from the force of the water. 'Quite a potent display, isn't it?' he said.

Claudine was staring dreamily at the fountains and at the stage. She had been subdued when she had met Andrea and had accepted his kiss in an absent-minded way. When he asked, 'What are you thinking about?' she smiled and shrugged.

'There's something on your mind,' he said.

'I'm looking at the stage and thinking about the way it used to be, when I was with the comedy theatre. I didn't have any grand parts, just columbines and shepherdesses. I wasn't there for long – they said I couldn't remember my lines, but it wasn't true. It was just that the part would take me over and I would think, no, she wouldn't have said that. And then I would be lost. But I still feel nostalgic sometimes when I'm watching a play, or even just looking at a theatre, like this one.'

'The stage is there, waiting for you. Take possession of it,' said Andrea.

'I have forgotten everything I ever learnt,' she said.

'It doesn't matter – just walk on to it. Francesco and I will watch you and applaud at the right moment.'

She laughed. 'Then you're a perfect audience. I never could abide people who sat on their hands.'

She walked towards the stage, which was separated from the auditorium by the water channel of the fountains. Stepping across the channel, she moved around the area as if testing it out, paused at the centre and turned to look out at the auditorium. She stood for a moment in thought, then said, 'This is from *Le Mariage Forcé*.'

'*Brava!*' called out Francini.

'Be quiet. I haven't begun yet.'

She put her hands to her ribcage as if to test out her breathing and began to sing, '*Si l'amour vous soumet a ses lois inhumaines . . .*'

'You'll like this,' Francini muttered to Andrea.

> 'If love binds you to his inhuman laws,
> Choose to love someone full of charms.
> Let the chains you bear be fair ones
> And since we must die . . .'

322

Claudine stopped. 'No, that's too gloomy.'

'We can bear it,' called out Francini. 'Continue!'

'And since we must die, let our death be beautiful.'

'*Brava!*' cried Francini.

Claudine bowed and said, 'I can't remember much more. There was a dance that followed.'

She began to step to the side, pointing her feet and raising her arms in a delicate arc, with a hop, then stepped forward and back. For a while she seemed to have forgotten the watchers, so absorbed was she in her performance. For Andrea, the scene before him, of Claudine dancing among the fountains on the pale sand, against the green of the hornbeam hedge, would remain forever etched on his mind. She pirouetted, her petticoats floating around her, her small feet moving more and more quickly, then she leapt in long strides across the stage. Suddenly she stopped, her hand on her stomach.

'What's wrong?' called out Andrea.

'Nothing, I've got a stitch.' But her face was white and the distracted look when he had first seen her that morning had returned.

'I know what that's about, I should do with eight kids of my own,' muttered Francini, as Andrea reached her side.

'It's just that I haven't danced for so long,' said Claudine.

'*Brava, la diva!*' said Francini. 'Now I'll have to turn off the fountains before we empty the *étang*. Next time, Signora, we'll find you a larger audience.'

As Francini left, Claudine said, 'I shouldn't have done that, I'm so out of practice. Let's walk for a while.'

They walked slowly down the shaded path of the *bosquet* towards a clearing where a gilded fountain glinted in the sun. 'Are you happy?' Claudine asked inconsequentially.

'Of course I'm happy,' said Andrea. There seemed to be no reason not to be, walking in a magical garden, his arm round her waist, aware of the warmth of her body through the boned stays. They came to the *bassin* of Ceres and paused before the goddess lying among wheatsheaves in the centre of the pool, surrounded by plump, gilded Cupids. Around the rim of the *bassin* were pigeons, squirrels and tiny ants, all moulded out of painted *métail*.

'The goddess of fecundity,' said Andrea, smiling, until he saw Claudine's stricken face. 'What's wrong? There's been something on your mind all morning,' he said, and then, as she looked up at him through her welling eyes, 'You're pregnant, aren't you?'

She nodded. 'Yes,' and burst into tears.

Afterwards the cause of her misery was all too clear, but at the time it seemed that Claudine was being perversely despondent. His heart leapt at the thought of the new life inside her. His own child, his son, his reason for being alive – to live and to give life. He could see the boy already in his mind, playing on the piazza in Murano, where he himself had played. He could anticipate the pride his father would feel in the new generation. Perhaps this new life would heal the breaches of the past. For the first time in years, he felt drawn back towards his roots. 'Why are you crying? I'm not going to desert you,' he said, drawing her to him. 'We'll get married, whether the Marquise is content or not. You didn't think that I would abandon you or the child, did you?'

She raised her face and looked at him intently. 'Do you mean that?'

'Of course. It doesn't matter about the dowry. I don't believe any time is going to be convenient for her, so why wait until you're ancient?'

Claudine laughed and wiped away her tears. 'Who knows, she may come up with a dowry anyway, now that we are forcing her hand. Let's move away from here, this place has become too public.'

They were indeed attracting curious looks from several courtiers who were taking a stroll around the fountain. They wandered through the *bosquet* to a more secluded glade, where there was a stone bench under the trees. As they sat side by side, she said again, 'Are you happy?'

'Of course I am.'

She leant her head against his shoulder. 'I'll enjoy telling Madame,' she said. 'I'll tell her today, if I can possibly get her to attend for one moment. When shall we meet again?'

'I'll return in three days' time.'

'Then we can start arranging the marriage. Where shall we meet?'

He was about to say the mirror pond, in sentimental remembrance of their early meetings, but something seemed not quite right about the choice. 'By the fountain of Apollo,' he suggested.

'By the fountain of Apollo, then,' and she kissed him on the lips.

'Can you feel anything there, yet?' He placed a hand on her stomach.

'Don't be silly, it's far too soon.'

'When?' he said, the word meaning a whole succession of things. When was it conceived? When will it quicken? When will it be born?

'I must go,' she said in sudden confusion. 'Madame will be waiting.'

'The fountain of Apollo, at midday,' he called after her and sat for a while in the shade of the *bosquet*, his mind taking in his new status in life. Husband, father, householder. He could see the dreams he had chased in the past were chimera. Now there was work and family in the near future. He was leaving the airy element of possibilities for the earth of certainty. He was beginning to find contentment.

Forty-Three

MONSIEUR BELIEVES in excess. It is all that is left to him in this life. Prevented from taking part in government, sidelined from the battlefield, all he can do is spend as much of his brother's money as he can, as outrageously as possible. He enjoys seeing Louis wince at his latest costume. Today he is in a fetching shade of rose, embroidered with gold and silver thread. Lace flounces decorate the knees of his breeches, threaded with crimson ribbon. Lace foams from his throat and his sleeves like the cascades at Saint-Cloud. Pearl and ruby earrings tangle with his wig.

Monsieur is accompanied by his close friends, the Marquis d'Effiat and the Chevalier de Saint-Eustace. The Marquis is weighed down by his ostrich-plumed hat, the Chevalier more restrained in hunting green. Monsieur's dogs are sporting ribbons in shades of pink and red, to complement Monsieur. He should have been attending mass with the King before lunch, but decided to plead a breakdown in their carriage. So his little party spends the intervening time making a tour of the gardens, which Monsieur pronounces as still inferior to Saint-Cloud, despite the hard work and ingenuity of the gardeners. 'It's the situation. Versailles has no situation,' he explains to d'Effiat's nodding plumes. 'One of my brother's biggest mistakes. And look at these feeble fountains. They have to keep them turned low most of the time. They don't have the water, you see. There's a little man who runs ahead of the King to turn them full on and then someone turns them off again when he has passed by. I ask you!'

The Marquis, who has heard this all before, continues nodding, like a toy dog at a fairground. They saunter down the Allée Royale towards the *bassin* of Apollo. The gilded sun god appears to leap from the water in his carriage drawn by four surging horses, while four tritons blow conch shells to announce the rising of the sun.

Monsieur pauses to take in the full glory of Apollo. 'Now that,' he says, 'is one statue I should like to take away with me. Look at the physique. Magnificent.'

'There's another choice physique,' Saint-Eustace mutters.

'Where?' and then, seeing Andrea near the fountain, 'If that isn't little Monsieur Ne Me Touches Pas. He's obviously waiting for someone.'

'Should we have that Italian thug arrested?' says Saint-Eustace, a shade nervously.

Monsieur smiles. 'On the contrary, I think I know who he's waiting for. This could be fun.'

ANDREA HAD arrived early at the *bassin* of Apollo and was passing the time in studying the statue from all aspects. It was Le Brun at his flamboyant best, the design executed by the *métail* sculptor, Tuby. The face of Apollo reminded him of the painting he had seen Le Brun working on. The classical face bore a passing likeness to the King. The golden body was naked but for some draping carelessly thrown over shoulder and thigh. Apollo was leaning forward holding the reins of the four horses in one hand as they reared out of the water, a consummate horseman. Like the King, in fact, who could check his warhorse with a flick of the wrist.

He heard some yapping dogs and looked up to see Monsieur approaching him with two of his courtiers. Flight was the best defence and he turned to go, in order to avoid the embarrassment of a meeting. Monsieur was already calling out to him. He waited uneasily, half expecting an attack from Monsieur's men . . . but no, there was Monsieur standing before him, looking as amiable as if their last encounter had never happened.

'If it isn't our man of the mirrors,' said Monsieur cordially. 'I think of you each time I look in them. They are true works of art.'

'You're too kind, Monseigneur.' As Andrea made a discreet bow, he noticed Saint-Eustace's quizzical expression. He, too, as the man who must have tended Monsieur's bloodied nose on that night at Saint-Cloud, seemed unsure what to make of this unexpected friendliness.

'What do you think of the Apollo? I saw you admiring him; handsome, isn't he?'

Andrea smiled. 'It's the best sculpture in the garden.'

'Of course, the King thinks it's himself. Le Brun has convinced him of it. I don't think the face is at all like. Actually,' and here Monsieur paused and looked up at Andrea's face, 'I would say it's more like you in its classical beauty.' His eyes glinted mischievously at Andrea's discomfort. 'But of course in other ways, the King does resemble Apollo,' he continued. 'In his love of music, for instance. That's very evident. Music follows him wherever he goes, as if he's a travelling opera. And then there's his love of the chase, of women as well as deer. My good friend the Marquise de Montespan has been thoroughly ensnared.'

'I don't think I should hear this . . .' began Andrea, to discourage Monsieur's gossip, but the little man simply twinkled his black eyes at him.

'The King's appetite for love and his potency are impressive. The dear Marquise thought of herself as Venus and now she has become Ceres, as fertile as the earth. And if that's not enough, he has also got her maid with child. I ask you!'

Monsieur's eyes, diamond hard, bored into Andrea, alert for any change of expression. 'Which maid?' Andrea muttered, unable to take in his meaning.

'Why, Mademoiselle des Oeillets, of course. The one you were flirting with in the labyrinth. It's a deceptive place. Lovers think they have found private corners and don't notice the gaps in the hedges. But you should congratulate yourself on sharing similar tastes to the King.'

'With child?'

'The King only has to look at a woman and she conceives. You didn't think it was your child, did you? I hope the little minx has not been deceiving you.'

Andrea felt as if he had been winded in the stomach. He clenched his fists, experiencing an almost irresistible desire to bloody Monsieur's nose again, but that would have only resulted in Monsieur's triumph. Instead, he said, 'Excuse me, I don't wish to hear any more,' and turned on his heel, wishing fervently that he had done so in the first place. As he strode away, he heard Monsieur crowing to his friends, 'That was nice – I enjoyed that. And now it's time for dinner.'

Poisonous little viper, thought Andrea. But the poison had entered his ears and however much he told himself that Monsieur had lied out of spite, doubts festered inside him. He walked away from their meeting place until he was aware that Monsieur and his friends had left and then returned to wait, turning his back on the statue, which seemed to him now an image of arrogant power.

He saw her hurrying down the *grande allée* towards him. She was slightly out of breath as she arrived and stood there, fluttering her hand like a fan across her face and bosom. As always, she explained, just as you're about to leave something else is required of you.

'Who required it – the Marquise or the King?' he asked.

He could see a light of comprehension in her eyes but she said, looking puzzled, 'What do you mean?'

'Let's go somewhere more private,' and he walked off in the direction of the woods.

She followed after, calling, 'You're going too fast, Andrea. Wait for me.' He looked briefly over his shoulder at her and continued walking. 'Such politeness!' she exclaimed. 'What's got into you?'

Under the trees, to the west of the mirror pond, he stopped and waited for her to catch up.

She arrived, panting slightly, and said, 'What's the matter with you? I can't go running after you in my condition.'

'It's your condition I want to know more about,' said Andrea. 'Don't lie to me – have you been to bed with the King?'

'How dare you!' Claudine's eyes stared like a baleful cat. 'How can you say that? Who's been talking to you?'

'Then there's something to talk about, Claudine.'

'Not at all, I just want to know what's put this stupid idea into your head.' She stood before him, jutting her chin defiantly, her hands on her hips.

'They say you're with child by the King. Is it true?'

'Some enemy is spreading rumours about me. Of course it's not true. I'm furious that you should believe it.' She began to cry, then battered at his chest with her fists.

'*Doucement, doucement*, everyone will come running,' he said, restraining her flailing arms.

'Good, then you'll be shamed for treating me like this' and she subsided on to the ground, burying her face in her hands. He sat down beside her and waited for her sobs to ease.

'It's not true,' she said at length. 'Who told you?'

'Monsieur.'

'Monsieur! What does he know? The King tells him nothing, the Marquise would never tell.'

Andrea said softly, 'Who would, then?'

She muttered, almost to herself, 'That bitch Thianges.'

'So then there was something,' he said, even more quietly.

'Stop it!' she shouted. 'It was nothing.'

'You seem very agitated over nothing. But I can understand how it happened, Claudine. The King comes to Madame de Montespan's apartments whenever he wishes. Madame de Montespan may be out playing cards, she may be indisposed or pregnant. And you are there. What could be easier for him, for a man to whom no one says no? You couldn't refuse him, could you, Claudine?'

'It wasn't like that,' she said, beginning to cry again.

'When did it happen, Claudine?' The anger welled up in him. 'How many times? Is it still going on? Is it his child you are carrying? Or don't you know?'

'It's your child, I'm sure of it,' she said, an intransigent set to her mouth.

'I don't know that I believe you. The King thinks it is his. That's what Monsieur said.'

'Monsieur is a troublemaker and jealous of the King. You should never believe anything he says.'

'But you yourself have admitted you lay with the King. In so many words you have acknowledged it. Does Madame de Montespan know about it?'

'What does Madame care? Better me than some lady with power and influence.'

The pieces of a complex puzzle were coming together in Andrea's head. The Marquise wouldn't have cared, for Claudine was under her control and through her she could maintain control of the King. 'What does the King think of all this?' he asked.

'He thinks it's a great secret between us and that Madame would kill him if she found out.'

'As gullible as all men,' said Andrea. 'What fools we are to be taken in by women's deceit.'

Claudine leapt to her feet, her face pale with anger. 'Yes, what fools you are – you think with your balls and not your brains. And then you blame us for having indulged you. You make the rules and you expect women to follow them like nuns, but you have no intention of keeping them yourselves. In this world outside the convent, especially in this court, we have to deceive in order to survive.'

Before she turned to go, she fired one last shot. 'As it happens, it was worth the deception.'

Andrea watched her walk away down the path, her petticoats frou-frouing agitatedly around her legs. He called after her, but she did not look round. He remained for some time, leaning against the tree trunk, trying to adjust his mind to the ruination of their love.

Forty-Four

IN THE days that followed, Andrea was distracted by
thoughts of Claudine. On the one hand she was a
little whore who had been set on gulling him into
marriage, not knowing or caring whose child she was
carrying. On the other she was the victim of a corrupt
court where everyone submitted to the King's least
whim. He remembered her at the mirror pond, that
first time, looking after him, drawing him back to her
as he made to leave, or her walking towards him
through the long grass near the menagerie, a basket of
food she had taken from the court kitchen under her
arm. Of her dancing alone at the Théâtre d'Eau with
the ghosts of her past. He had known her and not
known her, for there were the times when he had not
been with her. When, for instance, she had been
carrying out her maid's duties, duties which had
included satisfying the King. At that point Andrea
would clench his fists and feel a sense of desolation.
The child, his child, so he had thought, what would
happen to it?

Then one morning he woke with the strong sense that he should see her again. For their love to end in rancour was a betrayal of what had gone before. They should part in a spirit of Christian forgiveness, rather than anger. Once again he borrowed the grey mare, Mouette, and rode off towards Versailles. It was a late summer's day, the leaves dark and heavy at the end of the season. He remembered another journey, in springtime, just as the leaves were unfurling, when everything had seemed right with the world. But it was hard to remain despondent now, with the sun shining down on him, warming his head and his back. He imagined Claudine, tearful and contrite, pleading for another chance, himself magnanimously considering it. No, he told himself, never anticipate what might happen, yet he could not help feeling a fresh optimism welling up within him.

At Versailles, no one asked you your business. There were too many workmen coming and going – carpenters with planks of wood, stone masons with their bags of tools, painters, plumbers and plasterers. There were the people who serviced the kitchens – water carriers, milkmaids, cheesemakers, fishmongers and butchers – before even considering those who were tied to the chateau – the servants, the gardeners, the pages and footmen, the courtiers. As long as you weren't in rags or a lunatic, no one took much notice.

Andrea knew the chateau well enough not to need to ask his way to Madame de Montespan's apartments. He knew they were situated on the right side of the marble courtyard and he reached them without difficulty. The door to the antechamber was open, but as he entered, he met his first obstacle. A large woman in black with a shrewish face, who had been sitting near the window, rose to her feet and said, 'Can I help you, Monsieur?' Her expression suggested that help was the last thing she intended to give.

'I am looking for Mademoiselle des Oeillets, Madame,' he said and saw her face close as if a curtain had been drawn.

'Mademoiselle des Oeillets is not here,' said the guardian of the antechamber.

'When will she be back?' he asked.

'She is no longer here. Mademoiselle des Oeillets has left the service of Madame de Montespan.' The woman enunciated her words as if Andrea might be simple-minded.

'Ah,' he said, thrown by this information. Then, as she looked impatient, 'Where may I find Mademoiselle des Oeillets, do you know?'

'I cannot tell you,' said the woman, which left unclear whether she couldn't, or wouldn't, divulge the information.

'In that case, Madame, would you be so good as to ask Madame de Montespan whether I may see her.'

'I am afraid that Madame la Marquise is indisposed.'

'I am sorry to hear that, Madame. But I am very anxious to find out the whereabouts of Mademoiselle des Oeillets. Have you any suggestion as to how I can obtain this information?'

'I suggest you write a letter,' said the woman in black conclusively.

'Thank you so much for your help, Madame. Au revoir.' Andrea turned away immediately to hide his chagrin, muttering as he left, 'You're one woman the King is unlikely to fuck.'

ON THE Grand Canal the two gondolas that the Venetian Ambassador had presented to the King were moored and beside them lounged one of the gondoliers. Andrea hailed him in Italian and said, 'I suddenly feel homesick for Venice.'

'Ah,' said the man, '*Venezia* . . . it seems a world away. I miss it too. The journey here was murderous. We had to haul these gondolas over the Alps, through the snow. Out of breath the entire time. Two of my comrades got frostbite and died. One fell down a crevasse. But there you go . . . their loss – God rest their souls – the King's gain. These gondolas are his greatest joy. They go out in them in the evening, sometimes a party of them, sometimes just himself and La Montespan, the length of the canal, all the way to the little porcelain palace to breathe in the scent of the flowers. They may be there till after midnight, I've known them spend the whole night there, listening to the nightingales . . . Well, that's their story . . .'

'How very pleasant.' Andrea smiled. 'Are they likely to take the gondolas this evening?'

The man shrugged. 'Who knows? We have to stand by, just in case, in our little Venetian sailor suits, ready when needed. I'd take you down the canal myself, but there would be hell to pay if the King or one of his guests wanted the gondola and I wasn't there.'

'It doesn't matter, I'm happy to walk.' Andrea left the Grand Canal and turned back towards the northern gardens. On the great parterre outside the chateau courtiers were drifting about, forming and re-forming groups, like so many starlings flocking together in their hunt for insects. Under the terrace was a great dark cave, outside it, mounds of earth and men shovelling earth and rubble into carts. They were bare-chested, glistening with sweat, their faces grimed with dirt. Directing the operations was Francesco Francini.

'What's this latest upheaval?' asked Andrea.

'Reservoirs, underground reservoirs the length of the terrace. To feed the parterre d'eau above. It's a catastrophe. We've taken water from the ponds to the south as well as Clagny, but it's still not enough.'

'The things you do for your fountains . . .'

'It's the battle of Versailles. The King goes off to war, we stay here and fight the elements. Victory will only come when we can have the *grandes eaux* playing all at once, each fountain at its full height. Nature enslaved to our art.'

Andrea wandered over to the *bassin* of the dragon, the fountain of which was playing at a height of around eleven metres. It would, Francini had boasted, send up a jet of nearly thirty metres if the King were present. The wounded dragon's open jaws spouted water at the heavens. Surrounding it were Cupids with raised bows and arrows, riding swans which hissed forth jets of water. According to Francini, the statue was based on the legend of Apollo killing the python, but the dragon symbolised the dark forces of disorder the King had overcome at the time of the Fronde. Now the King controlled all France in a harmony of order, down to the smallest lives. The King controls me, thought Andrea, and my life is in complete disorder as a result.

The sun was sinking low in the sky. Andrea considered what he should do next. He could write a letter to the Marquise, but he was unlikely to get a reply. He could approach her when she left her apartments, but if she was with the King he would only cause untold trouble for himself, for Claudine and possibly even the Marquise. And what was it he wanted? Something had broken that could never be mended. It was best to leave the pieces where they lay. Yet it was unfinished business and what he needed to find out, above all, was what the Marquise knew of it, and what had happened to Claudine. They were not matters that would be revealed by letter.

He heard the sound of trumpets and a commotion on the terrace. The King was making his evening appearance. He and his chosen guests made their progress down the *grande allée* to the Grand Canal, followed by a band of musicians. As the King and the Marquise were helped into their gondola, the musicians stepped on to a raft moored nearby. The strange procession moved off, the gondoliers navigating their craft smoothly along the gleaming water, the raft following behind with Monsieur Lully leading the violinists, the music filling the air with a haunting sweetness. The courtiers who had not been invited to join the party stood near the Grand Canal watching them into the distance, before drifting back to their own amusements.

Andrea was also moving away when a voice exclaimed, 'If it isn't the Chevalier of the Burning Mirror!' and a hand clasped him on the shoulder. He turned to see the Chevalier de Saint-Cyr, whose

weather-beaten face was now disfigured by a deep
livid furrow running down his right cheek. He raised
his hand to the scar, as he saw Andrea notice it, and
said, 'In the service of the King, at Maastricht. I can tell
you, there was not much left of the man who inflicted
it that day.'

'It really is the Chevalier of the Burning Mirror!'
echoed the girl who was with him.

'My niece, Mademoiselle de la Claise,' said Saint-
Cyr. 'She is entirely unimpressed by my exploits on the
battlefield, but *bouleversée* by young men who set boats
on fire.'

'My heart was in my mouth,' said the girl, who
looked no more than fifteen.

'You weren't the only one. I felt the same while I was
waiting for the wood to start burning,' said Andrea.

'Come and join us in the Bosquet de la Girandole,'
said Saint-Cyr. 'We have a table set up with a few
friends for a little fête champêtre.'

How easy to forget everything in a matter of
moments, when there is food, wine and company.
When there is an admiring, pretty face, when there are
jokes and badinage, when the night air is like a warm
caress. Andrea felt a lightness in his head from the wine
and a feeling of camaraderie with Saint-Cyr's fellow
musketeers. Time slipped by pleasantly, while the sky
darkened and the moon rose over Versailles. When
they parted company, Andrea wandered back towards
the Grand Canal to clear his head. The gondolas and
the raft were back at their moorings, and there was no
sign of the gondoliers. The temptation was too great.
In a moment he had stepped into a gondola, slipped its

rope from the moorings and cast off into the Grand Canal.

He used the long oar in the way he had learnt from the gondoliers of Venice and the wine, far from impeding him, had given him the skill that comes from blind confidence. The gondola moved through the water like a magic craft, its prow carving through the reflected moonlight. On either side of the wide expanse of the canal rows of lime trees masked the wild *bosquets* behind them, in which the nightingales sang. There must, Andrea thought, be at least a hundred of them. Close by, he could hear a counterpoint croaking of frogs. He remembered a bewitched evening at Saint-Cloud, listening to the nightingales at the manoir. Now he was gliding towards another hidden place, the porcelain palace built for the Marquise.

At the mooring post near the Trianon de Porcelaine he left the gondola. The tiles of the building gleamed in the moonlight; along the ridge of the roof, etched against the night sky, porcelain birds perched as if resting there after flight. There was a paved courtyard in front of the Trianon, with a guardroom on one side of the gate and a chapel on the other. It appeared deserted and no light was burning in the windows. Andrea moved forward quietly, until he was standing in the courtyard. No one challenged him, the nightingales continued their full-throated song and he moved closer. He could smell the scent of jasmine and followed his nose around the side of the building, through a wrought-iron gateway into the garden. There were massed wallflowers and stocks in the borders, tubs of orange trees, frangipani and tuberoses, and over every archway and bower, festoons of white jasmine, the clinging scent infiltrating his lungs and the pores of his skin. He sat for a while in the bower until he became dizzy from the heavy air. How can they stand so much sweetness, he thought, and, seeing an open window, stepped inside the miniature palace.

He was in a salon, the walls of which were tiled with porcelain. The moonlight slanted through the windows on to the polished tile floor. He was aware of some other living thing in the room with him. He heard small sounds, a rustling, a scratching, a little chuckle. Drawing aside a curtain that concealed an alcove, he met the eye, small, round and sleepy, of a blackbird, perched on a branch in an aviary. He pulled aside another curtain to reveal a second aviary containing canaries, which blinked back at him and began hopping from perch to perch. Nightingales outside, caged birds inside – there would be birdsong at any time of the day or night in the porcelain palace.

A double door at one end of the salon was half open. He moved cautiously towards it and peered inside. He could see from the hangings that it was a bedchamber and he was looking directly at the bed, its silk curtains furled back on either side. With a sudden shock, he caught sight of a man staring back at him. As he moved, the man moved and he could see now his own image in a mirror, which extended the width of the bed and about two metres above, framed like a picture by the silk.

In the bed someone stirred and he saw a mass of hair rise from the pillow. A hand drew back the hair to reveal the face of the Marquise, blinking at him in the moonlight like one of the birds. 'What's this?' she said. 'Did we have an appointment?'

At that point there was no way of quietly retreating from the room. 'Yes, we had an appointment several years ago,' said Andrea.

The Marquise sat up straight in bed, her eyes wide and startled. 'What are you doing here?'

What indeed? He could think of no answer, beyond 'I was drawn here.'

'Why did no one see you? Where was the concierge? What about the sentry in the guardroom?'

'There wasn't a soul.'

'Drunk, no doubt, the lot of them. And you, too, I suppose. Are you also drunk?'

'Not now. But I think I may be dreaming.'

The Marquise smiled. 'That's always a fine excuse for rash actions.' She looked at him as if trying to read his mind and then, 'You haven't come here with bad intentions, have you?'

'Marquise, of course not. How could I ever? You must know that.'

She lay back against the pillows, alertness lulled by the residue of sleep still drifting through her body. 'Now I remember,' she murmured. 'The woodcutter's son . . . cutting his way through the forest of thorns to rescue the princess at the manoir. And I was wandering through a dark wood, having lost my way. All so long ago . . . You've changed, Andrea, since then.'

'You're so beautiful that you frighten me.'

She laughed. 'I remember, too, your outrageous compliments. In that you have not changed. Since you're here, take a seat and tell me what you want to know. I heard from one of my ladies that you have been asking for Claudine.'

Andrea looked around for a chair that wasn't occupied by clothes. The Marquise, he could see now, was wearing only a shift. Her dress was draped carelessly over a chair, together with her discarded stockings. On the floor nearby her petticoats lay where she had stepped out of them. There was a shoe, kicked off with some force, it seemed, over by the window. Never had a bedroom looked more in need of a maid's attention. He found an embroidered tabouret and subsided on to it, his mind dazed by their unexpected meeting. The familiar scent of tuberose caught his nostrils. In the moonlight, her face was pale, but her eyes had become dark and lustrous. One hand lay on the bed sheet, slim-fingered and graceful as a perfect sculpture.

'So, our Claudine has been a naughty girl,' said the Marquise. 'I'm not at all pleased with her. Nor, I may say, with His Majesty.'

'We were to have married. I believed myself to be the father of her child. Did you know the King had been lying with your maid?'

The Marquise nodded, with some irritation. 'Yes, but only when it was too late and then one has to accept the inevitable.'

'Where is she now?'

'Do you still want to marry her, Andrea? What if such a thing were to happen again? She's in a convent, where she can discreetly await the birth of the child without anyone at court speculating as to who is the father. I think that's the best thing, in the circumstances. The other solution was for her to marry you, which she would have done if it hadn't been for Monsieur's runaway tongue. Do you still want to marry her?'

'I'm no longer sure of anything. She betrayed me.'

'Ah, the pride of a cuckolded man,' said Athénaïs, yawning and then raising a hand to stifle it. 'Well, at least you're not tearing around the state apartments denouncing the King . . .'

The bizarre quality of meeting the Marquise, alone, without the King, had been troubling Andrea and he had an uneasy sensation that at any moment they would be surprised. 'Where is the King tonight?' he asked. 'He was with you earlier.'

The Marquise sat bolt upright, her cheeks flushed with anger. 'Need you ask? He's with that dwarf with the blackened teeth. When Royalty calls, Royalty attends. Because he had promised her earlier . . . One moment we are taking in the scents of the evening in the garden. We'll stay here all night, I say. Not tonight, he says, I promised Madame la Reine. So, go then, I say, I'm staying here. If you prefer an ugly face, if you prefer a stupid mind, if you prefer the smell of rotting teeth to the scent of jasmine, then go. So he went, in rather a bad temper.'

Andrea laughed. 'Marquise, he was driven away by your sharpness, not by desire for the Queen.'

'He's got an heir, why does he still go to her? Why are those filthy religious bigots trying to turn him away from me? Andrea, even thinking of it makes me angry again. Get me that flask of wine on the chest there. Take a glass for yourself.'

Picking up the flask, half full of red wine, Andrea noticed two glasses, both used. He smiled to himself as he imagined the King taking a fortifying gulp of wine before announcing his intention of joining the Queen. But when he turned round to give the Marquise her glass he saw she had got out of bed, a dressing gown thrown over her shift, and was standing near the window. Two glistening tears rolled down her cheeks.

He paused, a glass in each hand, unsure whether the tears preceded a storm, and the image of wineglasses flying through the air came to mind. He held out the glass hesitantly. 'You have no need to cry, Athénaïs,' he said. 'You have all you ever wanted.'

She drank her wine and looked at him pensively as though she, too, was trying to understand her sorrow, as to why, inundated with love and riches, she was racked with uncertainty, as if she would wake one morning and find the palace vanished like a dream and herself on the hard ground.

'Do you remember,' he continued, 'I said I would do anything to make you happy? You said it was a dangerous promise.'

She put the glass down on the window ledge and murmured, 'So why don't you keep your promise?'

He stared at her, uncomprehending, for a moment, moved towards her, then paused, as if not believing what she had just said. She smiled at his tremulous uncertainty and slid her arms round his neck, drawing him to her. Her mouth opened under his, tasting of wine. Her hands roved around his chest and inside his shirt, like fire on his skin. She whispered, 'Keep your promise. Make me happy.' Then she dropped her dressing gown from her shoulders, raised her shift over her head and stood naked in front of him.

Afterwards he could only remember a blur of passion. The urgency of his blood coursing through his body, her limbs entangled with his, their devouring mouths. Then the extraordinary sight, as he was on his knees, astride her, raising her body towards him to immerse himself in her flesh, of seeing his face suddenly in the mirror, convulsed with desire. As they rose and fell, one moment above her, the next below, the twin lovers in the glass behind the bed rose and fell with them, until they lay bathed in each other's sweat, exhausted and at rest, out of range of their reflections.

'So, are you happy?' he said at last.

'Yes.'

'Then so am I. Athénaïs, if I were to die at this moment I would be happy.'

They lay entwined in the bed and he laughed at the memory of their reflected passion. 'I never imagined the King would find such a use for mirrors . . .'

'Ssh.' For a moment he thought she might be angry at what he had said but then she raised her hand to silence him. 'I heard one of the guards coughing. They do that to show they're on watch. Go out through the garden and keep well away from the canal. You'd better go now, before it gets light.'

Andrea pulled his clothes on and stooped to kiss her, until she pushed him away. 'Every moment you're here gets more dangerous,' she said. 'You must go.' She walked with him to the door by which he had entered and said, 'Through the gate at the end of the garden.'

'We'll meet again?'

She smiled. 'Tonight never happened, Andrea. But I'll think of you always, I'll remember the man who kept his promise.'

The perfumed garden heightened the dizziness of his senses. He found the gate and opened it quietly. He could hear voices near the canal and as he left the shelter of the garden wall, he saw two guards examining the gondola. He edged towards the woods, praying to whichever god existed to protect men from the consequences of their sins.

PART THREE

Toads and Diamonds

Versailles and Paris
1675–80

Forty-Five

BENEATH THE mask of humanity, the face of the beast. Le Brun likes the phrase. It illustrates perfectly what he wants to say in his painting. The humane nobility of the victors, the face of the beast in the vanquished. You can see it in the eyes, in the tortured faces, the mouths stretched in horror. Colbert examines the drawings for the *grande galerie* and makes a few suggestions. As the envoys of the vanquished will no doubt be arriving in Versailles for an audience in the future, he writes, it might be as well not to render the defeated so abject. He should emphasise the glory of the King without humiliating his foes. Reluctantly, Le Brun modifies his drawings.

The Dutch war has dragged on for too many years and is draining the nation's finances, but it's no reason to stop building. There is in the meantime another war going on, no less than the war between God and the devil. That snake in the grass, that turncoat whom Athénaïs had plucked from obscurity and introduced to riches, that widow of the third rate-poet, Scarron, is trying to undermine her position with the King. Athénaïs has a shrewd idea of what she is up to – the conversations with the King about his children have now strayed into the realms of religion and her erstwhile friend has been subtly pointing out the impossibility of Louis being the most Christian King of France while at the same time being a double adulterer.

It is a war that, like the Dutch war, flares up and dies down according to the energy and commitment of the participants. The Marquise uses her armoury of weapons to secure her position. She demands a home befitting her and her children, and the young architect in a hurry, Hardouin Mansart, is called upon to design it. The new palace rises at Clagny, near the gates of Versailles. Athénaïs diverts her energy from battling with La Scarron to supervising several thousand workmen on the house and gardens. It is a declaration of power, but it is not enough to restore the faltering passion of the King. Other weapons are necessary. She recalls Mademoiselle des Oeillets from the convent.

So, on a chilly day in early spring, a chastened Claudine arrives to join the household again, while her baby is farmed out in a nearby village. During her months at the convent her clothes have been adapted to conform to modesty, the bosom subdued by starched linen, the hair hidden under a linen bonnet, like a Dutchwoman. Underneath the starch she is simmering with anger, but for a different reason from her mistress. She was so close to marriage and then it was ruined by none other than the King. She doesn't feel any more well-disposed towards him than Madame de Montespan is to the Widow Scarron, particularly as on the one or two occasions they happen to meet, he maintains a courteous but distant façade, as if the man who had tumbled her on to the bed were unknown to him. Well, what can you expect from a most Christian King?

The Marquise is angry, too, at the presumption of the Scarron to call God to her aid. The devil has been effective in the past and he will be again in future. Claudine will be her proxy in a mass and also purchase the necessary powders to fan the King's diminishing ardour. There is not a moment to be lost, for God is in the ascendant and Louis, no doubt encouraged by the Widow, has ended carnal relations during Lent. She has to be seen to agree that this is the right and godly thing to do, so she retires to Clagny to pray, fast and have long discussions with her confessor.

THE AIR in Paris, despite the newly paved streets and the work of the street cleaners appointed by La Reynie, was acrid from the urine of animals and people that soaked into the earth under the cobbles. The smell was worse in the summer but even in March, Claudine had to hold a scented handkerchief to her face, particularly near those secluded corners beloved by pissers. And the smell at Madame Voisin's was enough to make you gag. The tribe of cats had multiplied. They were everywhere, on tables and chairs, prowling along windowsills, scratching for fleas, yowling and mewing like the devil's creatures.

Madame Voisin received Claudine in her consulting

room like an old friend. She enquired after the health of Madame de Montespan and smiled with sugary tenderness at Claudine. Mademoiselle des Oeillets was always most welcome, she said, whether she was there for the Marquise or on her own account. What help could she give on this occasion? Absolute discretion assured.

Discretion was important, said Claudine. They needed powders for love, powders for potency. In the strictest secrecy.

'Of course. But there is something else as well?' suggested Madame Voisin.

'Madame la Marquise wants a mass said for her. And there are also some other powders. Those that do harm.'

'You mean a *poudre de succession*?' Madame Voisin's face was impassive.

'Not too strong. Just to teach a lesson. To give someone who did me wrong a very nasty headache, for instance.'

'You have to be careful in measuring such powders, or it will be more than a nasty headache. And the mass, when will the Marquise be free to take part?'

'She has asked for me to be her proxy. And to do it as soon as possible, there's not a moment to be lost.'

'Father Mariette is not here, he's at Saint-Séverin, but I have staying with me the Abbé Guibourg, who is a master of these ceremonies. He will need a little time to prepare.'

Claudine placed the Marquise's purse of gold louis on the table. 'It's a matter of urgency,' she said.

Afterwards, Claudine wished she had waited for

Father Mariette. The Abbé Guibourg was of repugnant appearance, with jowls that sagged either side of his fleshy mouth, nostrils eaten either by disease or by snuff, and a wall eye which reminded her of a goat. He smelt like a goat, too. The ceremony was performed in the chapel adjoining Madame Voisin's house by the Abbé, assisted by a depraved-looking choirboy.

The Abbé required her to undress, to strengthen, he said, the power of the mass. Two braziers burned by the altar, which was draped in a black cloth embroidered with gold stars, pyramids and tongues of flame. Claudine lay on the altar, thinking, the things I do for Madame. She heard the Abbé intoning in a strange language. She heard the names of Astaroth and Asmodeus. She lay there, her eyes closed, her mind hazed by the wine Madame Voisin had given her beforehand, for courage. She heard the Abbé's breath, an old man's wheeze of air passages impeded by phlegm. He hawked and spat close to her head. Charming, thought Claudine. She heard the sound of a hand rubbing against cloth, quicker and quicker. She opened her eyes. It was as she had suspected, the Abbé was clutching his member through his robes, a lascivious expression on his face as he stared at her breasts.

Claudine sat up, her mind suddenly clear of the wine, and said, 'I'm not having you ejaculating over me, you dirty old man. One spurt and I'm off.'

'Please, Mademoiselle, you're breaking the spell,' protested the Abbé, his erection subsiding instantly.

'Father Mariette managed it without recourse to his cock. Straight mass, or no money.'

'As you wish, I hope it will be as efficacious.' The Abbé muttered something to the choirboy, who poured dark-red liquid into a silver chalice. He held the chalice over her body, said another prayer very rapidly and raised the chalice to his lips. She caught the smell of it, as of an unclean butcher.

After the ceremony she emerged into the street outside Madame Voisin's feeling tearful and abused, in no mood to return to the Marquise. She lingered uncertainly for a few minutes, then she saw a pony and trap that was for hire and asked the driver to take her to the faubourg Saint-Antoine. They agreed a price and she sat back against the wooden seat, jolted as the pony trotted over the cobbles. She had not seen Andrea since that day at Versailles, but now it seemed only one person could be of comfort to her, the man she still thought of as her lover. At the mirror factory they told her he was out on business. She waited for an hour, but the day was beginning to draw in and she had to be back at Versailles before dark. She left a note and departed for the Louvre where she caught the last coach back to Versailles. Whatever the devil may have done for the Marquise, she thought, he has not served me very well.

Andrea returned an hour later to find her hastily scrawled note. Like all her letters, it was mispelt and hard to read. But the message was clear enough. She was frightened and she needed to see him. There had been some unpleasant business at Madame Voisin's. She begged him to get in touch, to write or come to see her. He could find her at Versailles, she was back with Madame.

Andrea thought about it for a while. He had, as a result of his night with the Marquise, woven a web of deception around himself. He was not sure he could dissemble if he were confronted with both women and the behaviour of either in such circumstances was unpredictable. Yet Claudine was asking for help and not to reply would take a hardened heart. He was aware the callous indifference of the court was seeping into his soul and to ignore her would be an acceptance of their ways, a denial of those letters he had penned to his *gattina birichina*. False pride was holding him back, he told himself, combined with a fear of running into more trouble. He wrote the letter, sealed it and put it among the despatches from the mirror factory to Versailles.

Two days later the letter had arrived at Versailles but had not reached its addressee. It remained in the pile for the attention of Monsieur de Louvois's postal censor, marked with a query.

Forty-Six

A LARGE and boisterous party from the court attended the execution of the Marquise de Brinvilliers – first beheaded, then burned, for crimes that everyone gossiped about with delighted horror. It was the talk of the summer of 1676. Her father and two brothers had died from poisoning, her husband's health was wrecked. She had experimented, too, on people she visited in hospitals. Under torture she had confessed it, itemising the poisons she had used – antimony, arsenic and a herb from Italy highly recommended by her apothecary. Before she was taken to the place of execution, she wept from the agony she had endured at the hands of La Reynie's interrogators and from the sheer injustice of it. After all, she said, most people of quality did what she had done when it suited them. It seemed unfair she should be the one to be singled out for punishment.

Le Brun had attended the execution and had drawn a portrait of Madame de Brinvilliers just before her death. He brought it in his portfolio to Versailles for the interest of the King. It was standing on an easel in the middle of the Mars drawing room. Andrea looked at the pale upturned eyes, the mouth half open and downturned in her misery. 'It's like the expression of your soldiers being killed in battle,' he said.

'It's always the same,' said Le Brun, 'the agony and the disbelief that this can be happening to you. We prepare ourselves with priests and prayers, yet we cannot comprehend the state of non-existence.'

'But after death we go on to heaven or to purgatory,' said Andrea.

'You're a simple soul, Monsieur de la Glace. As for me, immortality is in my work. That at least I can be sure of.'

'Which is why the King is building Versailles.'

Le Brun looked at him with derision. 'The King knows his devoutness will gain him immortality. He is building Versailles for the glory of France. The King and France are so intertwined that one cannot be separated from the other. Every Frenchman carries inside himself a piece of the King. You're a foreigner, you wouldn't understand.'

'I've been in France for over ten years now. I think I may have a rough idea.'

Le Brun laughed. 'You're not under the impression you've become French, are you?'

'I no longer feel entirely Italian.'

'Well, there you are, neither one thing nor the other, floating in the ether of unbelonging. But I can tell you one thing,' he added decisively, 'you will never be one of us.'

'The master speaks,' said Andrea. 'I bow to your superior French reason.'

Le Brun had returned to the easel and the anguished face of the Marquise de Brinvilliers. After contemplating her for a while he said, 'Isn't it curious that in the throes of agony and ecstasy we have a similar expression? The darts of love can make us look as if we are undergoing torture. How fortunate we can't see ourselves at such moments, don't you agree, Monsieur de la Glace? What has happened to your little maid, by the way?'

'There was a falling out.' Andrea had turned his face away from the observant eye of the artist.

'So that's why we see you so rarely, nowadays. *Tant pis*. They're not here at the moment, anyway. The Marquise has taken herself off for a cure at Bourbon-l'Archambault. She departed with her niece in a coach and eight, with six of her women following in another coach and eight, a mule train of luggage and a dozen or so horsemen. A truly royal procession, like a real Queen of France. She will no doubt return more beautiful than ever – in the full summer of her reign, with her reconquest of the King. Her power over Louis is unearthly. I can see it emanating from her, like some supernatural radiance.'

Le Brun smiled at Andrea's studied indifference. 'A falling out with the maid, eh? You're very close over your matters of the heart. Come and have a look at the terrace, they've started building the *galerie*, to house your mirrors. That will be your bit of immortality.'

FROM TIME to time Andrea wondered at Claudine's silence after he had sent the letter. There had been nothing in it that could have offended her, but maybe the Marquise had seen it first and destroyed it. Or perhaps Claudine had thought better of seeing him again. The court had now moved to Fontainebleau for the autumn's hunting. It was a clear message to him. Their lives were swallowed up by the complexities of court life, to the exclusion of outsiders.

From time to time, he also thought about the Marquise and the night at the Trianon de Porcelaine. He wondered if she thought about him, whether one day he would receive a letter from her. But there was only silence, which in itself was another message – the voracious emptiness in her which could only be filled by all the trappings of royalty was greater than any love she might have felt for him. That night, she had said, never happened, though the disturbing reflections lived on in his mind.

At the mirror factory, orders were coming in ever-increasing numbers. First there was Royalty, then the *grands seigneurs*, then the minor nobility, the *grande bourgeoisie* and so on, until it seemed *le tout* Paris had to have mirrors on their walls. The factory took on two more apprentices, whom Andrea trained. One of the best mirror makers, who had been there since the Venetians had left, became ill with the same symptoms that had afflicted Guillaume and was pensioned off. He was reluctant to leave his place of work and would sometimes return, rambling incoherently. As he didn't interfere with the running of the factory, no one took much notice until he went home again.

Andrea began working on a new experiment, about which Monsieur du Noyer was sceptical. Suppose, he said, you could cast glass on a flat surface, instead of blowing it. Eventually you would be able to make a large mirror all of one piece. Du Noyer thought it was doomed to fail. How could you keep glass at the right temperature, if you were spreading it out over a large surface? That was what they would discover by experiment, said Andrea. If we succeed, we will ensure the supremacy of our factory against all rivals.

We don't need to worry about competition, said du Noyer, as long as Monsieur Colbert is Minister and we retain our royal warrant. But you may go ahead with the experiment, provided the orders don't fall behind.

A metal tray was constructed, with sides to hold in the molten glass and a roller fixed to the sides to distribute the glass evenly over the surface. It would have worked with a pliable material like clay but molten glass was too volatile to changes of temperature. The glass cooled and cracked as it was rolled. There were uneven waves as the pace of the roller varied. Du Noyer shook his head over the complete waste of time.

'Have patience, Monsieur,' said Andrea. 'How many years do you think it took before men learnt the art of glass blowing? Eventually this will work and then no one will believe there was any other way of making mirrors.'

'I'm not prepared to wait until the next century. In the meantime we have to prepare the mirrors for the *grande galerie*. Each mirror has to be perfection itself. Each will be inspected by the King. You will be far better employed by putting aside experiments for the future and concentrating on the job in hand.'

Andrea complied, up to a point, but continued his

quest in his spare time. He rejected du Noyer's caution but he himself was no longer the defiant young man who had clashed with his father. He could see the need for harmony between tradition and innovation. One could not exist successfully without the other.

Forty-Seven

THE FILES at the office of Nicolas de La Reynie were growing thicker by the day. Ever since the Brinvilliers case two years before, he had been gathering evidence of poisoning. There was a whole network of murderers operating under various guises, as apothecaries, fortune tellers, alchemists, purveyors of blessings and masses. A careless word by one of them to an agent of La Reynie's had been enough to set the process of inquiry under way. Those arrested and interrogated were quick to blame someone else, if they thought that might end their torture. La Reynie sat in his office, head in his hands, in despair at human nature. Lives were being bought and sold all over Paris. No one was safe. The man who brought light to the darkness, whose system of watch had frightened the criminals off the street, now saw that the real danger to the citizens was in their own homes, among their relatives. As the inquiry continued, the roll-call of names grew more illustrious. From Madame the butcher's wife who was tired of her husband's brutality, to Madame la Comtesse, whose ailing and very rich uncle was most inconveniently refusing to die. He was moving closer to the circle that surrounded the King himself. How truly ironic, La Reynie wrote to Louvois, that the latter-day Garden of Eden the King was creating at Versailles harboured serpents.

As far as Athénaïs was concerned, the only serpent in the garden was the Widow Scarron, now Marquise de Maintenon, taking her name from the estate she had bought with the King's largesse. La Maintenon, she knew, was pouring poison into the King's ears with her constant homilies on the joys of morality. Athénaïs had dominated Louis with her body, the Maintenon sought control of his mind. Madame Voisin's powders seemed to be losing their effect. Once they had restored the King to vigour, now they seemed only to give him violent headaches. The Marquise was feeling the cold draught of insecurity, as if she were finally losing the power within her. Claudine was less than helpful, dressing her mistress's hair carelessly while she prattled on about the actors in the Paris theatre companies. You might have thought her early stage experience would have put her off, but no, on she went, while combing the Marquise's hair, about this actress or that and how she would have played it differently. Athénaïs told herself to be patient, the girl was restless because she had messed up her marriage chances.

The terrace was now enclosed with a great vaulted roof, forty metres high and seventy-three metres long.

The arched windows were still open to the elements, in order to disperse the dust of the building works. Le Brun's men had begun painting the scenes of Louis's victories at one end and would work steadily through the seventy-three metres to the other, section by section. Already the King was bringing visitors round to see what was essentially still a building site. The carpenters carried on hammering and sawing, the masons chipping away, the plasterers plastering, the gilders gilding, their work more important to them than the splendour of the spectators.

'You would think we were running a theatre,' complained Le Brun. 'Everyone wants to come and gawp at men working, as if we were some kind of circus. And I don't need any more helpful hints and suggestions – as if these cretins can judge anything when the place is rigged out with scaffolding. They've been peering at your mirrors, you know, imagining they can see flaws when it's simply that the glass is covered with dust and greasy fingermarks. I'd kick the whole lot out if only the King would let me.'

Andrea had come to see the first completed mirror arch. Soaring from floor to the swagged cornice, like a great silver window that reflected the room and the light pouring in through the real window opposite, it seemed to have an almost otherworldly glow. Each mirror was born in the furnace, given life through the breath of the glass blower, given sight by the amalgam of mercury, ground and polished to perfection. The spirit of the mirror maker was alive in each glass. Andrea thought of the mirrored windows stretching the length of the gallery, one after another, all seventeen ablaze with the sun. 'It will be the greatest sight in Europe,' he said.

'But of course,' said Le Brun. 'It has the éclat of genius – mine, the King's, even yours, my dear André. It will astonish the foreigners more than all the King's glorious victories on the battlefield.'

Andrea smiled. Which mirror was the work of which man could not be guessed at, yet somewhere among them was one he had worked on, after he had learned of Claudine's betrayal – one of the glasses over which he had cursed again and again, 'May the King see himself as he really is.'

AT THE end of the great courtyard of Versailles the road led to Paris and Saint-Cloud in one direction, to Saint-Germain in another. Andrea had ridden in the direction of Paris for only a few minutes when he saw an open carriage drawn by six horses on its way to Versailles. He waited by the side of the road for it to pass. He could see three people in it, two women and a boy seated in the middle. One of the women was Madame de Montespan. As they drew nearer he noticed the changes that the last five years had wrought. She had put on a lot of weight. Her face was still beautiful, but the neck and chin had thickened, obscuring the curve of the throat. She was dressed in blue, with a lavish quantity of lace. Beside her was the boy, slim and pale, around nine years old. Next to him sat the other woman, in black, a silver crucifix glinting on her bosom. The two women were perfectly still, apart from the jolting of the carriage, staring in front of them. The boy likewise looked ahead, an uneasy expression on his face. Now Andrea could see the faces of all three clearly. The woman in black had well-defined features and hooded eyelids over dark, intelligent eyes. There was an air of coolness and self-possession about her, in contrast to Madame de Montespan. As the carriage approached, Athénaïs glanced in his direction and he felt the shock of those azure eyes again. But the emotions they conveyed were so different from her former radiance that he was shocked anew. The Marquise was desperate. She was angry, she was defeated and she was afraid. He raised his hat, for he had seen a glimmer of recognition in the midst of her inner turmoil, but the carriage had passed by.

Andrea rode on to Paris, his thoughts similarly in turmoil. The sight of the boy, who must have been the Marquise's eldest son by Louis, had raised in him an almost visceral longing for a son, for his son, for Claudine's child to be his. By now he must be around five years old and would be showing evidence of his parentage. But Claudine's silence indicated that the King was indeed the father, and that Louis had acknowledged it and made the necessary arrangements for his upbringing. He thought back to the passing carriage and the expression on the Marquise's face. It was of disbelief at what was happening to her. Like the princess in the enchanted wood for whom diamonds dropped from the leaves of the trees. And then she wanted more and shook the magic tree, and the diamonds turned to toads.

BACK AT the mirror factory, one of the men told him, with an air of concealed excitement, that Monsieur du Noyer was asking for him. Andrea wondered why such a routine enquiry should have produced this frisson, but went to du Noyer's office in an easy frame of mind. Du Noyer was sitting at his desk, examining an order book. As he looked up from his work he said, 'Come in and sit down, please. Would you close the door behind you?'

Andrea knew now that something was wrong, but although he felt uneasy at du Noyer's behaviour, his conscience was clear. Du Noyer sat back in his chair and looked at him silently for a moment. Then he said, 'Some officers from Monsieur de La Reynie were asking for you earlier. Have you any idea why they should do so?'

'It's a mystery to me,' said Andrea. 'What did they want?'

'They questioned me at length about the death of Guillaume and about the illness of Maurice. They wanted to know the symptoms and what I thought had caused them. Then they started to ask me about you – about your temperament, your relations with the men, whether you fell out with them, whether you went to mass, what you had been experimenting on in your studio.'

Andrea looked at him in amazement, at the realisation that he was a man under suspicion.

'Apparently Maurice has been talking in the taverns to anyone who would listen, making accusations against you. He said you had been poisoning him and that you had also killed Guillaume.'

'You don't believe it, surely?'

'I told them Maurice was mad and it was all a figment of his diseased mind. They suggested he was mad because of the poison. They kept coming back to you and to your being Italian, as if foreigners made them doubly suspicious.'

Andrea felt a chill to his heart. To have lived so long in France and to be under suspicion for not being French was an affront. 'There are many Italians living here,' he said, 'helping to enrich France with their talents. Are we all to be treated as criminals?'

'I'm only reporting what they said, not agreeing with them,' said du Noyer. 'You must know that Paris is seething with rumours about this poisoning business. They have arrested dozens of people and now they're following up every lead. They asked whom you knew at court and whether you had any liaisons there. Then they told me to say nothing to you and that they would return.'

Andrea gripped the sides of his chair, as the room seemed to sway around him. Du Noyer's face had become blurred and indistinct. He heard him say, 'Are you all right?'

'Just shocked,' said Andrea, trying to breathe steadily. The idea of being questioned by La Reynie's men was unnerving. At what point did the interrogation become torture? 'Thank you for telling me,' he said. 'It's as well to be prepared. Was there anything else?'

'No, that was all and I'm very sorry,' said du Noyer. 'I'm sure there are no grounds for suspicion, but in this present atmosphere of hysteria, anyone can find themselves accused.'

Andrea rose to his feet, saying, with a faint smile, 'I'll have to lie down for a while to recover.'

'I'm sorry,' du Noyer said again and then, as Andrea

reached the door, 'By the way, does the name Madame Voisin mean anything to you?'

'Never heard of her,' said Andrea.

'That's good. Apparently they thought you might have had some dealings with her. It's a nasty business, going right to the centre of the court.'

As Andrea left the office, suddenly the memory came back to him. Madame Voisin – the woman with the cats. Claudine coming out of her consulting room with little packages. He had been there, of course. He remembered the name now and a chill went through his body, as though a cold steel trap was closing on him.

Forty-Eight

CLAUDINE HAS finally made the great leap. It was, in the end, quite simple. She got one of the actors to make an appointment for her with the theatre manager at the Guenegaud, where Molière's company had found their home since the playwright's death. She recited one of Doriana's speeches from *Tartuffe*. The manager examined his nails as if they were of more interest. Then she sang a song from *George Dandin*. He smiled sympathetically and, before she reached the last note, he asked, 'What else do you do?'

'I can keep costumes in good repair, remove stains, make alterations.'

'Very useful.' He sighed. 'What else?'

'I can play the greatest Marquise in the land,' and, as he continued to smile patronisingly, she launched into a tempestuous scene. It was almost word for word what she had heard from Athénaïs on that occasion when she had ruined her dress. The manager laughed. 'No prizes for guessing who that might be. You can join us,

Ma'mselle, as long as you look after the costumes better than you did for Madame de Montespan.'

Abandoning the shelter of the court, though, was harder than she had expected. The Marquise had given her money, she had a pension for her child from the King, but life outside was a challenge. It was difficult to know who was honest, who was likely to gyp her. She moved from one lodging after the landlady had made extortionate demands, from another after she realised someone had been searching her room. Eventually she found a place north of the Palais Royal. It was a clean and well-kept house, where the landlady was kind to both her and the child.

Her son was now five years old. He had cried when she had removed him from his foster-parents near Versailles and, for the first month in Paris, the fetid air had disagreed with him. The landlady's maid helped look after him while Claudine was away at the theatre, but there were times when he was left alone and she would have a sudden sickening vision, while she was standing at the side of the stage with the prompt book, of him climbing on to a window ledge, or wandering out into the street to be kidnapped. Her landlady had told her of the increasing number of child abductions, for slave-running, black mass sacrifices, even for cannibalism. Claudine shivered at this talk. Clearly, Paris was unsafe and unhealthy for a child. It would be better to send him back to Versailles.

Letters sometimes arrived from the Marquise with orders for scented gloves or ribbons, and occasionally a commission for some more powders from Madame Voisin. Then one day she received a letter that obviously had been written in some urgency. Would Claudine immediately go to Madame Voisin for as large an order as possible. Immediately, wrote the Marquise, meant the instant she had read the letter.

As if I am still your maid, thought Claudine. But her years of service had conditioned her to comply almost unquestioningly with her demands. She told the landlady's maid she would be out for several hours and left for Madame Voisin's. It was a journey she had made several times during the past few months. On each occasion Madame Voisin had treated her almost like a daughter. Those who have psychic powers, she said, have a bond. She had even once suggested that Claudine might like to go into partnership with her. 'Not as long as that old goat of an Abbé is around,' Claudine had said.

On this day, as she drew near to the villa, she sensed that something was wrong. The shutters, instead of being fastened back, swung to and fro in the wind. Instinct told her to turn back, but then she saw some of the cats outside, mewing disconsolately. Madame Voisin's favourite, a pretty white cat, ran towards her, as if recognising a friend. Claudine picked her up and the cat nestled in her arms, looking up at her with a green gaze. 'Mignonne, you have eyes like mine,' she said. It seemed, from their miaowing, that none of the cats had been fed. The front door was half open and she walked inside to find herself face to face with a man in the blue uniform of one of Monsieur de La Reynie's officers.

'Come in, Ma'mselle,' he said. 'We were expecting you.'

There were men all over the house, ransacking it like an invading army. The officer who had confronted her on the doorstep kept asking her the same questions. Name? Occupation? Reason for being there? How long had she known Madame Voisin? Eventually another officer, who had been listening, interrupted, 'We know all that. You had better come with us for further questioning.'

She sat very still in the closed carriage, the two officers opposite, watching her, she thought, like two cats that had caught a mouse and were savouring the idea of playing with it. The one she had met on the doorstep was thickset, dark and brutal-looking, the other, fair, thin-lipped and supercilious. They looked as if they worked as a team. She saw, when the carriage drew up, that they were in a courtyard and she judged from the distance they had travelled that it must be near the Palais Royal.

In the room where they took her, she was overcome by an urgent need to empty her bladder. One of them produced a chamber pot and she asked them to leave the room for a moment. 'You're not at court now,' the dark one said. They stood in the open doorway chatting to each other while she relieved herself. The thin-lipped one turned while she was adjusting her petticoats and said, 'Is Ma'mselle quite ready for us?'

Then the questioning began. Why was she at Madame Voisin's? What were the properties of the powders? How long had she known Madame Voisin? How often had the Marquise seen Madame Voisin? It was clear that they already knew a certain amount and that they were looking for confirmation of their suspicions.

Madame de Montespan's letter to her, she learnt, had passed through the office of Monsieur de Louvois, as did all post to and from Versailles. Which was why they had been expecting her. Madame Voisin, Father Mariette, the Abbé Guibourg and various other confederates were already under arrest, and were beginning to talk. So, they suggested, Mademoiselle des Oeillets would make it a great deal easier for herself if she were to confess all she knew rather than oblige them to interrogate her more intensely.

Claudine repeated her replies to the questions again and again. The powders were nothing more than those relating to women's monthly problems, or to do with morning sickness. The doctors' remedies of bleeding and purges were too violent for many women, so they had recourse to Madame Voisin's herbal medicines.

'Would you call spleen of a toad herbal?' asked the thin-lipped officer, and the dark one said, 'If this was all to do with women's problems, why was the King given these powders?'

'I know nothing about that. I never gave the King anything,' she said.

The thin lips parted into an unexpectedly broad smile, showing tobacco-stained teeth. 'Nothing at all, Ma'mselle? That's not what we hear.'

The Marquise had taken part in a black mass with the Abbé Guibourg, stated the dark one.

That's not true, Claudine said immediately. She has never met the Abbé Guibourg.

'The Abbé thinks differently,' said the officer. 'He thinks he performed a mass over her naked body.'

'Completely untrue,' said Claudine. 'The Abbé is lying. And I have never met him either.'

The men looked at each other. Then the thin-lipped one said, 'It's just as well you haven't met him, Ma'mselle, for he's not very pleasant. These masses he performs, do you know where the blood comes from?'

'I know nothing about masses.'

'There is a trade in babies, live or stillborn, and young children. I'm sure you have heard about it. Some of them end up with the Abbé. He cuts their throats and drains them of blood for the blasphemous chalice. Why, Ma'mselle, you're not looking well.'

Claudine had half fallen from her stool, retching. 'I have a child of my own,' she said eventually.

'So you must know how important it is that monsters like the Abbé should not be at large. We must work together to make sure such people are caught and punished, Ma'mselle. We believe you're not telling us all you know.'

'I have nothing more to tell. I was sent to Madame Voisin for powders for Madame de Montespan, for her health. That's all.'

The two men conferred together for a moment, then the dark one turned to her and said, 'You have an Italian lover. He used to visit Madame Voisin with you.'

'Only to keep me company. And I haven't seen him for some years. He's no longer my lover.'

'Aah,' said the thin one in mock sympathy, 'what a shame.'

'After he visited Madame Voisin with you, there was some nasty business at the mirror factory,' said the dark one. 'He goes to see poisoners and then workers at the factory die. Odd kind of coincidence, isn't it?'

'He thought it was to do with the mercury. He was extremely distressed about the men.'

'Poisoners weep many tears. It's part of their subterfuge.'

Claudine began to cry. One of the officers, she didn't see which, was humming a tune to himself. 'Where's your Italian now?' the dark one asked suddenly.

'I haven't seen him for years. I suppose he's still at the mirror factory. Why don't you go and ask him?'

'Don't worry, we're on the trail. Monsieur de Louvois is taking a particular interest. He doesn't much like foreigners bringing their criminal activities into France.'

The two men seemed to have become bored with their questioning. The dark one yawned loudly, the thin one stared at the ceiling. There was silence for a moment and Claudine thought of cats pretending lack of interest in their prey, waiting for the mouse to scuttle away, before they pounced again.

'Time for dinner,' said the dark one. 'What shall we do with her?'

'Excuse me, Messieurs,' said Claudine. 'I have a child waiting for me at home and he also has to eat.'

'You should have thought of that earlier,' said the thin one. 'But we'll be kind, for the sake of the kid. We know where you live, anyway, so don't try and skip off or we'll have you slammed up in jail.'

'Thank you so much,' said Claudine, moving towards the door before they could change their minds. '*Au revoir, Messieurs – et bon appétit.*'

★

ANDREA HAD returned to his lodgings, a couple of streets from the mirror factory, rather than eat with the men. Since La Reynie's officers had arrived there was an uneasiness between him and his colleagues. Du Noyer assured him that no one believed the rumours, but his imagination was already hearing whispers behind his back. Of course, that's what Italians are good at, isn't it? Poison is their favourite weapon.

He sat by the window of the salon de jour, which overlooked the street, and read the letter that had arrived from Venice two weeks before. It was from his brother, Federico. Their father had been taken ill, suffering an apoplexy that had nearly killed him. He had partially recovered and walked with difficulty, his left side semi-paralysed. He was determined to get back to the factory, but the family feared for his health. And he had begun to talk of Andrea, whom he had refused to mention for years. There had been tears in his eyes and, though he was too proud to say it, Federico was sure he was missing him. It was like that, as a life began to draw to a close, one wanted to mend the rifts of the past.

Andrea felt a prickling of tears in his eyes as he read the letter. He had written back as soon as he had received it, but had said nothing to du Noyer, for he remained undecided as to what he should do. If he returned to Venice, would he ever see France again? He looked down at the bustling scene in the street outside. A coach and a cart were trying to pass each other and, though there was enough space, an acrimonious dispute over precedence had erupted between the drivers. The clatter of hooves and steel-rimmed wheels over cobbles, the shouts of the street hawkers and the water sellers, the charged atmosphere of too many people crammed into the same space, had all infiltrated his blood. And then there was the atmosphere at court, charged in a different way, from too many people circling around the dazzling centre, moths around a flame. The intoxicating sense of being present at the creation of the most splendid palace in the world, of being among great artists and masters of craftsmen; and at the very centre of the palace, of which he had become a part – the *grande galerie*, progressing mirror by mirror. What he felt about the King mattered less than what he felt about the *galerie*. To leave before the seventeenth mirror was complete would be to miss creating the wonder of a lifetime.

Life here in Paris, life there in Venice, ran through his mind as he looked out of the window. He noticed a woman hurrying along the street, her head obscured by the hood of her cloak. She disappeared from view as she passed under the window and then he heard voices downstairs, footsteps on the wooden stairs, a knock. He opened the door and saw Claudine standing there.

'May I come in?' she asked.

For a moment he could do no more than stare at her. At the feline eyes, the pale skin, the mouth that he had known so well, its provocative little smile, now with an uncertain tremble to it. Instinctively he stepped forward to embrace her and then remembered the restraint of five years of silence.

She looked at him questioningly and stepped into the room. 'May I sit down? I'm tired from the journey,' she said.

He showed her to the chair by the window and sat

on the window seat beside it. 'Claudine,' he said. 'I can't believe it. Five years there was nothing from you, and now – what brings you here?'

'As I recall it, there was nothing from you,' she said. 'I left you a note – you must remember that. You never wrote back or tried to see me.'

'I did write – I wrote to you at Versailles and you never replied,' he protested. 'I had to draw my own conclusions.'

'The letter never arrived,' she said. 'You can't trust the post at Versailles, I've since found out. There are half a dozen little snoopers who read everything. I assumed you were still angry with me.'

'I was.' With the hood of her cloak down and her face towards the daylight, he could see the shadows under her eyes and the tired lines round her mouth. Yet despite that she had not changed as greatly as the Marquise. She was not yet defeated.

He began to say, 'Tell me what has happened to you since . . .' but she stopped him.

'Andrea, later. You're in great danger. They're going to arrest you.'

'Who are? Why?'

'Haven't you heard of the affair of the poisons? Don't you know about the arrests?'

'I know that one of our workers, who is mad, has accused me of poisoning, and that La Reynie's men suspect me because I'm Italian and was seen going into Madame Voisin's house. I'm angry that being a foreigner makes me guilty in their eyes.'

'It's not only that,' she said. 'There is something at the core of it which concerns Louvois. He is undermining Colbert and he's using every weapon at hand. That's why he's taking such a close interest in the case. Some of Colbert's friends at court are implicated in the poisonings. One of Colbert's daughters is married to a nephew of Madame de Montespan.'

Andrea shrugged. 'What have Monsieur Colbert's friends at court to do with me?'

She looked exasperated. 'The mirror factory is Colbert's achievement. He brought you over from Venice. You have become his protégé. Think of your experiment with the burning mirror. I was there that day. I saw the way Louvois looked at you. I thought at the time he was jealous because you're handsome and he has a face like a pig. Now I know he has plans to destroy the factory and rebuild it as his own. He's not happy unless he's destroying – the war wouldn't have dragged on for so long without him.'

Andrea remembered the force of enmity that had emanated from Louvois on that day. He said, 'I almost believe you, Claudine.'

'You'd better believe me,' she said fiercely. 'You must leave Paris immediately, you must leave France. Your innocence won't help you. After they've tried out their instruments on you, you'll confess to anything. Get out now before it's too late.'

'If I go,' he said, 'you must come with me. I can't leave you here. You're in danger as well.'

'After all this time, is this some sort of proposal?' She was laughing and crying at the same time.

'What about the boy?' He was no longer able to contain the question that had been on his mind since she had arrived.

Her expression froze. 'That's what most concerns you, isn't it? What do you want to know about the boy?'

'Is he my son?'

She hesitated a moment, then, 'Yes, I'm sure of it. He's beginning to look like you.'

Now he was laughing, clasping her to him and kissing her hands, breathing in the old familiar scents of warm skin and perfume. She had taken on a new power over him, that of the mother of his child. 'What is his name?'

'Louis François.'

Andrea recoiled, as if he had been hit. 'You call him my son, yet he's named after the King. And you call him my son?'

'I had to name him Louis. How could I have got a pension for him if I had named him André?' she said.

'So the King has been paying for the welfare of my son?'

'Yes. Why not? He's got enough money.'

Andrea burst out laughing. 'I love you,' he said. 'My *cattiva* Claudine never misses a trick. I want to see my son. Bring him here and we'll leave together.'

She looked uncertain. She would be arrested if she tried to escape, she said, and then he would be caught as well.

'Then leave without any luggage, as if you're just going to market with the boy' – he hesitated over the name – 'with François. I'll get us a place on the coach for Lyon, then on to Nice, and we'll be in Italy.'

'I'll bring you your son.' She kissed him hard on the mouth, her hands entangled in his hair. She sighed, a dark, longing sound from the depths of her, then drew back, looking into his eyes, and said, 'I thought you'd be married by now. Has there been no one else in your life?'

'One or two passing fancies – nothing important.'

'I'm sure they'd be delighted to know they were passing fancies of no importance. Men!' She shook her head, laughing and reproving at the same time.

'I'll go to Monsieur Colbert now and get my permission to leave,' he said. 'You promise you'll return?'

'I promise.'

'I'll be waiting.'

He listened to the footsteps receding down the stairs and then went to the window to watch her walk along the street. He glanced up and down to see if there were any other watchers, but no one seemed to be paying any attention to the lone woman in the grey cloak.

IN THE main hall of Monsieur Colbert's office there was a portrait of him, wearing his star of office, his shrewd dark eyes looking at the artist, as if assessing his talent. This was the Colbert that Andrea remembered. It was a different Colbert from the man he saw now in the office on the piano nobile. The Minister was heavier, his hair was greying, but more than the signs of age, the vital spirit in him seemed subdued. The penetrating gaze which Andrea had expected when he looked up from his papers was diffused, as if a bright all-seeing mirror had been turned to show its opaque reverse. A deep sadness emanated from the man.

He listened as Andrea explained that family circumstances obliged him to return to Venice. He would need to be away for some time, depending on the health of his father.

Colbert nodded and said, 'You won't be coming back.'

'Probably not, Monseigneur.'

'You will not see the completion of the *grande galerie*.'

'It's unlikely.'

'Family must come first, of course. That's the primary rule of mankind. When are you leaving?'

'I should like to leave immediately.'

'Then I won't stop you from doing so. Dessaix, will you prepare the necessary papers of discharge.'

'Right away, Monseigneur.'

A spasm of pain passed over the Minister's face. 'Will you excuse me, Messieurs,' he said and left the room.

Dessaix looked sympathetically at his departing back and confided, 'Monsieur Colbert is not well. He has the most terrible stomach pains. He works too hard and never stops to eat. And he takes the whole weight of the state on his shoulders.'

'I'm sorry to hear it,' said Andrea. 'He has always treated me kindly.'

Dessaix smiled. 'He has a warm heart under his coldness. That's one of the troubles, he feels everything passionately. Every mood of the King affects him. Over ten years ago he warned that Versailles would cost too much money, but the King insists on going ahead, he puts Monsieur Colbert in charge of the building works, then criticises him for the amount it has cost.'

'The King wants perfection and perfection costs money.'

'Nevertheless, the King loves Monsieur Colbert, in his way. A few months ago the Minister had to be confined to bed and His Majesty came to visit him. He told him, "Colbert, unhappiness is what makes people sick. Be cheerful and you'll get well." '

Andrea laughed. 'The King sounds wiser than his doctors.'

'Monsieur Colbert would be as cheerful as a lark if he could persuade the King to spend less money,' said Dessaix, then broke off abruptly as the Minister returned to the room.

'Are you preparing the papers?' asked Colbert.

'Right away, Monseigneur.'

Colbert sat down heavily at his desk. 'I shall give you some money for your leaving and for the journey,' he said to Andrea. 'When you get to Venice, go and see the French Ambassador there. I shall instruct him to arrange a pension for you.'

'I am truly grateful, Monseigneur.'

'Of course,' said Colbert, the old glint returning to his eyes, 'you will leave us everything you have been working on at the factory – which has all been in our time and at our expense. The papers relating to your work on the flat glass, together with the construction.'

'Monsieur du Noyer thought it a waste of time. But I can't take anything with me.'

'Monsieur du Noyer is too busy meeting orders to look to the future.'

Dessaix placed the discharge paper and a leather pouch of money on the desk. The Minister signed the paper and added his seal, then rose to his feet and handed the paper and the pouch to Andrea. 'Now all that's left to say is bon voyage, Monsieur. I hope you will not have any regrets at your decision.'

'I shall regret not seeing you again,' said Andrea.

'I'm sure there are others you will regret more,' replied the Minister with a wintry little smile. 'Adieu, Andrea, God be with you.'

BACK AT his lodgings, Andrea packed his bags and put aside some money for the concierge. It was early evening, the blue hour between daylight and darkness. He lit some candles and began writing a letter to Monsieur du Noyer, apologising for his hasty departure. There was a knock at the door and, occupied as he was with his reasons for leaving, it came like a blow to his heart. He opened the door with trepidation, half expecting the call from La Reynie's men.

On the threshold stood a young boy and the concierge. 'A lady arrived with this lad and told me you were expecting him,' she said.

'Why did she not stay? Was it the same lady who was here a few hours ago?'

'No, Monsieur, it was her landlady. She left a letter for you.'

Andrea took the letter, his eyes on the boy, who was looking up at him. The child's eyelashes were dark and extraordinarily long, the eyes grey with a dark rim round the iris. His hair was light brown, curling to his shoulders. 'Where did you get those eyes from?' Andrea murmured, meeting the almost hypnotic gaze.

'He has lovely eyes, doesn't he?' said the concierge.

'That's the first thing I noticed about him. Here's a bag of his clothes too that the lady brought.'

She handed Andrea a small rucksack. He looked down at the boy. 'That's all you've got in the world, is it?'

'Maman packed it,' said the boy, showing the first tremor of emotion, as his lips trembled slightly.

'He will be hungry. I'll bring you some *potage* I have cooking downstairs,' said the concierge.

'Thank you, Madame, that's very kind of you. Now, step inside, young man.'

The boy walked into the salon de jour, looking around him curiously. He went to the window and peered down at the street, then his eyes took in the chair, the table nearby, the fireplace, the large chest in the corner. Finally they came to rest on Andrea, looking him up and down. He asked, 'Are you my papa?'

'Yes,' said Andrea, squatting down beside him.

'Then I'll call you Papa,' said the boy and put his small arms round him.

Andrea blinked back his tears and asked, 'What shall I call you?'

'My name is Louis François,' he said solemnly.

'In Italy that would be Luigi Francesco.'

The child laughed, wrinkling up his nose. 'That sounds funny.'

'You'll get used to it.'

'What is Italy like?'

'We're going to Venice. It's different from the rest of Italy. It's a city in the sea. The streets are canals full of water, and instead of using horses and carts, we travel by boat. The houses rise from the water and you moor the boat by their side. The lagoon is calm and shining as a mirror, and the sky is like a great bowl overhead, extending over the sea to the far horizon.'

'Can we go tomorrow?' asked the boy.

'We can, but it will take us several weeks to get there. It's a long journey overland.'

The boy looked at him contemplatively as he took this in and said nothing for a while. Andrea opened the letter. It had been written hurriedly, words abbreviated. Claudine was under house arrest, forbidden to leave, under pain of being locked up in some lousy jail. The landlady was bringing his son over. He must leave with the boy immediately. The word 'immediately' was underlined twice. She ended, 'After what I have seen and heard in Paris, I'm afraid for my child. He will have a better life with you in Venice. Look after him. I love you. Claudine.'

There was nothing about joining them, as if she was expecting the worst. 'Maman sends you her love,' Andrea said. 'She says you'll be happy in Venice.'

The concierge brought in a casserole of leek and lentil soup, and Andrea sat the boy at the table. His chin came only to the table top, so he fetched a book and some cushions for the chair. They ate their soup, occasionally glancing at each other across the table. When they had finished, Louis Francois continued his exploration of the room. Stopping at the desk, he examined the paper and crayons, and picked up a drawing of a face that Andrea had been working on, copying Le Brun from memory.

'He doesn't look very happy,' said the child.

391

'He isn't. He's been fighting and he got the worst of it.'

'Draw me something,' said Louis François. 'Draw me a horse.'

Andrea sat at the desk and drew a horse's head, its nostrils flaring and mane flying.

'No, draw me a whole horse.'

'That's enough for one day,' said Andrea.

'No, I want a whole horse. Draw!' commanded Louis François, holding out a crayon.

'Excuse me, where's your please and thank you? Who do you think you are, little man?' He almost said, 'The King?' then stopped and looked more closely at the boy. The jut of the chin, the head raised imperiously, was this how the King had been as a child?

Louis François lowered his head and said, 'I'm sorry, Papa. Will you draw, please?'

'It's enough for today, François. Time for your bed, we have a long journey tomorrow.'

Later he looked in on the boy, sleeping on one side of the bed. In the candlelight his skin seemed to have a luminous translucence, like an aura. This is where children come from, thought Andrea, not from us, but from heaven. He watched the boy stir in his dream, the pupils of his eyes flickering under the closed eyelids, then got undressed himself and into the other side of the bed. For a while he lay awake, listening to the soft breathing beside him. It came to him at that moment, like a voice in his head. He is his own person, not to be stamped with a father's mark.

★

THEY LEFT next morning at daybreak. The pony and cart were there, as he had ordered, to take them south-west, across the Seine to the city gates near Saint-Germain-des-Près, from where the southbound coach left. The sky began to lighten. The sounds of the waking city were all around him, wheels on cobble-stones, the shouts of the water sellers, the buzz of humanity regaining consciousness. The pony's hooves struck the ground in a rhythmic trot, the harness jingled and the driver cleared his throat of phlegm. Sitting next to him, François held on to Andrea's sleeve with one hand, looking around him in wonderment.

Then the bells began to ring out. As they passed the fortress of the Bastille its bell sounded, deep and resonant, like some great creature stirring in its lair. The great bell of the Louvre added its heavy tones and soon all over the city the church bells started to peal, like an early-morning chorus to greet the sun. They passed Notre-Dame, their ears ringing with the noise, and then over the Pont-Neuf, past the statue of Le Vert Galant. The pony and cart slowed down as they moved through the street sellers setting up their stalls along the bridge. The slanting light glanced off people's faces, emphasising the shadows and contours with an intense clarity. As they reached the left bank, the bells of Saint-Germain-des-Près added their bronze notes to the clamour.

François turned to Andrea and said, 'Are we really leaving?'

'We are,' said Andrea, but he knew that part of him would remain, that the bells in Venice would remind him of Paris, just as the bells today reminded him of that early morning, so many years ago, when a young man set off for Saint-Cloud, elated, confident and unaware that he was to be trapped in a fairy tale. Once upon a time there was a woodcutter's son and a beautiful princess, and a clever white cat. And a king who wanted to create a world of mirrors.

Epilogue

NOVEMBER 1684

A STEELY grey morning. In the grounds of Versailles the gardeners sweep up the leaves from the *allées*, scattered by disorderly nature during one of her storms. In the *grande galerie* a dozen men are polishing the parquet before the laying down of the Savonnerie carpets. The *galerie* is ready on time, a matter of pride for Charles Le Brun, who has rallied his army of plasterers, painters, sculptors and metal-workers with an exacting timetable. The date of the inauguration is fixed for 15 November. Two days beforehand a letter goes to the King, who is at Fontainebleau with the court, to say that all is on schedule and the seventeenth mirror is being installed. The King writes back to express his delight.

Le Brun can afford to make a leisurely appraisal of his work before his kingdom is finally relinquished to the sovereign and his army dispersed. Even on the grey November day the *galerie* is full of light, reflected from the mirrors and the crystal chandeliers. The carved silver furniture shines with opulent solidity.

The gilding of the capitals and cornices gleams richly. Several maids are adjusting the folds of the white and gold brocade curtains at the windows. Looking up at the vault, he sees his masterpiece – thirty compositions depicting the triumphs of Louis. There is the young King in the centre, being crowned by a gold laurel wreath. His gold and silver armour reflects the gold and silver of the furnishings below. You and I are linked in immortality, Le Brun says to the portrait. Each of the workers and artists has his piece of eternity here in the *galerie*, from the great Tuby to – and he pauses a moment as a picture comes to his mind of the mirror maker standing in front of the first mirrored arcade, looking not at his reflection but at the glass itself, with the fiercest concentration. André de la Glace, thinks Le Brun. That was a strange business, something to do with the Montespan maid – what was her name? – and the King. It was a nice bit of scandal at the time.

BY EVENING the *galerie* becomes a different world in the light of a thousand candles. The reflections of the flames tremble in the mirrors, so that it seems any moment it may dissolve like an insubstantial dream. Then the courtiers arrive and the *galerie* takes on their life, the mirrors reflect their silks and velvets and jewels, the heat of their bodies heightens a temperature already warmed by candlelight.

They are all there – the princes of the blood, the *ducs et pairs*, the *ducs d'épées*, and a mass of marquises, comtes and comtesses, barons and chevaliers. There is not a soul at court who would miss the inauguration of Louis le Grand's *grande galerie*. Like actors in a drama, they all have a part to play.

Earlier there had been a comedy to entertain them – *Le Bourgeois Gentilhomme*, which most had already seen, but since Molière's death there have been few new plays of note. The little comédienne from the company at the Guenegaud had a way of sending a sidelong glance at the audience at each catastrophe on stage, stealing the limelight from the other actors, but delighting the audience. Le Brun looked at his programme. Of course, Mademoiselle des Oeillets, that was the one.

In this drama of the inauguration, some of the leading actors are missing. The Queen is no more. She died the year before, a victim of the royal doctors' incompetence. She is not greatly missed. And the dour-faced, black-clothed figure of the great Minister Colbert is no longer to be seen. He, too, died the previous year. Louvois has taken his place, strutting in his brocade coat through the throng, bestowing a haughty stare here, a condescending nod there. His arrogance only falters as he passes a middle-aged woman, dressed unobtrusively in brown silk, whose hooded eyes look enquiringly at him. He bows low, suddenly humble, and as he raises his head a glance of complicity passes between them. They each, in their own way, have a conduit to the King. Madame de Maintenon moves on, gliding through the crowd until she sees the extravagantly dressed and voluptuously overweight former Reine Sultane, to whom she nods coldly and passes on. Athénaïs looks after her in contempt and observes to her sister, 'I hear she doesn't bring him much joy in bed. She's rigid as a post, dry as a drain in a drought.'

'Ssh, Athénaïs, please,' says Gabrielle de Thianges. Madame de Maintenon is not yet out of earshot.

Athénaïs could not be excluded because, after all, she is the mother of the King's children, but she carries with her an aura of unresolved scandal. No one knows whether La Montespan was guilty or not in the *affaire des poisons*, because she was never called for questioning. But the King remembered the headaches he had suffered and worse than poison was the thought that without his knowledge she had been feeding him aphrodisiacs. It was a mortal insult, to be concealed at all costs from the *canaille*. So Athénaïs, unquestioned, lingers on with a substantial pension. A few faces from the time of the *affaire des poisons* are no longer at court – the Comtesse de Soissons, the Marquise d'Alluye and several others, exiled from France for life, to escape being tried for murder. Their names are never mentioned. It is as if they did not exist.

Now the King has arrived at the entrance to the *galerie*, his eldest son, the Dauphin, and his brother, Monsieur, on either side, behind him the rest of his children. The King is dressed in cloth of gold and silver, his wig luxuriantly curled. Monsieur glitters with jewels. The royal party begin their progress through the *galerie*. And there is the first mirror arcade, gleaming in the candlelight, like a great reflecting eye. The King pauses in front of it, remembering as he does so the Louis of many years ago, standing in front of the Venetian mirror, tracing the image of his face on the glass. He looks at the mirror and another face stares back at him. He is confronted by an ageing man, the powder emphasising the lines on his face, the mouth tight and downturned. He does not like what he sees. There must be something wrong with the mirrors. They are too clear. There is his great *galerie des glaces*, mercilessly showing to him in each of the seventeen mirror arcades, as he processes the seventy-three metres of its length, a face he would rather not see. The procession continues, the King playing his part in the evening's drama to perfection – his comportment noble, majestic, every inch the greatest monarch of Europe. The court bows in an undulating wave as he passes through and at every mirror his eyes are reluctantly but compulsively drawn to the image. It is there before him, the truth, revealed by the brilliant mercury. He can conquer everything except time.

THE GREY November weather extends over the continent. The canals of Venice shine like polished steel. There have been a few stormy days, but now a calm has descended over the lagoon. A crowd has gathered in the *campo* of the Basilica of Santa Maria e Donato. It's a happy occasion, a christening. The young woman, surrounded by her family admiring the lace-festooned bundle of new life she is holding in her arms, is radiant. The man beside her, in his middle years but still handsome, smiles with pride. Beside him, one hand holding on to his sleeve, is a boy of about nine. One of the boy's friends shouts, 'Ciao, Francesco!' and he lets go of the man's sleeve to run after him.

Ciao! That word of new beginnings. A picture comes to mind of him walking across the same Campo

Donato on an early summer day not long after he had returned. A woman's voice, raucous-edged, shouting, 'Ciao, Signor Andrea!' He had turned to see a dark-haired young woman wave to him. The first thing he noticed was the white teeth of her smile and then, as he drew closer, her amber eyes. She was wearing a dress of patterned blue and red, edged with lace, and as he glanced down to take in the whole picture, he saw her red shoes and white silk stockings.

'Don't you remember me, Signor Andrea?' she demanded as he drew near. 'I used to ask you for mirrors.'

Then he recalled the dark-haired little girl and her small friends, waiting outside the factory to pester him for broken pieces of mirror. He gazed at her in confused disbelief for a moment, saying, 'But you've grown . . .' She began laughing at the ineptness of the remark and he continued, 'You've grown quite beautiful, Signorina.'

She stopped laughing and said crossly, 'And you've grown older,' turning away. But she was there again on the *campo* next day, and then in the church, and soon everywhere. He said, on their wedding night, 'To have travelled everywhere and then to have found you were here all the time.'

'Not all the time but at this time – this was the only time that was right for you, when you had stopped gazing at the horizons.'

It's strange, though, how his wife, Giulietta, seems part of his past as well as his present. Her eyes, with their slanting amber light, like a cat's, remind him of Claudine. And she has a temperament. Her fits of temper are as highly charged as those of the Marquise. She is hugely extravagant. He trembles at the thought of the bills when she and her two best friends go off on a shopping expedition to Venice. She may have no title, but she is a natural *principessa*. And now she is the mother of his child.

He is only sorry his father is not alive to see this new grandchild. But at least he saw Francesco. The boy is growing up and sometimes puzzles him with his behaviour, which ranges from loving affection to imperious command. 'Don't worry about him, Andrea,' said his father indulgently, as Francesco stamped his little foot at being thwarted. 'You were just as difficult when you were young.'

The contentment he feels at his life is something new. He thought growing older would fill him with regrets, but it seems instead to have calmed his restless soul. Venice has taken back the renegade, despite their threats of reprisals. The entire bag of Colbert's louis went to accommodate the officials and it was agreed, in the end, that much water had flowed since under the Bridge of Sighs. He is in charge of the factory now and is changing its course. There is less call for mirrors, as the French have their own, but no one can make glass in as elaborate and fanciful patterns as the glass blowers of Murano. Andrea designs some of the goblets and vases himself, in the florid style of Le Brun. There is one large standing bowl painted with men in battle. It's known as the bellicose cup.

Sometimes he thinks if he were not surrounded by so much beauty in Venice, he might miss the splendour of Versailles. Here the buildings are the work of many generations, monuments to many men. Versailles is the monument to one. His image lies under Andrea's conscious mind, the Sun King, known now as Louis le Grand. And it is the Sun King who continues to haunt Andrea in his dreams, like a golden icon. One night in his sleep he saw Le Brun's statue of Apollo rising from the fountain and then, as happens in dreams, there was a metamorphosis and it was Andrea who found himself enclosed in a carapace of gold. He was inside a skin of precious metal, golden armour from which only his eyes were free. But it wasn't armour, the gold had become his skin, constricting the flesh inside in its rigid mould. At that moment Andrea realised he was no longer himself, but Louis, and the body struggling to be free of the constriction of gold was so welded to it that it was part of him. He raised his hands to the gold mask over his face, feeling through the metal the warmth of the blood inside. And then the metal began to contract against his flesh, tighter and tighter. His cry woke Giulietta, who held him as he clutched at the air. He murmured, 'Now I know what it's like to be him,' but when she asked more he said, 'It was only a nightmare – best forgotten.'

He thinks of the dream now as Francesco asks him for a story. The child is lying against the linen pillows looking up at him with those grey, long-lashed eyes that flood Andrea with helpless love.

'Tell me a story,' says the boy. 'Tell me about . . .'

He stops for a moment and Andrea says, 'About the little white cat . . .'

'No,' says the boy, 'I want an adventure story. Tell me about . . . Tell me about the man who flew too close to the sun.'

'Not tonight,' says Andrea. 'It's a long story and I'm tired.'

'Tomorrow, then, Papa?' says Francesco.

'Tomorrow. I promise.'

'I'll be waiting.'

Those final words to Claudine. I'll be waiting. Her footsteps fading as she descends the stairs, her grey cloak merging into the stones of the street. The boy smiles up at him, his mouth like a ghost of his mother. Then he closes his eyes and falls asleep, so he doesn't see Andrea's tears.

ACKNOWLEDGEMENTS

I am grateful to Arts Council England for their financial assistance, which gave me great encouragement and the time to complete the book.

I should like to thank Dr Sue Thorpe and the Royal Literary Fund Fellow's Scheme which appointed me writer in residence at the University of Greenwich, for similarly making it possible for me to find time to work on the novel.

The Mirror Makers has evolved over a period of time. I have, from the time of first reading *Alice Through the Looking Glass*, been intrigued by the reflective qualities of mirrors. Several visits to Versailles increased my fascination for the role they play in defining identity. At the same time, the character of Athénaïs de Montespan lingered in my mind, after visiting a remote chateau on a lake in the La Brenne region of France, where she was reputed to have lived at one time. Then I read *The Mirror and Man* by Benjamin Goldberg, which includes the story of what is probably the first incident of industrial espionage, when Jean-Baptiste Colbert persuaded a group of mirror makers from Murano to come to Paris, despite threats of reprisals by the Venetian authorities. My grateful thanks to Richard Gollner for drawing my attention to the book, and to the chapter on the mirror makers.

I should like to thank the archivists of Saint-Gobain International for making available to me documents of the factory on faubourg Saint-Antoine, which grew into the great Saint-Gobain conglomerate that created the glass pyramid in the courtyard of the Louvre – a tribute to Colbert's success.

The books I read on Louis XIV, Versailles and Paris during the seventeen century are almost too numerous to list, but Westminster Library, through its referral system, and the Institut Français were excellent at meeting my requests (though some of the most treasured histories from local libraries are no longer available, probably due to the mania for getting rid of old books). I should also like to thank Pierre-Henri Eulert for his enthusiasm in finding books published in France on the Galerie des Glaces and the building of Versailles. Special thanks to Anna Haycraft, for her encouragement and advice, and to my agent Mike Shaw, and editor Paul Sidey, for having faith in the book from an early stage.